HEART
OF A
STAR

Michael,
Thank you so very much for being my
very first book sale & my very first fan!
Lots of Love,
Casey Mansfield

CASEY MANSFIELD

ISBN-13: 978-0615967820
ISBN-10: 0615967825

Book design by Casey Mansfield
Front cover design by Casey Mansfield and Dennis Lloyd, Sr.
Back cover design by Casey Mansfield
Front cover image © Pop Catalin Sebastian | Dreamstime.com
Back cover image © Pawel Nawrot | Dreamstime.com

Printed in the United States of America

This book is dedicated to my loving family – Glenn, Noel and Kaylee. You are my first dream come true. Thank you for allowing me to make my second dream come true.

And to my Mom, my Dad, Joanne, Denny, Melissa, Bobby, Heather, Tommy and the entire Mansfield family. Family is what you make it, and I'm glad to call you mine.

To God for the talent, the dream and the patience.

Special thanks to everyone who helped to make this book what it is. To Glenn for the many nights of letting me read to him in the midnight hours. To Kristina Marlowe, my first and favorite W.P. To Amber Sepulvado for her eagle-eye and endless hours of last-minute editing. To all of the ladies who helped by reading and editing and offering words of support and encouragement. To the band Oasis for their incredible music and inspiration, and to all of my friends who are fans. To David Heilman and the members of the band The Dig for letting me 'interview' them about life on the road and the music business, and for their musical inspiration. To the members of the Supernova Heights forum for their everlasting knowledge and love of a band. And to everyone who supported my writing along this long journey... A very heartfelt Thank You!

PRELUDE

There are moments in your life that are ingrained in your heart forever. Long after your mind tucks the memory away and you've moved on with your life, your heart never forgets those moments. For me, it was the look in her eyes.

Glassy charcoal eyes that begged me.

She didn't have to say a word. Her eyes said it all.

She drew in a quivered breath, shaking her head and squeezing her dark eyes shut, wringing the tears down her cheeks like a sad, sullen dishrag. Her fingers, which had only seconds ago been interlaced with mine in any attempt at compassion that she might drag from me, now wrapped in a tight fist that she smashed to the table. "You can't make me do this!" Her voice was trembling, desperate. "I can't. *I won't!*"

I could feel my own eyes widen, but I remained in my chair, my body stiffening as her hands covered her face. A part of me wanted to reach out to her, to offer her my shoulder, a warm embrace, words to console her. But what was I to say? Was it even my place?

Instead, I chose to try to reason with her. "You said yourself that he'd kill you if he found out. This way, he'll never know. It's the only solution."

She leaned her head against the wall, looking upwards for an answer that wasn't there. "You're only worried about your career," the words stung more than I'd ever have admitted, "your *fucking* music."

I couldn't deny it; I had no valid argument against the accusation. But I had another that was far more convincing, even to a woman on the brink of hysteria. My eyes blinked rapidly, but it was the only movement I'd allowed my own body. "I'm not even eighteen. I don't know the first thing about what to do with a baby."

She calmed, and for but a brief moment, she was herself again. She regained her composure, transforming instantly back into the woman who'd seduced me three months prior, standing in the front row as I played guitar at our first sold-out venue.

I'd never been that drunk before, but after that show, there was enough liquor backstage to do in an entire football team. She had her eye on me the whole show, and I had recognized her instantly when a security guard escorted her to our dressing room, nodding in my direction before she slipped something into his pocket with a wink of those incredible brown eyes.

She was older than me, there was no doubt about that, and I'd found myself trying to guess her age several times during the show. Once she was up close and under incandescent lighting, I placed her to be a good ten years my senior. And hell, she was hot. I had known right away her breasts were nothing that God had created, but I found myself putting my guitar down quickly so that my hands would be free – just in case.

The entire show, she'd been with him. He stood there, arms crossed over his chest, tattoos flexed, glaring straight ahead like he was bored while she screamed and danced and sang every one of our songs. And while he hadn't followed her backstage that night, I found myself now wishing that he'd had.

"I could leave him," she offered, her hands digging deeply into my shoulders. I fought off the urge to close my eyes, lean my head back and enjoy it. "I could go live with my sister in Brighton."

I shook my head. I couldn't let her talk me out of this. We'd already discussed it once. Hell, it'd been her idea. I'd just agreed to it, and now I was sticking by it. It was my first decision as a man, I'd told myself. And it was the right thing to do and what was best for everyone.

"What kind of a life would that be? For you or the baby? You'd be living your life in fear, hiding from him all the time..."

She stormed back over to the other side of the table. "At least I'm *trying*. It's like you have your mind made up, and you won't consider any other options!" She swept her arms at the chair, sending it tumbling across the floor, just missing a glass curio cabinet which housed several antique-looking china dolls. It looked like something out of the fifties, which matched the décor in the rest of the house. It made me want to get out of there even faster.

I held strong to the reason I'd knocked on her door in the first place. We'd already made the decision - made it together - I reminded myself, mostly so I wouldn't have any guilt when I walked back out the door. I'd no idea at the time how much that guilt would follow me for the rest of my life.

I slid a check across the table. It was already made out and signed. "This is for the expenses." This was the one that was on the books. My manager had insisted that it be on record, for legal and PR purposes, he'd explained.

The second check was from my personal account. It was down to the last penny of what that account held, and would close it out for good. Tomorrow, I was starting fresh. A new account, a new bank, and a new life. That check was also quite a bit heftier than the first. But I didn't care about the money. The band was doing well and I'd easily make it back in a few months' time. What mattered to me now was that she was taken care of. And safe.

Her eyes turned warm and soft as she sniffed back the tears. "What's this one for?"

"For you," I told her, "To start over."

ONE
Natalie

So this was going to be the time of my life, I thought, as I packed up my suitcase rather haphazardly. Hell, I would just be repacking it anyway. My OCD would eventually kick in with a vengeance and I'd have it emptied in no time, then organized with the greatest of finesse. But for now, clothes were flying through the air from my dresser into a pile inside the open suitcase.

There were six of us going on this trip, five of my best friends in the world, five people who thought they knew me better than anyone, and by all rights, probably did. Yet almost everything about me and my life back in London was hidden behind a smoke screen of secrets, so much so that if I merely told them in words alone, they'd never believe the truth. Back here in the States, I was so far removed from all of it that I had a hard time believing it myself most days. Here, life for me was ordinary. I went to college, I had a job, and I had my friends, who were my only family while I was on this side of the Atlantic.

I had met Rachel Garrison when we were nine years old, just after I'd moved to the States. All throughout our years at our prestigious private school, Rachel and I dormed together, studied together, and got in a fair amount of trouble together. She was my family when I didn't have my own to turn to.

Even when Rachel and I decided to go to college not far from home, we remained roommates. Her parents had supported our efforts to work through the last two of our high school years, and we saved every penny toward our rented two-bedroom townhouse located a little outside of the rough side of the city, just far enough on the right side of town that we could safely walk to the train station in the dark. That was enough for us, for now. We were very happy with the life that we had made for ourselves. After all, we were outside of the dorm life that most freshmen embraced, but had restricted us for the many years we had spent in boarding school.

So here we were, in the summer before our junior year of college. I was the youngest in our group, just about to turn twenty-one in four days. Now I could partake legally in the clubs that I had been frequenting for the past two years, much thanks to my fake ID, which I owed very much to Rachel's cousin, who I somewhat vaguely resembled in the fact that we both had shoulder length dark hair.

I was just about ready to zip up the suitcase, positive that I could just call it a night with a glass of red wine, when Rachel poked her head in my door and tossed her cell phone on my bed. "It's Ray-Ray" she said, "wants to know who's driving first thing in the morning, and can we please stop at the diner for breakfast?"

I rolled my eyes as she ducked back out of my room, leaving Ray-Ray on the cell to be tended to. "Can't you eat before you leave the house?"

A heavy sigh came through Rachel's phone. "Eat what? Josh got rid of all the perishables so nothing goes bad and stinks up the house while we're gone."

One more thing that I had to do before bed, I noted, thanking God that Ray-Ray's roommate was as much of a clean freak as I was. I cringed at the thought of hamburger meat rotting and green in the fridge when I came home twelve days from today.

"Look Love, if you're gonna be in a car with me for two whole days, you're gonna wanna make sure that I'm well-fed, happy, and maybe not as horny as I usually am." He tried as best that he could to imitate my fading British accent, but as always, he did a sad job of it.

I thought very carefully about what I was going to say before I responded, but I had to make it quick, lest he jump in with another quip. "I can help you with the first two, but the last one, you're on your own."

"Ah Natalie, you'll be begging to differ before the end of this trip." And then the phone went dead.

I shook my head as I tossed the phone back on my bed. Whatever vibe Ray-Ray and I had going between us lately couldn't have been described as sexual. He was, after all, my best friend next to Rachel. But I also couldn't deny the fact that the little innuendos and jokes between us lately had been increasingly flirtatious in nature. I wasn't sure what to make of it, so it seemed easier to just ignore it. Anything further might complicate things, and the last thing I wanted was any more complication in my life.

He and Rachel and me went way back to freshman year of high school. We were, for all intents and purposes inseparable, the three of us. Ray-Ray had been the first to see Rachel and I drunk. Or maybe it was him who had gotten us drunk.

It had happened just outside of Philadelphia, the summer between our sophomore and junior year. It was the only little piece of woodland that we really knew about, in a small suburb about twenty minutes north from where our boarding school was. There was a creek that ran alongside the highway. If you pulled into the small stone parkway, then walked about twenty or thirty yards through the woods, you could cross the creek via a rock wall. It was on that rock wall that we enjoyed our first case of beer, the three of us. Sure, Ray-Ray consumed more than half of it himself, but between Rachel and I, we weren't sure who was who after a certain point. Somehow, the summer night ended with the two of us girls in the creek, letting the ice-cold water pour over us through the rock wall. We laughed until well after midnight, soaked to the bone, freezing cold but not feeling any of it, with Ray-Ray pulling us out of the water when it was way past time to go home. Rachel and I huddled in the back seat of his car, wrapped in a small blanket that he had found in the trunk, still laughing as he cranked up the heat on the ride home that hot summer night.

Of course, Ray-Ray's version of the story always involved some form of girl-on-girl action, whether it be sloppy wet kissing, or shameless sex steaming up his windows. It was completely unfounded, but depending on our mood and who he happened to be telling, sometimes we'd correct him, and other times, we'd let him have his little fantasy. I had a strict belief that our real friends would know the truth from Ray-Ray's imagination, and screw the rest of them. The public believes what it wants to anyhow.

I had to sit on my suitcase to zip it shut, but after a few minutes of fighting, I managed to win the battle. Dragging the thing down the stairs, it made its final resting place by the front door.

I found Rachel leaning up against the doorway between the living room and kitchen, eating an apple. Even when she was leaning, she seemed amazingly tall for her five foot nine inch frame. Dark brown hair fell, long and wavy, over her shoulders and down to her mid-back. She'd sweep a handful of it out of her face, only to have it fall forward again. Then she'd complain, to which I'd only laugh. Rachel couldn't have a bad hair day if she tried. The girl made sweat pants and t-shirts look casually elegant. "That dive diner over by Second and Beech is open twenty-four hours. If we get our sorry asses up by five, we can meet Ray-Ray and Josh before we pick up the rest of the crew."

I cocked my head to one side, in fake amusement. "Can't you swallow before you start talking? You've got apple falling out your mouth…"

Rachel nearly choked as she laughed at me. "That's why I love you, Nat. You're just brutally honest. Say it like it is, spare no expense for my feelings."

"I lost sympathy for your feelings when you agreed to start off this trip by going to the diner with Ray-Ray. We're on a schedule," I reminded her, as I moved into the kitchen to start mass cleanup on the refrigerator, "we are supposed to have everyone picked up and be on the road by seven am sharp so that we can make it to Nashville by nine pm. Then we have to leave Nashville no later than nine am so that we can make it to Dallas by nine pm."

Rachel tossed her apple core over my head toward the trashcan, then shoved her hands into the pouch of her Abercrombie hoodie, and resumed her position leaning now against the kitchen wall. Her brown eyes were wide with conviction. "And that will still give us an entire night to rest, and the next two days then to tour, shop, have fun, whatever. Then we'll have three nights of concerts, and whatever happens after that happens. I love not having any plans. That, my friend, is what vacation is all about!"

"But there might be traffic, or construction, or an accident. Anything could hold us up, and we'll need that next day as a buffer in case…"

Rachel put up her hand. "Stop right there, Natalie McKinney, just stop right there. You are getting way ahead of yourself, and I'm not going to let your paranoid imagination jinx our trip. We've planned too hard and saved for way too long to make this little trip a reality. You're now going to enjoy it, even if it kills you."

With a sigh, I shut the refrigerator door. She was right,

and I knew it, but there was more than just a vacation for me. For them, this was all just a trip to see 7 Year Coma, our favorite band, play live, to hang out in Dallas for a few days, and enjoy the drive there and back.

But my friends, my very best friends, those who knew me better than anyone in this world, had no idea of what I'd been planning for weeks now. They had all pitched in for the tickets as part of my twenty-first birthday gift. They were good seats, by all means; about fourteen rows back from the front of the stage on the first of three sold-out nights that the band was playing in Dallas. They were all ecstatic when I opened the envelope, and I put on the most surprised look I could conjure up at the moment. It was very touching, because I knew the cost of the tickets, and the trouble they must have gone through to get them. It meant a lot to me, but it also meant I had to alter my plans a bit to make everything work out just right.

Through the help of a very good friend of mine, I had managed to arrange for six front row seats on the opening night in Dallas. But when I saw the look on their faces as I opened my birthday gift, Rachel's especially, I didn't have the heart to tell them about the front row tickets. Instead, I called Sammi frantically later that night, and she was able to pull some strings for me. When she finally called me back, she revealed, "I can do six seats in the third row on the second night, Natalie. That's about all I can do on this short of notice. The Parlstein Group was very happy to change their plans and accept front row on opening night instead. It was actually a good PR move, come to think of it..."

"That'll be fine Sammi. I just have to not mention that I traded first row for third, or it'll be a lynch mob of five after me."

Sammi laughed that hearty laugh that she has, and I smiled as I pictured her. She was an Irish redhead straight from Dublin, in her mid-thirties, with a heart of pure gold. I had known her since I was a kid, and now kept in touch with her usually through emails or random phone calls throughout the year. "And third row still comes with backstage passes, Natalie. That is, if you want them..."

That part I was still deciding. "You're a hell of a saleswoman, Sammi. I'm forever in your debt."

I hadn't yet told my friends about that "other" birthday gift. I'd have to find the right time, somewhere over the course of the next few days.

Opening my closet, I pushed aside the row of neatly organized clothing, revealing the black leather case. My heart jumped just a little as I grasped the neck of the Gibson Acoustic, feeling the strings press down under my fingers. It was pure beauty to me, just the feel of the instrument in my hand, and every time I took it out, I reveled in the mere pleasure of owning something that could create such pure bliss with each chord struck. It was the only thing that was ever a constant in my life, albeit hidden away from those who knew me best in this world.

I had bought my Fender first, when I was seven, because it was about all I could afford on my meager allowance. Then after about two years of vacuuming carpets, scrubbing toilets, and weeding the garden at my aunt and uncle's place, I had earned enough for an Ibanez. My goal was a Gibson CSR Solid Rosewood Series Grand Concert Acoustic, which I finally achieved at age sixteen, after having graduated to a real job at a local coffee shop with Rachel. It was my proudest achievement to date, though I kept all of my guitars hidden away, for the most part, and only played to Rachel on rare occasion.

Tonight didn't involve working on a new song, or practicing some of the many I had already written. Tonight was purely about hearing the music that my fingers were inventing with each stroke. Revitalizing senses that hadn't been tapped into all day.

By the time the guitar found its home back in the closet,

I was truly ready for our trip. I was going to miss my guitars, I thought, as I closed the closet door.

The first drops of rain were tapping on my bedroom window, a rhythmic ominous sound. The sound alone was enough to make my spine tight and my head ache. The forecast earlier was for an eighty percent chance of rain, with some pop up thunderstorms in our area. By tomorrow, it was all supposed to clear out, making for beautiful driving weather. I had checked several different sources, and felt good about tomorrow's outlook. I just had to survive the night.

I pulled the shades down on the windows and closed the curtains. Sliding my hand into my nightstand drawer, I pulled out my headphones, my only comfort on a stormy night. As they so often were on nights like this, my dreams were peppered with images from my younger years, most of which I had chosen not to remember during lucid awareness. It usually started just after I had reached the deepest part of sleep, as both my body and mind were finally starting to fully relax.

Flashes of lightning, roars of thunder would fill my dreams. Every sensation was touched in these dreams – down to the taste of my own blood, thin and metallic, on my tongue.

It was always the same house, the same hallway where I stood with the same wood door encased in faux-fancy molding with the old-style copper doorknob. And as hard as I fought against the temptation to open that door, I was always driven to turn that knob against my will. The door would swing open as if by sheer force, and I'd hear the blood-curdling screams of a voice I'd long since forgotten. The room, pitch black, even when I knew it wasn't supposed to be, had such a compelling draw that I needed to step in, I needed to move forward into the blackness.

I needed to stop the screaming.

TWO
Natalie

The morning came way too soon. I felt like I had just drifted back off to sleep by the time the alarm clock disturbed my dreams. The room was still all too dark, lit only by the dim glow of the streetlights outside of my window. My hand came down hard on the snooze button, but I knew there was no chance in hell that I'd be going back to sleep, even if just for a few minutes. My mind was already racing. Jump in the shower, blow dry and style my hair, put on my favorite, most comfortable pair of jeans and pull a sweatshirt over my t-shirt, load the car, and hit the road. The itinerary had been engraved into my brain for weeks now.

We pulled up at the diner at 5:30, and though we arrived much later than I wanted to, I was especially pleased to see Ray-Ray and Josh waiting patiently at a booth for us. Josh was leaning his blond head against the back of the booth seat, his eyes closed and his fingers drumming the tune of some song playing inside his head on the white marbled Formica table.

He had never been a morning person, and was known for his frequent mood swings when sleep-deprived, so I knew all too well to tread lightly around him early in the morning. We had all found it particularly amusing when he announced that he would be enrolling in pre-law at St. Joe's University just prior to us graduating prep school, but so far his partying habits hadn't interfered too much with his career path, so the last laugh might have been on us in the end. Lately all that had been on Josh's mind were preparing for the LSAT's, which were coming up in the next year, and getting into a good law school.

We knew Joshua Van Arden through Ray-Ray, who was his best friend throughout boarding school, and now they rented a historic twin together just outside of Philly, not too far from Rachel and me.

We were never quite sure why Ray-Ray had enrolled in St. Joe's. Maybe it was to stay close to his friends, and the city that he loved. It definitely wasn't for the Business Administration program that he was enrolled in. That also remained a mystery, as none of us could ever see Ray-Ray in an office cubicle. He could barely sit still long enough to get through his classes.

"Why are you even bothering to look at the menu, Natalie?" Sitting next to me, Ray-Ray pulled the slightly egg-coated bi-fold from my hands. On impulse, I wiped my hands on my jeans, mentally noting that I needed to pick up more anti-bacterial gel to restock my purse somewhere along the way. "You know you're just going to order the same thing you always do. Western Omelet with cheese, extra ham, side of wheat toast with strawberry jelly, a large iced-tea and a coffee. You're as predictable as my grandmother's medicine cabinet."

Even I had to laugh at that one. "Okay, I'm not sure what that means exactly... Maybe you should just chalk it up to knowing everything there is to know about me, Ray-Ray. You're such a good friend that you know me inside and out."

I realized as soon as the words came out of my mouth that I should have chosen better language around Raymond

Montgomery. He caught his head in his hand as he leaned on the table, and said, "I think I'd like to know the inside of you a little better. If that's an invitation to..."

"No, it's not."

He looked like a three-year-old who had just been scolded, but recovered quickly. He wore that wide grin on his face, and his eyes had too much sparkle for that hour in the morning.

"Do you really need an invitation to a party that you've been to before?" Josh asked dryly, as he stretched, then tossed a smile in my direction.

Even Rachel cringed a little behind her menu. "I think he's got you there, Natty." She ignored the hand signal that I had flashed in Josh's direction. "Apparently Ray-Ray's the kind to kiss and tell."

The wide smile returned without a moment's hesitation as Ray-Ray turned to face me, "Only the ones worth telling about, Love."

I lowered my voice in mock-secretism, "So you didn't tell him about Rachel then?"

I laughed as she returned with her own sign language just before our waitress came over to stop the conversation from going any further down the toilet. Ray-Ray threw his arm across my shoulders. "My girlfriend here would like a western omelet with cheese, extra ham, side of wheat toast with strawberry jelly, a large iced-tea and a coffee."

Nearly two hours later, we were pulling up to Callie Thorne's parent's stone farmhouse. Her father had helped her pull her two overstuffed suitcases to my car, while she managed the two additional bags that were packed to the brim, one slung over her shoulder and the other she clasped with two hands. He kissed her on the cheek and eyed Josh up at least twice before wishing his daughter a good trip, then turned back down the long walkway to the house without a word to any of us.

I found myself staring a bit longer than I wanted to as Callie's dad made his way to the old farmhouse. Callie, for as frustrated as she always was with her father, was lucky to have him in her life. She was lucky to know who he was and to spend time with him. She just didn't know it.

She had grown up in a strict Roman-Catholic household, and was smack in the middle of the birth order between her five sisters and two brothers. She had attended a Catholic High School, and now commuted to a Catholic University. Personally, I was surprised that Callie hadn't run off to school in California, or as far away as she could have gotten from her parents, but she had a strong sense of family loyalty, no matter how much she complained about her strict family life.

She rebelled silently though, becoming a bar tender at a nightclub in Blue Bell, where she eventually met Josh. Her parents were under the impression she was a waitress at a nearby country club, so apparently she had left out some details when she told them about her summer employment.

I would have given my left arm to have had her upbringing. To have both a mother and a father, under one roof, and grow up with your siblings all around you, making memories, arguing, sharing laughs – it was something I had longed for my entire life.

Josh made no reservations about greeting Callie with a heavy kiss right there in front of her parent's house, although I doubt he had the balls to do it before her father's back was turned. Callie's long, strait blonde hair reflected the early morning sunlight that was peaking over the crests of the rows of corn that overran what would have been her family's front yard. Her black framed glasses and grey DeSales sweatshirt screamed studious college girl, which was exactly what she wanted her father to see as she left for our trip.

"You two can make out all you want in the car, but we have a schedule here, and we're seriously behind thanks to

Mr. Montgomery back here." I nodded in Ray-Ray's direction.

We picked up Nathan last and realized very quickly that we needed to address the luggage situation if Nathan was going to have room to both sit and bring his suitcase along. Callie and Rachel had packed way more than enough for a month-long trip, let alone two weeks. Both Ray-Ray and Josh had packed surprisingly light for almost two weeks, and I silently prayed that there were at least enough pairs of underwear each that they could change daily. But that still left us with way too much cargo for six passengers in my Suburban.

Nathan laughed at the sight of the suitcases strewn across the lawn and sidewalk outside of his mother's house. "I'll bet they're half yours, Natalie."

I wrinkled my nose in protest. "You obviously underestimate the tools that it takes to create the beautiful creature you see before you." I did a half-curtsey to accentuate my point.

He smiled at me and cocked his head to one side. "Somehow I doubt that you can improve on nature that much." He gave me a quick wink before jumping into the back seat.

Resuming my spot in the driver's seat, I turned to face my friends. "I need to stop at Mocha Joe's before we go. Gotta get my Triple-X Special for this trip." Extra-large coffee, with extra cream and extra sugar was a staple on any morning that I saw the dawn.

From the back, Ray-Ray shouted a little too loudly with the windows still open, "I'll give you a Triple-X Special Nat!"

That was our Ray-Ray, I thought as I shook my head and pulled out onto the street. There was just no telling what would come out of his mouth. He kept us laughing, even if it meant laughing at ourselves, which it usually did.

He had been the former tight end of our high-school football team, with a medium build. He had relaxed a bit on the obsessive exercise now that he was in college, and usually only hit the gym once a week, but his forearms and chest were tighter than ever, and I had to admit, that hit a weak spot for me. He had dark brown hair, which he kept purposely messy these days, and these deep dark eyes that always had you guessing what was going through his mind.

Girls often found him physically attractive, as he had a fairly solid frame, and they loved that relaxed, disheveled look he had going these days. He tried to claim that he was 'rugged', but I often told him that he missed that mark just a bit and had fallen into the neater side of sloppy.

The first two hours of our trip were filled with silent voices, random radio music, and somewhat haphazard scenery. We were headed west in Pennsylvania, through areas of the state that I rarely saw. I had been through Harrisburg a time or two, but only having driven through it. The first thing I noticed was that the roads were in terrible shape. Bumps and potholes littered the pavement. It made me wonder why our taxes were so high if the roads mid-state were in such poor shape. I had never followed politics much, but this part of the road trip made me vow that as soon as I got back, I would start reading the newspaper a little more often.

Despite the road conditions, my heart held a fondness for Pennsylvania. We had it all here really, especially having lived on the eastern side of the state for the majority of my life. We were two or three hours from the beach, depending on which beach you liked the most. We were two hours from the Poconos, which had all the best skiing that the winter had to offer. We were four hours from New York City, if you happened to want to enjoy all that NYC had to offer. The best part, of course, was that we were just outside of Philadelphia, which truly was the best city in the world. I could boast that really, even after having visited hundreds of cities all over the world.

Philly just housed that old-world style mixed with the new world excitement. It had ships, tall buildings, trains, planes, clubs, dive bars, nightlife, historic museums, parks, sporting complexes, a zoo, and anything else that you could ever want in a city.

"Nat-a-lee!" Ray-Ray's voice abruptly disturbed my thoughts. I looked in the rear-view and saw him leaning forward, his head right next to Callie's, who was unfortunate enough to be seated directly in front of him. "Can't put 7 Year Coma on for us? How are we supposed to get psyched up for a concert if you aren't gonna blast their music?"

Ray-Ray was about the biggest fan of 7 Year Coma that I knew. It was almost scary, his obsession with the band. He had been following them since the time they first became famous in the States, which was about two years after they had topped the charts in England. He knew every word of every song, even the ones that no one else had even heard of. He prided himself on knowing every little detail about every member of the band and he often amused us with his random band trivia. 'Coma Trivia Challenge' was his favorite game to play, especially when incredibly drunk, or high, whichever he happened to be at the moment.

We had all been to at least one live show, with Nathan finally getting to attend one last year while the band was touring Boston. Callie had gone twice before, when she and Josh first started dating. The rest of us had attended as many of their concerts as we could afford, with Ray-Ray claiming to have seen the most with a total of fourteen. I had the added privilege however, of having been the only one of us to see the band in concert outside of the US, and most notably in their home country of England.

The band had a tendency to travel the world on each tour, and only managed to land precious few concert dates in a small part of the States with each tour. This year happened to be the west coast through the southern border tour, which ended in Houston, Texas. After that, the band was traveling back to England for a short break before heading back out to tour the rest of Europe.

I flipped the radio from FM to CD for Ray-Ray. The first CD that the band released, entitled *Metabolic*, poured through the speakers. Personally, it was one of my favorites, as the band was still young, their voices fresh and full of energy. It hit a nostalgic nerve somewhere deep inside me, bringing me back to when I was about five years old, and still living in northern England.

The couple that stood in the doorway looked like strangers. He wore a scowl below his bald head, a rust colored t-shirt over sagging jeans, and smelled of stale liquor. Her eyes were dead brown, a complete contrast to the way her dark hair shined in the sunlight pouring through the window of my mother's living room. She was pretty enough, but distant. She made my sister Katie suddenly appear warm and loving, even as Katie was prying me off of her leg.

"Natalie, you're going to go stay with Aunt Hannah and Uncle..."

"Leo," Aunt Hannah responded, "This is my husband Leo."

I grasped tighter to Kate's leg, which under any other circumstances would have her shouting at me. She pulled my wrists apart and crouched down next to me. "It's just for a short while. Until Mum's better. You know she's not well."

Mum hadn't seemed sick. She wasn't in bed. She was out in the back garden tending to the flowers that she loved so much. She had even just gotten back from a trip to the United States. She told me she had been looking after my dad, and if I was a good girl, I might even get to go and meet him someday. That news had me dancing and giggling right along with her.

She had spent many a night telling me stories about the man who was my father. He was a movie star, she told me, who lived now far away, across the ocean. She had taken several trips to go and see him, and she told me that he couldn't wait to meet me.

"No!" I screamed when Aunt Hannah tried to take my

hand. *"I want to stay here with Mum! And I want to meet Dad! I can go live with him!"*

Kate stepped back and let them pull me out the door, toward the waiting car. It took little more than a stern look from Uncle Leo for me to climb into the backseat. As the engine turned over and they pulled away from our drive, a familiar song poured through the crackling speakers of the worn car. 'Find My Way Home', 7 Year Coma's latest number one, was my only sense of peace as the house and the family I loved grew smaller and smaller in the horizon.

Screeching tires in front of me had me snapping back to reality, and back to the States, in no time. For miles ahead, it was a sea of brake lights. And the next exit wasn't for another ten miles.

"It's time for 'Coma Trivia Challenge'!" Ray-Ray boomed from the back.

Callie groaned and sunk down in her seat, pulling the hood of her sweatshirt over her head and stuffing her hands in the sweatshirt pocket. "It's too early in the morning for trivia."

Ray-Ray performed a drum-roll on the back of her seat with his hands. "That's okay Cal. You won't get very far anyway. You're not that good." He ignored the sign language that she flashed him, and continued with his rant. "Everyone else is in though. You all know the rules. One wrong, you're out. Last two standing name the stakes, winner gets that and possession of the trophy. Best out of three breaks a tie."

"Ray-Ray, you always win. Why don't we just save ourselves the trouble and let you pick what you want right now? And that damned guitar pick is hardly a trophy." Rachel turned down the music. We all knew she was only bluffing. The girl lived for a challenge.

Off came her seatbelt and she turned herself around so that she was kneeling backward in my front seat, facing our friends, and leaning her back up against the dash. Traffic had started moving again, though very slowly, and I hoped to God that I didn't have to hit the brakes, for fear that she'd go through the windshield.

Through the rearview, Ray-Ray looked shocked, and whether he was pretending or not, I couldn't tell. "That guitar pick, Missy, was left behind on stage by Rylan Porter at my very first Coma show in Philly. I had to wait for an entire sold-out crowd to leave the venue, dodge past multiple security guards and stage dive to grab that thing before a roadie swept it away. Rylan Porter used that guitar pick. It's sacred."

"Whatever," Rachel rolled her eyes, "I'll go first."

Ray-Ray sat quiet for a moment, contemplating his first question. Without seeing him, I knew he had an inquisitive look on his face, was biting his upper lip in deep thought, his eyes in a narrowed gaze at his opponent. This was all part of his tactic, we knew, his staring down his opponent. Finally, he nodded, clearly impressed with his silent decision. "Multiple choice, since this one is tough."

Rachel scoffed. "No multiple choice. I can take whatever you can bring, baby."

"Who or what was the song *Sorry I Wasn't* written for?" It was a classic Ray-Ray trick question. He'd ask what he thought we would think would have an easy, obvious answer, yet the true answer was something completely off the wall. I was actually curious to hear what his multiple choices would have been, but once Rachel made up her mind, that was it.

"Good one, Ray-Ray. Very good." Rachel clapped her hands in mock applause. "This is one of the few songs not written by the very talented Porter brothers. *Sorry I Wasn't* was written by Lucas Mason and was based loosely on the fact that he was turned down at the alter by his former fiancé a few years after he signed on with 7 Year Coma."

In the back, Ray-Ray scowled. "I forgot you were a Lucas fan."

Rachel did her little victory seat-dance while Ray-Ray scoffed. "I was hoping you'd get that song confused with the more popular *Gutted*, written by Rylan Porter, which has a similar theme. It's rumored that Rylan wrote the song for his estranged daughter."

Now it was Rachel's turn to roll her eyes. "You're obsessed. There's no proof that Rylan had a child. He's never admitted it in a single interview. This mystery daughter is a myth, a legend. So let's move on." She cleared her throat to be sure we all had her attention again. "Okay, Natty-girl, this one's for you then. I would like to know if you can tell me what type of electric guitar that Lucas favors over all others."

"Bitch." I hissed. I liked to pretend that the questions were difficult. Sometimes it did require a bit of acting on my part, I had to admit, and somehow I always ended up throwing a question somewhere in the middle of the game, then spending the rest of the time just enjoying listening to my friends challenge each other. Somehow though, today felt different. Today, I didn't feel like letting Ray-Ray win. "That would be a Martin, my dear."

Rachel's jaw dropped just a little, but she quickly recovered, and I knew that she didn't think I noticed her glaring at me, ever so slightly. I suppressed a silent smile. "My turn then. And I think I'm gonna knock Joshy out right in the beginning of the game."

We continued on for a good forty-five minutes, back and forth, until one-by-one, they were all out of the game, and finally it was just Ray-Ray and me. It had never ended up with the two of us before, and for once, I was inviting the challenge. This time, I was not going to back down, and it felt good. It felt free. For just a little while in my car, amongst my friends, I was actually just me.

"Okay Nat. It all comes down to this. What are the stakes?" Ray-Ray was on the edge of his seat, excited that for the first time ever in the history of the game that he was met in the final round by someone other than Rachel or Josh.

"You're the Defending Champ. You call first." I was glad we were now in cruise-mode on the highway, somewhere in Virginia at this point. I wanted to concentrate on the game. I could tell my friends were excited as well, more for the fact that this was something different than the norm. Rachel was standing on her knees, hugging the back of the passenger seat. Nathan's lips were curved up in a smile. Josh was leaning forward, his head on his hands, elbows on his knees, and even Callie next to him had pulled off her hood and was sitting cross-legged, snacking on a bag of chips.

Ray-Ray cleared his throat, adding to the drama. "Natalie, if you don't win this tournament...."

"It's a tournament now? It's come to that?" Callie cried, as she crumpled up her empty bag and tossed it in the back seat toward him.

I silently cringed, making a mental note to pick it up at the next rest stop. The thought of crunched chip remains mashed into the floor of my car made my skin crawl. "Get to it Ray-Ray. We might get to Texas before this game ever ends."

"Okay then. If I win...." He paused for effect, "you sleep with me."

The car went silent. The road before me narrowed. Why hadn't I seen that coming a mile away? I refused to let my heart race any faster than it already was. I quickly gained control over the fact that the temperature was raising in the car by the second, and beads of sweat were forming on the back of my neck. I flipped the air conditioner on and drew in a deep breath, letting it out slowly.

Suddenly, a smile formed on my lips. Out of nowhere, I glanced over at my best friend. I was about to throw her to the wolf. "If I win, you sleep with Rachel."

Rachel's jaw dropped. "No way! You two can't pull me into this, I'm out of the game!"

Josh, pulling out his law school savvy, held up his hand. "Actually Rachel, that is not an official rule. The only rule regarding the final bet is that winner takes all. There are no rules that specify who can or can't be involved in the final stakes. Besides, Ray-Ray has won every game since the beginning of time anyway. And if I recall, Natalie hasn't made it past the third round, ever. Odds are on your side."

Rachel turned around and slumped down in her seat. "Natalie, I swear to God that if you win this, I will never speak to you again."

In the back seat, Ray-Ray looked like a kid on Christmas morning. I could tell he was contemplating whether he should pick a hard question or an easy question. Either way, he won. I silently cursed myself for setting him up like this, but on the other hand, the stakes had to be good, and I had to admit, it was an ingenious scheme on my part. I just had to make sure that I didn't lose.

Ray-Ray requested a few minutes to prepare his question, which I granted. I didn't need the time, I just wanted him to pick out a good one. Besides, Rachel's scowl was amusing me, and I was happy to add to any drama that she was about to bestow upon the rest of our friends.

"Hit me, Ray-Ray. Do your worst." I challenged, as I turned the Suburban into the rest stop. We had been on the road for a full three hours now. I pulled into a parking spot and eyed up my friends. They were all entranced in anticipation, waiting for the next move.

"Okay, that's enough! If he has any more time to think, he's gonna have an unfair advantage, and the whole game's lost. We'll need to have a do-over..." I couldn't help but smile, and that was the only reason why I couldn't turn around in the driver's seat to face the rest of my friends.

The temperature in the car had risen about five degrees since I had slid the gearshift into park. I turned the key in the ignition just slightly toward the windshield enough to roll down all of the windows that I could.

Rachel still hadn't spoken a word, though I could feel her hot glare on me. As much as she pretended that she was mad, I knew that it was all just for my benefit. The truth was, Rachel had spent one wild night with Ray-Ray back in our junior year of high school. She told me about it the next day, giddy as I've ever seen her, with a sheepish grin on her lips and blushed cheeks as she relayed her story. She'd had many boyfriends since that night, but I've never seen the glow in her eyes like when she had told me about her and Ray-Ray.

I was surprised how vividly I remembered it. The air was slightly chillier than it should have been for mid-April in Pennsylvania. It was almost to the point where I wished I had my winter coat with me as I stood outside the local WaWa pumping gas into my little Civic. Cars were buzzing around in the parking lot, and the gas pumps were all just about full. WaWa had the cheapest gas and the best coffee in the area, so Saturday mornings were usually busy there all day long.

Rachel appeared around the back of the Civic and leaned up against it, rubbing her hands together and acting as though there was still snow on the ground. "So I slept with Ray-Ray last night." It came as casually out of her mouth as a conversation about what she had for dinner the night before.

I pulled the nozzle out of the tank and replaced it on the pump. As I screwed the cap back on, I said, "Like slept over at his dorm or..."

"Slept with him, slept with him." She jumped in. She was now fiddling with the strings on the hood of her blue windbreaker.

I had to laugh. "Rach, he's like our brother. That's practically incest!"

Rachel rolled her eyes and turned back around to get into the passenger seat. Once we were both back inside the car, she slid her hood over her head and pulled the strings tight to hide as much of her face as she could, then slumped down in the seat.

Feeling a little bad for her, I couldn't help but ask the question that was suddenly bouncing through my mind, "Sooooo, how was he?"

I could see her wide smile underneath her hood. "Wow."

We both wound up laughing, as I turned the key in the ignition to drive across the parking lot to go get our coffee inside the WaWa. It was so strange at the time, my two friends hooking up. Even if it was just the one night, now there was something that bonded them.

"I've got it." Ray-Ray's declaration finally came from the back seat of the Suburban. "I've got the question. I'm ready."

I turned to face him. "You sure?"

He nodded, and cracked his knuckles. Anticipation filled the car. All eyes were now on Ray-Ray. We ignored the cars moving around us, finding parking spaces, pulling back out onto the highway, and people walking back and forth. None of it seemed to matter. Suddenly, our own little soap opera was playing out before our very eyes.

"During an interview in his home city of London in June of 2007, JT Porter claimed to have written most of his songs while under the influence of what drug?" With his arms crossed over his chest in proud victory, Ray-Ray's brown eyes pierced me through his dark, straggly bangs.

I could tell that there were five other brains with wheels turning in them right there in the car. Amazingly, it both amused me, and saddened me at the same time. Every other time that we played this game, I would have just automatically chosen the obvious answer. Even if they didn't care about 7 Year Coma, the answer that any American would have seen on TV or read in a magazine would have been quite obvious. The usual answers of marijuana, cocaine, even heroin, were on the tip of anyone's tongue. It just made sense. That was easy for the public to believe that anyone famous could have easily been wrapped up in such a debacle. And not to say it wasn't the case, on occasion, with JT Porter.

But the truth may lie somewhere between what everyone else believed, and what I was about to say. I smiled slyly at Ray-Ray, seeing no one else in the car at the time. This was just between me and him. And I loved every second of this. I was about to match Ray-Ray in the final round of his own game.

"Prozac, or so he claimed."

"Damnit." Rachel muttered under her breath. The air in the car was getting heavy, and there was no breeze outside to pour in through the windows. She pulled the ponytail holder off of her wrist and placed it in her mouth as she gathered her thick brown hair in a messy bun on top of her head. Tying it all together with a few quick turns of her wrist, she began to coach Ray-Ray. "You know she's going to throw you a question about Dax Crowley, so be ready. Get that one-track simple mind of yours focused on her Lover Boy, and you're golden. And Ray-Ray, please, please, please don't blow this one..."

Nathan turned to face him, and mumbled something that I couldn't hear, but it made the guys immediately burst into laughter.

I tossed an apologetic glance over at Rachel, as I prepared to seal her fate with my question. The crowd sat in quiet anticipation. *Shit,* I thought, *this was going to be good.* I couldn't help the smile that crept over my lips.

"How many siblings does Rylan Porter have?"

Rachel breathed a sigh of relief. She reached over to hug me, throwing her arms emphatically around my neck and squeezing as hard as she could. "Thank you Nat. Thank you so much. Good God, I was actually worried." She sunk back down in her seat and put her feet up on the dash, taking the last few sips of her cold Mocha Joe's.

I said nothing, just watched as a confused look appeared on Ray-Ray's face. "For real? That's your question?" He was quiet for only a moment, and then suddenly his eyes grew wide and he practically stood up in his seat, nearly hitting his head on the roof of the car. "Oh my God, Natalie. *Holy shit,* you actually *want* to sleep with me!"

I held my poker face. "Do you have an answer or not?"

As much as Ray-Ray was a fan of the band, he idolized Rylan Porter. He knew everything that was publicized about his life, from which guitar was his first, to the exact number of songs Rylan played lead on for each of their twelve records. He knew all of the songs that Rylan had written and released, even those that weren't on the albums. He hailed Rylan as a musical genius, which none of us could argue. This would have been a no-brainer question for him any day of the week. Ray-Ray leaned over the seat, hovering between Callie and Josh, to get as close to his opponent as he could possibly manage from the back seat of the car. "Two."

The guys cheered, as though this had suddenly become a team effort or something. As Ray-Ray gave out high-fives, I cleared my throat, trying to get their attention.

"I'm sorry, but that would actually be an incorrect answer."

Rachel rolled her eyes, and I believe she may have called me a liar, but it was a little hard to hear over the celebration going on in the back corner of the car.

"Nat, trust me, he has two siblings; JT of course, and a sister named Kathryn. That's something that even Callie might have gotten right." Josh defended his friend, then started to push open the door to make a break for the much-needed rest stop, "It was just a really bad pick for a final question."

A small wave of cooler air crept in, but I was paying no attention, as I defended my answer. "He has three siblings. A brother and *two* sisters."

Ray-Ray laughed. Josh turned back to stare at me in disbelief. Rachel's scowl had returned. Everyone else was looking from Ray-Ray back to me, trying to figure out what was going to happen next.

Nathan spoke up first. "Where did you read that?"

I shrugged my shoulders. "Insider knowledge. I've spent enough time in London, which I remind you, happens to be where Coma hails from. Think about the bands that come from the Philly area. If you're a fan, you go to the places that the band started playing at before they were big. You talk to people who may have known them before the rest of the world did. You know things that other people don't know. Call it town gossip, if you will."

It was Josh who came to my defense before Ray-Ray could open his mouth to object. "Maybe she's right, it's not outside the realm of possibility that there's another Porter sibling. It's highly unlikely that we wouldn't have heard about it until now, especially with Ray-Ray obsessing about the band's every move. But... maybe she does have some sort of insider knowledge. I'd say she has the burden of proof if the championship goes to her."

I smiled at Josh, grateful to have someone on my side.

Ray-Ray wasn't having it though. "See Natalie, you have to be able to back it up, and you can't. Google it, consult Wikipedia, whatever you want, but the fact is that you're just wrong."

"I'm not completely confident that the Internet is the most reliable source for facts," I told him, "but I will prove it to you when we get to Dallas."

THREE

Rylan

"What's that?" JT's sunglasses appeared over my shoulder, well before the pilot had turned off the seatbelt light. I had long let go of the notion that I'd ever have a peaceful flight with my brother occupying the same plane. He was a seven-year-old trapped in a thirty-five-year-old's body. He'd once been detained by the airport security after slapping a flight attendant's ass, throwing a full glass of vodka in another's face and verbally assaulting a second-class passenger - all in the same intercontinental flight. That was back in the days before he gave up most illegal drugs. Now, he was only a mild disturbance when trapped on an enclosed transportation device.

I looked back down at the letter in my lap. It was one that I had wished would never come. But you can't stop the inevitable. It was a river that we had dammed up, hoping it would hold forever, but knowing that the day would come when it'd be released. Now I was forced to deal with bones I'd buried a lifetime ago.

"Notification of Estate Sale." The lawyer had a certified overnight letter sent, knowing that I wasn't in the country, and along with it came a voicemail that it was coming. Leonard Kaplan had been killed by a fellow inmate several months ago in his prison cell. His home was being sold at an

Estate Sale, and while prepping and cleaning the home, they'd come across some personal effects of his late wife. The lawyer informed me that he'd have those items packed up and sent to his office, then he'd ship them to me when I returned to London.

JT slid into the seat next to me, snatching the letter to give it a quick once over. A few seconds later, the paper was flying back in my general direction. "Rubbish," he mumbled. "That cunt should've gotten the chair long ago for what he did."

I looked out the window, clear blue sky and clouds below us. The sun was shining above the plane, and it made me grateful for the time we spent up here, away from the chaos that was our lives far below. Here, there were no photographers in our face, no tabloids, no lawyers with Estate Sale notices.

"Find anyone to replace that wanker in Lull yet?" If anyone knew how to change a subject, it was JT.

I merely shook my head, slipping the envelope back into my jacket pocket. "Sammi's had a few leads, but the bastards keep rejecting all of them. We're running short on time. Anyone new that we bring aboard is going to need practice with the band before we sign them to open for us, and the European tour isn't long after we get back from the States."

One look in JT's eyes told me he had succeeded in getting my mind off of the letter. That bastard. But it was only a mild distraction. She was already on my mind. And so was that night, playing as it did, over and over again for the past twelve years.

I could never remember what the hell it was that we were doing the night JT's phone rang, and the moment he hung it up, he was dragging me by the sleeve toward the door. JT didn't know frantic, and it made the hair on the back of my neck stand up the way he was rambling on about us having to find her before he did.

It was barely moments later when we were on our way to the train station, only to find her being loaded onto a stretcher, shards of glass glittering like hundreds of tiny diamonds on the floor around our feet. The entire wall of windows at the station had been busted out from his gunshots, and her blood was spattered in intricate webs on the floor tiles, turning the diamonds into rubies. Later, they'd all be photographed and collected as evidence, but for now, they were pieces of a little girl, who lay broken and shattered on an ambulance gurney.

She was my responsibility, I reminded myself, climbing into the back of the ambulance with JT. I should have protected her from this. It was a hell of a time for fatherly instincts to kick in.

When we arrived at the hospital, they immediately rushed her back to surgery to remove the bullet that was lodged in her abdomen and bleeding extensively at that point. And while she was under the knife, detectives had come in to talk to me, in their crisp white shirts and black pants and annoying badges. One of the women from the police department tried to tell me as sympathetically as she could that they recommended a rape exam be done immediately after her surgery, before she woke up.

Good God, I argued, she's a child. Do they really think that...?

Yes, she told me, curtly. The rest of their team was already at Kaplan's house, looking for evidence. And oh, by the way, did I know that his wife had been found murdered? It was a virtual blood bath at that house, and it would take some time to sort out exactly what had happened and in which order. The body, they'd told me, had been found on the bed, with multiple stab wounds. Maybe the girl knew something about it? I didn't want them questioning her on it - that was for damn sure. She had been lucky, they had assured me.

Then when they told me the extent of her injuries, I wasn't so sure. She had two broken ribs, a deep gash from a kitchen knife in her side, and the gunshot wound that ironically, was only inches above where he had driven his knife into her. The surgeon speculated that he could repair both wounds with minimal scarring.

Whatever, I thought, just bring her back to me in one piece.

She had lost a lot of blood, and that was the biggest concern right now. The knife wound was at least three hours old, and the bullet that ripped through her added to the blood loss. There were multiple scratches and cuts over her upper body. Her face and arms suffered a few of the deeper cuts, where the shattered window wasn't slowed by her clothing. There were also deep purple bruises that were beginning to form where he had beaten her. And some of those were days old, they told me.

I couldn't sit still thinking about it.

JT had been there, thank God, when the doctor and the detective came to talk to me about the surgery and the results of the rape exam. It was actually the first time ever that JT had to hold me back. Not that it was the detective's fault, but I was about to kill the messenger.

"We weren't able to gain enough recent evidence, Mr. Porter," she explained, "but there are definite signs of...."

I was on my feet and lunging at her before JT had grabbed me around the waist. I never saw anyone move so quickly as that detective for the door. I'm sure she was used to it; they had to get this reaction a lot when they delivered this type of news. I was sure if JT wasn't busy holding me back, he'd have been going after the detective himself.

When they brought her back in from recovery, she was awake, but still heavily sedated, and shaking from the anesthesia. The nurse offered her warm blankets, which she kept kicking off. She was struggling to sit up with all of the wires and IV's that were attached to her. She reminded me of JT on a bad day.

The detectives insisted on questioning her right away, despite my protests. She completely denied that he had ever touched her inappropriately, and claimed he had never hit her before tonight. She remembered walking in, hearing something in one of the rooms, but couldn't say what. It was all a mess of confusion in her head.

The lead detective asked her again if he had ever touched her. "It's okay to tell us, you won't be in any trouble."

"No", she insisted, "Never."

She drifted in and out of sleep during the whole ordeal, and finally I told the detectives to get lost. I'd get in touch if she had any more information to offer.

I clenched my teeth, wanting so badly to tell her I was sorry. Sorry this happened to her, sorry that I put her in the position for something like this to have happened in the first place. She shouldn't have lost her childhood, lost her mother. She shouldn't be fighting for her life.

And when the machines around her starting beeping loudly, and nurses and doctors in their clean white coats came rushing in, pushing JT and me out, I knew I could never forgive myself.

It was a weight I'd carry around for the rest of my life.

FOUR
Natalie

We made it to the Virginia-Tennessee border around five pm, which was a little later than I had anticipated. After we stopped for dinner, I decided it would be okay to let Josh drive for a while, and I took over Ray-Ray's spot in the very back of the car, leaning my head against the side window. I very much enjoyed watching the scenery instead of the road.

It was a beautiful summer evening, and I almost wished that we weren't spending it cooped up in a car. The air outside was growing warmer and warmer the further south we headed, and even though the sun was falling in the western sky, the temperature in Tennessee was about where it was when we had left PA.

"So Natty," Rachel gave up on flipping through the stations, finding only a vast array of country music to choose from, "What're you wishing for when you blow out the candles this year?"

I smiled as I leaned my head on the back of the seat in front of me, knowing this question would come sooner or later. She asked me every year, and every year I told her the same thing. I wished that I could be with my family for my birthday. But as a kid, our private school started two weeks earlier than the public schools, which meant that my birthday greetings were all over the phone, and birthday gifts arrived in the mail.   All of my other friends enjoyed birthday celebrations with their families, who were all close enough for a short trip home if their birthday fell during the school year. I was invited each year to both Rachel's and Ray-Ray's, and had always longed for them to be able to come to a birthday celebration with my family. But this year would be different.

I was sure I had surprised them all when I answered, "That you guys enjoy meeting my family when we get to Texas."

I think Rachel even gasped. "Your family? For real? I was beginning to think that you'd made them all up…"

I couldn't help my smile. Seeing them for the first time in almost three years was enough to make it feel like Christmas was coming. It left a nervous energy in the pit of my stomach, just the thought of it, but it was also something that I had been looking forward to for many years now. "Well, not my whole family, but my brothers," I left out the part that they were really the only ones I considered family anymore anyway. "They'll be in Dallas for a few days while we're there, so I thought it might be fun to meet up."

I hadn't quite told my brothers about the trip yet either. I was hoping that my oldest brother would be receptive of the surprise visit, as we hadn't exactly spoken to each other in several years.   He'd sent texts at Christmas and on my previous birthdays, and I'd done the same, but after our last epic argument, neither of us had ventured as far to pick up the phone and actually speak to each other. But I missed him. There was a piece of my life - a large one - that was missing without him in it.

By the time we pulled into the hotel, I was tired but wound up all at the same time. After we checked in, the guys went to go find some alcohol to bring back to the rooms.

I stood outside in the hot Tennessee summer air, leaning over the railing outside of our second floor hotel room. The highway was just over a row of tall trees, and I stood there for a few minutes listening to the sound of the cars flying by.

We had made memories today, and as I thought about them, I smiled. I hadn't laughed as hard or as much as I did today in a long time. I thought about our little trivia game, and the arrangement that Ray-Ray and I had gotten ourselves and Rachel into. Unbelievable. Nothing would come of it, of course, and it would probably be the first time in the history of Ray-Ray's game that the final stakes would never really be settled. Of course, we'd keep that between us. We couldn't have the others thinking that they could bail out on the final stakes. It would ruin everything that the game stood for.

I thought of Ray-Ray, Rachel and I. The three of us had a friendship that was entirely unshakable. We all depended on each other, we all brought each other up when one of us was down, and we all loved each other more than anything else in the world. And we were the cornerstone of the rest of the group.

Out of the corner of my eye, I saw my Suburban practically sliding sideways around the far corner of the hotel parking lot. The tires squealing, it almost sideswiped a minivan before managing to move in a forward direction again. I could see the four of them laughing their asses off as Josh pulled the car into an empty spot somewhere below me.

As they got out of the car, Nathan stood next to it, threw his head back, and emptied the bottle of beer that he had in his hand. They were clearly already lit. I made a mental note that none of them would ever get behind the wheel of my car without passing my own personal sobriety test.

"Excuse me, Mr. Javerek," I shouted down to Nathan, "Was that an open container in a moving vehicle?"

Nathan looked up at me with a crooked smile. Flashbacks from Romeo and Juliet came to my mind, but I quickly dismissed them. He's engaged, I reminded myself, picturing Dori with a target on her back. "No ma'am. The vehicle's not moving anymore."

"Do I have to come down there and frisk you guys?"

Ray-Ray was pulling two full cases of beer out of the trunk. "Baby, you don't have to come down. I'll be right up!" He followed the other two up the stairs, each one of them with massive amounts of alcohol in their arms. Wine coolers for the girls - lots and lots of wine coolers - a few bottles of hard liquor, including rum, vodka and tequila, were all being unloaded into the girl's hotel room.

I turned and followed them in. Callie was in her pajamas, a towel wrapped around her wet head, and Rachel was wearing what she wore to bed every night, a t-shirt and sports pants. Nathan, who had found the pack of plastic shot cups in his suitcase, tossed them to Ray-Ray, who pulled off the plastic wrap and lined up six cups on the desk. "Rum or Tequila, ladies? What'll it be?"

We held up our cups to toast as Ray-Ray announced, "To the first night of the best trip of our fucking lives."

By midnight, there were more empty bottles than full, and most of the hard liquor had made it into the plastic shot glasses. Most of my friends had retired to bed, but I was still way too wound up to think about sleeping yet. My nerves were wreaking havoc on my mind, and there was no way I'd be able to settle down enough to rest properly.

I had returned to my spot on the balcony, leaning over the railing outside of our hotel room. I was pretty sure that everyone else was asleep, but when Ray-Ray slid over next to me, I realized that my judgment might have been slightly impaired.

We stood there a while, drinking our beers without saying a word. It was a nice night, and even if I was drunk off of my ass, I was still able to appreciate nice weather when it presented itself. Maybe it was the inborn Brit in me that made me love the warm weather wherever I could find it, but I decided right then and there that somehow, someday, I wanted to move where the climate was warm all year round. At the moment, Nashville was looking good. If I could only become a country singer, I thought, and then laughed out loud.

Ray-Ray looked over at me, but didn't say a word. He just continued to sip his beer, very casually. His dark hair was almost covering his eyes tonight, with an occasional warm breeze blowing them out of the way just enough long enough that I could catch a glimpse. He claimed there was a slight Irish side to him, to which he attributed his sense of humor and love of alcohol. Much like most of what came out of Ray-Ray's mouth, we took a lot of it in stride.

Ray-Ray had grown up relatively well-to-do, but never really paid much attention to his own upbringing. He had a successful father, who had made a good amount of money on Wall Street in his early years, then settled in as a partner at Montgomery, Banks and Morton in the Bucks County area. Ray-Ray's parents lived alongside the Delaware River in New Hope, known for its eclectic shopping, sophisticated wineries, and upscale restaurants. His mother was a middle-aged socialite, spending her days planning local charity events, and her nights entertaining her husband's colleagues, local business units, or political figures. Ray-Ray's younger sister Janelle was finishing her senior year at the same prep school that we had all attended. My understanding of Janelle was that she took after her brother more so than her parents. Ray-Ray considered that to be a personal victory.

It amazed me that he was as carefree as he was, and I often wondered myself where all of that free spirit came from. Ray-Ray set the standards, he didn't follow them. There were so many times that I thought Ray-Ray would get kicked out of school, but he had the gift of charm - inherited from his father - that he used to his advantage. It didn't hurt that the headmaster at our prep school was an undersexed single woman in her late thirties. There were many rumors, most of them likely started by Ray-Ray himself, that she and Ray-Ray had an arrangement of sorts that kept him in school until he graduated, which he did somehow without issue. And from what I remember, the headmaster was in attendance at the graduation party that Ray-Ray's parents had thrown.

I looked back over at him, seeing the guy that I had known back then, now two years later. He hadn't aged very much, just grew his hair a little longer, and maybe built up a little more muscle in his forearms than he had in high school. He was still the same old Ray-Ray, though he was now two years into his Business Administration degree at St. Joe's University in Philly.

We both spoke at the same time.

"Ray-Ray."

"Natalie."

He laughed and toasted me with his bottle. "Ladies first."

"Fuck," I told him, finishing my beer, then handing him my empty, "Then we're screwed, aren't we?"

He took my bottle, and handed me his, which was only half full. And warm. "Then beauty before age."

I decided that would do, took a sip and then giggled. "I forgot what I was going to say..."

He didn't hesitate. "I want to take you out for your birthday when we get to Texas."

I cocked my head to the side, my vision a bit more blurry than I'd had wanted. "I know, you guys bought me tickets to..."

"No, that's different." Ray-Ray interjected. "I want to take you out, just you and me."

I felt like I was looking at him as though he had two heads, and I had to take a moment to collect my drunk, impaired thoughts.

"Every woman deserves to be taken out for a great dinner on her birthday, especially when it's such a monumental one." He took his beer back out of my hand and finished it off, all the while never taking his eyes off of mine.

Damn, he was good, I thought. It made me wonder why he and his last girlfriend broke up, actually. For just a moment, I saw him as this hopeless romantic, throwing a pickup line out there to the girl of his dreams, hoping it hit its mark. He was confident, borderline cocky, but something in his eyes held back, as though there were the slight possibility that she'd say no.

I do remember when she had broken up with him, after almost a year and a half of on-again-off-again dating bliss, that he had rung up Rachel and me, and we went out to our favorite pub to play pool, drink beer, and vowed to stay single the rest for the of our twenties. To this day, Sydney is still considered a curse word in our vocabularies. She was, after all, the closest that Rachel and I ever came to losing Ray-Ray.

Sure, it started out innocent enough, but before we knew it, he was canceling our poker night to go to dinner with her parents. Movie night was replaced with date night. Friday nights of drinking at our favorite pub or local hangout soon became weekends spent with Sydney's friends. We'd only see Ray-Ray when he didn't have a "previous engagement". We weren't even sure if he knew what that phrase meant, but visions of a pristine dominatrix heiress came to mind whenever Rachel or I even thought about Sydney.

And the news that she had broken up with him had come to us wrapped in a bittersweet package. We were relieved that we would have our friend back, but felt his devastation and pain. We were women, after all, and had each felt the agony of breakups as only a woman could see them. However, the joy of having Ray-Ray back in our lives trumped everything, even our distaste for Sydney.

The breakup had been about nine months ago, and Ray-Ray hadn't really dated much since then, other than a random date here or there.

"Let's do it." I agreed, "But I have to warn you. I have

expensive taste."

Ray-Ray laughed. "I'll do my best, Love. Just keep in mind, I'm a college student."

"With very, very rich parents." I reminded him.

FIVE
Natalie

The car erupted into cheers when we crossed the border from
Arkansas to Texas. "Fuck yeah!" Josh shouted, "Do you guys
realize we're that much closer to fourteen fucking rows away
from the greatest band of all time?"

"After the Beatles." I reminded him.

I could feel their hot stares, especially Ray-Ray's, who I
was surprised had not all-out swerved into the opposite lane.
"What?" I contended, "I'm from London! I'd be a hypocrite to
my country and people if I was not a Beatles fan." Which for
the record was the truth. I often contended that I had been
born twenty years too late. I'd have given my left arm to see
Lennon live. Yet I'd take 7 Year Coma, in Lennon's absence.

As a young child, I had often aspired to play the guitar
like John Lennon. Of course, I had been taught by who I
considered to be the best guitar teacher (other than Lennon,
perhaps) in the world. From the time I was a young girl in
London, I had a guitar in my hands. It was never something
that I had gone without for long in my life, as my first guitar

had made its way from London to the States, then as I grew old enough to earn allowance, I had saved enough for the first guitar I'd ever purchased with my own money.

"So I heard that JT Porter was considering a solo career." Josh threw out there, rather nonchalantly. Josh loved to argue, and he knew that the words that he had just uttered were pure blasphemy in present company. The sly smile on his face showed it too.

I often wondered how it was that Josh and Ray-Ray lived together without killing each other sometimes, especially when Josh came out with comments like that. I hadn't realized that my mouth had opened and words had just started pouring out until it was too late. "You know that's never going to happen. JT depends on Rylan's musical direction to create his songs. He's also too grateful and loyal to the band."

It was that very moment that Ray-Ray hit the brakes. Maybe not as hard as he would have if traffic in front of him had come to a stand-still, but I could tell he had that urge to no longer concentrate on the road, as he was staring at me in disbelief more than he was looking at the blacktop in front of him. "Who are you?"

I shrugged it off good-naturedly. "I've been reading a bit in preparation for our trip." Suppressing the smile that was fighting its way through my teeth, I fought not to look over at Ray-Ray. I already knew that his dark brown eyes were narrowed in suspicion, as they always were when he was the slight bit thrown off or confused. The wheels inside his head were turning full speed right now, and I loved it. I loved every second of it. Casually, I pressed my finger against the black button on door, lowering the window, and letting in the warm breeze and Texan air. I slid my hand out of the open window, allowing my fingers to fight the eighty-mile an hour breeze that blew through them.

As we pulled up to the Elyad Suites, just about twenty-five miles north of the center of Dallas, I found myself surprisingly impressed. Before us stood a colossal white stone building with a grand entranceway and eight stairs surrounding the glass doors leading the way into the lobby. Inside, orange-red marble and thick Brazilian Rosewood wrapped its way throughout the room before us. Abstract ivory carved statues of mythical creatures tapered the walkway to the solid marble welcome desk. Behind it, an anorexic thin woman in a cotton stretch seersucker blazer, with blonde hair pulled tightly behind her head, forcing a smile at us.

I had to find the humor in it all, a group of six twenty-something's, with me, their spokeswoman, in sweat-garb left over from a nasty hangover, approaching the front desk and claiming, "Reservation for Winters."

My friends were in tired awe, and with the "Guest Services Specialist" practically in repulsion, I leaned my head on my elbow on the exotic marble counter, just thinking about the crisp white sheets that I was about to slip into. Her eyes lit up slightly as she looked me over not once, but twice, then back at the computer. A smile quickly curled her lips and she slid a printed receipt my way. "Please sign here, Ms. Winters. There will be complimentary room service, on the house, throughout your stay at Elyad Suites. Also, you and your guests will have a personal concierge service throughout your stay at our establishment. Please feel free to ring them, anytime day or night. Would you like to select your breakfast menu tonight before bed, or would you prefer to have breakfast in our private dining hall in the morning?"

This was information overload, I thought, as I resisted the urge to turn back to my friends for decision making support. I had to play the part, at least for a few more minutes, though I was anticipating some pretty weighted questions in only a few moments. I had prepared some canned answers though, and I hoped that it held me over until I absolutely, positively, found just the right moment to open up to all of them. Until then, I had to continue to play a role that I clearly wasn't qualified for. Good naturedly, I said to Professional Twiggy Barbie, "We'll dine privately tomorrow, thank you. Must I make a reservation this evening, or just ring you in the morning?" I didn't have to try very hard for the accent to seep through.

Moments later, she slid me three sets of key cards, gave me directions to our rooms, and bid us goodnight. I turned to my friends, who since the first time I had known them, were speechless. Not one word was uttered as I walked past them and toward the grand elevators at the far end of the lobby. It took a few moments before the group gathered behind me as I waited for the ivory doors to open. Once we were alone in the elevator and on our way up to one of the top floors of the building, Josh broke the silence.

"What parallel universe did we just step into?"

I smiled sweetly at him. "Don't you like the hotel, Joshy?"

"It's not that, it's just that I was expecting Motel 6 or HoJo and we end up at the fuckin' Ritz-Carlton."

"Elyad Suites, actually." I corrected him, as the elevator doors swung open, and revealed a majestic hallway, with burgundy walls speckled with gold foil. Large cherry wood tables stood valiantly under wood framed mirrors, illuminated by soft white lights housed in fancy wall sconces.

Even more impressive was the view just after I slid the plastic card through the box on the door. Two huge pillow-top beds in lavish burgundy comforters lay below overstuffed plush pillows centered the room. A large cherry wood desk sat against the wall opposite of the beds, with a matching cherry armoire, which housed the stacked entertainment center. Silk taffeta Goblet drapes lined the French doors to the balcony, which overlooked the fountains in the pond just outside, and beyond that, the entire city.

"Hell yes!" Nathan did a dive onto one of the beds. "Rachel and Natalie, if you care to join me on this bed, the rest can have the other bed...."

I revealed to them all three room keys, and their eyes got even wider. "So who the hell is Winters?" Josh snatched the key cards out of my hand, glaring at me suspiciously. I could now feel five pairs of eyes boring holes into my skull.

"What gives, Natalie?" Ray-Ray chimed in, as he headed toward the French doors for a closer inspection of the view.

I was quite pleased with my work, or Sammi's rather, and enjoyed for a few moments their total bewilderment. Well, maybe I enjoyed a few moments more than a good friend would have, but I couldn't help it, it had been a long, long time that I had been keeping my life quiet.

"I have a friend who hooked us up." I confessed. "Maybe you'll get to meet her."

"Does she work here?" Rachel inquired. She was standing next to me clasping the handles on her Prada bag that was slung over her shoulder.

"Nah, not at the hotel." I quickly changed the subject. "We can go check out the other rooms, if you want."

We found a rustic little Irish Pub down the road from the hotel. O'Shalley's offered four pool tables lined up in a row at the far end of the place, a large wooden bar with high stools in the middle, a few mismatched tables huddled near the bar, and a mid-sized rickety dance floor just in front of a make-shift stage at the other end.

There were a total of five Texans, regulars, most likely, drinking their beer from mason jars at the bar. This totally intrigued Ray-Ray, as it was his lifelong dream to be a regular at a dive bar someday. He jumped right in and ordered his own mason jar, then headed straight for the pool table. Josh was not far behind him. The rest of us ordered our drinks and settled into the haphazard tables just as a local band started their warm-ups.

The second that the only guitarist in the band struck his

first chord, the sound cut through me like a razorblade and I couldn't fight the goose bumps crawling all over my skin. Nothing made me cringe faster than an out-of-tune guitar. It was one of the first lessons I had ever learned, and it was ingrained in my heart and soul that before you played your first song, your instrument had to be in perfect tune. I had learned how to tune a guitar before I learned how to write my name.

It was either that or it was my OCD, but I wasn't sure that I could sit through a whole set without having a meltdown. I downed my nearly full mason jar in a few swigs and casually made my way up to the stage. Locking eyes with the shaggy haired guitarist, I smiled sweetly as I approached the stage. He smiled back as I thought of my approach. I let him take the lead. "Looks like we have our first groupie."

My smile widened, and I cocked my head to one side. "Nice Baby Taylor you've got there."

He raised his eyebrows, then he looked down at his guitar and shrugged. "We're just starting out, but she's been good to me." He tapped her on the top and nodded back toward me. "So you play then?"

I glanced back toward my friends to make sure they were all where I had left them, and nodded. "I do."

"What do you play?"

"I have a few. My favorite right now is my Gibson J-40." And I missed it. Terribly. Just the sight of his guitar in front of me had me longing for any one of mine cradled in my arms.

"Nice." He was legitimately impressed.

I smiled again, and took my hands out of my pocket. "Can I see yours?"

He didn't hesitate as he slipped the strap over his fuzzy head and passed the guitar to me as I stepped up on stage. I sat on his bar stool and leaned the guitar on my thigh. My fingers nearly melted as I let them slide down the strings. It was well broken in, and very loved. I picked at the strings for a moment, adjusting the tuners until they went back into range, hitting the notes on precision. Much better, I thought, breathing with relief as the notes rang true back through my ears at each pick.

After a few moments, I was happily strumming some chords, lost in the music. I hadn't even noticed that the drummer was tapping along lightly with my tune, and the guitarist was now in the audience watching me. It hadn't occurred to me that everyone in the bar was watching also, until I heard Rachel's voice shout out, "Nat, do *Wake Up!*" It was a great 7 Year Coma ballad, one I had played for her once a few months ago.

I smiled somewhat shyly and handed the guitar back to its rightful owner. He cocked his head as he took his Baby Taylor and slid the strap back over his head. "You know, you look very familiar. I've been watching you play, but I just can't quite place you. Can I ask your name?"

I did get this once in a while. "Natalie McKinney." I replied, and slipped back over toward our table before he could question me further.

Nathan came over to me as I was about to sit, handing me a fresh mason jar with one hand and swinging his other arm across my shoulders, pulling me tight against him. "Nat, when did you learn to play guitar?"

I took a few sips, letting the lager slide down the back of my tongue and fizz the whole way down. I answered him with a wink just as Josh and Ray-Ray were starting up another game of pool.

I was barely aware that my eyes had fallen upon Ray-Ray as he leaned over the table, lining up to take his first shot. There was something about the concentration on his face, the way he focused so intently on what he was doing, that had me intrigued. The way he laughed at whatever off-color comment Josh had just made, it made me wish that he was laughing with me.

My mind wandered back to that night two years ago, when I had showed up at Ray-Ray's door in my most fashionable pair of black workout pants, my favorite long sleeved faded gray T-shirt and my freshly cut shoulder-length dark hair in a neat ponytail tied just behind my neck. I turned the knob, and walked into the mini-foyer, which was really just a stone slab cutout in the corner of the living room of the renovated historic twin home that they rented. I always felt a shiver run down my spine and crawl all over my skin whenever I entered the house. Now was no exception, even in the fading evening daylight.

Looking throughout the room, the first thing that always caught my eye from the moment I walked in, was the overstuffed beige and blue couch in the middle of the room. It faced a large-screen Hi-Def television, and was matched on either side by reclining armchairs. There was a large wooden coffee table in front of the couch, made of dark cherry wood, which replaced their kitchen table most nights.

Josh was heading toward the living room from the stairs, his keys in his hand, and his backpack slung over his shoulder. "Hey Nat. Enjoy movie night." He said; as he quickly bent down to re-tie his sneaker. "Where's Rachel?"

"She bailed last minute. Had a date." I responded. "Where are you off to in such a hurry?"

"Callie's. Catch you later." With that, he was out the door.

I heard Ray-Ray rustling about in the kitchen, so I walked toward the back of the house to find him. When I entered the brightest room of the house, I found Ray-Ray on the floor, his head inside one of the bottom cabinets, banging through a mess of pots and pans.

"Lose something?" I had to speak loudly over the banging noises in the cabinet.

Ray-Ray managed to pull his head out of the cabinet. "Looking for the popcorn maker. Can't have movie night without popcorn." He dove back behind the wooden door and appeared a few moments later with both pieces of the prized popcorn maker. His next stop was the cabinet above the sink, where he pulled out two bottles of wine. One was my favorite, Cab Franc, and the other was a very nice looking bottle of Merlot, bottled two years prior, I noted.

"Rach will not be joining us this evening, due to a last minute date with a random hottie she met in class. So who is going to drink all of that wine, I wonder?"

"One's for you, one's for me." Ray-Ray didn't miss a beat.

I wasn't exactly thrilled that Ray-Ray had chosen the most graphic horror movie that had just hit the shelves at the local video store. He and Rachel were horror movie buffs, but I rarely watched them, lest I be up all night in terror. Ghosts and gore were two things that I just couldn't stand, and this movie seemed to have an abundance of both. I had seen the previews, and those alone caused me to lose two week's worth of sleep. Ray-Ray apologized profusely, claiming that he had chosen this one for Rachel. I forgave him, and promised that I'd brave it anyhow.

Only minutes into the movie, I was curled up at the end of the couch, hugging my knees, with nothing but a throw blanket and my glass of wine to protect me from the demons and knife-murderers that I was sure were stalking the house.

I hadn't even realized that I had jumped when the knife-wielding madman made his third surprise appearance, until Ray-Ray looked over at me, suppressing a laugh. The lights were out, and every little creek in the house was making me startle. "You're really freaked out, aren't you?"

Perhaps it was the sound of the air-conditioner kicking in upstairs somewhere, or the next-door neighbor closing the door a bit too loudly behind us, but I hadn't realized that I had turned a full one-eighty to make sure there were no ghosts or serial killers behind me, until Ray-Ray had mentioned it. I was too ashamed to nod, and too scared to say that I wasn't.

Ray-Ray extended his arm. "Come here, Nat. I'll keep you safe."

There was only a brief pause before I slid over next to him, pulling my blanket and my wine with me. He wrapped a warm, sturdy arm around me, and for only a moment, I felt what it was like to be loved freely. He was, after all, my best friend next to Rachel, and I tried as hard as I possibly could to ignore the fact that his cologne was filling my nose, my lungs, and my heart. All I knew for sure was that I was leaning my cheek up against his warm chest, and his strong arm was wrapped tight across my shoulders.

I continued to sip my wine, maybe a slight bit quicker now than before, but tried my best to enjoy the movie nonetheless. At least until he whispered to me loudly, "Hey Nat?"

I pulled back slightly so that I could look him in the eyes, my face only inches from his. I tried not to let the shivers run so quickly up my spine. I wasn't even aware that I holding my breath, but I did notice that my palms starting to sweat.

He continued to speak in a loud whisper. "Can you grab the popcorn?"

As the movie played on, we drank our wine, and finished off the popcorn. Though we were both into the movie, just as the main character was faced with her potential demise at the climax, I became particularly tense. It was just then that Ray-Ray pressed his lips against my temple.

It was only moments later that my chin had turned up toward him, and my eyes locked with his. I hadn't noticed that the bottle of Cab Franc had been almost finished, and so had the Merlot. Somehow there was also a bottle of Shiraz that had found its way to the table, but I couldn't place when or how it had gotten there.

All I knew at that very moment was that his eyes were inches from mine, and suddenly I was meeting him halfway. His lips brushed against mine ever so lightly, and he pulled back only long enough to see that my eyes were half closed and I hadn't backed away. I ran my tongue over my lips, tasting him and instantly wanted more. His hand had moved from across my shoulders to my lower back as he pulled me closer toward him. My fingers found their way to his chest, where they were starting to twist and tangle his t-shirt as his tongue slid across my teeth then into my mouth.

I was finding it hard to take in air, but the taste of him intrigued me. The fact that he had forgotten to shave this morning sent ripples down my spine every time his chin brushed against the soft skin on my face. And when he moved down to kiss my neck, I leaned back, letting him support me with the arm that he still had wrapped around me.

"Good God, Natalie," the words came from deep inside of his throat, and with his free hand, he cradled my head, his fingers falling through my hair. I wished to God at that moment that I hadn't cut three inches off of it so that it would have given him more to play with. "We need to go upstairs. Right now."

The very next afternoon I had found myself on a flight back to London for a family emergency. I didn't even have time to reflect on what had happened between us, let alone let him know where I had gone, but was instead thrown into a restless ocean of dysfunctional family affairs and emotions.

It was a full three weeks before I had been able to return to the States, and when I did, Ray-Ray and I made the logical decision that our friendship was eternally more important than the insanely fabulous sex that we had shared. Only a few short months after that, he started dating Sydney the Snoot.

I realized that I had finished my drink only when the bartender was setting a Captain and Coke in front of me. He must've read the baffled look on my face, because he pointed down at the end of the bar, and as I leaned forward, I saw Ray-Ray give me a wink before he downed his shot. With a sigh, I rolled my eyes, picked up my drink and walked over to him.

That wide smile was painted on his face again as he held up a fresh bottle of beer to toast my glass. "Thanks for the hotel room in the ritziest fucking hotel in the state," he paused, then added, "that I get to share with Nathan..."

"I was kind enough to get you separate beds."

"Thank you for that." He nodded toward the dance floor and threw an arm across my shoulders. "Why aren't you up there?"

I looked up at him, eyeing him suspiciously. "Dancing?"

He frowned, cocking an eyebrow to show his disappointment. "Guitar. From what I heard tonight, you have a bit of talent, Love. If you didn't suck so much at Karaoke, you might have a career on your hands."

I shook my head and pulled away from him. "It's just a hobby. Nothing serious."

To say the words aloud made me cringe inside. Conflicting emotions set rage against each other, and I could almost physically feel my life up until now clashing against my future. Sooner or later, I told myself, I needed to tell him. I needed to tell all of them. But I didn't want to do it while I had been drinking. That much I knew.

We got ourselves a table and I had just placed an order for jalapeno cheese fries when Josh tapped me on the shoulder with the blunt end of a bar dart. "Let's go, McKinney. You and I have some unfinished business."

I was on my feet in a matter of seconds, and food was now the furthest thing from my mind. "Wish me luck, ladies." I said, as I grabbed my bottle of lager and followed him to the opposite end of the club toward the lonely dartboard in the lonely corner.

Josh absolutely could not stand losing at anything, let alone a bar room game, and especially not to a girl. Never mind the fact that I was a Brit. Of course, he had blamed it on the alcohol when he lost twice in a row only a few weeks ago in a dive bar somewhere off the beaten path on the way home from a club. We had seen a great band that night, and the drinks were dirt cheap, but when we had gone out to the parking lot, we discovered that there had been a pretty violent fight, and Josh's car had been scratched by some drunk bar slut. Still, the only thing that Josh could focus on the entire ride home was that he had lost at darts.

He started off the game tonight by throwing a near bull's-eye, twice in a row. He raised his eyebrows and took a long swig from his beer bottle.

"Doesn't look like you brought your game with you

today." His comment followed my dart hitting the wall next to the dartboard, then sliding pathetically down to bounce onto the floor.

My skin crawled at the thought of touching it, but I sucked in my breath and ignored the fact that the floor around it was slightly sticky with beer that had probably been spilled long before tonight. I found calmness by taking a long sip of my own beer. "You don't rattle me Van Arden. You just keep your mind on your own game and don't worry about mine. We both know what happened last time."

He gave me the finger subtly before throwing his next dart, which barely made it into scoring range. He managed to win the first game, but not by much. "Best out of three, I'll go get us refills."

We sat at the empty bar in the back of the game room with our fresh drinks, and the shots of Captain that Josh also managed to sweet-talk the bartender into. Josh was leaning casually on the bar, his blond hair just long enough that the ends curled slightly in the humidity of the room. He held up his shot glass to mine. "Your twenty-first."

I tipped mine toward his and we downed the liquor.

When he set his glass down on the bar, he paused a moment, then looked over at me. "I hear you have a date with our boy Ray-Ray tomorrow night."

I set my own glass down, trying to let the rum settle before I responded by shaking my head perhaps a bit too emphatically. "It's just dinner."

Josh winked, then took his beer and headed back toward the dartboard. "If that's what you want to believe..."

He was already eyeing up his next shot when I approached him.

"One second," I told him, "What did you mean by that?"

He only smiled slyly and shot a perfect bull's eye. Then he turned to face me, rather proud of himself, and sucked down half of his beer in one long swig.

I set my darts down on a nearby table and pulled up a chair, waiting for his answer.

After a few moments, he gave in and sat down across from me, setting his darts down next to mine. "You know, I really can't tell if you're just playing dumb, or if you simply don't see it." He eyed me up to see if I'd react, which I intentionally didn't, and only responded with a nod. He knew I wasn't playing anything with him. I never did. I just sat there with my arms folded on the table and waited for him to continue. After a moment he asked me, "Do you know why Ray-Ray and Sydney broke up?"

I struggled to remember an event that I hadn't really ever delved into. Ray-Ray had been pretty tight-lipped about the whole thing, from what I remember. I didn't recall him ever saying anything more than that it was over and he wanted to go out with Rachel and me for drinks. I finally just shook my head and shrugged. "I don't think he ever mentioned the reason."

Josh nodded, knowing full well what the answer was before he had even asked the question. He then leaned forward, and lowered his voice. "He called her by your name when he was in bed with her one night."

I choked on my beer, and Josh let me recover before he pushed my darts over toward me. "So game on, McKinney."

I blew the next game. Not intentionally, but the entire time I was throwing darts, I was properly convincing myself that Josh was only winding me up to win the game. It was an innocent mistake, I told myself, if there was any truth to it at all. Which I was sure there wasn't. I was one of his best friends. It could have just as easily been Rachel's name that he called her. It just happened to have been mine.

When we returned to our table, the girls hung their heads in shame. "Next time." Callie promised, as I scowled and sat down.

Ray-Ray was sitting on the other side of the table, one arm around Rachel, the other around Callie. A quick tickle twisted my stomach ever so slightly when my eyes met his, and I abruptly looked away. I had hoped he hadn't noticed.

"Aw come on, Natalie. Don't be like that," Ray-Ray toyed with me, "We all now know your true talent is with a guitar, not a dartboard."

Just hearing him say my name, it was somehow different now. I was trying not to picture the scene, him and Sydney, somewhere in the throws of passion, and he calls her by my name. Rachel would die when I told her. We'd have a proper laugh over that one. Even if it wasn't true, which I doubted it was, it was still worth a good laugh.

SIX
Rylan

The calendar on my phone was set to count down the final days of the tour. This one was wearing me down quick. Probably had a lot to do with all the things going on outside the tour. Once we got back, I could focus on sorting it all out. But for now, the main goal was just getting the band back to London in one piece.

JT wasn't exactly making that easy. Between his impromptu hook up with that up-and-coming advertising agent, or so she claimed, and his even more spontaneous decision to come off his prescriptions, I couldn't keep up. He was up, he was down, and he was leaving a trail of trouble every direction he turned. And his kind of trouble usually came with price tags and severe consequences. We had cancelled two shows when he and his new girlfriend split from the rest of the band and disappeared in Vegas. And when he all out attacked a photo-journalist, sending the kid to the hospital in need of seven stitches and a personally injury lawyer, it required forfeiting our one and only day off between cities to reschedule yet a third cancelled show while we posted his bail.

Sammi, as usual, ran cleanup for us. She made things disappear, though I'd rather not ask her how. That was one reason why she was with us. She was the best at what she did. But even she was growing worn by JT's antics. We had been discussing it last night over dinner. Something had to be done, though trying to control him was like trying to dam a tsunami. Pointless. All you could do was just get out of the way and do what you could to fix it afterward. And yet somehow, Sammi had managed to keep both the girlfriend and the antics out of the eager eyes of the press. God bless Sammi - the woman had a power that was unmatched, even in our business, and we were incredibly lucky to have her - myself in particular.

The best part of my morning was about to happen, as it did most mornings, like clockwork. The alarm in the bedroom of my hotel suite would go off, loud obnoxious music pouring through a tiny speaker, sounding like shit, but music to my ears all the same.

Then, exactly ten minutes later, the door would open, and she'd be leaning against the door frame in my t-shirt and nothing else, her copper red hair still tousled from the pillow and sticking out in every direction, her eyes fixed on me. I'd cross the room, sweep one arm around the small of her back, then the other I'd slide behind her neck, kiss her gently once for good morning, then, needing so much more of her than just that, I'd pick her up and we'd fall right back into bed. The clock on the nightstand would read exactly 8:11 am. That's how she operated, much like me, on a tight schedule.

This morning, just as I was about to pull my t-shirt up over her head, a cell phone went off on the nightstand, buzzing furiously against the wood. I considered ignoring it, as my hand ran along that light, soft skin that tasted so good when we made love. But Sammi couldn't. It could be anyone: venue managers, the media, record producers, or any myriad of all the hundreds of people that she corresponded with on a daily basis. A missed call was a delay that could potentially ruin a show, and cost us upward of a half-million.

She reached for her phone, took a quick look at the caller ID, and wiggled out from under me before she held it to her ear.

I nibbled on her free ear as she talked. "Right then, the Westshire Room. That'll be much appreciated." She slid the phone back on the nightstand and without turning, reached her hand behind her to run her fingers through my hair. "We've arranged an after show party with the editors of Rolling Stone Magazine tomorrow night here at the hotel. I'm putting you in charge of getting JT there."

I was glad she couldn't see me roll my eyes at her, but I couldn't hide the displeasure from my voice. "I hate these things…"

I was sure she was rolling her eyes right back at me, but she kept her tone even keel. "We need to do a better job of marketing the band in the States, Rylan. Record sales are falling here. America is a major market, and even though you're huge in the rest of the world, you're not where you could be over here."

"Fuck the States," I grumbled, standing up, "they wouldn't know good music if it bit them in their ass. The record companies pay a fortune for these semi-talented half-wits who play canned music and make it big as long as they conform to whatever's popular at the moment. And that's all these kids over here know. It's a damn shame."

She had heard it all before, I knew. It wasn't the first time, and it wouldn't be the last that the American music industry would fire me up. "So I guess you won't be looking for an American to kick-start Lucas' brother's band then?"

I growled at her, my eyes narrowing. "Don't wind me up, Sammi. You won't like the consequences."

She made a sound like a giggle, but it came out more like a sensual purr, and it had me crawling all over her again.

My lips touched the bare skin on her belly, my tongue tracing a crooked line up between her breasts, firm with hard pink nipples that loved to be clenched between my teeth. My fingers ran from her wrists up the delicate skin of her inner arms, and back down her sides to hook the bottom of whichever one of my shirts she was wearing through my fingers, lifting it up over her head and slinging it off to the floor. And as I came back down, my lips played casually over hers, teasing and playing against her chin, her cheeks, her neck, until I finally chose a spot to dive into. This morning the soft skin just under her ear smelled of the slightest bit of a new perfume, and I let my nose brush against it over and over as I gnawed at her neck.

Her hips rose against me, as though she might try to fight me off, and she gave a half-laugh-half-moan, "Rylan..." Her long fingers dragged through my hair, then clenched tightly as I thrust into her. The heat that surrounded me was enough to make me want to start and finish in one powerful blow, but I pulled back and paused just long enough to nearly send us both over the edge before driving back into her, deeper and harder this time, dragging the next moan from deep in her throat before I covered her mouth with mine. She tasted sweet, sweeter than most mornings, and I indulged in the every sense that I could pull from her. She made it all worth it for me. The long hours, the tireless travel, all the bullshit drama, she made it all disappear the second her breasts, sweating with pleasure, pressed against my chest.

Every muscle in my body was rock hard against her soft, porcelain skin, and if I didn't know my Sammi as I did, I'd have been careful as not to break her. But it had never been like that between us. I'd known her for years before ever once touching her, and I'd long known by that point that the woman was tougher than most men I knew. But her body said otherwise.

Her body was feminine to the core. She held a class and an elegance like no other, and in the bedroom, this was far more apparent. But I knew what she liked, what drove her to the brink of insanity, what made her bite her bottom lip and turn her head to the side, clenching her eyes shut, curling her toes and grasping me tighter than any woman ever had, enough to force it out of me in a way that I couldn't control any more than she could.

"Rylan..." she repeated, breathing heavily and sliding out from underneath me. I never grew tired of hearing her say my name. I let my eyes lay upon her, enjoying the sight of what I'd done to her, damp hair and glistening skin that made me want more of her already. I loved the sound of my name on her lips. I could listen to it all day. Fuck the show tonight. The fans could pull up our band on any number of internet sites, slide a CD into the player, tune us in on their car radio. But I had to rely on hearing Sammi's voice only when I was with her. And I wanted her all day, all night. Was that too much to ask? To blow off work just one night so that I could spend the day in bed making love to the most beautiful woman in the world, listening to her over and over say my name in that sweet, sensual whisper?

And that was it. I wanted her again. Already. I leaned in closer, about to kiss her neck, my fingers tracing downward, below her belly...

"We've an interview with the local rock radio station in a half-hour."

I froze for a moment as she slipped off the bed and headed for the shower. "I fucking hate my job."

She tossed me a half-grin through the doorway to the bathroom, "No you don't."

SEVEN
Natalie

When the alarm went off at 8:02 on Thursday morning, it was officially my twenty-first birthday. Ray-Ray had made a reservation at Worthington's, an upscale high-end seafood restaurant located in the heart of Dallas. I was excited, as on the rare occasion that I enjoyed seafood nowadays, it usually consisted of all-you-can-eat crab legs at a local chain restaurant. The last time that I had been treated to such an affair was at our high school graduation, when Rachel's parents took us to a restaurant near Wilkes-Barre, where you could choose your own trout from a stream that ran right through the dining room of the restaurant.

The morning began when Rachel and I decided to venture on a little shopping trip in Plano, a large suburb just north of Dallas.

In the northern suburbs of Dallas, it was very much populated with strip malls, apartment complexes and businesses, as well as very new construction just about everywhere we looked. It amazed both of us how flat the land was around the buildings, and when you were lucky enough to catch a glimpse of some of the open fields, they rolled on for miles and miles without a mountain or a hill disrupting it.

We ended up at a large three-story mall, where we started our day with a late "breakfast" at The Cheesecake Factory. Rachel explained that on vacation, this was allowed. She rationalized that calories did not accumulate on vacation at the same rate they did back home, so we need not worry about fitting into our bathing suits again tomorrow because of cheesecake enjoyed for breakfast today.

I didn't think that Rachel ever needed to worry about calories anyhow; the girl barely had an inch to pinch on her. She was also highly addicted to the high she got from exercise, running three miles religiously each morning, taking aerobic classes after her college courses during the school year, and participating actively on our school's tennis and lacrosse teams. During the summer, she eased up just a bit and found solace in random physical activities like swimming or biking.

We chose the curbside seating outside the restaurant. We placed our orders rather quickly, and sat in silence for a while, basking in the sunshine and freedom of our vacation. When the waitress returned with steaming mugs of froth, I couldn't resist the urge to dive right in.

Rachel laughed as I licked the whipped cream off my lip only seconds after the waitress had delivered the steaming cups to our table.

"Nat, what is it that you want to do with your life?"

It was a typical Rachel-like question, and if I didn't know her as well as I did, I might have accused her of having smoked an early morning blunt.

I thought for a few moments, wondering how deep I really wanted to get this fine morning. But here we were, just me and her, on the cusp of all things great and new. And without Rachel, I never would have made it even this far. She'd gotten me through the aftermath of the worst years of my life, and helped to ease the pain in the years thereafter when I'd been convinced that I was a burden to my own family.

I was finding it hard to tell my best friend that there was anything that I could possibly want more than what she had already given me. But she opened the door, and I dared to step inside. "I want a career," I glanced up at her, "in Accounting. I want to be a tax-accountant and crunch numbers behind a computer the rest of my life in some boring office with a tiny desk and no windows."

Rachel gave me her "get serious Natalie" look – the one where she lowers her head slightly, looking at me through the top of her green eyes. "Nat, your career right now consists of working part time in a pizza shop on campus and going to school for that fabulous future. That wasn't what I meant."

I played along, because I knew I wasn't going to get anywhere arguing my point. When Rachel had an agenda, it was best to just go with it. Otherwise, we might have ended up outside the café all day. "What should I be focusing on then at this point in my life, Dr. Garrison?"

She rolled her eyes and sipped on her coffee casually, then folded her arms on the table and leaned forward. She meant business. "A relationship."

"A relationship?" I couldn't help rolling my eyes. This was out of nowhere. But I could tell she was serious, so I tried to straighten up and look her in the eyes with about as much decorum as I could muster.

"I'm just saying that if you're going to focus on anything right now, why not a relationship? Your longest relationship didn't even make the six month mark, and that's hardly what I'd call long-term. But you've got the right guy in front of you and either you're completely oblivious to that fact or you're simply not interested in him, and quite frankly, it's driving me slowly insane."

I laughed entirely too loudly, drawing a few stares from the passing Texans on the street. "Nathan? Please, he's engaged and totally off the market..."

She interjected, giving me an impatient stare. "I'm talking about Ray-Ray, and you know it."

I thought very carefully about what I wanted to say next as not to further offend her. "Ray-Ray and I are friends. And that's all it's ever going to be."

"Do you ever see the way he looks at you, Nat? Do you ever see that look in his eyes, like you are the only woman in the world? He doesn't give me that look, or any other woman, for that matter. Just you."

I pondered this for a moment. Maybe he did hold his gaze a little longer on me than the other girls. So what? It didn't mean anything. But I let myself entertain this prospect, more to humor her than anything else, and maybe even myself, just a bit. "He was pretty good in bed."

I saw a slight smile cross her lips. "True." She sipped her coffee casually, oblivious to the pang of jealousy that ripped through my veins. I shook it off. It was probably just the caffeine surge under the hot sun. After all, I had no reason to be jealous of something that neither of us had.

I ran my finger around the rim of the coffee cup, not daring to look up at her. "So why didn't you two ever hook up again?" It was a question that I wasn't sure I wanted to know the answer to.

She took a while to answer, almost to the point where I thought she was going to just bypass the question altogether. But finally she relented, "It was good Nat, but it was just sex. Ray-Ray's got the ability to be a passionate guy, but there was just no spark. It was just physics between us." Although the answer was carefully crafted, there was an air of honesty in her voice, laced with solemnity as she continued. "From everything you've told me about that night, there was no lack in chemistry there. I'd be willing to venture that there's a whole lot more if you just put yourself out there."

I laughed, more as a reflex than anything else, and felt my cheeks getting warm in the hot Texas sun. "You're being ridiculous. Ray-Ray's like our brother. That's it, there's nothing more. You're reading way too deep into things that aren't there."

She shrugged. "So maybe I am. But then again, it wasn't my name that he said in bed…"

EIGHT
Natalie

Rachel was following me around as I prepared for my dinner date with Ray-Ray. She claimed final veto on my wardrobe, hair and makeup, which was nothing new. Every article of clothing that I held up for her inspection received the same reaction, a shameless shake of her head, until I was finally through everything that I had packed, and not one potential outfit.

"I see you in black this evening." She decided, opening the closet where she had unpacked everything she had in tow the second we had opened the door to our room. She flipped through a few hangers before producing the perfect Ruched black dress, which I had never seen her wear. Then I saw that it still had the tags on it.

"Happy Birthday!" She exclaimed, holding the dress up in front of me.

I tried to ignore the triple digits on the tag, but did happen notice that it was exactly my size. I eyed her suspiciously, but snatched the hanger from her hand.

Moments later, I was making my grand appearance, twirling in front of her.

The dress fit perfectly, I had to hand it to her, she knew me well. And indicative of a Rachel-induced outfit, there was plenty of visual cleavage, and more leg than I might have shown on my own. There was also quite a bit of my back exposed, which made me slightly chilly in the air-conditioned room. But I felt like a diva in my new dress, and slid in front of the mirror so that she could work her magic with my hair and makeup selections.

By the time Ray-Ray knocked on our door at eight sharp, I was ready to pose for the cover of Vogue magazine. I hadn't looked this good since high school prom, when Rachel helped me prepare for my date with Jay Stowing. And even I had to admit; I looked much better now than I did then in my purple Jessica McClintock gown that Rachel had decided to also purchase, in a much shorter version.

Standing just inside the doorway of our hotel room, Ray-Ray only managed a whistle when I twirled for him. When I came full-circle, he extended a single long-stem red rose, which I smiled and took. "There aren't words." He said, not once taking his eyes off of me. He was dressed black dress pants and a neatly pressed sea-blue button down and matching silk blue tie. His hair was gelled and the instant I was close enough to him, I caught the musky-sweet scent of a new cologne. It had me wanting to get closer, to put my head on his shoulder and draw in this new, exciting scent.

The Irish in me had my ears burning instantly, forgetting for a moment that this was Ray-Ray, and not my high school prom date. Yet the feeling was there, that off-set jitter in my stomach, a mix of wonder and uncertainty about where the night would take us. Our eyes met briefly, and for an instant we held each other's gaze, and I found myself having to look away, afraid that he'd see that subtle nervousness that was starting to take over.

"You know," Rachel broke the tension, "I don't recall

getting a fancy dinner out of my twenty-first birthday."

Ray-Ray's eyes snapped over to hers momentarily. "I did so take you out for your birthday. And I'm hurt that you forgot."

Rachel scowled at him. "You took me to Applebee's Ray-Ray."

He raised his eyebrows; "You were dating Dustin McCoy. It was his job, not mine, to wine and dine you."

He held out his elbow for me to take, and as I did, I turned and glanced at her over my shoulder. "Don't wait up." I joked, as we headed out into the hallway. I made sure to take in a deep breath as the door closed behind us, just in case the open air of the night faded his cologne.

Worthington's was much more than I had expected. The restaurant sat in the center of town, at the top of a building that stood twenty-seven floors high, with rooftop dining overlooking the beautiful city of Dallas. The mere beauty of it took my breath away, and I couldn't help being mesmerized by the view. I couldn't wait until the sun went down so that we could enjoy the city lights.

It was still close to ninety degrees, even with the fading sun in the western sky, but a gentle wind blew through the evening air, providing momentary refreshment. I was trying to study the selection on the menu, but the atmosphere was captivating me so much that even when the waiter came to deliver our dinners, I was caught off guard.

Ray-Ray had been schooled in the fine art of proper etiquette, and ordered a sophisticated sounding bottle of wine, followed by two house special dinners. It was then that the scenery suddenly faded into the background. Only three feet of breezy white cotton tablecloth lay between us. Not sure that I had ever actually seen him in a tie before, outside of one of his parents' functions, I smiled and looked down at my hands, folded and resting on the table.

When the waiter returned with a bottle wrapped in a white cloth, he poured a mouthful in my glass. I waited for him to pour some for Ray-Ray, but instead, he stood there holding the bottle and waiting for me. A quick glance at Ray-Ray's eyes told me that I was supposed to sample a taste, which I did, then nodded my approval. I couldn't help but notice the smile that had formed on Ray-Ray's face as the waiter poured a half-glass for each of us.

When the waiter left us, Ray-Ray chuckled. "Cute."

I drew in a deep breath, letting the air flow easily through my lungs. A wave of contentment surrounded me as gentle as the light breeze that was reserved only for the rooftop diners. The spray of red roses in the center of our table cast an elegant fragrance, light and airy, and I closed my eyes and drew in the sweet scent just a little deeper.

When the waiter returned with my plate, I couldn't help but stare in awe. A red lobster tail, split open with the succulent white meat pouring over the sides and decorated with butter and seasonings, sat upon a bed of crisp green leaf lettuce. Seven oysters rounded the edge of the plate, and though I had never really tried one before, they peaked my curiosity.

I smiled as I thought of the irony of the situation. This was, without a doubt, quickly turning out to be the most romantic evening that I had ever had experienced. It was fit for a romance novel, I decided, as I took in the scene. Rooftop restaurant, red roses, delectable dinner, expensive red wine... And there, across the table from me, was Ray-Ray.

I wondered what was going through his mind right now as he looked back at me. Did he see the irony in all of this as well? Or was he just enjoying taking his best friend out for dinner on her birthday? I almost wanted to just come right out and tell him what Rachel had told me earlier. I wanted to laugh with him as he told me she was just crazy, and let him tease her all throughout the next day for merely suggesting such preposterous notions.

Yet I had to admit, I had often imagined being swept off my feet by monumental acts of romanticism such as this.

Ray-Ray definitely had that going for him, and a woman could get past that wall of wittiness and sarcasm that made up his everyday persona if it meant that this was what lay behind that wall.

I thought of all the women that never got past that wall. They never gave themselves a chance to meet that guy who would be there at three am if you heard a strange noise in the house, or who would hold you and let you cry on his shoulder after a huge blowup with your sister, or who would pull an all-nighter to help you pass a Calculus test the next day.

Those women were missing out, I thought, as I took another sip of wine, and enjoyed the warm Texas night air just a little. While it certainly wasn't an uncomfortable silence between us, something popped into my head out of nowhere, and I couldn't resist the smile that crept across my lips.

"I have a very important question, one that I've wanted to ask you for a long time." I said to him, suddenly. His dark eyes shot up at me, wide and curious under brown bangs that should have been cut a few weeks ago. I paused a moment, to let his imagination run for only a moment or so. "Why do we call you Ray-Ray?"

His mouth opened slightly, and his eyes narrowed. Somewhere deep inside me, the butterflies took flight. I lived for these moments when I could throw the unexpected at him and actually hit my target. He gained his composure, and crossed his arms on the table, leaning in ever so slightly toward me over his lobster. "Well, I have to attribute it to the fact that my parents are truly jackasses when it came to naming me. They picked Raymond after my great grandfather, which was fair enough. But when it came time to pick my middle name, they wanted to use my mother's maiden name."

"Which was?"

"Reymont."

"Ouch."

Ray-Ray nodded, never taking his eyes off of me. "My

turn."

"Your turn?"

"My turn," he repeated, "Now I get to ask you a question that I've wanted to ask you for a long time."

I took my fork and began to dig into the lobster. It was soft and meaty as it graced my tongue. It was a nice momentary distraction while I waited for Ray-Ray to continue with his question.

He sampled a bit of his own lobster, and then downed an oyster like it was a shot, wiping his hands on his cloth napkin. "So I've known you now for seven years, and throughout those seven years, you've never talked about your family. I know you have two brothers and a sister, and that your mother lives in London, and that's the extent of it. Now we're finally going to meet your brothers, which is great, but I know nothing about them. Why is that?"

I don't think the question really sank in until almost a full minute after he asked it. It hadn't been what I had been expecting at all. I really wasn't sure what I had been expecting exactly, but it definitely wasn't that. I responded by finishing off the full glass of wine, not caring at all that it was meant to be sipped. Within seconds of my empty glass touching the table, the waiter was filling it again. Once he stepped away from the table, I leaned back into my chair and sighed.

"I'm not really sure what to say," I confessed, feeling the temperature rise as the breeze seemed to move elsewhere suddenly. "I've never met my father, but I'd like to someday. My mother lives in London near my sister, who is forty and married with two girls. My brothers are in their thirties and they travel a lot for work. I haven't seen them in a few years."

Ray-Ray hadn't moved an inch, and was still looking me straight in the eyes, challenging me. "You somehow failed to answer my question."

I picked up an oyster, eyeing it suspiciously. The inside of the shell was pretty, like an opal, but the small wad inside sat in a shallow pool of slick substance that looked absolutely unappetizing to me. Yet somehow it appealed to me more than answering his question, so I tilted my head back just as he had done and let it slide onto my tongue. The first sense I had was that it was slippery and salty, then as I instinctively chewed, it was soft and a little sweeter, and just as I swallowed, I was rewarded with almost a melon-meets-cucumber flavor that lingered even after I set the shell back down on the plate.

When I was about to reach for the third oyster, Ray-Ray slid his hand across the table and held mine down gently, those coal colored eyes fixed deep into mine. "Why can't you just open up to me? Don't you trust me?"

I cringed, and it was more than just a little. I shot back quickly, "Of course I trust you." Then apologetically I added, "Look, I've barely told Rachel about my family, or my life back in England. It's behind me. With the exception of my brothers on rare occasion, you and Rachel are my family."

I started feeling the tenseness that had suddenly snuck up into my shoulders and neck ease up as I went on, hating the feeling that I had to explain. It wasn't anything I talked about, not with anyone.

"I wish I had a typical family, and I wish I had been able to grow up at home. Hell, I wish I could have gotten to know my family the way that most people do, but the truth is that I've had to be happy with the bits and pieces that I was lucky enough to get over the years. I spent some summers with my brothers, and they were some of the best summers of my life because for a few short months, I got to at least pretend I was a part of my own family. And even that's gone away these past few years, since my oldest brother and I don't get on much anymore."

He tilted his head, inquisitively. "How come?"

I let out a hard breath. This was deeper than I'd ever gotten with anyone outside of the mirror before. But there was something about the way that his eyes fell warm and gentle and caring on mine that made me feel... safe.

"I wanted to find my father. And my family didn't think he was worth finding."

Ray-Ray nodded, understandingly, yet with a slight bit of concern. "Is there a reason for that?"

I shrugged. "They claim that he was neglectful, even abusive when he was around, and then he eventually just abandoned them altogether." I drew in a deep breath and let it out slowly. "And I know how that sounds, I really do. Why would I want to meet someone like that? But I want to see for myself. I want to make my own decision on whether or not to have him in my life. At the very least, I just want him to at least know that I exist."

I could see the wheels turning in his head. There was so much more I knew he wanted to say, but was filtering. Surely, if the situation were reversed, I'd have a lot to say on the subject. And it'd be all against pushing the issue and meeting his father. But he only had half the story. And there were answers that I needed to get.

He gave my hand a quick squeeze before letting me back to my oyster. The breeze had returned, a bit stronger now, and I had to hold it back with one hand to keep it out of my face as I downed the next shellfish.

In typical Ray-Ray fashion, he lightened the mood with a joke. "I'm now sitting here finding myself wondering where you get your stunningly gorgeous looks from." He took a quick sip of wine as I blushed, then he continued, "Since I've never even seen any pictures of your family, do you look like your mother or your father more?"

I caught myself after an impulsive laugh. "I've always been told that I'm a dead ringer for my oldest brother, who I guess looks more like my father." I paused for a moment then added, "And actually, I'm pretty sure you've seen pictures."

As our plates were being cleared, I was instantly attracted to the far edge of the building, where the sun had long set, and the city lights were shining through the darkened sky.   As Ray-Ray paid the bill, I found myself wandering to the edge of the building to take in the full view. Straight down below us there was a street side café with white string lights lining an invisible ceiling above the curbside tables. Off in the distance, lights of every color decorated the buildings and the streets. It went on for miles through the flat land that the city stood on. It took my breath away to see such man-made beauty amongst such natural landscape.   More impressive was the night sky directly above me, painted with sparkling stars, that carried on infinitely further than my view of the city.

I was lost in my own amazement when I felt Ray-Ray's arm slip around my waist as he appeared next to me. There was a tingling in the pit of my stomach, an excited jump, as though I was just about to step onto a roller coaster. "We have one final thing to do before your birthday is over."

Instinctively, I rolled my eyes. I had just realized that we had almost gotten through an entire evening without one off-color comment or innuendo out of Ray-Ray. It was almost as though I was out with someone else for a few hours.

He turned and faced me, and with one hand still on my back, he held out his other hand. "You owe me one dance yet."

I cocked my head to the side and listened to the sound of the rustled voices of the other diners in the restaurant. And almost instantly after he had said it, I heard a few faint strums of an acoustic guitar behind me. I turned on my heel to see that a young guitarist sitting on a stool had suddenly appeared out of nowhere, and was softly playing Coma's *Take Me There*.

I took his hand with a smile, and let him take the lead. As the music floated through the Texas night air, I let my hips sway to the sound of the guitar, and let my body feel every chord. My left hand rested behind his neck and my right was held safely in his hand by his shoulder. His fingers cupped mine with a calming warmness like I had never known. With every strum of the guitar, my body moved intuitively closer to his.

I wasn't even aware that I had been holding my breath until I forced in a slow, deep flow of air into my lungs. Even that wasn't much relief, and as it turned out, he had been moving even closer to me, until every free part of us touched one another as we danced on the rooftop that night. I leaned my head against his shoulder, and let him hold me just a little tighter. I found myself wishing that the guitarist would just play all night long.

For longer than I could remember, I was completely lost in that moment, wanting, without realizing it, that I didn't want it to end. Everything about being in his arms felt so right, so safe, and so much of what I had been missing for too many years.

He leaned his head down close to my neck, and I could feel his every breath. Just behind my ear, he left a single, light kiss. As he slowly brought his head back up, his lips careened against my cheek until just before he was close to my lips, he pulled back and looked straight into in my mesmerized, half-open eyes. I hadn't realized that my lips were already slightly parted, anticipating his kiss, until his mouth finally met mine, first with a soft nibble on my bottom lip, then a deeper, passionate sweep of his tongue. And that was all it took for me to answer back by wrapping my arms around his neck, and leaning in toward him, holding on as his hands slid down to my lower back, holding me tight against him.

I wasn't sure how long the kiss lasted. All I knew is that when we finally pulled away, the guitarist was playing a new song, and I was out of breath. Ray-Ray smiled as he looked deep in my eyes, and placed one last quick kiss on my lips, before he turned to the guitarist and addressed him with unintelligible words and a handshake.

The kiss had taken me by surprise, there was no doubt about that. What surprised me more, however, was how I was feeling about it. I couldn't figure out how I was so suddenly shaken, suddenly infatuated, suddenly turned on by my best friend. This wasn't supposed to happen, I reminded myself. I wasn't supposed to be having any of these feelings for him. Yet one look at him as he held out his hand to lead me out of the restaurant had me second-guessing where my priorities should be right at that moment.

A short while later, I was sitting in the passenger seat of my own car outside of our hotel. Ray-Ray turned the car off, but instead of getting out, he turned to look at me. He didn't say a word, just smiled. It was so uncharacteristic for us to have any kind of awkward silence between us, and we couldn't help but laugh.

A bashful smile crept up to his lips. I had never seen anything like it on Ray-Ray before, and enjoyed the moment only long enough for the realization to click in on what he was about to say. "I have something I need to tell you, Natalie. And I know how this is going to sound, so I'm just going to come out with it." He drew in a deep breath. "I'm in love with you."

I was sure I had stopped breathing.

Love?

Where had that come from?

Of course he loved me. We were friends. Best friends. And best friends loved each other.

But best friends didn't kiss. Not like we had tonight. And they also didn't have sex on movie night after a lot of wine, either. And they sure as hell didn't keep thinking about that night if they were just best friends. I was panicking for the proper response. I looked around nervously, out the window, perhaps for an answer that just wasn't there.

I could tell he was interpreting my silence as a bad thing. His body had stiffened; I could feel it in his hands as they were still holding onto mine. He was biting his bottom lip, and his eyes were narrowed, as if he was trying to look deeper into mine to see if he could tell what was running through my mind. Finally, when I couldn't conjure up a single word to say, he simply nodded and said, "It's okay, Nat. If you don't feel the same way, you can tell me."

I shook my head. "I'm just overwhelmed right now. There are a lot of emotions involved with this trip, and what if it's just that we're feeling these things because we're in a whole different world than back home? What if we're just caught up in vacation romance?"

"I didn't know there was such a thing." He looked taken back. "Natalie, I've been in love with you for a long time now, well before we left home."

I couldn't speak. Literally. Words no longer knew how to form on my tongue. I hated feeling like my emotions were getting the best of me. I was a master at self-control, and not once had I ever let a guy get to me. Rachel and I would laugh at the way girls like Callie would fall head over heels in love, then fall completely apart when it didn't work out. I'd never let myself get in that deep.

He waited for a response that never came. Finally, closing his eyes a moment, he gave my hands a quick squeeze before letting go. There was a hint of disappointment in his voice that ripped my heart in two, as he replied, "No problem, Nat. I won't make this any weirder between us than I already have."

He turned to get out of the car, and I reached for him, with a quiet desperation. "Ray-Ray, wait." My heart was racing suddenly, and I wanted to set things right. I didn't want to leave things like this, and I hated that hurt look that he tried to hide behind the nonchalant expression that he now wore.

He gave me a half-smile over his shoulder, then held up his cell phone. "I think we were just summoned by text message to the pool. Supposedly our friends miss us just a bit."

I slid out of the car, watching him walk toward the front door of the hotel. "Ray-Ray..."

"See you at the pool then?" He didn't wait for me to answer as he slipped through the doors and was gone.

NINE
Natalie

I made my way into my empty hotel room. My mind was numb, and my heart was heavy as I opened my dresser drawers. I held up my blue bikini, wrinkled my nose at it, then dropped it back into the drawer. I didn't feel like swimming. I didn't feel like being in a crowd right now. And I sure as hell didn't feel like pretending right now either.

So I slid on a pair of denim shorts and a tank top instead of my bathing suit. I pulled back the curls that Rachel had labored over into a loose ponytail, and traded the cute black slinky heels for the comfort of a pair of flip flops.

I tapped the screen on my cell phone and located Sammi's number, praying that she picked up, although my hopes weren't very high. The night before the concert began she would most likely be busy with a million things to do. I tried not to be upset when I got her voicemail, and left her a message anyway. It was probably crazy of me to think that she'd have time to squeeze in a drink.

I flopped down on the bed and flipped through some

of the channels on television. Nothing was appealing to me in the slightest. My mind kept wandering back to the kiss. What was I thinking? Was I even thinking at all? I had let my emotions get the best of me, overcloud my thoughts and my rationale. But it felt so damn good…

My mind was racing fast, and I was barely aware when the cell phone buzzed on the table next to me. Relief escaped my lips in a single word, "Sammi!"

"Natalie! You're here, I take it?" It never sounded so good to hear her voice, even with the loud music in the background behind her. This was typical for Sammi. If she wasn't promoting a concert tour, she was with the band, who were usually partying when they weren't playing or practicing.

I simply laughed a relieved, happy laugh. "I'm here. Hey, I'm sure you're probably busy right now, but I was hoping maybe we could meet for a drink?"

"I can sneak a way for a while. In fact, I've heard this hotel has a great bar if you want to meet me there in about ten minutes."

And exactly ten minutes later I was walking into the hotel bar. It was located on the first floor, down a long winding hallway, past the Grand Ballroom, which I didn't know the hotel had, as well as the office that professionally coordinated the wedding plans for the hotel, and a room entitled "The Parkway on Bel Air". I literally missed the bar the first two times that I walked through the marble floored hallways, but on my last circle through, I found the plaque on the wall that simply read, "W.G. Bristol Bar Room".

The bar itself was very dimly lit, but I found Sammi sitting casually on a bar stool, already sipping her martini with the utmost class in her skinny jeans and well-filled grey halter-top. Her red hair that had once been long and flowing, was now cut short in a sleek, professional-style ponytail. Her eyes were boldly splashed with bright green shadow in a cat-like pattern and matched her halter-top with exact precision.

She wore trendy black Lafont frames to complete her look. And the moment she saw me, she set her drink down, stood up very casually, and smiled as she pulled me into a hug.

"God, you're so grown up and beautiful!" She told me. When she finally pulled away, she had tears in her eyes that she had to lift her glasses to dab away with a bar napkin.

"It's only been three years. I couldn't have grown up that much..."

I ran my hand over her ponytail and laughed, "Last time I saw you, your hair was so long..."

Sammi laughed too. "I had to! These boys give me no time to do my damn job let alone my hair anymore. I thought it was tough when they first started out, but it only gets worse with age..."

I sat down on the bar stool next to hers. "I hear ya." I had cut my own hair shoulder-short just about two years ago, and kept it that way ever since.

I ordered myself my standard Captain and Coke with a lime, and smiled sweetly at the very, very hot bartender, then giggled like a kid with Sammi when he turned to wait on his customers at the end of the bar.

Sammi and I exchanged none of the typical small talk that two friends would exchange after just seeing each other for the first time in three years. Instead, she got right down to business. "So who is he and why the hell would he break your heart? Doesn't he know that you have two big brothers who would kick his ass in a heartbeat?"

I sucked down the CNC a little too fast, and set the empty glass for the bartender to refill. "There is no 'he'," I corrected her but when I saw her skeptical glare I added, "But I think I may have broken his heart."

I relayed to her the whole story, which took up the better part of an hour and four martinis of her time.

Sammi simply smiled at me when I finished my story, and slipped the bartender her black AmEx card. When he handed it back to her, she leaned in and told him loudly enough for me to hear, "Make sure anything that Room 415 orders before seven am goes on this card." She then leaned in toward me as she slung her purse over her shoulder, "You're a beautiful young woman and you're gonna break a few hearts. Just make sure that when you do, it's because you're protecting your own."

With that, she kissed me and left the bar room. I found myself wondering why she wasn't dating anyone. Sure, she had relationships off and on throughout the years, but I never heard of her dating anyone recently. She was a great catch, I thought, though she was married to her work. She'd need someone who was completely understanding of that, and didn't mind her being on the road for as long as she was. Or maybe she just needed someone who liked to travel and see the world. With the money that Sammi made, she could easily support a one-income relationship. Something else to ponder, I decided. Since I was obviously not an expert in the love department, maybe I could at least solve everyone else's romance issues.

When I got back to my room, Rachel was sitting on her bed, pillows propped up behind her, one arm wrapped around her knees and pointing the remote at the TV, and in her other hand was a glass of white wine. She looked very cozy in her favorite white hoodie, and short black sweat shorts. Her dark hair was straightened and pulled back into a loose ponytail, and long wispy strands fell out around her face. Rachel never had a bad hair day, which often made me jealous when I fought with mine so much to stay in place.

As I shut the door behind me, her eyes moved cautiously over to where I stood. She didn't say anything for a moment, taking in a long sip of her wine. "We missed you at the pool tonight, Natty."

My eyes fell to the plush carpet as I slipped my feet out of my flip-flops and enjoyed the soft comfort that wrapped around my toes. I wouldn't have minded just a small welcome mat of this piece of heaven next to my bed at home.

I ventured across the room to the wet bar and turned over a Bordeaux glass. Even though I was going to share Rachel's Riesling, I loved the feel of how the broad bowl filled my small hand, which at the moment was aching to be strumming chords emphatically on a guitar. This will have to do, I decided, and began the process of self-medication; alcohol and my best friend.

I crawled over my bed until I was sprawled out comfortably, lying on my stomach, parallel to my perfectly fluffed pillows, leaning my head and arms over the edge of the bed as not to spill the wine on the burgundy bedspreads that I had fallen so deeply in love with at first sight.

"So," Rachel waited until I was settled before she began, "Ray-Ray was a perfect gentleman. He didn't admit to anything further than third base."

I rolled my eyes, and reminded myself that I should have known that was coming. "Rach, I'm...." Obviously phonetically challenged, I thought, then confessed, "God, I don't even know." If it had been anything other than a glass of wine in my hand, I might have thrown it across the room. Saving the wine, I settled for burying my face in the pillow that I had been using to prop myself up on. "What the hell is wrong with me?"

Rachel's voice remained calm during my near-crisis, "So why don't you start at the beginning? Honestly Nat, he really didn't tell me anything, so I'm starting fresh here. Just start talking, and we'll work through this together."

By the time I had finished reviewing the events of the night with Rachel, she was just finishing her last sip as I was telling her, "So then he tells me he's in love with me."

I paused and waited for her reaction.

"And then?" She stood up and poured herself a fresh glass, then topped mine off as well.
"And then what? What am I supposed to say to that?"

With a heavy sigh, she took a long drink right from the wine bottle that she still held in her hand, finishing it off. "Do you want to be with him?"

She set both the bottle and the glass down on the nightstand, then folded her hands on top of her head. My eyes laid solidly on the perfect mahogany tabletop as a drop of wine slid down the bottle and onto the surface. I couldn't concentrate on anything else until I had lifted the bottle, wiped away any trace of moisture from the table, and set the bottle back down on a napkin.

Did I want to be with him? Of course, that answer was simple on one level. The easy answer was that I did want to be with him. I very much enjoyed being with him. The real question was if I wanted to be in a relationship with him. "How would I know? I haven't had time to think..."

"Natalie!" Rachel nearly jumped back to her feet, her arms swinging through the air. "Can you please, just for once, stop thinking? You need to start feeling. Just because he's in love with you doesn't require you to be in love back to start a relationship. You can just try it and see where it goes."

I sipped my wine carefully as I pondered this. My eyes narrowing, I tilted my head to the side and looked up at her, and as I did, I caught the scent of his cologne that still lingered in my hair. Instantly, I missed him. I wanted to be that close to him again, to take in the scent of his cologne, to take him in.

She sat cross-legged on her bed, cradling her wine glass.

"I keep thinking what happens if we do start something, me and Ray-Ray, and they we have this horrible break up, and we're never friends again? Then I've lost him entirely."

Rachel threw her pillow at me, nearly spilling my wine. "What if the world ends tomorrow? What if the earth opens up and swallows us whole? What if you had fallen off the roof of that lovely four-star restaurant he took you to tonight..."

"I get it, Rach." Only it wasn't as simple as she was making it out to be, I was sure of it. "So what do I do about it?"

She finished off her glass of wine in several large gulps, making a point to set it back down on a napkin coaster, then slipped under the covers and settled her head down on the pillow. "Tell him the truth about how you feel, Nat. He deserves that. Then let whatever happens happen." She yawned, "You may be surprised."

I flicked off the light, retiring into the soft cloud of a bed that the Elyad Suites offered. Laying down never felt so good. I slipped off to sleep, enjoying the fading scent of Ray-Ray's cologne in my hair.

Thunderous drums pounded through my head, flashes of lightning quick and hot and furious created a strobe effect as I stood at that same wooden doorway. My hand burned as it touched the copper doorknob, and as hard as I tried to pull my arm back and run down the hallway, my fingers grasped the hot metal and pushed open the door, revealing the dark room. Lighting flashed both inside and outside of the house. Through the bolts of white-hot electricity, blurred faces swam through the air, coming in and out of focus. The one that kept coming closer and closer burst into full color as it passed in front of me, shrieking at first, then roaring with the thunder. Leo. It was always him.

The shadows that danced and moaned behind him were unrecognizable in the dark, though their voices were familiar to me. I wanted to run to them, tossed between an urge to help them or save myself and by running away from them all, but my legs wouldn't cooperate. They were weighed down and tired, and even when I tried to lift them and push forward, my feet stuck to the ground, keeping me held captive.

The thunder was growing louder, and I tried to focus on the faces swirling and screeching behind him. I wanted them to help me, but they were sifting through the air, out the window, down the hall, saving themselves and leaving me alone with my uncle.

Hands grabbed at my arms, holding me down, and I

struggled to free myself, throwing punches and kicks wildly through the air. I wanted to run, but I was pinned down.

"Natalie!" Rachel's voice cut through my nightmare.

My eyes flew open, and I pushed myself up in bed, tangled in the sheets, hot sweat dripping from my hair and beading up on my face. My heart was racing away from me, my chest rising and falling with uncontrollable breaths, as I looked around the dark room to be sure that we were alone. He was gone. The shadows were gone. It was just Rachel and me.

Sitting next to me on the bed, she shook her head and pushed my hair out away from my face. "You've had this dream since we were kids Nat."

I tossed an apologetic look toward her as I got up and went over to the sink. "I know. I'm sorry I woke you up."

"I think you need to focus more on figuring out what it means. Maybe then they'll stop." She climbed back into bed as I held a glass under the running water. I didn't want to focus on the dreams. I wanted to get a peaceful night's sleep.

TEN
Natalie

The next morning Rachel was pulling me out of bed at ten, which I personally considered to be the crack of dawn, especially when we had a long night ahead of us. She had clothes already picked out for me. "We're all meeting for breakfast," she explained, as she pulled the covers off of me, "And then as long as we are back by five for the concert, the rest of the day is our's to do what we want with."

I mumbled something that even I couldn't comprehend, and reached for the comforter that was no longer there. *Who the hell had fired me and appointed her Itinerary Nazi?* I buried my pathetic, sleep-deprived, half-heartbroken head under the pillow. Shit, I thought, I had almost forgotten about the last part...

Yet with a splash or two of cold water, and Rachel's rendition of hotel room made coffee, I was almost presentable to my own friends in my barely-there tube top that matched the belly ring that hung just above my low cut denim shorts. I even faked a smile, just for her, as I eyed myself in the mirror.

I knew exactly what she had on her mind when she had pulled these clothes from my dresser. "If it helps," she offered, throwing a sympathetic arm across my shoulders, "Ray-Ray looked pretty damn hot at the pool last night. I forgot how ruggedly sexy he looked half naked..."

I groaned, ducking out from under her arm and out the door as she laughed at me.

I found myself at our table a few minutes later, after what amounted to a really rough elevator ride. There was a small glass of orange juice and an ice-cold bottle of spring water that had appeared in front of me while the rest of my friends were scoping out the breakfast buffet that the hotel had to offer. My hand was the only thing that was holding my head up, as I briefly reminisced about CNC's and limes, followed by Riesling, and then concentrated on sucking my OJ through a straw.

Ray-Ray set a steaming cup of hot coffee in front of me, extra cream, extra sugar, then took a seat next to Josh at the other end of the table. I tried to ignore that fact.

I let the caffeine take hold and I even took a few samples of Callie's muffin that she swore she picked up just for me. It was chocolate chip, which happened to be my favorite.

Pulling myself together, I sat up strait in my chair. "I wanted to just say thank you all for my birthday gift tonight." I had clanged my spoon on my OJ glass like we were at a wedding. "And I have a little surprise for you guys as well." There were five sets of eyes pasted to me suddenly. "My friend who got us these lovely hotel rooms invited us all to a party tonight here at the hotel, after the concert."

I noticed that Ray-Ray and Nathan were looking at each other before Nathan spoke up, "We actually had plans tonight, but thanks for the invite..."

Rachel jumped right in, reprimanding him before I could say another word. "That's a hell of a way to say thank you. You can just change those plans to another night. We'll be down here for a whole week yet."

Nathan laughed, then looked at Ray-Ray and shrugged. "That works." Rachel glared at him with a disgusted look on her face, and I suddenly had a feeling that she knew something that I didn't know.

We continued with breakfast, and a few minutes later I caught only a part of the conversation that was going on at the end of the table. All I had heard was Nathan mention something about going to a strip club, followed by Rachel's perturbed response, "Ray-Ray, you're an idiot!"

He simply brushed her off with his smile and a witty comment, and as she sunk down in her chair looking more than slightly irritated, Ray-Ray piped up, "So who's in for a little pre-concert festivities?"

7 Year Coma fans were known for smoking pot at their concerts, or at the very least, arriving at the venue relatively stoned. Some have even argued that their music was enjoyed on a whole new level when one was high. This was also a long-standing tradition among most of my friends, who often snuck away shortly before the concert for a smoke.

Ray-Ray often informed us that if it weren't for marijuana, and other various drugs, most of the songs that we have grown to love over the course of the past few decades would not have come about, and rock and roll as we knew it today would just not exist. He contested that mind-altering agents opened parts of the mind that normally we don't have access to on a daily basis. That ninety-percent of our brains were unused, but housed some pretty serious talents, and that the only way to access those abilities were through the mind-altering effects of marijuana. And therefore, since most of those songs were written, recorded and often played live while the composers were high, they should also be enjoyed while high.

Sometimes I found myself wondering why Ray-Ray

had not enrolled in law school with Josh.

So that afternoon, I sat in the back seat of my Suburban with Rachel and Nathan, as Josh sat shotgun and Ray-Ray was at the wheel. Callie, who was not a fan of drugs of any sort, had stolen off to the beach solo. The rest of us found ourselves the perfect secluded parking spot, overlooking Lake Lewisville. We were surrounded by thick woods, chock full of short trees and Texas weeds peeking through the gravel.

Ray-Ray had parked the car only inches from the sandy beach. We could watch the small waves lap at the sand, one right after the other, methodically. Off in the distance, we could see a cluster of boats hovered together on the far side of the beach. There were easily a hundred or so sunbathers and partiers on the boats and in the water, making me wish that I lived even remotely close to such a wonderful mix of beauty and carefree fun.

With the windows of the car rolled down, Rachel leaned back and stretched both legs out the window. "You gonna light up Ray-Ray, or make us wait until Nat hits her twenty-second?"

Ray-Ray turned to face her. "Oh, I thought you said you were bringing it?"

Josh reached under his seat and pulled out a small black zippered case, shaped like an oversized letter envelope, made of thick canvas. Inside the case was a flat tin, which housed a Ziploc baggie with exactly nine neatly rolled joints. He pulled out two, resealed the baggie, then returned the case to its spot under his seat.

He lit one up, then handed it to Ray-Ray, then he lit the other and took a long drag before handing it to me. I took in a long, slow, deep breath, letting the warm sweet air fill my lungs, and held my breath as long as I could before letting it out the open window as slowly as possible. I snuck in one more quick puff before passing it off to Nathan.

We had two going, one clockwise, one counter clockwise. Though Ray-Ray was, out of all the guys, the one who could absorb the most alcohol and pot without it affecting him, he always skipped every other pass if he was driving. He'd reward himself by smoking an entire joint himself later on, usually once we got to where ever it was we were going.

"Dori let you out of your cage long enough to join your old friends for a few days of debauchery?" Josh threw out to Nathan. I saw right away that this was a double-edged sword, one that Josh was good at, as the competition quickly shifted from Ray-Ray and I to Harvard-pre-med-against-Temple-law student. I did admire Josh's ambition, but often wondered why he would jump into the snake cage holding a rat in his hand.

Nathan reached across Rachel's lap and pushed the door open to welcome in some much-needed breeze, however we were met by a rush of air that was warmer than what had been in the car to begin with. "Yeah, I'm pretty whipped these days Josh." Nathan leaned his head back and enjoyed an additional rush of contact high. "That's why I'm sure as hell going to have as much fun as possible while I'm down here."

We all knew enough about Nathan's fiancé Dori to know that she didn't so much let him go out to see a movie without her knowing who he was going with and when he would be back. Smoking pot was well out of the question, and it was rare that Nathan could ever sneak away to partake anymore, now that Dori was in the picture.

"I'll see what I can do to make that happen then." I promised him, with a smile, thinking about the party later tonight.

But Nathan raised his eyebrows and smiled back slyly. "Does that mean you're gonna join me and Ray-Ray at the strip club then?"

Out of the corner of my eye, I saw Ray-Ray squeeze his eyes shut tight and heard him mutter a muffled curse under his breath as he turned around and faced the steering wheel.

Nathan looked over at him, slightly confused. "What?" He turned back to me and asked, "You can't tell me you're offended by strip clubs Nat. I know you too well."

I turned to look at the rearview mirror, where I could see Ray-Ray looking up at me from the driver's seat, waiting to see my reaction. I simply took a long drag on the joint that Nathan had just handed me, let my breath out the window slowly, then leaned up front to hand it to Ray-Ray. "I'm not offended by strip clubs. You guys are both young and single, you can do what you want...." I paused just a moment for effect and looked Nathan in the eyes, "Oh wait, you aren't both single, are you?"

"Harsh, Nat." Nathan responded, with a smile.

I smiled back and shrugged. "Some women are offended by it, but if I had a boyfriend, I wouldn't really mind so much, because I'd know he's coming home to me."

"Or with you." Rachel added dryly, causing a roar of laughter in the car.

Nathan sighed and flicked the last bit of second joint out the window. "Well Natalie, any guy would be lucky to have you."

"Before or after he left the strip club." Josh tossed in. I couldn't help but smile at the glare I caught through the rearview that Ray-Ray sent in Josh's direction as he turned the key in the ignition.

A half hour later, I was standing in my hotel room shower, letting the hot water drench my dark hair. I reveled in the time alone where I could contemplate my feelings without interruption. Working the rich lather of coconut and mango shampoo through the thick strands that were falling over my shoulders, I focused on Ray-Ray, and that night too many years ago now that we spent together.

What was it about that night? What was it about him? Of course there was the obvious. He made me laugh with that quirky sense of humor that he had. I trusted him with my life. He could be sweet, and obviously romantic. He was attractive. And at that thought, I couldn't help but giggle, which was followed by that silly little tingle I was feeling these days whenever I thought of him in that sort of way. When did that happen, I wondered? When had that transition occurred, where I stopped seeing him as just a friend and started seeing him as attractive?

But all that aside, there had to be more than that. What was it? It started to drive me crazy, to eat away at me, the same way all of my little obsessions did. And it suddenly bothered me more than a chip wrapper in my car or a dart on a sticky floor. I realized that I was just about out of lather in my hair when I felt my nails scrape along my scalp. And it was just then that it occurred to me, as the shampoo worked its way into the shallow scratch I had just dug into the back of my head.

He was safe, and he made me feel safe. He wasn't going anywhere. He had been there, without fail, since the day I met him. And I knew him almost as well as I knew Rachel, and far more than I knew anyone in my own family. When he held me, I felt security, for the first time ever. I felt loved. I felt that no matter what I said or did, he'd still love me for who I was. And wouldn't let go.

Rachel was right. I needed to tell him how I felt. I needed to tell him the truth.

All of it.

ELEVEN
Natalie

The crowd outside the stadium was a rowdy one. A group of women standing by the entrance immediately caught the guys' attention. Security was telling one woman that she had to put something on over her translucent white t-shirt, and as we walked past, it was apparent that the only thing keeping her from being completely revealed was the '7 Year Coma' logo splashed across the front of the shirt.

We had arrived early enough to make sure that we saw the opening band, though usually we skipped the opener altogether. This particular band, Lull, happened to have a few hits here in the States, which made them appealing enough to other fans to come early. Callie and I had been listening to their albums for some time now, and she was psyched about seeing them play live. I'd never told my friends, but I'd seen them twice in England, back before they were famous. I'd also been practicing their songs on my guitar for a while now. If they continued in the direction they were headed, they had a chance at being a headlining act someday.

The lead singer of Lull was also the younger brother to Lucas Mason of Coma, and though the bands had two completely separate sounds, the talent and promise was evident in Lull. They weren't the caliber of Coma yet, and they were far more Americanized, but I'd been taking the time over the years to learn their songs, and quite enjoyed playing them on my guitar.

Our tickets were ripped one by one as we funneled through the front gates to the arena. Once inside, we followed the signs to the front access, closest to the stage. My friends were buzzing with excitement as we shuffled along the aisles, after having to show our tickets yet again to one of two guards at the front entrance.

It was already hard to hear each other, as other fans were already starting to get rowdy. "I can't believe how much of the stage we can see!" Callie had been the first to get to her seat, her blonde hair bouncing along with her. "I can actually see the logo on the drum set." She snapped a few pictures on her phone, sending them immediately to friends back home.

"Who needs a beer?" Ray-Ray was anxious to join the rowdy fans.

I glanced at my watch. The opening act, Lull, was due on in about ten minutes. "I'll go with you." I offered, pushing past the fans that had already filled our row. I was hoping we'd get a chance to smooth things over a bit between us.

We moved toward the exits near the front of the side stage. Ray-Ray was clearly mesmerized being so close to the stage, his eyes wandering past the stage crew to sneak a glance at the instruments that were set up and waiting to be played.

Just as we were about to push our way into the crowded hallway, I heard Sammi's voice call my name. I stopped and turned suddenly, causing Ray-Ray to nearly collide into me.

Sammi stood near the entrance to the back stage area,

talking into the mouthpiece of her headset, waving me over to her. She held up a finger as we approached her, so that she could finish the heated discussion she was having. "Look, I realize that's a bit unreasonable, but your job tonight is to make the band happy. So find a way to make it happen!" She slid the mouthpiece up and away from her face before giving me a quick hug and explaining, "Your brother is in one hell of a mood tonight. I might just fire him myself."

I laughed somewhat uneasily as I stole a glance at Ray-Ray, who suddenly looked very impressed, if not a little confused. "Sammi, this is my friend Ray-Ray. Ray-Ray, this is Sammi, my longtime friend, the one who got us the lovely hotel rooms that we're staying in."

Ray-Ray, eyes wide, extended his hand to greet Sammi, who smiled as she shook his hand, but then quickly snapped the mouth piece back into place. "Well you've got about four minutes to fix that, don't you? I don't care if it costs twenty-*thousand*, just get them onstage happy!" She apologized profusely before she turned and disappeared through the door that led backstage.

Ray-Ray stood there staring at me, his eyes wide and questioning. "I don't even know where to begin asking questions."

I smiled and started walking out into the hallway toward the beer counter, but the line was insanely long, and that gave Ray-Ray plenty of time to start firing away. "So how do you know Samantha Brockhaven?"

I wasn't foolish enough to try to pretend for a moment that Raymond Montgomery, 7 Year Coma's self-proclaimed number one fan, didn't recognize the band's manager. I thought very carefully about how I wanted to answer his question before I spoke. I didn't want to lie to him, but I also wasn't about to speak freely in the crowded hallway, with thousands of people around us. "We met in London when I was a kid, and we keep in contact."

His eyes narrowed as we moved forward in the line.

"She knows your brother? Does he work for the band or the venue, or what?"

I eyed the crowd around us. There were far too many people for me to just start blurting things about my personal life out. It was far too public, and far too risky. One mention of Samantha Brockhaven in a crowd of 7 Year Coma fans would draw a lot of attention. I responded quickly, and in a low voice that only he could hear. "Yeah, she knows my brother. Can we talk about this later? I promise I'll tell you more, I just don't want to right here."

He looked both suspicious and intrigued, but gave me a reluctant nod and nudged me toward the front of the beer line so that we could give our order.

We got back to our group, both of us carrying as many plastic beer bottles as we could. Of course, Ray-Ray couldn't keep quiet, and had to tell them who we had just run into, which sparked a whole wave of questions. "No, no," Ray-Ray jumped in facetiously, holding up his hand, "She doesn't want to talk about it until after the concert."

There was nothing more exciting to me than when the lights dimmed, and the headlining band took the stage. A wave of screams and applause filled the venue with a power that just couldn't be matched. The first few notes on the single lead guitar answered back through the speakers, the lights on the stage exploded, revealing the band, who went right into their first song. It was pure bliss.

When JT Porter, who alternated the position of lead singer with his brother Rylan, stepped toward the mike and started singing, the already deafening screams from the crowd only became louder. We could barely hear his voice. By the time he reached the chorus, the audience was singing along to every word.

7 Year Coma had a stage presence that could not be matched by any other band. They refused to have the pyrotechnics that had become popular among other rock bands in recent years. They didn't dance on stage, or jump

around trashing their equipment, but their energy came through their musical talents, and the chemistry and interactions with each other on stage added to the music, it didn't distract from it.

JT's vocal range and slightly raspy voice gave him a distinct sound that set 7 Year Coma apart from any other band out there. It would have been enough if he was just the front man to the band, but when his brother Rylan took lead on a song, JT often moved back to play the drums. And when JT wasn't on stage, he obsessed himself with his song writing. Along with his brother Rylan, the two had written over ninety percent of the songs for 7 Year Coma, letting the other band members try out their songs on their more recent albums. At age thirty-five, JT claimed to have written hundreds of songs, only a few select choices made it to their albums.

Where JT provided the band's signature sound, Rylan provided untamed heart and soul to every song that he sang. He didn't have the vocal range that his brother owned, but the power behind his voice made their fans crave more. There was a deep emotion in his voice, and every time he came near a microphone, you couldn't help but wonder where it all came from. When he wasn't singing lead, Rylan sang backup to his brother, as well as played lead guitar on almost every song.

Rylan was the oldest member of the band at thirty-eight, and was by all means the best guitarist I've ever heard. It didn't matter if it was acoustic, electric, bass, if it had strings, he could play it. And he played better than anyone. Magazines, music critics and fans all hailed him as the best in today's music business. He was what the other musicians strived to be. He played the way he sang, with full passion, as though it were only he and his guitar in the room. It didn't matter if it was a recording studio or audience of thousands, it was just Rylan and his guitar.

Rylan was also the clear leader of 7 Year Coma. He had created the band, coming up with the name and handpicking each member with impeccable precision. He once told an interviewer that he had had a vision of what he wanted his band to be, and he wasn't going to stop looking until he achieved that vision. It took him almost a full year to recruit for his band, but it was well worth it in the end. He truly had created one of the biggest bands to ever come out of London.

Eli Emerson played the drums like he was bored. He always wore the same monotonic look on his face. His frizzy blond hair was equivalent to a white-man's afro, and was very uncharacteristic for a thirty-six-year old man. It was the most surreal thing I've ever seen anyone wear, and I often wondered why a guy would pay money for a perm in the first place, let alone pay the money just to ruin it like he did.

Dax Crowley was the rhythm guitarist. He was thirty-seven and rugged to the core, with dark dirty blond hair, or light brown, I could never be sure. He had a permanent five o'clock shadow that drove me insane. Me and twenty million other women all across the world. Twenty million and one if you counted his wife, which I much preferred not to most of the time.

Lucas Mason was thirty-six, and played bass, but could pick up on any instrument wherever he might be needed. There was talk of him singing lead on a song two albums ago, but it never played out. So, Lucas' fans were still waiting to see what would happen next.

The five of them together claimed title to England's top band for the past two decades. While they had more of a cult following now here in the States, they held several Top Ten songs on our charts consistently over the past two decades as well. They were also huge in many countries worldwide, such as Japan, Germany, and even South America. They constantly sold out large venues on their world tours, and tonight was no exception.

My favorite part to any Coma show, hands down, was Rylan Porter's guitar playing. Whether it was a solo lead or the occasional rhythm guitar, he simply commanded the crowd. The music didn't just flow from his guitar, he forced it out of the instrument. And he did it in a way that made it seem natural and easy, like it was what he was born to do. When he played, it mesmerized and inspired me. I wanted to capture half the talent that he had, even if only for just a moment.

When the rest of the band left the stage at the end of the show, JT jumped down into the pit, and on the monitors we could see that he was all but making out with a beautiful blond in the front of the crowd. Security was all over him in an instant, pulling him back up onstage, to which he only laughed and saluted the fans as he followed the rest of his band offstage.

The lights snapped on in the venue, and my ears buzzed painfully as people started flooding toward the exits. It took us longer to get out of the building and the parking lot than it did to get back to the hotel.

"So Nat," Callie pressed, as we reached the hotel lobby, "I want to hear this story that Ray-Ray started telling us."

I smiled and nodded. "I know, but we've a party to prepare for. I promise I will talk, but right now, I need a quick shower and a change of clothes. Let's meet back down here in about an hour?"

Sammi was already waiting for us when we arrived back in the lobby. She was dressed in a silver satin v-neck smock top over black sateen cropped pants. On her feet were silver snakeskin platform sandals, and she carried a matching silver patent croc convertible clutch. Her short red hair was neatly slicked behind her ears, with a slight curl on each side to frame her chin, accenting the 2-carat diamond solitaire earrings that she wore in each ear.

I was having a hard time containing my excitement as I was finally able to introduce her to my friends, and as she extended her hand to each one, she repeated their name with a smile. She once told me that was her trick to remembering all of the hundreds of people that she met during the course of her career.

Ray-Ray jumped in full force, barely waiting until she had released his hand to ask, "So what's it like working with 7 Year Coma?"

She smiled at him, noting that she gets this question a lot, and answered honestly, "It's very trying sometimes. Days like today, for example, when just about *nothing* goes the way that we planned it. But it's also very rewarding. They're a great group of guys." She winked at me, then motioned for us to follow her, as she made her way past the front desk toward the oversized hallway that had led me to the bar room the other night.

As we walked along, Josh pulled my arm, slowing me down behind the rest of the group as we followed Sammi through the corridor. "Nat," he whispered to me, "Is the band going to be at this party?"

I simply shrugged my shoulders and whispered back, "Anything's possible Josh, why?"

He nodded up toward Ray-Ray, who was walking next to Sammi and picking her brain about how she became a manager for the biggest band in the England. "Cause he'll never forgive you for letting him meet his favorite band in that shirt."

I laughed out loud about Ray-Ray's lime-green button down shirt, just as he slowed a few steps so that he could talk to us as we walked along. He was clearly having a hard time containing his excitement. "She said that the band is staying in our hotel. Do you realize that 7 Year Coma might have walked this very hallway? I could be standing in Rylan Porter's footsteps right here." He stopped in his tracks, just to prove his point.

I bit back the urge to tell him that he had already been much closer to his idol than merely standing in the hallway where the rock star had walked.

Josh couldn't help but jump in. "Ray-Ray, if we run into them, maybe when Rylan's done signing the girls' tits, you could ask him to autograph your cock."

Ray-Ray raised an eyebrow at us. "He'd have to use his middle name to make it worth my while…"

Sammi pulled on the iron rod handle to the double etched-glass doors next to the plaque on the wall that read, "Westshire Room", revealing a dimly lit lobby with a matre dee standing behind a mahogany podium. "Brockhaven." Sammi told him, "Party of seven." There was an air of authority in her voice as the businesswoman in her came out.

"Of course, Ms. Brockhaven." Was the response from the man in the slim tuxedo and slicked black hair. He held his hand out for Sammi to take, and led her around the corner. He turned back toward the rest of us, "Right this way, please."

When we walked into the private party room, we entered another dimension, one that I was familiar with in another life. The room was large, and was darker than it was light, but the bar area was lit up in white and green lights, highlighting the bar and the bar stools, as well as the array of top-shelf-only liquor behind it.

The rest of the room was lit sporadically with various blue, green and white club lights. There was a large dance floor in the center of the room that was only about half full. I scanned the crowd, recognizing no one so far. Tall tables were placed sporadically around the dance floor and the bar area, and in the far corner of the room were several private round tables with leather booths surrounding them.

"Please feel free to enjoy the open bar," Sammi told us, as we looked around, taking it all in. "They'll be around with appetizers in a bit."

I spotted the bass player from Lull, one of the opening bands, standing at the bar and laughing with a group of busty blondes. Callie recognized him also, and whispered to Josh, who nodded, his eyes wide.

I slipped my hand into Rachel's, and turned her toward the dance floor, which was made entirely of three inch thick Plexiglas, illuminated with blue lights that blinked on and off to the beat of the music. "Think that'll fill your dance fix for a while?"

"Shit, if you find me off that floor even once tonight, kick me in the ass."

All around us, women were dressed in flashy club gear, low cut shirts, short skirts, everything worn skin tight as though it were liquid latex poured onto their bodies and molded just before they walked in. Jewelry was anything from gaudy costume to high end and flashy. They were here for one reason: to hook up with a band member, even if just for one night.

It had long been rumored that 7 Year Coma hated these type of parties. The stiff, upper class groupies, the media and publicity, and the restrictions imposed on them by management and PR - namely Sammi - to portray themselves respectively. It went against everything that they stood for, a hard rocking, we-don't-give-a-shit group of guys that could care less about what the public thought of them. "Once in a while these events are necessary," Sammi explained to us. "The record companies want to meet the band that they were putting their money and their reputation into."

I scanned the room, looking for faces that I'd recognize. My friends were all doing the same, taking it all in with a quiet awe. A man in a suit, sticking out like a sore thumb in this crowd, was sitting at the bar drinking a heavy drink in a low ball glass, no ice, chatting it up with an obvious groupie. Next to him sat a clean cut man in polo shirt and khaki's, an off-duty golfer who'd been let in on a thick wad of bills no doubt, flirting shamelessly with the bartender, a sleek blonde in a black rubber dress.

And just beyond the golfer, I spotted him. He was sitting at one of the booths, laughing, his hand cupping a half-filled tumbler. He was dressed in a navy green jacket covering a plain black t-shirt, slightly worn jeans, and his dark brown hair hung just above his ice-blue eyes. He could have been anyone in the room, the way he was relaxed in his seat, enjoying his drink and chatting with his company. He had one of those full on laughs, the kind where you could tell that he wasn't faking it just for the sake of public relations. And the look in his eyes was genuine, if not a bit tired.

Behind me, Ray-Ray had spotted him as well, nearly toppling me over to get a closer look. "Holy *shit*! Sammi, is that...?"

"It is." She tossed a quick, inquisitive look in my direction, to which I smiled and nodded ever so slightly before she followed with, "Did you want to meet him?"

If Ray-Ray answered her, I didn't hear it. Instead, the look on his face was one of quiet awe, as we began closing the fifty-foot gap between Ray-Ray and his idol. I could almost hear his heart pounding through the crowd.

I stayed behind Sammi as she led us over to row of booths, then casually slid her hand onto Rylan Porter's back, interrupting his conversation.

"Gary, Kevin, would you excuse us for a moment?" Sammi addressed the other two men who were seated at the table. They smiled at Sammi, gave a quick nod to Rylan, and were instantly gone. "Ry, I have some friends that I want you to meet."

Rylan stood methodically to greet us, and I stepped out from behind Sammi. He opened his mouth to speak, but the instant our eyes met, he blinked several times as if he didn't trust his vision.

"Natalie... I thought you weren't able to make it this time around?"

His eyes fell quickly over to Sammi before they returned to me. Sammi explained ever-so-briefly, "Natty asked if I could keep it a secret." She gave me a wink before excusing herself to tend to the lack of appetizers that she'd been promised.

We stood for a moment, five feet in between us - a divide that felt eternal - until finally I took a step forward and he pulled me into a tight hug. His chest caved with the tentative breath that he'd been holding, and he gave me one last tight squeeze before letting go. The words could be spoken later, but for now, we put a silent cover over the past three years, and enjoyed the moment as though the waters were still.

He held me next to him, his arm across my shoulders, and pressed a kiss on the top of my head. "How are you? Did you just get here tonight? You flew in then…?"

I had to laugh at his erratic rambling, and wiped my damp cheek on my palm. It was so good to see him again, and the years that had passed since we'd been together last seemed to slide away quickly. "We drove. Just got in last night."

"Fuckin' one hell of a surprise…"

I took a good look at him, noticing that in the three years since I had seen him last, he had aged about eight. He had been touring for the better part of those years, and being on the road takes its toll, he often told me. His dark hair was short, and still thick, with a few traces of gray cropping up at the sides, and there were signs of shallow wrinkles around his stunning blue eyes, which were still as sharp and bright as ever.

"Fuck my manners," Rylan apologized as he extended his hand to Callie.

I quickly interjected. "Mine too. Callie, this is my brother Rylan." I hadn't expected to get so caught up in the moment, yet my friends were still standing there with shell-shock painted on their faces.

"Your brother…" Rachel's voice came from over my shoulder, as she quickly started putting pieces of a deliberately intricate puzzle together. I turned to face both her and Ray-Ray, who were standing behind me.

They both wore the same look on their face, and it wasn't the wide-eyed, star-struck smiles that my other friends were donning. They were both clearly thinking, calculating, as though they were rewinding high-speed back through the years of our lives together, looking for clues that should have led them to this very moment. But the truth had been well-buried, intentionally masked, but I was certain that throughout the years, if viewed in retrospect, there would have been enough opportunity to piece it all together.

I mouthed the words; "We'll talk later," to both of them, then turned quickly to resume introductions without missing a beat.

When I introduced my two best friends to my brother, his dusky smile deepened. "I feel like I already know the two of you," he told them, as he turned to Rachel and said, "Rachel, the pictures don't do you justice. You're far more beautiful in person."

Rachel blushed, then went to deep crimson as he took her hand and pulled her into a tight hug like she was his long lost sister. Still holding Rachel under one arm, Rylan then turned to Ray-Ray and extended his hand. "You must be Ray-Ray. Natalie's not shut up about you since the moment she met you."

While I wanted to simply die at that very moment, I was far more amused at the surprised look on Ray-Ray's face. I could see the wheels in his head turning, as he looked at Rylan, then back to me. I knew he saw it. He was seeing my face for the first time in a whole new light. Standing next to Rylan, it was hard to miss the identical blue eyes, long nose and high cheek bones. His face was a little more square than mine that was oval, but the genetics were unmistakable.

Rylan motioned for us to join him at his booth. "Make yourselves at home. I'll get some more chairs."

He returned with two more chairs for Ray-Ray and Nathan, then slid in the booth next to me, throwing his arm across my shoulders and looking around at my group of friends. "You all look a little stunned."

Josh spoke up, "Well, Natalie failed to mention she had any ties to our favorite band," he sent a glare across the table at me, and added, "for the last *seven* years."

Rylan smiled and settled in a bit more into his seat.

"Eh, it's just a job. Pays the bills."

"You're such a liar," I smiled at him, "It's your whole life and you know it."

A waitress, dressed very professionally in a black uniform, took our drink orders. When everyone had finished, Rylan motioned for her, and she leaned in so that he could whisper in her ear. "No problem, Mr. Porter." She responded, "I'll have that right out for you."

A few minutes later, she returned, followed by a waiter dressed also in an all-black uniform. Both were holding bottles of Dom Pérignon Rosé Champagne, and yet another waitress quickly rushed to place crystal flutes in front of each of us. Once each flute had been filled and the wait staff had exited, Rylan tipped his glass toward mine. "Happy birthday, Natalie girl."

My friends held up their glasses and toasted as well, and as I sipped the bubbly champagne, I tried not to choke on it before it slid down my throat. I turned to Rylan. "I'm sorry, but I can't stand champagne."

He gave me an amused look, raising his eyebrows. "I can't as well, but at four-fifty a bottle, we'll just pretend we do tonight. Besides, whatever we don't drink, JT's sure to finish off."

"JT!" I threw my hands up on top of my head, and started to scan the room that was beginning to get crowded, "Is he here?"

"He'll be by later," Rylan promised, "He's attached himself, so to speak, to this young ad agent that he met at a video shoot a few months back, and she managed herself a front row ticket to every US show since LA. He's gotten his own bus for the pair of them, and that's where they usually head to after the show. He hasn't even checked into his hotel room yet, from what I've heard..."

I held up my hand. "Thanks, that was more than what I needed to know. Sammi said he'd be here."

Rylan nodded. "He'll be along. Sammi made it clear

that this party was mandatory tonight. Though now I know it had nothing to do with our record promotions in the States." He finished his champagne in one long swig, and followed it with a sour look on his face, just as the waitress was bringing our drink orders. He took his Belvedere on the rocks right off of the tray, and chased the champagne with a sip of the top-shelf liquor.

He followed by asking each of my friends what they were going to school for, and I enjoyed listening to them tell him about each of their lives, how they knew me, and answer the other random questions that he threw at them. They seemed truly amazed at how much he already knew about each of them. Rylan had a true talent for details, and remembered all of their names just from the initial introduction. Although, I had been telling him and JT bits and pieces about my friend's lives since I had met each of them. After so many years, my brothers probably felt like they knew my friends personally.

I sat there wondering what was going through Rachel's mind, and feeling waves of guilt wash over me as I looked at my best friend. Did she feel as though I had lied to her all these years? If she did, would she accept my explanations of why? She looked as though she were having fun though, laughing along with the rest of my friends as my brother told us stories of some of the crazy things that had happened to them during this last leg of the tour.

For the first time in my life, I almost felt normal. I had gotten a chance to meet all of my friends' families, in one setting or another. Though some of them I knew better than others, I had at least been formally introduced, and gotten a chance to put a face with a name. It allowed me a unique opportunity to catch a glimpse at their pasts, to see a bit of what made them who they were today. It was as though a missing piece of the puzzle had been placed by sitting there tonight with my friends and my brother, laughing and sharing stories.

After a few more drinks, the girls and I decided to find our way to the ladies room. We found it in the far corner of the club, and as soon as we were inside, they ambushed me. Callie took the lead, in an unexpected maneuver.

"You sneaky bitch!" She hissed, and hit me on the shoulder with her clutch. Rachel stood next to her, as I was helpless with my back against the row of sinks set in a large marble countertop. "Why in the hell didn't you tell us?"

The dreaded question, I thought, the one that I had been prepared for my entire life, in the event that I had been exposed without warning. Yet with all of my preparations, and though I had practiced my speech thousands of times over the course of the years, I found myself without words at moment. My eyes locked on Rachel's, whose wide eyes were locked on mine.

I shook my head. "It is a long story, as you can imagine..."

"We'll take the Cliff Notes, Nat. Just give us the five minute run-down." Callie offered, and I was grateful for the soft tone in her voice.

Nodding, I made sure to look them each in the eyes as I gave them the abridged version. "My family moved me to the States to keep me away from the press. They wanted me to live a normal life, outside of the public eye. We've lied to the press for so many years, and me being over here, on this side of the ocean, it made it easier. I don't have cameras on me at every waking minute like I do when I'm with my family. As we got older, I thought so many times about telling you all, but I never knew how... or when. I mean really," I choked back a laugh through the tears, "Would you guys have even believed me? It all seems so preposterous..."

Rachel was quiet for a moment, and I could see the wheels behind her eyes turning and calculating. It took forever before she reached out with both arms and pulled me into a hug. I buried my face in her shoulder, apologizing to her profusely. She pulled back and looked me in the eyes, and offered me a tear-stained smile.

"I saw a picture once in your nightstand back at school. I went to hide a bottle of JD, and it was right there in a beautiful silver frame when I opened the drawer. I thought I had broken it when I dropped the bottle in, so I took it out just to make sure. It was JT and Rylan, but it wasn't one of those cut out magazine pictures. It looked like it was outside of someone's house. I just never put it together that you actually knew them."

I simply shook my head, and suddenly felt so ashamed. All those nights that I had lay in bed, feeling so lonely that I didn't have my family to turn to, I could've just flicked on the light and poured my heart out to my best friend, my sister. She had been there all along, and instead of taking it for what it was, I chose to feel sorry for myself, just because I could. I should never have held anything back from her, and it tore a hole in my heart that I had for so long.

"Rach, I'm so sorry..." I hadn't even realized that Callie had slipped out of the ladies' room at some point, and though I had no recollection of when, I was grateful that Rachel and I were alone. We found our way to a small cushioned bench in the vanity side of the room.

She dabbed at her eyes with a wad of tissues. "Stop feeling guilty, Nat. Just for once, can you believe enough in yourself to trust your decisions? You're a good person, and I'm not mad at you. I'm just in shock. You'd be too if you just met Rylan Porter for the first time."

She gave me a quick wink, and we both laughed. I hugged her one last time before standing up. "I knew even if you were mad, you'd forgive me pretty quick when I introduce you to Lucas Mason."

She joined me in the mirror. "Honey, if I meet Lucas looking like this, I will never forgive you.

As Rachel and I stood waiting for the bartender to fix

our sour apple martinis made with Grey Goose vodka, I heard an all-too familiar voice come up behind me from out of nowhere. "There's our girl!"

I had only enough time to turn halfway around before JT Porter had me in a backward bear hug and was swinging me in dramatic circles, apparently not caring if he knocked anyone in the club over with his little sister. When the room stopped spinning, I blinked my eyes several times until I could bring him back into focus.

He stood there in front of me, a good nine inches taller than me, wearing sunglasses in the dark club, and his hair peeked out haphazardly all around from underneath a knit hat. His face didn't show the wears that Rylan's had, but I doubted that JT would ever age. He had that Peter-Pan boyish charm about him that kept him in a good amount of trouble, yet somehow he never seemed to care.

He enjoyed life to the fullest, though most of the press implied that he enjoyed it way too much. Sometimes I think that his own headlines were an inspiration for him to top his own crazy antics, and JT was not one to resist temptation. It was that energy that kept the band in the spotlight, and they all knew it. However the rest of the band felt about JT's dramatic tribulations, they knew it was a part of what kept them in the public eye in between tours and record releases.

JT ran both hands over my hair, and tilted my head up toward him. "God girl, you're stunning. When did you grow up on us? Let me buy you a drink...."

"It's open bar." I told him.

He gave me a quick wink, "So they're on Rylan then." He caught a glimpse of Rachel next to me. "Ah, this must be your partner in crime."

Rachel and I both giggled. It wasn't the first time someone had accused us of this. I formally introduced them, but before I could finish, JT had grabbed my best friend and dipped her, placing a solid peck right on her lips.

She stood, only slightly taken back, and looked back

over at me, straightening herself out again. "Well then, that's almost as good as it's been in my dreams..."

"Oh no," I reminded her, "Your dreams were always about Lucas."

Rachel blushed, and JT wrinkled his nose. "That cunt? I've just lost all respect for you..." He gave her a quick wink, then turned back to me as Rachel went to grab our martinis. "I like her."

"Me too. I'm lucky to have her."

"And her you." It was a rare compliment, so I took it for what it was worth, as he continued with his uncharacteristic sentiments, "I missed you Natalie girl. You sticking around a while?"

I nodded, sipping the martini that Rachel handed me. "We'll be here about another week."

He took a drink from his own glass, and unidentifiable straight-up liquor with a few sporadic ice cubes floating at the top. "Good, you'll have time to meet Candace then."

Ah, the elusive ad agent that Rylan had made mention to earlier. "She's not here tonight then?"

"Nah, she went to our bus to call it an early night. You'll see her tomorrow."

Rachel found the whole conversation very interesting, as she quietly sipped on her martini. I could tell she was feeling quite good. "Your new girlfriend is sleeping on a bus? It must be one hell of a bus if you're giving up these hotel rooms."

I laughed, and couldn't help throwing a dig at JT. "Rach, most of what you read in the tabloids is total shit. Except for the fact that JT Porter is banned from almost every hotel in the country. That's completely true."

"Sod off," he told me, then made sure Rachel knew the truth. "It is one hell of a bus, I'll tell you that. And I haven't been chucked from a hotel since my late twenties." With a quick change of subject, he took Rachel around the waist, "Let me introduce you to my mates, since Natalie's clearly not able to tell fact from fiction."

I punched him on the shoulder and followed them across the room, where Dax, Eli and Lucas where gathered in a corner booth, drinking and carrying on with some of the members of the opening band.

"Shit JT, does your missus know you're hanging out with beautiful women while she's off in the bus?" Lucas was never one to be quiet off stage, which occasionally caused some rivalry with the younger of my two brothers.

JT introduced Rachel to them and there were stars in her eyes when Lucas stood up and hugged her. He leaned down and whispered something in her ear, and whatever he said caused her jaw to drop instantly, her cheeks to blush, and she instantly turned and gave me less than a gentle shove. "I can't believe you told him..." She hissed.

I laughed, rubbing my arm. She had quite a swing.

Dax jumped up from the table and pulled me into a tight hug. "When did you become such a hottie?" I nearly melted right there in his arms. It didn't matter that I had known him since I was a young girl, he had taken my heart the moment I first saw him. "Fuck, JT, you better keep your eye on this woman."

Rachel said that she absolutely had to go get the rest of our friends, mainly because Ray-Ray would kill us if he left tonight without meeting the rest of the band. It gave me only a few minutes to catch up with the rest of the guys before the chaos began.

I took a moment to take it all in. It had been too long since I had seen the rest of the band, and it didn't occur to me until just then how much I had truly missed them. They were an extension of my family, my other big brothers, and my heart was aching to see them again.

They were all still happily married, which I was glad to hear. Life on the road could be tough, so I had been told many, many times. But Eli announced that he and his wife were expecting their first child in a few months, so Sophie was resting at their new home in Madrid. Lucas and his wife Layna had been married for five years now, though Layna rarely traveled overseas. Dax's wife Jules however, very much enjoyed touring with the band, it was rare to see her stay home during a tour.

I busied myself by introducing my friends to the rest of the band. I could tell they were thoroughly enjoying themselves, if not a bit overwhelmed by the whole night. It was almost two am, and I was beginning to feel the effects of the long day.

I found a door which led outside to a beautiful Japanese rock garden. During the day, I imagined that it would be an ideal spot for wedding pictures, though now it looked to me like a good place for a cigarette.

Enjoying a few moments of peace, I marveled at the fact that it was suddenly quiet, save for the occasion passing car on the street leading to the hotel. At this hour, I was still surprised to see the few cars that did pass by. It seemed the perfect night for reflection, and I wish I had more time than the quick fresh air break that I claimed to have needed.

I lit a cigarette that I had pinched from JT, took a long drag, then closed my eyes as I leaned back against the stone building. I felt worlds away from where I had been when I woke up this morning. And I felt like I still had worlds to go before I could fully explain everything to my friends, and I still wasn't sure I could tell even Rachel the full truth.

I knew there would be questions. Why had I kept this from them? How could they not have known all these years? The last one would be infinitely easier to answer. It was much easier to hide your identity when you spent precious little time with the only people in the world who knew who you really were. And in those rare opportunities that a photographer had a chance to snap a picture, the moments were left up to speculation by puzzled reporters. Tabloids had a field day with those pictures when I was a kid. But the public would have to settle on their own imaginations, as no one was revealing the truth.

The first question would be the tough one. And I wasn't sure it was one I could answer honestly yet.

Still, there was an incredible weight that had been lifted; I could feel that much already. I would no longer have to hide photographs of my family, keep the cherished international phone calls private, or hold back when it came to talking about my brothers.

I took in another long drag, letting the smoke out slowly, and tried to enjoy the stars sparkling above my head. About twenty feet away, music escaped from the party into my private little reprieve. I looked over to see Ray-Ray slip through the open door and into the rock garden. As soon as the door closed behind him, there was nothing but the still night and the sound of his footsteps on the stone and gravel as he crossed through the garden to where I stood against the wall.

"Mr. Montgomery." I greeted him, tapping out my cigarette on the wall behind me and letting it drop to the stones where I stood in the dark.

He wore a look of mock suspicion as he approached and said, "Ms.... Porter." He leaned up against the wall next to me.

"It really is McKinney." I corrected him, feeling a sting of guilt that even my own name was now in question. But rightfully so, I reminded myself.

"A rose by any other name." He said, as he looked up at the stars above us, "Still not as gorgeous as Natalie McKinney-Porter."

I smiled and tried to suppress a laugh. Where did he come up with this stuff, I wondered?

We stood there for a while in silence. I wasn't sure if he was just overwhelmed from the shock of the night, or if he was just taking advantage of the quiet solace as much as I was. I looked over at him, standing just about six inches away from me. His dark eyes were hard to read in the Texas moonlight, but he seemed to have good thoughts running through his mind, as his lips curved ever so slightly upward into a subtle smile.

"Not to sound cliché, but I'm dying to know what you're thinking about right now." I stood in front of him and folded my arms across my chest. I had to struggle slightly to keep my balance on the rounder rocks in the garden, but he reached out and steadied me with a hand on each of my arms until I was able to gain solid footing again.

"I'm standing here thinking that tonight was one of the best fucking nights I've ever had, really. It's not every day that you get to meet your all-time favorite band. Then to find out that one of your best friends is related to the band, well that's a pretty fucking wild revelation."

"*One* of the best nights?" I inquired, a bit taken back by this. I had expected the rest, but that part jumped out at me. "Just 'one of'? How can that be?"

He gave me a crooked smile as he cocked his head to the side. "'Best night' still goes to the night that Natalie McKinney slept over and I was lucky enough to wake up next to her the morning after. You're gonna have to try a little harder than 7 Year Coma if you want to top that night, Love."

I smiled back at him, taking a step closer so that I was only inches away, gazing up into his eyes. My hands placed flat on his chest, I turned my chin upward and stood on my tiptoes, brushing my lips against his. For a moment, he accepted the small peck on his lips, but he hesitated as I nibbled his bottom lip.

Everything about me right then and there wanted every bit of him. Memories of the night that we spent back at his placed were spinning through my mind. And the question "Why not?" kept ringing in my ears. My heart was pulling in every direction just to get to him. I couldn't keep it from racing out of my chest, and I sure as hell couldn't keep my hands from pressing into him just a little more. My fingers were burning to dig deeper, and a hot sweat was beginning to form on the back of my neck.

Pulling back slightly, he took my hands off of his chest, holding them in his. His eyes questioned mine as he asked, "Nat, you sure you want to do this?"

I nodded, a slow smile forming on my lips, as my heart skipped several beats. "I'm sure."

"Because this isn't about a one night stand, then we part ways tomorrow..."

"I know."

He looked as though he were reading my eyes, trying to see straight into my heart before his arms instinctively wrapped around me, pulling me against him, and his mouth covered mine with a hungry kiss. His hands kneaded my body, everywhere that he could reach, and I arched up toward him, throwing my arms around his neck and running my fingers through his hair as I kissed him back with just as much hunger.

He moved down to kiss my neck, that spot just behind my ear, then toward my shoulder, which drove me absolutely wild, and made me wonder if he somehow knew just what he was doing to me. "I need you." He said in a low groan, still nuzzling my neck, "Stay with me tonight."

"But what about Nathan..."

"I'll stay with you then."

"Rachel..."

"Fuck. Can we get our own room?"

"Doubtful. I hear that 7 Year Coma's staying here..."

He sighed heavily and leaned his head back against the wall.

I leaned my head against his chest, looking up at him before suggesting, "My car?"

He choked back a laugh. "No chance in hell I'm making love to you in your car. The idea turns me on more than I can even tell you right now, but I'd opt for a cold shower and some patience before I'd let that happen. That's not to say that down the road..."

I took a step back. "Okay, I get your point." I took a deep breath and let it out slowly, and ran my hands through my hair in frustration. Parts of me were aching in ways that I couldn't control, and it physically pained me to step away from him, but I knew if I didn't, we'd have been tearing each other's clothes off right there in the rock garden.

I'd have to talk to Sammi in the morning to find out if there was any way she might be able to come up with just one more room in a packed hotel. As much as they tried to keep their location under wraps, it always had a way of getting out somehow. Even choosing the high-end hotels anymore didn't seem to cure the fact that fans would pay top dollar just for the slightest chance of running into their favorite band in the breakfast room or the hotel lobby.

We headed back upstairs to our rooms, and he kissed me goodnight when we got to my door. It was a kiss like he hadn't kissed me before, deep and warm and passionate beyond what I felt like I could break away from. So much so that when he stepped back and my eyes fluttered open to meet his, my tongue was still tasting him on my upper lip.

"If you find that Rachel ran off with Lucas, call me and I'll be right over." He told me, as he turned toward his room.

But when I opened the door, Rachel was sound asleep in her bed. I crawled into my own bed, and hit the pillow with solid exhaustion.

TWELVE
Natalie

It was one of the best night's sleep I'd had in a long time. Even after only a few hours of rest, I felt wide awake when I heard Rachel's alarm go off at eight am. While she was in the shower, I stepped out onto the balcony to enjoy the morning sun.

Today was a brand new day. I'd let go of the secrets that had been holding me back for so long. There was no more having to wait to take phone calls from my family, no more having to dodge questions about my childhood or how my trips to the UK had gone. It was freeing.

I was toweling off after my morning shower when I heard my phone ring on the nightstand by my bed. In one swift motion, I wrapped the towel around me and dove, soaking wet, across the comforter for the phone. I wanted it to be Ray-Ray, and was almost disappointed to see Rylan's number appear on the screen.

"Hey Ry."

"I'm ordering room service for brunch. Do you have

some time?"

I found it strange that my heart sank just a little. I hadn't really seen him in so long, yet I had been looking forward to seeing Ray-Ray at breakfast this morning. "Sure, I'll be up in a few."

I had to show ID when I reached the top floor of the hotel. It was a standard security measure anytime the band stayed at a hotel. They had to pre-approve any visitors to their floor, even those related by blood.

Rylan's suite was breath-taking, even bigger than most I've seen. It was clear that the last few years had been successful for the band. The suite itself was easily four times the size of our oversized rooms, and had a full kitchen, a large seating area, French doors that opened to the bedroom in a loft above an iron spiral staircase, and another set of French doors that opened up to the balcony. Just inside the kitchen sat a large cart on wheels, laced with a crisp white tablecloth which presented a mini-buffet of everything from Belgian Waffles to finger sandwiches, exotic fruits, and fresh-baked rolls.

Rylan stepped into the suite from the balcony, dressed in a pair of cargo shorts, a long-sleeved dark T-shirt pulled up at the sleeves, and sandals. He wore his sunglasses on top of his head, and his bright blue eyes were wide and alert, even for having been up as late as we had all been last night.

"Did your friends have fun last night?" He asked, motioning for me to dive into the buffet as he poured us each a mug of tea. I was hoping for coffee, but didn't see any.

"I'd say. They sure as hell were surprised. I think today I'll have a lot of questions to answer."

Rylan smiled, handing me my tea. We ate on the balcony, enjoying the already ninety-degree temperatures that greeted us even before noon. It was a peaceful, quiet view. We were about twenty-five stories off of the ground, and had a magnificent view of the Texas landscape, spotted with the occasional palm tree, and a large two-story high fountain below us.

After brunch, Rylan took our dishes inside, and returned with a pack of cigarettes. He leaned up against the railing so that he was facing me, pulled one out of the pack with his teeth, then handed me one before I could ask him. He flipped his sunglasses down to cover his eyes from the sun that had just peaked over the top of the building.

"I know you don't so much as check the balance, but I put a small deposit into your account for your birthday."

I rolled my eyes. It had been an ongoing debate over the years. Even the years that we hadn't spoken, the balance would sneak up on "my" account. "That's not why you called me to have brunch with you, is it? To discuss finances?"

I caught the start of a smile before he cut it off. "No, Natalie, hard to believe I just wanted to spend some time with you. It's been too long."

Cringing with a little guilt, I nodded in agreement. I wondered for a moment if he would bring it up. It would be the normal thing to do, apologize. But Rylan Porter was as stubborn as they came, and if I expected anything more than what I knew him to be, I'd turn up disappointed in the end. Instead, he offered what I knew was his version of an apology.

"We'll be home for Christmas this year, if you want to spend a few weeks back home."

I'd spent the last three with Rachel and her parents in a cabin at the lake in the Poconos. It was a beautiful way to spend the holiday, but it wasn't the same without my family. I was sure Rylan wouldn't have understood the loss that I felt, the emptiness of not sharing those family traditions; the stories that we laughed about each year that never got old no matter how many times you'd heard them, or watching the reaction on their faces when they opened your gift. I would've loved to have seen the look in JT's eyes when he opened the coffee table picture book that I'd bought him on drummers in world-famous venues.

"I know you're an adult now, technically, but you can

still come home whenever you want. I'm not turning your room into a guitar closet anytime soon."

The thought of my bedroom at Rylan's place lifted my mood. The entire upstairs of the townhouse that Rachel and I shared could fit inside my bedroom in London. I held a fondness for it, as it was the one room in Rylan's house that was warm and feminine. And my bed made even those of the Elyad Suites seem like a cheap motel mattress. The second you laid down on it, it was like the entire bed would fluff up and hug you. One night's sleep on it was enough to cure even the worst of insomniacs.

"I'll consult my travel agent and get back to you." I said, not quick enough to duck his swing. He caught me right around the neck and pulled me into a hug. It got to me sometimes, how close we really were, even if we were rarely together anymore. Families, normal families who grew up together, probably never cherished those moments the way we did, those rare precious gems of time that popped up here and there over the years. I had been foolish these past few years, and I knew it. But not now, I promised myself. I would take advantage of every moment I had with my family. It would be all too soon before I'd be saying a tearful goodbye, and watching him head back across the Atlantic again.

"I'm glad you came, Natalie." He pulled another cigarette out of the pack and lit it, and as he drew in a deep breath of tobacco, I noticed his fingers tightening around the iron railing. He let the smoke trail slowly between clenched teeth before saying, "I have some news I wanted to share."

'News' was typically in the form of a new record coming out, an exciting extension to their tour, perhaps Australia, or the purchase of an epic new guitar he'd had his eye on for a bit. I settled back against the wall, preparing to be blown away by the newest revelation.

"I'm getting married."

All that I could offer was a half-laugh and, "What?"

I could tell he was finding amusement in the stunned

look that was creeping across my face, so much so that I actually began to believe he was kidding me. I rolled my eyes and smiled, half-relieved at the thought that he was pulling my leg. But his expression never changed, and he waited in quiet anticipation for a reaction that I couldn't provide.

He flicked his ashes over the rail. "In September of next year, when the tour is finished."

My eyes grew wide as the slow realization that he was serious began to sweep over me. "Ry, I didn't even know you were seeing someone." Though I had to admit, my sources were limited to my brief conversations with JT, which obviously proved me nowhere, and the media, which had been inbred in me to never trust. "Who?"

The smile that crossed his face was unlike any other I'd ever seen on him. It was a crazy kind of smile, a little wonderment and a little like that of a kid in love. "Sammi."

My foot slipped out from under me, and I had to catch my balance quickly by grabbing onto the rail. He laughed, though I couldn't tell if it was at me, or at this revelation. It was good to hear him laugh, it really was, but shock was setting in as I found it hard to conceptualize the whole notion of him marrying his manager. The thought seemed almost incestuous.

"You're not serious. How've I not known about this?" She wasn't even wearing a ring.

He flicked his ashes over the railing. "We're keeping it very quiet until after the wedding. You know how the media tends to get over these things."

My eyes narrowed at him. "That's not what I meant, and you know it." I couldn't keep the hurt tone out of my voice, though I had to admit I wasn't really trying hard either. "How long have you been seeing each other?"

He leaned a bit harder on his elbow, and wiped a line of sweat from his forehead. I was ignoring the fact that my skin was reddening by the second under the direct rays of the sun. "I don't really know how to answer that Nat. About a decade, maybe?"

"Are you fucking kidding me? You're joking…"

"Not exclusively, of course. It just kind of evolved over the years. It hasn't been like a normal relationship."

'Normal relationships' really didn't exist in his world. I knew that. All one had to do was look at our own relationship as evidence. Yet still, I found it incredibly hard to believe that there was absolutely no indication prior to today that he and Sammi had been having this surreptitious affair. There was no way that I could not have known. They wouldn't have been able to hide it from me for that long. Surely there'd have been some indication in all that time of their relationship.

His eyes held an apologetic regard. "It's not a big deal really."

"You're getting *married*, Rylan. It's a big deal."

"Well, maybe let's not go three years without talking, Natalie." He flicked his cigarette butt over the railing and set his eyes on mine.

"Like it's all my fault? All I wanted was…"

He held up his hand, and I instantly rolled my eyes. Typical of Rylan, cutting off the conversation when he was done with it. This happened every time I brought up the subject of our father.

"Hey, not now, al'ight? Just be happy for us?" He caught the impatient glare that I couldn't hide, and trying another approach he added, "For Sammi?"

He knew how to get me, that he did. But even if he'd asked on behalf of him, to be happy for his sake, I couldn't deny him that. And I was, no matter that it hadn't begun to sink in yet, I was happy that he was happy. It brought a sense of peace that I couldn't deny either one of us. I felt I owed him at least that, for all he'd done for me over the years.

THIRTEEN
Natalie

I found my friends just settling in down at the pool, where they were occupying two adjoining cabanas.

Callie had already stripped down to her pink string bikini, and Rachel was setting her sarong on a beach chair, revealing a beautiful green two-piece. The three guys were completely distracted by anything that walked by in a bikini, and I had to refrain from making any sly observations to that fact.

"There better be a bathing suit under that tank top, McKinney." Ray-Ray warned, from the far side of the second cabana. He had just pulled off his t-shirt so that he stood bare-chested in a pair of black swimming shorts. He alone was enough to distract my thoughts, but I felt a certain comfort in the presence of my friends. They were always able to make me feel better.

Wishing that I had swung by my room beforehand to change, I merely shook my head, and dipped my foot into the luke-warm pool water. I turned to face Rachel, and was about to ask her for the room key that I had forgotten to take with me, when I felt a strong arm around me, knocking me off balance, and sending me flailing helplessly into the pool, pulling me under the water.

When I came to the surface, Ray-Ray still had his arm

wrapped around me, and was laughing along with my other friends. Not sure if I was irritated or amused, I splashed him, only causing him to laugh more, and wrap his other arm around me, holding me close against him.

"You had to know that was coming," Callie accused, "I'm actually a little disappointed that you didn't."

I wriggled to try to free myself, unsuccessfully. He had a good grip. "Shame on me." I muttered, giving in, and just enjoying the feeling of him holding me for a moment. His skin was hot and wet against mine, and it was making me wish we were alone in the pool all of the sudden. I felt him take a deep breath before releasing his grip, and I wondered if he was wishing the same thing.

Rachel lowered herself into the pool. "So, third row tonight? You must have some pretty good connections, my friend."

"That's right, only the best for my friends." I had to use both hands to brush my wet hair out of my face. I wasn't in a hurry now to get out of the pool, even though the water was pulling at my clothes. It was a small sacrifice to get to be within close proximity to Ray-Ray.

"Wouldn't front row have been 'the best'?" Nathan spoke up. He was sitting on the edge of the pool, legs dipped casually in the water.

"Any more surprises we should know about?" Josh inquired, sending a spray of water cascading in my direction. "You're not secretly married to Dax Crowley or anything... Are you?"

I wiped my face with the back of my hand somewhat ungracefully, and leaning back against the wall of the pool, sank down until the water covered my shoulders. It was a welcome refreshment from the blazing sun above us.

"Time will tell, my friend." I gave him a quick wink, trying to keep my eyes off of Ray-Ray. He was a surprise I hadn't been expecting.

When we were ready to leave to go back to our rooms,

Ray-Ray offered me his towel. "It's kind of my fault you're in this predicament, so it's the least I can do."

I raised an eyebrow. "Kind of?" I took the towel and started drying off my drenched clothes. It was almost a hopeless cause, as my denim shorts were holding more water than I could ever dab out with a towel.

He studied me for a moment, amused at my attempts to stop the incessant dripping. "If you just take those off, you'd probably dry off a lot faster…"

I wanted to tell him right then and there that I would take them off back up in his room, but we still had this issue of no privacy whatsoever. I gave in and handed him his wet towel back, then rung out the front of my tank top onto the concrete pavement around the pool. "You know," I announced, "I might just sit out in the sun until I dry out a little more. I'll meet you guys around five or so for dinner at Tributes?"

I wasn't even sure that they were paying much attention, but Rachel waved her hand at me as she slipped into pace next to Nathan. Conveniently, Ray-Ray offered to stay behind with me, under the pretense that his towel was now too wet to dry off as well.

I wasn't quite sure that anyone of our friends bought the excuses, or maybe they just didn't think anything of it. It didn't matter to me either way. All that was on my mind at that moment was spending some time with Ray-Ray.

He immediately pulled a beach lounge up next to mine, so that there were no less than a few inches between us, as we lay out under the Texas sun. He rolled over on his side, propped up on his elbow so that he was facing me. He ran his hand along my hip and down my thigh, as far as he could reach. "I can't get you off my mind, girl."

I smiled, without even trying. I loved this whole other side of Ray-Ray. It was as though I had known it was there all along, but never really was on the receiving end of it. Up until the last few days, I never realized how much I wanted to know that side of him. "We have to find ourselves some time alone."

"No kidding. Not an easy feat when you've got six other friends hanging about."

It seemed to happen every time I was in close proximity to him anymore. This insane urge to touch him, running my fingers over the rippled muscles on his arms. Or to taste the heat radiating from his skin. It was overpowering, and I was having a hard time fighting my own self-control.

He leaned down toward my face, his mouth gently nibbling at my lower lip just enough to test the waters, to which I answered by parting my lips just slightly, to allow him to touch his tongue to the tip of mine. I leaned in to taste him more fully, enjoying the feel of his hand on the back of my neck, caressing my skin and grazing my hair with his fingers.

"How do I get you alone?" He groaned, nuzzling my neck.

My head was leaning against him now, my hand on his chest, loving the feeling I got from touching his bare skin, and wanting so much more than what I was getting at that moment.

"What if I gave Rachel my credit card and told her to go on a shopping spree? We'd have days alone in your room then..."

Ray-Ray's suggestion had me laughing, but I knew that we were going to need to find some time alone together soon. I hated that we were victims of circumstance, having to settle with stealing brief encounters such as this.

We met in the hotel's restaurant for an early dinner before the concert. Ray-Ray and I found ourselves at opposite ends of the large circular table, which was probably for the better, I decided. I wasn't sure I'd be able to keep my hands off of him if he was sitting next to me. I found it equally hard to keep my eyes off of him, though.

Tributes was a nice restaurant, and we seemed just slightly out of place in our concert attire. The guys were all wearing t-shirts, Josh and Nathan had their baseball caps on, and both Rachel and I were wearing practically obscene-lengthed denim shorts with cleavage-bearing tight shirts, and Callie had on a mini-dress that she had purchased on a shopping trip before we left Pennsylvania.

Josh and Callie were sharing a plate of grilled scallops, sitting close enough to each other that you could barely slide a piece of paper between them. There were times that you could almost swear they were oblivious to the rest of us, which brought about a slight pang of jealousy from deep within me as I felt the five-foot distance between Ray-Ray and myself.

Callie held her fork to her mouth, nibbling a scallop as she asked me, "What's happening after the concert tonight? Is there another party?"

I nodded. "There's usually some sort of party after every concert. Sammi called me earlier to let me know it's going to be a little more casual than last night's party. Rylan invited us to his room afterward, so I don't think that he's planning on staying at the party long."

I usually enjoyed the more intimate get-togethers at one of the band member's suites anyway. The parties could be fun, but in my opinion, they weren't much different from being in a club, only you were there among incredibly rich and famous people. At least when we were in a hotel suite, we could actually have a decent conversation, and catch up on lost time. They were a lot more laid back, and by far, a lot more real to me.

We settled into our third row seats at the concert venue only moments before Coma was about to come on stage. Nathan and Josh made sure that each of us had a beer in each hand before the first screams came from the audience as JT sauntered onto the stage. He appeared to have been drinking just a bit prior to the show, which always made for an interesting concert.

While I had been front row for their shows before, back in England during my teenage years, it had been a long time since I had seen the band play this close up. I had almost forgotten how amazing the power of both the music and the fans were. It was completely surreal when JT's voice came through the microphone so loud and so clear. The music was so much more enjoyable when you were this close to the stage. When Rylan struck the first few notes on his Gibson, the sound sent shivers down my spine. Looking at my friends, they were ten times more mesmerized than I was. I found myself smiling, happy that they were having the times of their lives.

Around the fifth song or so, Rylan took the lead on one of my personal favorites, *Not At My Door*, and I couldn't help singing along. About half way through the song, when Rylan had reached the chorus, I caught Ray-Ray studying me, his eyes narrowed and his mind clearly calculating.

"What?" I asked, knowing full well that he could only read my lips from where he was standing next to me.

He leaned in close to me, and shouted into my ear, "You were right." I returned a puzzled look, to which he responded by pointing up at Rylan. "You look just like him. Even your face when you sing looks just like his."

I closed my eyes and laughed heartily. I had always been told this when I was younger, and told by those who knew us both as I was growing up, I had also been told by random strangers throughout my lifetime. A number of times, I had been approached randomly by someone who would say, "Has anyone told you that you kind of look like that rock star, Rylan Porter?" Yet, never once had Ray-Ray Montgomery, 7 Year Coma's biggest fan, ever suggested it.

I was still laughing at the irony of the situation when I turned back to face the stage, just as JT was resuming the lead on their next song, 'Wasn't My Idea'. He wasn't more than two lines into the song when he pointed directly at me, then waved his hand, motioning me for me to come up on stage. The crowd around us had erupted into cheers, and I could feel myself being pushed toward the stage.

I emphatically shook my head, hoping that he'd let that idea slip away just as quickly as it had possessed him. I was completely okay with his spontaneity on stage, so long as it didn't involve me. Yet I also knew my brother well enough to know that once he had an idea in his head, he didn't let it go so easily. He grabbed the mike off of the stand, something that he rarely did, and walked to the edge of the stage, then jumped into the pit directly before the front row. Three security guards had instantly surrounded him to assist with crowd control, as the entire crowd pushed forward. JT reached his arm out toward me, and with the help of the security guards, he was able to grab a hold of my arm and pull me up toward the stage, all the while without missing a word in the song.

He replaced the mike, lowering it a few inches, and despite the adamant refusal in my eyes, I blended my voice with his just as we got to the chorus.

It was completely surreal. I had sung the song a million times alone in my car or around the house, as did any other fan in the world, but being up on stage in front of tens of thousands of people was incredibly invigorating. There weren't words to describe the energy that was coursing through my veins at that very moment. While my body was frozen in complete shock at the fact that I was singing to a sold out venue, I was still able to somehow project enough vocal ability to possibly sound somewhat decent.

My heart was racing with a sudden panic, irrational fears that I was going to forget the words in front of the thirty thousand people who had paid hard-earned money to hear my brothers' band play for them. What was JT thinking? What was I thinking?

I could barely see with the blinding spotlights shining in my eyes, and I suddenly knew why JT was never without his sunglasses on stage. Yet I could see Rylan off on the far side of the stage, still playing his guitar, his eyes locked on either JT or me, I couldn't tell which. Even as he provided the backup vocals, his eyes were transfixed on the two of us.

JT sang into the mike, clear and strong and unwavering; the sound of his voice inspired me to propel my own voice out into the crowds. As many times as I had heard my brother sing, either in the studio, around the house, or from the audience, it was completely different experience to stand next to him and hear him sing into a microphone before a sea of fans.

Taking a deep breath, I matched every note, a few octaves higher, but in perfect tune, creating a whole new rendition of the song. My only regret was that I wasn't in the audience at the same time to experience it like the rest of the fans were, with an unbiased ear.

As the song ended, JT gave me a quick wink, before he helped me off stage, making sure that I made it safely back to my friends before he returned to the mike to announce the next song. My friends enveloped me in a group attack, all of them shouting to me the second that I returned. I couldn't make out what they were all saying over the sounds of the crowd and the music, but they were barely able to contain their excitement.

Ray-Ray's arms slipped around my waist, as he hugged me from behind and shouted into my ear, "You're absolutely amazing, Natalie McKinney!"

I could barely catch my breath, knowing that I had just had a small taste of my brothers' dream. It had all happened so quickly, and I was still having a hard time convincing myself that I had actually been up on stage. The rest of the concert was almost a blur for me, and I hadn't even realized when the show had ended.

After the show, we headed straight for the party, and I was still reeling from the excitement of the night. I kept running the moment through my mind, over and over again, not wanting to let the feeling go.

"Natalie!" Callie shouted, as we headed back toward the Westshire Room at the hotel. "You can *sing!*"

I tried to hide the smile that crossed my face. "Did I do okay?"

"All these years, you've sucked. How all the sudden did this just come out of nowhere?" Nathan, brazen as always, inquired.

Rachel jumped to my defense. "Obviously she didn't *suck*, she just had us all really snowed over." She threw her arm around me as we headed down the hallway to the party.

I greeted the matre dee with a smile. He returned with a nod, and pulled open the door to the club. It was packed, crowded with at least a hundred people already. I lead my friends to the nearest empty table, explaining that it would be a bit before the band would join us. There was a meet and greet for one of the local radio stations, and the band was giving away a signed guitar.

I was disappointed by the fact that Josh and Callie were sitting in between me and Ray-Ray, and by the look on Ray-Ray's face, he wasn't quite so happy about the seating arrangements either. I glanced over and saw Nathan and Rachel at the bar, toasting each other with a double shot. I tossed a glance over to Ray-Ray then nodded in their direction. "Looks like they've got a head start on the rest of us."

When they returned to the table, they had brought with them a drink in one hand and another double shot in the other. Nathan slid in next to me, and placed the shot glass in front of me. "This one's all yours, Cutie."

Rachel, sitting across from me, was already raising her glass. "To my best friend the rock star. Don't forget us little people when you are rich and famous, Natty."

I held up my glass to hers and downed the Rumplemintz while it was still ice-cold. At least if I kissed Ray-Ray later, I'd have minty fresh breath, I mused.

It was a good half hour of heavy drinking on our part before the band started to arrive. We saw JT first, standing at the bar with his arm around a beautiful blonde woman who was dressed in a gorgeous green top, straight black pants and black heels.

I practically climbed over Nathan to get out of the booth, and made my way over to the bar. When I caught his attention, JT greeted me with a hug and a kiss, then introduced me to his girlfriend. "Natalie, this is my missus, Candace."

She stayed hidden behind her sunglasses, despite the dim lighting of the club. "You were amazing tonight, Natalie. JT said this was your first time on stage?"

I couldn't help the smile that spread across my face, as the excitement that I had felt in front of the crowd tonight crept through me in a giddy wave. "Thanks…"

JT jumped in quickly. "Yeah, Rylan was pretty pissed about the whole thing. I caught hell for it after the gig."

"What for?" I questioned, slightly taken back.

"'Cause I didn't clear it through him. He's just pissed he didn't think of it first." JT winked at me before finishing off his drink. "It was worth it, Natalie girl. The crowd loved you." The bartender had replaced his drink before JT even had the chance to set it down. I had him order me a Lager bottle while he had the bartender's attention.

I hadn't realized how long the three of us got to talking, but we were mid conversation when Rylan interrupted by slipping his arm around my neck. "Nice job tonight." He ignored the smirk on JT's face, and reached between us to grab the drink off the bar that the bartender had immediately slid his way.

I narrowed my eyes, studying Rylan's face with some intensity for a moment, but was having a hard time reading him completely. "Are you saying this as a professional musician, or as my big brother?"

He was very matter-of-fact when he replied, "I don't

wear that hat when it comes to business. You can ask JT any day of the week."

JT scoffed and pulled Candace over to the other side of the bar. I stood there for a moment taking in the marvel of just having been complimented by the man who Rolling Stone magazine had just last month declared the number one guitarist of the decade. Those kind of things didn't happen every day, no matter who you were.

Rylan's voice lowered a bit as he took the bottle of Lager out of my hand and set it on a nearby table. Crossing his arms against his chest, he looked me straight in the eyes. "I want you to go with us to Houston." He told me. "Come onstage with us for a song or two. Just like tonight. Nothing too serious, just singing with JT, or even backup, but I think this would be a good experience for you."

I wasn't sure I had heard him right at first. "Are you serious?"

He blinked a few times without changing his expression otherwise. "You'll need to practice with us every chance we have between now and then, but yeah, I'm serious." Then he added, "And we'll see what happens from there." He pressed a quick kiss on the top of my head, then walked toward the group standing nearby that had been waving him over.

My mind buzzed at the thought of what he had just proposed. Me, singing onstage with 7 Year Coma. The idea itself was blistering. As much as I'd dreamed about being onstage since I was a kid, not much could really prepare you for the moment that your dreams would become a reality. And what was really making my stomach flutter was the "we'll see what happens from there" part. What did that mean exactly? Would he maybe let me write a song for Coma? Or would he help me produce my own album? The questions were endless, and I had to take a few deep breaths to calm myself down.

I joined my friends at the bar, where I slid in next to

Ray-Ray. After telling them the news, they had no issues with leaving Dallas for Houston. Ray-Ray gave me a sly smile as he handed me a fresh pineapple martini.

"She does put out much easier if you get her drunk first, Ray-Ray." Rachel tossed out there, as she sipped casually on her own rum and coke. Her wide eyes were slightly glazed, and I could tell that she and Ray-Ray had been taking full advantage of the bar while Nathan and I were dancing.

"Sounds like you know." He threw back at her.

"I'm so glad this phone has HD video." Nathan joined in.

"Not a chance in hell. You couldn't afford the rights to that video, baby." Rachel winked at him. I noticed that she held his gaze a little longer than usual, but before I had a second thought about it, Rylan came over to let us know that he was heading up to his hotel suite for the "after party".

It was a much smaller, intimate crowd that was invited back to his suite, consisting of the band, their significant others, and my group of friends. This was the type of party that I lived for, when a group of us could just sit around, drinking, smoking, playing guitar and keeping things low key. I had been to a few of these gatherings, even before I had reached my pre-teen years, and it was, to me, even better than going to the concerts.

There was easily room for our gathering in Rylan's suite. He opened the cabinet doors to the wet bar, revealing a fully stocked, top shelf only spread. "Help yourselves." He offered, then headed across the room to take a guitar out of its case, and find himself a comfortable spot on the couch.

I bypassed the bar and followed him over to the couch, not taking my eyes off the guitar. It was a Gibson, dark wood around the body, and its pattern was one that I've never seen before. It was stained dark around the edges, and lighter toward the saddle, the pickguard appeared to be almost a tiger stripe, and it had a gorgeously finished rosewood fingerboard.

When he strummed out a few warm-up chords, chills ran down my spine. It was one of the most beautiful sounds I had ever heard, each note rang out strong and deep, and if angels played music in heaven, I was now sure that it wasn't harps that they used.

Rylan glanced up at me and smiled. "It's a 1942 J-45 Legend."

A small gasp escaped my lips as I sat down next to him. He began the fast-paced chorus of *Satire Sheets*, one of the band's first releases that had hit number one on the charts in the States almost fifteen years ago. Then, in true Rylan Porter fashion, he blended in one of his personal favorites, a ballad that had first given him credibility as not only a guitarist, but a true singer, *Broken Windows*, and finally ended with another fast-paced B-Side title *Get the Hell Out, Love*.

The whole room had now fallen silent, and all eyes were clearly fixed on Rylan, who simply looked at me and said, "Not bad, eh?" My wide eyes gave him his answer, and he chuckled. "Try not to drool on it, Love. I just picked it up last week."

I looked up at him, my eyes pleading. "Three chords, Ry? And I swear to God that I'll give it back to you after that." I just wanted to feel it in my hands for only a moment. I wanted to know what it was like to have such a glorious instrument on my lap long enough for me to even try to replicate even a small part of what I had just heard.

I saw him considering it, really thinking hard about it. He was very particular about his guitars. They were like lovers to him, and he didn't like to let others touch them very easily. He held up three fingers, then removed the strap from around his neck. "Take off your jewelry first. This baby set me back almost ten thousand. Euros."

That wasn't hard for me to believe. I pulled off my rings and unhooked my necklace, setting them both down on the coffee table in front of us. Rylan sat the guitar as carefully

in my lap as he would have placed an infant, making sure to
hold onto it until I had the strap secured around my neck and
both hands on the instrument. As he pulled his hands away,
and the full weight of the guitar rested on my body, I
contemplated my three chords.

I finally settled on the three opening chords to the
chorus of *Broken Windows* that Rylan had just played. And I
hit each one with precision and passion, just as he had done
only a few minutes before.

It didn't matter that anyone else was in the room at that
moment. It was just me and the Gibson. And it was an
amazing moment to know that I had just produced three of
the most beautiful chords that I had ever heard myself play. I
looked to Rylan, who gave me a quick, approving nod, then
motioned for me to go on. "It's all you, Love."

I hesitated only for a moment to see if he would change
his mind before I finished the song. And when I struck the last
note, I looked up to see everyone staring at me, mesmerized,
just as they had been moments before when Rylan had played.
When I turned to face him then, to see what he thought, his
eyes were wide and proud.

"Who taught you how to play like that?" He asked
facetiously, as I removed the strap and handed the guitar back
to him.

I flashed him a quick smile. "The best guitarist in the
world."

He gave me a quick wink then nodded his head toward
the corner of the room. "Go grab the Epi and we'll give 'em a
real show."

I stood, but Lucas was already handing me Rylan's
Epiphone. It was a well-loved instrument, he had owned it
for twenty-five years now, and it was one that gave birth to
many of Coma's record-breakers. It was also the same guitar
that he'd use to teach me when I was young. Cradling the
guitar in my lap was like having a little piece of home in that
hotel room, bringing me back to the more pleasant days of my

childhood. The days where I'd sit - singing, giggling, strumming my small fingers on strings – they were rushing back into my mind and the feeling carried down through my arms as I warmed up the guitar with a few practice chords.

He began the intro to *Vinyl Highway*, a typically fast-paced song about the life of a musician on the road, but he played it at a slowed-down coffee house tempo. The song was unreleased, dating back about ten years or more, and it was one that Rylan had fiddled with many times in his living room, a fire lit in the background and a faint lit of marijuana in the air, but the song never saw the light of the recording studio. It was one he'd have me play a few times, slower, like tonight, or he would play with Dax accompanying him, but he never went as far to put it on a record. Die-hard fans, like Ray-Ray, would be clambering over each other to get their hands on rarities like this.

Yet for me, here in the hotel room, it was just my brother and I playing a beautiful song, captivating a small crowd of our closest friends.

Across the room, JT had lit up a joint, and the sweet scent of marijuana began to hang heavily in air. Only a few minutes later, I saw him give Candace a quick kiss before she discreetly left the room. She didn't seem to be much of a partier, from what I had seen of her so far, which really made me wonder how much she truly knew about JT's life style.

I joined him, and he passed me the joint over to me, throwing a heavy arm across my shoulders, "Guess I shoulda had a set of drumsticks in your hands a little earlier in life if I wanted you to take after me."

I inhaled deeply, then blew the smoke out. It didn't take much of what JT had for anyone to get high. He was always good for top quality marijuana, among a variety of other drugs. I glanced around for Ray-Ray and Josh, knowing that they'd appreciate some of this, but they appeared to be out on the balcony at the moment, talking to Dax and Eli.

"I do take after you. I write all of my own songs."

He flashed me a classic JT smile, the same one that had girls all over the world pining after him. His light brown bangs hung in long, thick wisps that swung in front of his eyes every time he moved his head. He nodded out toward the balcony. "Seems like you got a pretty decent guy there."

"Ray-Ray?" I asked, innocently.

JT tossed me a skeptical look. "You two dating or what?"

"Not sure yet." I was keeping an eye on the balcony to make sure that they were still out of earshot of our conversation. "What makes you think he's a pretty decent guy?"

JT pulled up a bar stool, and began to pour us each a drink, concocted of various mixed liquors, followed by a very small splash of club soda. "He looks out for you. Every time you're not standing next to him, he's got his eye on you." He paused, took a quick sip, and added another splash, "I'm glad you have someone like that in your life."

He handed me a glass, and took the joint out of my hand, placing it between his teeth very carefully and inhaling. His feet were tapping rhythmically against the carpeted floor, to the beat of the music that was now pouring through the speakers of the suite's sound system.

I took a good look at JT, trying to see the rock star persona that I had seen tonight, and that everyone else saw in him every day of his life. It was hard for me to see my brothers as rock idols sometimes, and yet other times, it was hard to see them as just my brothers.

Tonight JT sported the classic appearance of a rock star, with worn jeans, black shirt, and red leather jacket. He wore several gold and platinum rings on his fingers and a very expensive Jaeger-Coultre watch on his left wrist. He had his trademark Montblanc sunglasses on his head, completing his just-off-stage appearance that he was so famous for. He smelled of a conglomerate of Guerlain Imperiale and stage sweat.

Yet that was only the known side of John Thomas Porter, the side that he allowed everyone else to see. Only our family and the band knew the demons that lay beneath the surface, hidden down deep within his soul. Occasionally the public might get a quick glimpse, and that which could not be covered up was explained away as typical rock star behavior. JT wished that was the truth, and that the extreme mood swings were easy enough to forget when you turned the channel or flipped the page. But it was his reality, and ours.

As he finished off his drink and began to pour another, he started singing along with the stereo, which was playing 38 Special's *Caught Up In You*, and though it was obvious JT barely knew the words, he began singing along anyway. I couldn't help but join in when the chorus picked up, and before long JT was making up his own words, and I was trying to keep up with what he was coming up with. We were laughing more than we were singing, and anyone who was just listening in would never have guessed that either of us had any musical talent whatsoever.

By the time the song was done, Rylan shouted to us from across the room, "You two are an embarrassment to the Porter name!" JT and I looked at each other and started laughing all over again. I had spilled most of my drink on the bar, creating a sticky mess that I had absolutely no urge to clean up. I shrugged it off and refilled my glass with an unknown bottle of liquor and some ice, while JT headed back over to the living room.

I stayed at the bar, enjoying the ability to scan the room and take in the entire scene. It was just as I remembered it had been when I was growing up, and I felt a bit of nostalgia for those summer nights spent with my brothers and their band. Most kids remembered going to the shore or theme parks with their families, while I remembered after-concert parties with mine. This was my Disneyland.

I hadn't noticed that my gaze had gravitated toward Ray-Ray out on the balcony until Rachel appeared from out of nowhere and stepped up next to me. She didn't say a word, just began to pour each of us a drink, though I knew this was only a pretense for some greater cause. She nodded emphatically out toward the balcony. "Would you two just consummate this... whatever it is you have going on already? I can't take this anymore."

I looked around to make sure that no one was in earshot. Most of the guests were enthralled in conversation or too drunk or high to be paying attention to the two young girls collaborating at the bar.

I shot her a puzzled look. "One, I don't know what you're talking about. And two, even if I did know what you were talking about..." My eyes traveled back over to the balcony. "We're both sharing a room with someone else, which makes it impossible to consummate anything."

She leaned her elbows on the bar, casually sipping her drink. If I wasn't mistaken, she was drinking straight Captain Morgan on the rocks. "I can occupy myself for a few hours. You just say the word, my friend."

I splashed some soda into my glass, knowing that I wouldn't be able to stomach straight Captain in larger quantities than a shot glass. "I don't think we want just want quick and dirty. I want it to be right. I want the whole night with him... and the morning."

Rachel's smile changed from sly to sweet as she thought for a moment. Finally, she tilted her head to the side. "Why don't you two take our room and I'll spend the night in theirs?"

"With Nathan?" I looked at her skeptically, but she shrugged nonchalantly.

"Sure, why not? They're separate beds, and we're both grown-ups. I'm sure we can handle ourselves appropriately while you and Ray-Ray do anything *but* handle yourselves appropriately."

I slapped her on the arm, trying to repress the smile that was forcing its way through my pursed lips. I pondered the whole idea for a few moments, and looked back out on the balcony again. This time, Ray-Ray glanced back at me, and catching the look on my face, he sent me an inquisitive look, to which I simply smiled slyly and turned back to Rachel. "You're on."

"Thank God." She breathed a sigh of relief. "Because the sexual tension around here is unbearable."

I had talked JT into giving me another joint, which I took outside to the balcony to show off to Josh and Ray-Ray, who were still wrapped up in a conversation with Dax and Eli.

Dax was leaning against the iron railing, casually smoking a cigarette. "Natalie, I thought you were a good girl." He scolded, as I handed the tightly rolled drug to him to light for me.

I winked at him, as he handed me his cigarette so that he could light the joint. "You and I both know that's not been true for a long time." I took a drag off his cigarette before I gave it back to him, and nodded for him to pass the joint to Josh.

I pulled up a chair next to Ray-Ray, and casually tossed my legs over top of his, then stretched my arms back behind my head, enjoying the relaxing position that I had suddenly found myself in.

His cargo shorts left his thighs bare, and I loved the touch of his warm skin on the back of my calves. Our eyes met briefly, and in an instant I knew that he felt the same intense longing that was making me want to climb into his lap and start making out with him right then and there.

"So Dax, we want to hear more about Natalie not being such a good girl." Josh blew a puff of smoke out into the hot, dry air before he passed the joint back over to me.

Dax laughed, and I smiled back at him, giving him a nod. He raised his eyebrows and began, "Well, she had her first alcoholic drink at ten."

"Nine." I corrected. "If you're gonna tell the story,

make sure you get it right."

"She was nine. JT made her a... whiskey sour, I think?" He waited for me to nod, then continued. "She drank it like a pro, then promptly threw it up."

"On Lucas..." I added.

We all laughed, as Dax continued. "Then when she was about fourteen JT and I introduced her to pot."

"I was twelve."

Dax sighed, rubbing his fingers over his eyebrows. "Twelve. God, you were too damn young either way. I don't know what we were thinking."

"You weren't." I reminded him. "And when Rylan found out, he threatened to cancel the rest of the tour until he replaced both you and JT."

Dax laughed. "Yeah, he was pretty pissed. But then again, I'd be too if my little sister was drinking and smoking pot at twelve."

Ray-Ray and Josh were both staring at me, looking rather impressed. "What? I turned out okay." I suddenly felt the need to defend myself.

Ray-Ray's hand rested on my leg and leaned in to whisper in my ear. "You turned out more than okay, Love."

I wasn't sure if he knew exactly what it was that he was doing to me at that moment. Just the touch of his hand on my leg, innocent as it may have appeared, had thoughts of so much more running through my head. I was finding it hard to sit idly by while we had a hotel room downstairs waiting just for the two of us. My head was spinning, either with the excitement of the idea of the two of us alone or the effects of the alcohol and marijuana.

I leaned my head back on the lounge chair, closing my eyes, and listening to their conversation. A calmness swept over me as I breathed in the heavy night air, which covered me like a blanket. I embraced it, too content to fight off the deep sleep that I felt coming over me.

FOURTEEN
Natalie

"Where the fuck is JT?" Rylan stormed onto the stage, his arms flying in the air when he realized that our brother wasn't anywhere to be found.

The rest of us had been there on time, and were waiting and ready to go. Eli was doing a very light drum roll, which made me giggle, but Rylan only flashed him a look that told him he wasn't in the mood for humor. Lucas, perched at the keyboards, was flipping through a magazine and ignoring all of us.

I was just kind of standing in the middle of the stage, where JT usually stood, feeling kind of lost as I had been watching Dax warm up. Dax had been going through chords, ignoring Rylan's display of anger as though his outbursts happened everyday. He had a pretty good riff going, and I was wide-eyed with amazement at his talent.

"Nobody's seen him then?" Rylan scratched his head, looking around at the rest of the band. He gave up and pulled his guitar strap over his head. "Natalie, why don't you take his place at lead on *Just Friends*?"

I raised my eyebrows, but the rest of me froze. I loved the song, as it was one of their older ones, but I hadn't been prepared to sing lead, and on one of JT's songs at that. "Are you serious?"

As soon as I said it, I immediately wished I hadn't questioned him. He quit flipping the switches on his amp just long enough to ask me, "Are you in or out, Natalie? 'Cause right now I'm down one lead singer, and if you aren't up for this, we can just call it a day right now."

And right then and there I knew that he had no problem making the switch from brother to boss. It was something that had caused much friction between him and JT throughout the beginning years as a band. It was also an adjustment I was going to have to make immediately, like it or not. I sensed that Rylan wasn't very abundant with patience these days, so it was up to me to bend.

I stepped up to the microphone, adjusted it, and said loud and clear, "I'm in, Ry."

He nodded in my direction, then played the opening chords of the song. I counted the beat that Lucas was playing, and came in with impeccable timing with the opening lyrics. "Knew from the moment I met you, ya wanted more from me, knew from the moment I saw you, what this mess could be..."

I loved the way my voice sounded through the speakers, echoing off of the empty stadium where my brothers' band had played their last two shows. As I continued to sing, I closed my eyes, picturing the crowd of thousands, screaming and cheering as I stood in front of them, singing straight from my heart. I reminded myself that it had a lot to do with the fact that one of the best bands in the world was playing behind me. In my mind though, just for a moment, they were cheering for me, screaming out my name, singing the words to the songs that I had written myself. It was every dream that I had had over the course of the last twenty-one years of my life coming true in my mind right then and there.

As I sang the final verse of the song, repeating the last line, I heard a faint applause coming from the front row. When I opened my eyes, I saw JT standing up, clapping.

Rylan didn't even finish out the rest of the song, just threw his hand in the air, sending his guitar pick flying behind him. "D'ya even own a watch, you daft bastard?"

JT made his way up on stage and stood next to me smiling, intentionally ignoring Rylan. "I'm twenty minutes late and he's sacked me already, has he? Well, at least he's replaced me with someone who's got a lit'le talent." He reached around me and readjusted his microphone.

"I want Natalie to sing that one in Houston. She's done a better job of it anyhow." Rylan adjusted the tuning pegs on his Gibson casually, as though he hadn't just shot his own brother in the foot.

To my surprise, JT took it in stride. "Wha'ever. What's next on the set list?"

"Take a seat, JT. I want her to try *Reason of Insanity*." Rylan responded, further antagonizing him. That was one of the band's all-time biggest hits, and one JT's of personal favorites. It was a hard-rocking tune, sung with an edgy voice, one that only JT could pull off. It hadn't been written for a female voice, by way of lyric or sound, and it was one that I had never even tried to attempt, not even alone in my car.

My eyes shot up at JT, and I shook my head ever so slightly, as not to let Rylan see my adamant refusal. I wasn't sure that JT had even noticed my protest, as he was already wrapped up in his building friction with Rylan. "You're fucking mental. I thought you wanted her on backup before you just throw her into it? Or here's a thought for you, maybe you should *ask* her what she wants before you just go making demands and all."

Rylan's icy eyes went hot, and he instantly stiffened, his hands clenched on his guitar. "When the paychecks come out of your bank account JT, then you can make the decisions. But as long as my name is stamped at the bottom of every single fucking one, then it goes my way."

JT flicked him the finger and walked off stage, sending the microphone stand flying as he went.

"Where the hell are you going?" Rylan shouted after him.

JT never even so much as looked back, but we heard him yell back, "I'm on holiday!"

And that ended my very first practice with 7 Year Coma.

Rylan stormed off in the opposite direction, and as I looked over at Dax, he shrugged and slid his guitar strap over his head. "The fun part will be in convincing JT to show up for the gig tonight."

I wanted to laugh, but I knew he wasn't kidding. JT had a tendency to let his emotions take over at times, and since he was also stubborn as a bull, it made for quite a bad mix. 7 Year Coma had been forced to cancel quite a few shows due to JT's outbursts, which in turn pissed off Rylan. I volunteered to talk to JT, to which Dax wished me all the luck in the world.

He smiled, packing up his guitar, and nodded over in my direction, as I stood holding onto the microphone stand, watching him. The rest of the band had dispersed, content with letting the road crew handle their instruments. But Dax probably planned on using his between now and the show, and was taking care to make sure that it was properly handled.

Dax picked up his guitar case. "Talk to him Natalie. You're about the only one he'd listen to."

FIFTEEN
Natalie

My hands gripped the steering wheel as I sat there in front of the hotel, the cold air from the vents blowing through my damp hair. I shouldn't have been surprised with how much one could sweat walking from the air-conditioned hotel to the spot where my car was parked, but with the thermometer peeking toward a hundred and five, I was nearly drenched.

It was beginning to make me reconsider the plans Ray-Ray and I had made to sneak away to the lake. But the second he came through the doors from the lobby and out into the sunlight, making his way toward my car, I decided I didn't care if it was a hundred and ten out.

"What's all this?" I asked him, referring to his backpack as he slid into the passenger seat. A smile crossed his face as he pulled out a bottle of red wine and two glasses from the hotel room. "Nice." I told him, turning the key in the ignition and heading toward the highway.

When we arrived at the lake, the sky was looking slightly overcast, but my mood was bright. We found a beautiful secluded spot at the lake, where no one was around for miles, as far as we could see.

I spread out a throw blanket that I had in the back of my car onto the soft green grass growing alongside the lake. Kicking off my flip-flops, I enjoyed the liberating softness under my toes. I enjoyed it even more when Ray-Ray sat down next to me, and poured two glasses of Merlot.

Could it really be this good? I wondered, just about to hold the glass to my lips. Could I really be feeling this sense of complete happiness, of belonging, of romance, with my best friend? It was all so surreal, yet so... complete.

He held up his glass, interrupting my first sip. "This is to you, Natalie McKinney-Porter, and your debut as a rock star goddess on stage in Houston."

I winced a little. "Okay, you might be over-dramatizing just a bit..."

He responded by clinking his glass against mine and taking a long sip. I followed suit anyhow, and enjoyed the velvet taste on my tongue. He then leaned in and pressed his lips against mine, and I enjoyed tasting the wine on his tongue more than from my own glass.

"You take my breath away." I told him when we pulled apart. And it was true. I was having a hard time catching my breath. Every muscle in my body ached for more from him. It excited me immensely that during that entire kiss, nothing but our mouths had physically touched. Meanwhile, the rest of me was eager to make contact with every bit of the rest of him.

His eyes were still closed as his tongue ran over his lips. He drew in a deep breath and let it out quickly before he looked over at me. "I don't think you even have a clue what it is that you do to me."

He rolled over on his back, resting his head on his hands. I set my glass aside and moved over so that I was laying on my side next to him, against him, my left arm laying lazily across his chest and my head resting on my hand, supported up by my right elbow. I indulged a little in the warmth of his body against mine, ignoring the fact that all morning, the Texas sun had been casting enough warmth to supply several Pennsylvania summers with a heat wave for the next decade. And now, even with the dark clouds passing between us and the sun, the heat was immense. Yet I still welcomed the warmth of him against me, as long as it meant that we were touching in some way.

I hardly even noticed when the first drops of rain fell to the ground around us. I barely felt the splashes of water that hit my arms or my legs, I was so lost in his eyes, and in the anticipation of what was next to come.

My hand slid underneath his shirt, the skin of his broad chest burning against my fingertips until I could no longer stand having our clothing separate us. I pulled his shirt over his head and let him slip mine up over my arms before moving onto my jeans. My fingers curled against his bare chest, nails scratching slightly into his flesh, and I lowered my mouth toward his, longing for the taste of him again. His tongue plunged deep into my mouth, taking what he wanted, as he slid his hands so that they rested on each of my hips and I moved on top, straddling him. My back arched, feeling him hungry and needing between my thighs. I looked back down at him through half- closed eyes as my hips swayed back and forth over him.

Any hesitations I had of what would happen to our friendship if we dove into a relationship were washed away with the misty drops of rain that were caressing our naked skin.

With each touch of his fingers to my skin, and it didn't matter where on my body he touched, just the touch alone sent waves of electricity racing through my veins. My breasts swelled with the excitement that his hands were inching toward them, slow and tantalizing, causing such sparks of heated pleasure, dancing around my nipples, that I was no longer aware of any of my other senses.

The rain drenched our skin, washing away the sweat that was coating our bodies in the thick Texas heat. His thrusts, gentle at first, had become increasingly hungry, and he was taking every inch of me that I was giving him. I struggled to hold onto him, my hands sliding over every muscle on his shoulders, arms, his back, until I finally locked my wrists behind his neck and pulled him back into me, needing him with so much more than my body. The urges to pull him closer and closer and further and deeper into me came from everywhere at once – body, mind, soul and heart. The drive that I had to fulfill that empty space in my being, he was filling. Over and over again he was filling more than just a need for sex. And at the moment where we'd both reached fulfillment together, I was barely aware that he had entwined his way around my heart with such a hold that it would need to shatter to release him.

As the rain continued to beat down on the earth around us, Ray-Ray propped himself back up on his elbows, and flashed a pointed smile at me. "That was better than I had remembered."

I couldn't help the smile that set on my lips. "That was a tough night to beat."

My eyes turned upward. An eerie shade of black and green and gray sky had crept over us when we weren't aware. And even before the chills had a chance to set in on my skin, a sudden bold of lightning crashed not too far off in the distance, catching even Ray-Ray's attention.

"Hell hath no fury like a Texas storm." He said, and we were on our feet in a second, as the wind gusted from out of nowhere. We struggled our drenched clothes over wet skin, and rushed to gather the blanket, the wine and his backpack. Taking my hand, he led the way as we ran back toward the car and the thunder roared around us.

I threw him the keys as we approached my car. It wasn't until we were both inside that he looked over at me. "You okay?"

I nodded, but didn't say a word.

"What's wrong?"

A single flash of lightning lit up the air around us, with the crack of thunder filling our ears at just the same time. The blood had drained from my face entirely, and I could feel my shoulders shudder.

"The storm," he realized, "God, I'm sorry. We should have left when it first started."

Again, I nodded without saying a word. I couldn't have spoken if I wanted to; my body was frozen in the passenger seat of my car. The rain and the wind I could take, but the thunder and lightning paralyzed me. Every flash was a potentially deadly explosion, and the growl of the thunder that followed was only reassurance in that while it wasn't me that it struck this time, it would only be moments before the next bolt crashed to the earth in a hot fury, and I could easily be in its path. Here in the car, we were waiting victims.

As I leaned my head back, the memories started flashing before my eyes without warning. Or at least what I thought were memories. I couldn't really tell.

I felt Ray-Ray's hand cover mine. "What is it Natalie? Talk to me."

I squeezed my eyes shut, trying to block out the flashes of lightning, but the roar of thunder was something that I couldn't shake, as hard as I tried. The feeling of only the car between the storm and me was overwhelming, and I felt so small, so vulnerable at that moment.

"Hey," Ray-Ray reached over and tucked my wet hair behind my ear so that he could see my face, "You can trust me."

The wind was blowing the rain so hard that we couldn't have driven anywhere even if I could will my arms and legs to move. I hadn't talked to anyone about that night, not since I'd stopped seeing the therapist when I was twelve. Even back then, I wasn't able to get the memories in my head to come out of my mouth in words that would make sense to anyone else. And now, the only part that I could ever remember was the very end of the night, after I had gotten away. The terror of the storm that night was nothing compared to the terror that had ensued before I had escaped his fury.

Yet sitting next to Ray-Ray, I felt safe. I could let some of it go. Maybe if I shared it, got some of it out in words, I would feel freer. But I couldn't bring myself to do it, no matter how hard I tried. I'd never told anyone, not a soul in the twelve years since I'd left that house of hell.

I let the storm drag the memories back to the forefront of my mind.

My pulse was racing, my heart slamming against the wall of my nine year old chest as I found my way into the train station. Kneeling against the row of metal chairs that sat parallel to the glass windows that stretched floor to ceiling, I watched as the storm played like fireworks across the river, lighting up the night sky in sporadic bursts. The flashes of lighting painted the city's night sky, gleaming off the water across the street. The thunder that followed echoed off of the tall buildings that neighbored station.

That was all I remember up through that last flash. Everything before and after that was gone from my brain. An extensive white heat that seemed to strobe, like the flash of an old camera, was all that was left. The scenes played out in slow motion, my mind capturing each frame in still shots so that it could pick and choose later on which to play back for my memory. And they were all missing or out of order, save a few. There was the one of the bright white-yellow light, followed by the one of my head hitting the floor with a crack. The crack might have been the thunder, or it could have been my skull against the tile. I only remember the sound, not the feeling. And that was it. Two small images before it all went dark.

All the doctors, the therapists, the psychiatrists, they'd all said that it'd be unlikely that I'd ever be able to fully remember what had really happened. All that had ever come out of that night, and in the years preceding, were just bits and pieces. And whatever came to mind, there was no way of deciphering if it was actually even real or was just something that my mind had created.

Ray-Ray's hand tightened again around mine in the car by the lake, watching as the storm clouds moved to the other side of the water, leaving us unharmed in my car.

SIXTEEN
Natalie

The sun was shining hot and bright, and the buzz of generators hummed in my ears when JT opened the tinted glass door of his tour bus to let me in.

A wave of ice-cold air greeted me as I stepped up into what looked like a hotel suite on wheels. Overstuffed black leather couches lined both sides of the front of the bus, and matching black leather covered the benches on either side of the table in the kitchen area, which was complete with a stainless steel refrigerator, a double sink and ample marble top counter space. British rock was blaring through the speakers of an incredible sound system that ran throughout the entire bus.

Scattered across the table were dozens of sheets of scribble-covered paper. There was also a notebook, pages fat with writing, underneath a heavy blue-inked pen. JT was extremely picky about his writing instruments, even more than his drumsticks or microphones, surprisingly. He was also very protective of his writing time, and I could tell that I had interrupted.

He reached up and turned the volume down on a stereo system that made mine back home look like a cheap boom box. You never knew what you'd get with JT. It was almost as though there were two distinct personalities at play; the rock star and the guy who pretended he wasn't. Sometimes you'd catch him glammed up and ready for a show, other times he'd be in jeans, a t-shirt and sneakers, lounging about as though he were an everyday citizen.

At the moment, aside from the fact that he resided in a tour bus, he was completely everyday citizen in his jeans, light blue polo shirt and wire-rimmed glasses, with sandy strands of hair falling haphazardly in his eyes.

"Make yourself at home."

I fell into one of the couches, the black leather hugging me as I sunk in. I looked around the bus, noticing that we were alone. "Where's Candace?"

"Out shopping with Jules. I'll be lucky if I see her before the show tonight." He took a seat across from me, leaning back comfortably with one foot resting on his other knee, and folded his hands behind his head.

I raised my eyebrows. "Does that mean you're going then?"

"'Course I'm goin'. Those days of me getting mad and walking out on the band are over Natalie girl."

"Bet that makes Rylan happy. One more gig in the bank to help pay for his wedding."

JT shot me a half-smile. "He told you the news, I take it?"

I didn't answer him, just offered a half-smile of my own in return. I was happy for Rylan and Sammi, I really was. It just devastated me that I had to travel twelve states from home and force myself back into his life to be privileged enough to hear the news. Clearly they were keeping it quiet from the media, at least for now, but had I not made this epic road trip with my friends, I might have heard it on television or the internet before I'd heard it from his mouth.

"Think they'll have kids?" I knew Sammi was nearing forty, so if it was in their future, it would be in their near future.

I tried to picture Rylan as a father. Hell, it was a stretch to imagine him a husband. He'd always been married to his work. But maybe Sammi would change that in him, I mused. Maybe the two of them would settle down, take a break from the band for a while, have a kid or two...

JT's face grew dark. He pulled out a cigarette, pressed it to his lips and lifted a sterling silver lighter to his mouth. "Nah, and it's best not to bring it up with him either. Marrying Sammi's a big step for him, ya know what I mean?" He took a long, hard drag, letting it out slowly from the corner of his mouth. His thumb was tapping out the rhythm of Oasis' *I Hope, I Think, I Know*, playing in the background.

I wanted to object. I wanted to push him. But I knew better. I refrained from rolling my eyes as I gave him a quick nod.

"Good girl then."

Cigarette still pinched between his teeth, he resumed his position with his hands folded behind his head, and leaned back comfortably. His eyes were lost somewhere on the ceiling of the bus.

I slipped casually over to the table, eyeing the scrawled penmanship that lay waiting for its finish. Anyone who'd ever been fortunate enough to have a genuine JT Porter autograph wasn't privy to the fact that JT actually had a very beautiful and artistic writing style. My hand touched one of the sheets that had a significant amount of lyrics scratched across the surface.

What I saw brought chills to my skin. Profound words, sewn together in an intricate menagerie of wonder and crypticism. The depth of what he wrote was unlike anything that you'd ever hear through the speakers of your radio. I could almost hear his voice, echoing through a microphone, across a sea of awed fans.   There'd be the precious few thousand to understand what only JT Porter could convey.

"It's all rubbish." He mumbled, trading his cigarette for the bowl that had been sitting on the leather couch next to him.

I barely heard him, as my finger traced the words that he'd imprinted on the page. I reveled at the feel of it, the impression beneath my fingertip of his pen on the paper. He'd written with such force, such utter passion, and I felt that the unspoken words spoke strait to my heart. I hardly had to read them to feel the meaning behind them.

"I wish we were a normal family, JT."

Without turning, I knew he was smiling. "Everyone wishes they had a normal family. When one of us figures out the secret to making that happen, we should spread the knowledge worldwide. It'd be worth millions more than any of these records that we sell." He paused for a second, making sure I was listening, "Your family is who you make it."

And that line right there was what made him millions on his lyrics. The fact that his mind spun webs of rationale in a creative spin amongst the rest of the thoughts in his head both amused and amazed me at times. But it was a single sentence such as that one that rung through my head a million times before I understood the true meaning of what he meant.

SEVENTEEN

Rylan

Watching her onstage, guitar in her hands, was like looking back into a mirror to my younger days. That youthful energy in her playing, that confident reservation in her voice, it was a quiet reminder of where I had come from, where I had been. It seemed like a lifetime ago that I was where she was, stretching my wings for the first time, praying for that one chance to be discovered. Recognition was all we had needed, all we wanted. That chance to be something great, instead of just playing for those who had nothing better to do than to saunter on by, a five in hand, and give us a listen. Sure, we had our fan base, especially as we grew better, but it didn't mean shit until someone believed in you enough to make you big.

Her hand slipped a bit, and she fell a half count behind, then quickly recovered. But I could see it in her eyes. She was harder on herself than anyone else ever would be. Those types of things would happen, maybe a million times over in her lifetime, but it was how you recovered that made you a star. If the audience never noticed it, then that night was a success. But the second that they knew that you knew you screwed up, that's when it'd all go to hell.

She forged on, strumming away, her shoulders and knees loose, moving along with the music just enough to become one with it. *That's our girl.* Laugh it off if it was bad enough, but move right on from it. One way or another, you had to move on from it.

I sat across the table from Sammi, telling her about it later that afternoon.

"It's amazing, I'll tell you, the way that she just *finds* the music. No practice, no rehearsal, just plays like she's part of the band."

Sammi looked up from her tea, a quiet smile hidden behind the cup as she sipped. "You don't think that girl's been playing your songs everyday of her life then?"

I tossed the idea around for a minute, but shook my head. "Doesn't matter if she has or hasn't. It's different when you play with the rest of the band. They'll push you or pull you along if you let them. When you play solo, it's just you to contend with. Play with our lot, and it's a whole different game up there."

She finished her cup, stood, and walked across the room toward her ever-begging phone. Her thumbs moved madly across the keyboard and she set it back down on the table. "And if she can play with Coma, she's able to hold her own with any band out there. How is it again that she's going to school for, what is it, Accounting?"

I shot her a warning look across the table. Natalie and I had gotten in many an argument before I was finally able to get her to agree to go to a University. And I'd swear that she'd simply picked the first choice out of the catalogue when it came to what she'd major in, but it made no mind to me, as long as she finished her degree.

The music industry was a different world now than it was back when I'd first started. Nowadays, you'd be up on top for a few minutes of your life, make some money if you were lucky, then get thrown back on your ass. Our girl was going to have a solid education to fall back on if she needed it. But judging from what I'd seen today, she probably didn't need the added security of a Plan B.

EIGHTEEN
Natalie

I had almost finished my trek down the long hallway back to my room when I ran into Dax, almost literally, who was headed in the opposite direction. "Wrong floor." I informed him. "You want the high class rooms nearest the top of the building. Don't want to get caught mingling down here with the rest of us..."

He tossed me a crooked smile then caught me around the waist as I intended to walk right by him. "I was looking to mingle."

I slid the key card through the slot and pushed open the heavy hotel door. "Hope you weren't looking forward to mingling with Rachel." The room was empty, and it appeared that the cleaning crew had just done their daily sweep, as the beds were freshly made, and crisp towels were folded in the lemon-fragranced bathroom.

Dax made himself quite comfortable by flopping down on Rachel's bed, his long legs stretched out so that top to bottom, he almost took up the entire length of the bed. "How do you sleep at night? These mattresses are shite..." He immediately sat up and cracked his neck, as though he needed to seek the therapy of a chiropractor immediately for the slight infraction that he had just suffered.

I mouthed the words "fuck you" to him, then flopped down on my own bed, stretching out comfortably. "You've lost touch. These beds are the bees knees."

He laughed out loud. "An' here I thought yer lost the Londoner in ya."

I feigned a scowl from where I lay on the bed. "Never."

An instant smile appeared on his face. That smile melted hearts around the world, mine included. There was just something about Dax Crowley that would always linger in my heart. He was my first crush, my first fantasy. I wasn't sure that would ever really go away. The fact that I knew him personally never took away from any of that.

"So I know this is a big birthday for you, and I didn't want you to think that I forgot." He reached into his pocket and extended a small, neatly wrapped package in shiny blue and gold paper. I took it without saying a word, just letting the surprise in my eyes speak for themselves. "Just between you an' me, a'ight? You know how wives, an' brothers and boyfriends an' all get. But I thought you deserved something special for a special birthday, that's all."

I still hadn't opened it, just held the box in my hand in pure amazement, treasuring the thing like the wrapped box was the gift itself. "Dax..." I said, not sure what was about to come out of my mouth next.

He offered some assistance. "See, ya gotta take the paper off..."

I rolled my eyes as I pried at the tape, muttering all the while. Whatever breath I had was taken away as I lifted the lid on the box. Underneath revealed two stunning diamond earrings, each just a little larger than the diameter of a pencil eraser. Without being much of a diamond connoisseur, I knew enough to be aware that the sparkle radiating off of them was worth more than any jewelry that I already owned.

He stood up, his hand on the doorknob. "Now ya gotta little something to wear on stage in Houston. Might help ya feel like a rock star."

Before he could escape to the hallway, I was on my feet and throwing my arms around his neck, thanking him.

"Yer welcome." The door closed shut behind him, and my jaw was practically on the floor as I eyed up the diamonds. They were exquisite, and I couldn't wait to wear them. It made the allure of being on stage in Houston even more enticing.

I wasn't sure what to make of the whole thing, truth be told. I wondered briefly how Jules Crowley would feel knowing that her husband just bought his best friend's kid sister enough diamonds to pay off the car that she drove down here in. But it was all innocent, I assured myself. Dax was another big brother to me, and that was the end of it.

NINETEEN
Natalie

By the time I arrived at sound check for our first Houston gig, I felt airy and free. I had a bit of bounce in my step that I couldn't account for, but it gave me that extra bit of confidence that I needed to contend with a band with the caliber of 7 Year Coma. As much as they were family to me, when it came time to be on stage with them, still I felt as though I had to prove myself. Today however, I just wanted to have fun.

So far, only Dax and Eli were on stage. The rest of the band was nowhere in sight. As I walked by JT's microphone, I took the mike from the stand and kept on walking. Eli cracked up laughing, and Dax just shook his head. JT was a bit particular about his microphone, and the joke was that when he didn't have his drums, his mike was his instrument of choice to hide behind. I took it one step further when I started to sing the opening lines to *Stop for Breath*.

Taking my cue, Eli started tapping out the beat on the drums, and Dax followed by throwing out a few chords before

Lucas joined us on the keyboards. I gave the song my own spin, which was not only at a slightly higher octave than JT usually sang it, but just a bit slower and ridden with deeper emotion in my voice, tapping into a feeling deep down inside that I just didn't access on an everyday basis.

Stop for Breath was one of those songs that I had played over and over throughout my teenage years. Anytime that a boy had broken up with me, or a friend had hurt me, or I felt rejected in anyway, I played the one song that I felt could get me through the heartache. While most girls might play a song on their stereo, my solace was playing it on my guitar. I felt it incredibly relieving to take out my pain, my anguish, on the strings.

If I was alone in my car, I could sing the lyrics. It didn't matter that the CD wasn't in my player or the song wasn't on the radio at the time. The words were ingrained in my head. And my voice could carry the emotion straight from my heart, out into the world, where no one else could hear. It was the ultimate outlet for a young teenage girl who struggled with the definition of love.

Today, as I stood there on the stage that I would be playing on before thousands later on, I took the song that had long been the epitome of my high school years, and turned it into a true performance. I didn't even hear the rest of the band around me, I simply sang like I was meant to sing on that stage at that very moment.

And my audience turned out to be an audience of one.

As I replaced JT's microphone, I saw Rylan standing alone in the pit. He had been casually drinking a bottled water, but when I was finishing up the final verses of the song, I noticed that he was too mesmerized to move, and just stood there, still as a statue, taking it all in. Though he stood a good hundred feet from where I was standing, I could see the amazement, in his eyes.

Whether he'd intended to or not, he had created what he just witnessed on stage. If it hadn't been for him, I would have never picked up a guitar. And that love for the guitar lead to my love for singing. The talent would never have been cultivated had it not been for his persistent dedication to the art and the business.

I remember as a young girl just standing in the doorway of the living room, late at night, when everyone else had gone to bed, watching Rylan create new music. It was a magic that I was privileged to witness; a beauty that most could only imagine. It was like watching someone put together a puzzle, piece by piece, in an intricate form. The grace by which he composed was much unlike my brother JT, who concentrated immensely and scratched out lines that didn't work. Rylan took those lines that didn't work and hammered them out until they did. Each piece was molded until it fit. They came to him through a channel, a divine intervention that was meant to reveal a message of great proportion, and he was just the conveyer. Who was he to mess with divine intervention? He was only the translator.

And I was somewhere in between. I did a fair amount of molding and an equal amount of scratching out.

I casually walked off stage and joined Rylan in the pit to watch the rest of his band finish their sound check. He swung an arm across my shoulder, talking another long swig of his water. He didn't say anything as we watched, and he didn't have to.

I knew I had impressed him.

I can't say that I wasn't nervous before that first night in Houston. I knew my friends were out there in the audience, in the family-reserved section, supporting me, cheering me on. Yet there was a big part of me that was insanely afraid that 7 Year Coma's fans weren't going to accept a woman on stage with their band. This was definitely something different, something that they weren't accustomed to. Something that I wasn't sure that they were willing to accept. I wasn't sure that I was willing to accept it myself, even as I stepped onstage, right on cue, just as Eli started tapping out the first few beats of the third song on the set list. I slipped onto the then-darkened stage, inconspicuous and relatively unnoticed until the first chord on Rylan's guitar was struck, and the lights burst open, shining in my eyes and blinding me so that I couldn't even see the audience that we were about to play for.

The first song was completely surreal, and for the life of me, I will probably only ever remember bits and pieces of it. Between the butterflies in my stomach and the enamor of being on stage for the first planned time in my life, I wasn't sure that my feet were actually on the ground. I was afraid to imagine what my voice sounded like coming through the microphone, backing up JT's voice. I was hoping that his was enough to drown out my own if it didn't cut it.

Throughout the song, JT kept tossing glances over at me, smiling and nodding, letting me know that I was doing okay. He seemed to be lost in the moment, as he always was, just one with the stage, and it made me wonder if he could even hear me above the crowd. I tried to glance over at Rylan once or twice, but he was so completely involved with his guitar that I had absolutely no sign from him whatsoever if I was hitting the right notes.

By the time we got through the song, my heart was racing. I was sure that Rylan was going to signal me off stage, then tell me after the show that I just didn't have it in me to be a singer. Maybe I should just stick to guitar. Or worse, Accounting.

But what I saw when the music stopped was Rylan step up to his microphone and announce the next song, and JT stepped back and took his place on drums. "*Nobody Can Eva'*." Rylan's voice carried throughout the stadium, answered by ten thousand fans cheering. This was one of his faster-paced songs that he sang lead on. Normally, he'd play lead guitar as he sang, but tonight, I was playing lead and he was taking rhythm.

One of the stagehands brought me a Fender Strat, and I slid the strap over my shoulder, feeling it snug against my body. The instrument never felt so good as it did right then, the body of it leaning against my belly, its neck cradled in my hand. I suddenly felt at ease, with the guitar between me and the thousands of screaming fans, I drew in a deep breath and decided to drown out everything else around me. My brothers, the band, my friends, the crowd, all disappeared within an instant. It was just me and the guitar. The chords flowed as naturally from my fingers as the air flowed from my lungs. It was one of the most beautiful things that I've ever experienced in my entire life.

And yet only minutes later, hearing the crowd scream and cheer, sent a rush of lightning through my system that had my adrenaline pumping and my heart racing with excitement. It energized my body in a way that I could only describe as nearly-orgasmic. It was like a bolt of electricity shot from somewhere in my mind to my fingers, manipulating the strings with more passion and drive than I've ever felt playing alone in my room. And the fans were reacting. They were loving it. It only started the process over again. For the rest of the song, I felt like I was on fire. A hot, white heat that tingled in bursts of static energy over my entire body.

When I played the final chords of the song, I finally opened my eyes, and saw that Rylan had stopped playing his guitar, and was instead, applauding with the rest of the audience. As I hit the final note, extending it as long as I could, JT rolled the symbols lightly, ending the song. The crowd exploded.

Rylan stepped forward to his microphone after a quick swig of water. "She's pret'y good, is'n she?" He again clapped along with the audience. "Natalie McKinney, kids."

I smiled and gave a quick wave of appreciation as I exited the stage. I was immediately handed an ice-cold bottle of water and a towel to wipe off the sweat that I didn't know was dripping from my forehead before being led to the backstage dressing room. I had just sat down and was about to revel in the moment when Sammi burst through the door behind me. "Natalie, quick! Ry wants to talk to you. *Hurry!*"

The only time that Rylan left the stage was right before the encore, when the band took a short break, revving up the audience, and reappearing for three more songs. It was still too early for the encore, so I was a bit taken back as I slipped back into the hallway behind her, meeting Rylan by the entrance to the stage.

He motioned for me to move quicker. "Are you up to singing lead with JT? *Dreary Affair*, right after he's done with *Reason of Insanity*. Yes or no?"

I responded without thinking. "Sure."

He grabbed my arm and we hurried back to the stage. He had me wait while JT was just finishing up some random stage banter, something that he absolutely hated doing. JT could talk to the crowd in one or two lines, but to hold their attention with verbal conversation rather than singing, absolutely drove him crazy. It went against everything he stood for, so he had told us on many an occasion.

He was doing an all right job, and the crowd was loving it, but didn't hide his displeasure with Rylan when he returned to the stage. "Fuckin' take a break on yer own time, these people paid good money to have ya here on stage. Fuckin' tosser."

Rylan answered with a crooked smile and began playing the first few chords of JT's signature song. He had instructed me to wait until the song was over, then I was to count to five for the song change, and resume my place on the other side of the stage, where my microphone still stood.

The fans still hadn't died down when I reached five, but I stepped into position and waited patiently for my cue. The lights weren't shining quite as brightly in my eyes as they had been during the previous set, and this brought me a little relief. I wanted to see the crowd that I had been longing to play in front of for so many years. It was amazing to see their faces, so carefree and happy.

As Eli tapped out the first few beats, Rylan and Dax filled in with the opening chords, and Lucas strummed his bass. We had only run through the song once in an official practice earlier that day, but it was a classic Coma, and one that I had sang many times with JT just for fun over the years. I was now becoming every bit as comfortable on stage as I had always imagined.

I counted out the beats, listened for my cue, and sang in perfect timing with JT, the lyrics rolling off of my tongue as though I was always meant to sing the song. Despite the title, the song, *Dreary Affair* had absolutely nothing to do with love gone wrong. This was part of the genius behind JT's song writing. The title had been inspired by a quote he had once read. Of course, the song also had nothing to do with the quote, but that was also typical JT. No one could quite be sure exactly what the song truly meant, though many surmised that it described his experience with the band and life on the road.

Personally, I thought this one in particular was just a fun song to sing. And it worked well with the two of us singing together. We alternated between singing together and seesawing every verse. If we hadn't done it the same way a million times when I was growing up, we never could have pulled it off unrehearsed. But JT and I had a chemistry behind the microphone that allowed us to have a lot of fun, and still sound impeccable.

I poured my heart and soul into that song, allowing my voice to dip below the range I was accustomed to singing, and peak just a little louder and longer during the bridge, testing myself every chance I could. I wasn't sure how it all came together in the end, but when I opened my eyes after the last note, the fans were going wild.

I watched the rest of the show from the side of the

stage, just out of sight from the rest of the audience. It was where I had watched most of their concerts up until I was fifteen, when Rylan decided I was old enough to be in the crowd escorted by a plainclothes security guard. I enjoyed a few concerts from the family reserved seats that way, but found it much more fun to go with my friends and see the concert with them, even if the seats were so far from the stage that we could barely see the band.

I was escorted off the stage by security before the final notes were played and the band said their goodbyes. They wanted the band to have a clear pathway to the backstage area.

I didn't have to wait long. Rylan, who was usually the last one to come off stage, was now the first one through the double doors that led to the hallway where I was waiting. He lifted me off my feet and swung me in a full circle before setting me back down again. "Fucking amazing!" He turned to find JT and Lucas behind him. "Did you see our girl? Did you *hear* her?"

JT practically had me in a headlock. "I think she wants my job." He kissed me on the top of my head and let me go.

It was completely surreal. The feeling that I knew that they had been feeling for almost twenty years now, I was getting to experience for the first time. It was like coming off of the best high of your life.

I was still feeling that high way after we had returned to the hotel. I was sitting on Ray-Ray's lap, curled up in the armchair in the corner of the room. The lights were out, and we were enjoying the moonlight that was pouring in through the open curtains and the French doors to the balcony. There was the slightest hint of a breeze blowing in, and it brushed over our skin like satin sheets.

There was sex in the air, and as much as I wanted to jump back into bed with him at that very moment, I enjoyed just sitting there with him. His breath graced the back of my neck, causing goose bumps to creep over my arms and back. It was just as invigorating as the sex that we had just had.

"I can't wait until we get back home." He was murmuring into my neck.

I drew back a moment, a hesitant laugh bubbled in the back of my throat. "You're the only person I've ever met who wanted vacation to be over."

His hands ran down my forearms and with his fingers, he traced the lines on my wrists and palms. His touch was so light and unpredictable. His mouth was placing light kisses on my neck, just below my ear. This was driving me wild. "I want to experience reality with you in it."

I turned to look at him, to see his eyes, and the second I did, he pressed his mouth to mine. Everything about his kiss made me feel whole, like I had been missing pieces of him before this trip. But as much as he was looking forward to going back home, I was having an amazing time here. I didn't want this all to end. Reality was the last thing I wanted.

Any thoughts I had about "reality" were quickly being washed away with each sweep of his tongue over mine. Every breath he breathed was filling me with answers to questions that I hadn't yet asked. Worries and trepidations were gone before they sprung to my mind. The only one that ever lingered was the fear of losing his friendship if the romantic relationship didn't work out, and even that was beginning to lose its luster as Ray-Ray's hands slid, once again, up my shirt.

When I awoke in the morning, I felt only slightly hung over and even more infatuated than I had ever felt in my entire life. Shit, I thought as I pulled my arm away from his bare chest and pushed myself out of the crisp white sheets, we had graduated to 'infatuated'. I couldn't think about what was next. Just enjoy the moment, I told myself.

I stood out on the balcony, reflecting on the night before. It was still too good to have been true. In my wildest dreams, I had never imagined that it would feel so amazing to play for such a crowd, and for them to reciprocate with the cheers and ovation that they had was simply astounding to me. For my brothers, it had been gradual. This was all so new to me. I found myself wishing I had brought one of my guitars. If I had, I'd have settled myself down on a chair on the balcony and let the sun wash over me as I strummed through chords.

Ray-Ray joined me before I could further that thought, and had my mind wandering in all different directions. His hair disheveled, shirt non-existent, and boxers that he wasn't wearing moments earlier, he slid his arms around my waist and kissed my neck.

I was just turning around to kiss him back when there was a sharp knock at the door, followed by Rachel's shrill voice. "Rise and shine, its wake up time!"

I couldn't help but laugh. This was the wakeup call we received every morning when we took an impromptu trip to Jamaica for Spring Break our senior year of high school.

It was the one and only time that I had tapped into the money that Rylan had funded regularly into a bank account for me. The account had been set up initially as a "fun" account, so that I could concentrate on school and not worry about money for clothes, a car, or any of the other "essentials" that most teens worried about. My friends all had parent-funded accounts, which was not uncommon for my fellow private school students. Unlike most of them however, I had refused to touch mine. Not that I particularly enjoyed the odd jobs that I held throughout my high school and college career, but I didn't feel that I should be spending my brothers' money. They worked hard for what they earned, and I worked hard for what I earned. If I wanted something, I worked until I had earned enough for it.

But when the prospect of Jamaica came around, I had just drained my entire savings on my Martin guitar, a personal pride since Martin was a Pennsylvania-based company, and their guitars ran quite pricey. I decided that the Jamaica trip would be a consolation prize to the fact that nobody from my family would be attending my high school graduation.

Ray-Ray pulled on a pair of jeans and was zipping them up as he unlocked the door for Rachel. She made a point to eye him up from head to toe as she made a cat-like growl while walking by him, toward me.

Dressed in black athletic pants, sneakers, and an all too revealing tank top, she bent over and stretched her calves as she talked. "We're heading to breakfast. Are you too lovebirds coming with us or are you just having each other instead?"

Ray-Ray's eyes were fixed on her chest. "Are you sure that you didn't just throw on the work out clothes to hide something, Rach? You smell like condoms..."

She was upright in a second and tackled him onto the bed, to which he simply threw his arms around her and pulled her back down with him. "Admit it, Rach. You love me..."

I rolled my eyes. "When you two are done, you can join me for breakfast."

The breakfast room was moderately crowded, but it was easy to spot JT and Lucas, who were seated at a table in the far corner of the room. There were a circle of about five women cooing over them like teenagers, and between my brother and Lucas, I couldn't tell which of them were enjoying it more.

"Now that's the life." Ray-Ray commented as he opened his menu.

Rachel unfolded the napkin and placed it on her lap as I sat down across from her. "That'll be our Natalie someday. All famous with guys hovering around her..."

Ray-Ray faked a heavy sigh. "And I'll be the guy she dated for half a second. I might get a quick mention in a magazine somewhere, or maybe some random wannabe journalist will call me up out of the blue and ask me what Natalie McKinney was like before she was a star. And If I'm really lucky, Nat will dedicate a song to me someday, 'The Best I Ever Had'."

"Nah, it'll be called, 'Guy in the Lime Green Shirt'." I quipped.

He stretched his arm around my neck and pulled me over for a kiss. "As long as I get a song, Love. I don't care what you call it."

TWENTY

Rylan

When my eyes opened the morning after the first Houston show, my head wished that it wasn't quite the light of day yet. *Fuckin' Texas*, I thought, *Why the hell did it have to be so fucking hot?* I quickly shut the rest of the world back out, and, without looking, set my hand down on the nightstand, seeking out the three small orange and white capsules that I knew would be there waiting for me. I swallowed them, without water, and waited another fifteen to twenty before letting my feet hit the hotel carpet.

Mornings in our last city before leaving a country meant that I was having breakfast alone. And sex, that was out of the question. Even if I did catch a quick glimpse of Sammi, it'd be a brief and business-like approach, as she'd beg off to tend to matters of importance like ensuring travel plans were squared away, passports were in order, and security was extra tight at the airport.

My suite, for a change, was completely silent. It was a

welcome sound, those rare moments on tour that I was able to spend in the company of only myself. I tried not to let my mind drift to responsible things, things that always monopolized my head when I wasn't paying attention. Things like the affairs of the band, JT's mental state of mind the day before, Natalie's general well-being, my mother's health conditions, the bands that I was producing, our opening acts, and the like. There was a lot to juggle, yes, but right at that moment, I fought to focus on one thing and one thing only.

Breakfast.

Eggs, sausage, toast, whatever fancied my plate from the cart that room service brought to the hallway at the single click of a button. And right now, refueling was the only thing on my mind.

Until my phone rang. The damn thing buzzed nearly right out of my pocket before I decided to at least glance at the screen, where I saw a somewhat less than provocative picture of my beautiful redhead above Sammi's number.

I caught it before it went to voicemail, but just barely.

"Thank God you picked up..." She was saying, before I could even offer a greeting. "Lee Mason phoned me. The lead guitarist from Lull just quit."

My fork hit the plate with an unsettling clang. For as many months as I'd wanted to sack that tosser, ditching the band before the end of the tour was completely unacceptable. I was instantly prepared to barge right down to his hotel room and strangle him myself. But I knew full well I'd find it empty. Anyone in their right mind wouldn't stick around long enough to suffer the backlash of scorned band mates, an irate manager and a marginally homicidal publicist.

And as the irate manager, I was semi-homicidal at the moment myself. For months we'd prepped nearly seven different session musicians, and Lee Mason held issue with every single one of them, save the one we had on board with us now. But his refusal to let the guitarist fill the slot tonight left us with a hole where our opener needed to be, and precious little time to set in motion any of the other prospects that I had already had in the pipeline for the remainder of the tour. And that was all forgetting the fact that I had been looking forward to vacationing this upcoming break, not working it.

Lee's unique style as a front man was hard to follow, and even I held issue with what he perceived to be artistic ability. But if his style alone was a deterrent, his personality was the nail in the coffin. His band mates tolerated him because they grew up together, and that was the only reason.

"I'll start making phone calls to see if we can get a replacement band in for the remainder of the shows for the US tour, and get some auditions set up for late next week to find someone for the European tour." Sammi had taken the liberty of filling in my silence. The woman was always several steps ahead.

"No, I'll handle it. You focus on our band. Lull is my venture." I already had an idea bouncing around in my head; one that I didn't want her talking me out of. The best things sometimes came out of simple ideas, even if they were risky ones. But I usually had a pretty good knack for musical instinct, and if I could convince myself first, I was sure the rest would fall into place.

I was dialing my phone before I had the sense to talk myself out of it. Pushing my plate aside, I leaned my elbows on the table, supporting the phone with my shoulder. "Hey," I said, when I heard the click just midway through the third ring, "Can you stop by my room? We need to talk."

And I waited in quiet deliberation for the knock at my door. All the while, I convinced myself I was about to do the right thing. It'd be her decision, of course, but was I giving her a reasonable choice? Ask anyone in their early twenties if they'd want to continue to study for a career that you already knew they hated, or play in a rock band that was performing nightly at sold-out stadiums, and you'd get the obvious response. And I couldn't afford her much time to consider the issue. I needed an answer quicker than I could deliver the question.

A quick tap came at the door before Natalie poked her head in. "Everything okay?"

"That, Love, is going to depend on you."

TWENTY-ONE
Natalie

It was half past ten in the morning when Rylan and I found ourselves standing on the same stage we'd played at the night before. This time, we were surrounded by Lull's equipment, and everyone in the opening act with the exception of the lead guitarist. Mark St. Vincent had barely been able to hold his own, Rylan had informed me, and he played it off like it had been no great surprise when the musician announced his departure from the band in the early morning hours.

He had gone on to tell me that Lucas' brother, Lee Mason, had cutting edge vocals and exceptional guitar skills. Jasper "Jasp" McGurty was his wavy-haired bassist, and added a funky almost jazz-type sound to the band. Their drummer was a hard-rocking "top lad from up north", Steve Cronin. St. Vincent, Rylan told me, had been the only thing holding them back from becoming the next big thing.

Even Lucas had tried for months to get his brother to sack him, but the problem was bi-fold. One, they'd had nobody to replace him. Fruitless searches had turned up no one who could fit the bill. And second, St. Vincent had been with the band since their inception nine years ago, back when the boys were just starting secondary school. Their loyalty to each other was hard to crack through. They simply refused to give him the boot. Now they were screwed.

Just after I had accepted his offer, Rylan had phoned Lee, and told him to get his band together and meet him onstage, that he had a replacement for St. Vincent for the final two shows.

When we got to the arena, Lee was holding his hand above his coal-lined eyes, shielding out the sun and squinting in Rylan's direction as we made our way across the stage. "She's a girl."

"Hell of an observation." The words flew out of my mouth quicker than I could bite them back, as Rylan tossed me a quick warning with narrowed eyes.

Jasp swung his bass strap over his shoulder, plugging into an amp as though there were no negotiations going on in front of him. "Lee, she fuckin' handles a guitar better than you, so I'd shut your face." He extended his hand out toward me, "Can you play any of our songs like you can Coma's?"

"Everything on your set list and a few others."

Lee scoffed and reached for his guitar. "Two gigs with a girl in the band is enough to ruin us. Even if we are only in the States."

Looking at Lee, it was hard to see the similarities between him and Lucas. Blond-haired and blue-eyed Lucas was the pretty-boy that kept the girls latched onto 7 Year Coma. They were the girlfriends of the guys who wanted to go to the concerts to rock out to the music. They were the ones who flipped through magazines to catch a glimpse of moments of Lucas' private life that the tabloids had stolen. Lucas attracted a broad range of girls in their teens all the way up to the women who were ten years his elders. It was all-evident at their shows and in their fan mail. And the press loved him.

Underneath the pretty-party-boy exterior, there was a heart of gold. He was charismatic and sociable and patient.

Lee was everything but. He was inimical, and moody as all fuck. He would shift one way or the other more than any woman I had ever known. And couldn't lead his band worth a shit. From what I had seen, St. Vincent hadn't been the only issue with the band. They were all over the place, musically. Anytime that Lee tried to take control, he just ended up in a passive-aggressive fit that made them all stare at him cock-eyed and go their separate ways anyway.

His appearance also differed greatly from that of his brother. He was hardcore Goth, complete with his eyes painted with black liner and nails with chipped black paint. His hair, dyed black to match, had one thick streak of bleach blonde splashed across his bangs on the left side of his face. The rest of his black hair stood out in every direction, and I found myself wondering just how much it cost him in hair gel to attain that very style.

Rylan nodded somewhat impatiently in my direction. "You have two shows with her. After that, you have a month to get yourselves a new guitarist before we go back out on tour in Europe. I suggest you make the best of it."

He walked offstage, seating himself in the fifth row of seats, arms crossed tightly over his chest as he waited for the practice to begin.

Lee ignored me as he adjusted his microphone stand. "Let's go, Baby. Let's see what you have."

I raised my eyebrows slightly, wanting immediately to hit him with the guitar that I was plugging in, but began tuning it up instead. I started strumming the opening chords to *Liar, Player, Lover*, one off their most recent album. Jasp immediately kicked in with the bass, and Steve on drums. But Lee came in late on vocals, and I could tell he was fuming as he was putting extra emphasis on the opening lines.

Rylan was shifting in his seat uncomfortably. Bad music to him was like ice in his veins. He just couldn't take the sound. But he hung in there, until Lee caught up to us, and sat through the rest of the practice without offering one criticism. We ran through each song of the set, most playing at least twice. When we were finally finished, Lee walked off stage without a word.

Steve was toweling the sweat from his forehead. "Nice work," he stood up and threw his towel in Jasp's direction, "You know, for a girl."

I gave him a half-smile. "Yeah, you too."

Jasp laughed as he set his bass back on its stand. "Glad you're here. You're really saving our asses."

I caught out of the corner of my eye Rylan making his way to the stage. "Just convince your lead singer of that, and we might get through tonight without a hitch."

As Jasp left, Rylan gazed at his watch. "We don't have much time before your sound check. Let's get to work."

TWENTY-TWO
Natalie

Getting ready for the show that night, I was surrounded by my friends in Lull's dressing room, much to Lee's displeasure. I didn't care. In my mind, I was doing him a favor. Fuck him if he didn't see that. I was saving face, saving his band in a crisis. I didn't need him - he needed me. And I wasn't doing it for him anyway. I was doing it for Rylan.

Rachel was fussing over my hair. "I can't believe that hair stylist won't give you five-fucking-minutes of his time," she was saying as she further molested my already over-processed hair. I hated the fact that I looked anything like myself. Those who'd been to the show the night before would've never recognized me as the girl who'd played along with Coma. I was beginning to feel like an eighties-band-video-vixen before I finally put a stop to it and demanded she put away her hair spray and brush.

Across the dressing room, Lee was carrying on over how the stylist was gelling his hair into spikes that were going "in all the wrong directions". A make-up artist was dodging out of the way of the stylist to paint black lines across Lee's eyes, and I thought the two were going to get into it right there in front of the mirror.

Jasp and Steve were off in the corner, surrounded by a small group of friends, passing around a joint. At one point, Jasp caught my eye and offered me a hit, but I held up my hand. He nodded in my direction. "It calms the pre-gig jitters."

The corner of my mouth turned up in a crooked smile. "I don't get those."

"You will." He promised, giving me a quick wink before turning his attention back to his friends.

Ray-Ray was hanging close by. "You're not nervous then? Not even a little?"

He would have been able to see through any lie that I told him. The truth was, a few butterflies were beginning to turn my stomach into knots, but not enough to make me have to...

And with that, I was dodging for the nearest trashcan. I hit my knees hard on the tiled floor, and it was all I could do to keep my hair out of the way.

"Try again?" Jasp was at my side, a steady stream of marijuana smoke climbing from his fingers toward the fog in the room. With a low moan, I took his offer this time.

By the time our feet hit the stage, my stomach was fully settled and the nausea was replaced with the high of adrenaline, enough hormonal fuel coursing through my veins to have my hips swinging with the imaginary beat in my head and my feet barely able to maintain a solid connection with the stage. I had no idea how the crowd was going to receive St. Vincent's replacement being a woman, or if the news of his departure had even hit the public's attention yet.

Jasp, Cronin and I all took our places, with Jasp beginning the solo bass intro to *Boys, Toys and the Girls That*

Love Them. Lull's trademark entrance was that Lee was "fashionably late" to his own show. He loved nothing more than to hear the crowd cheering for him and him alone, hence waiting until the rest of the band had received their appreciation from the fans so that he could know that what he was hearing belonged just to him.

We were three songs into our seven song set when Lee knocked his microphone stand into the pit mid-song, mid-lyric. Instinctively, I picked up the vocals while he dropped back to share my microphone and resume his lead. We played it off well, and the lyrics allowed for us to play it up a bit as his eyes met mine when he sang, "I'd hide you in between my sheets, under the pillow 'til you can't breathe, let them all think what they'd want to think, I'd hide you away where they'll never see, and no one would know, no one would know, you're the secret between my sheets."

His eyes held mine in a way that I couldn't explain away in just a few song lyrics. Mesmerizing, perhaps yes, but captivating in a way that mine wouldn't let go. I had forgotten in those few short minutes that I didn't like Lee Mason, not in the least. I was lost somewhere in those coal black eyes, in the warmth of his breath on my cheek, in the mixed scent of leather and cologne that filled the air around us. I'd forgotten, as he sang those disturbingly enthralling words as though he were intentionally anchoring them into my soul, that he had insulted me both as a musician and as a woman, and in the same sentence at that.

But it all came back quickly when we'd finished our set, the screaming fans to our backs, he breezed past me, throwing a quick sneer in my direction, "Enjoy it while it lasts, Baby. One more show then you're on your way back to whatever hole it was you crawled out of."

TWENTY-THREE
Rylan

I sucked hard on three cigarettes back to back before I could finally concentrate on anything more than her playing. It took three cigarettes to get past the fact that she was on her own out there. And three cigarettes to get it through my head, again, that it was me who put her out there, and if this all fell apart for her, it was on my shoulders. But by the time I took that last drag, she had me sold. The audience loved her. Jasp and Cronin loved her.

And Lee needed her.

I reached for a bottled water, swigged down several gulps then swished the last one around before spitting it out behind the speakers. I wasn't worried about convincing Lee of anything. My money spoke volumes when it came to financing their tour and the recording of the album they were currently promoting. It was Natalie I was worried about.

This decision would alter her life, not to mention it would go against everything that I had argued for in her high school days. The last thing I wanted for her was to graduate high school and get into the music business. I'd wanted a degree for her. Higher education, so that she would have something to keep her out of this crazy life. Or at the very least, something to fall back on if she dove in anyway and it all fell to pieces.

After all, it wasn't me calling the shots while she was out there on the stage, it was the thousands of people who were standing in front of her at that very moment. The ones that had bought a ticket, most likely bought the album, and would, with any luck, buy a t-shirt on their way out. Those were the ones that determined if she was a success or a failure. And there was nothing that I could say or do that would change that. Not from where I was standing.

And with the next leg of the tour a short few weeks away, there wasn't a hell of a lot of time to get a backup vocalist and lead guitarist that would be up to speed enough to open for a band like Coma. Coma's audiences demanded a hell of a lot more than whatever-the-fuck-his-name-was that Natalie was replacing. They expected perfection, or damn near close to it, and they got that tonight. The cheers were eminent as they had hit the final notes in their encore.

My mind was made up. I needed her. And it was for more than just two shows. I needed her to finish this tour with them, maybe even sign with them, but definitely to finish this tour. The talent she had in her little finger was far more than enough to carry this band to where they needed to go. And it was enough to get her the recognition to branch out from there, if she wanted it.

It was a can't-lose situation.

I caught her around the waist as she came running off stage, followed by the rest of the band, adrenaline overpowering the exhaustion. It was a feeling like any other. One that I'd be experiencing myself in just over an hour and half when our own show ended, which gave me no time to get into a deep conversation with her now. So I'd just plant the seed. And see where it went.

"You don't have to be just their stand-in, you know."

She was breathless as she ran a hand through her sweat-drenched hair. She offered me a smile and a quick roll of her eyes, which were glistening with a high known only to those who have played their first real show. With an open hand, she pointed her finger back toward the crowd. "See, they came to hear you sing, not crack jokes." She planted a quick kiss on my cheek, and as she headed off behind the rest of the band, she called back over her shoulder, "Have a great show! I'll be out to watch in a bit..."

I watched as she ran to catch up to Cronin, and they disappeared down the hallway, laughing as he gave her a playful shove into the wall. I stayed behind, tapping into another cigarette as I watched the stage crew work to pull down Lull's set and put up Coma's.

If she decided that this was it, just these two shows and nothing more, that this wasn't what she wanted to do with her life, we'd be saying goodbye after the show tomorrow. She'd head back to Pennsylvania, and I'd be on a plane back to London. And that was fine - if it was what she wanted. But if there was any part of her that wanted to play in this band, she'd have to make the decision quickly, and it would involve leaving her friends then and there, and boarding a plane with us tomorrow night.

TWENTY-FOUR
Natalie

I sat at the breakfast table, alone and sober, half watching the hotel guests buzz around me at the buffet, half willing myself to eat the bagel and cream cheese that I'd toasted a half hour before. I wasn't sure why exactly I felt that the weight of the world was on my shoulders, surely there were far more epic crossroads in life than this, but as I sat there that morning, the decision itself felt colossal.

I'd spent most of the night talking it over with Rachel and Ray-Ray, both of them weighing heavily with opposing opinions. Rachel had practically pushed me out the door, swearing to call Rylan on her own and tell her that if I turned down the offer, she'd take it herself.

"It's all you've ever wanted to do, Natalie," she'd told me, "Deep down, you know that."

"But you don't have to go across the country to do it. You live three hours from NYC and three hours from DC. There are amazing opportunities in your own back yard." Ray-Ray was sipping heavily on Jack Daniels, propped up in the corner of the room on the lounge. He was putting on a good game face, but I knew. With every sip of his drink, he was closer and closer to speaking his mind, or his heart. And I wasn't sure that I could take that. Not right now. I was already wrestling with the heartache that went along with leaving him.

I could tell myself a million times over that it would only be for the few short months that tour lasted, and then I'd be back home again. But it didn't work that way. 7 Year Coma tours were known for being extended, shows being added on to fit demand around the world. And if Lull was as successful of a venture that Rylan lead into, we'd be along for the full ride. And who knows what might come after the tour? Maybe they'd sign me permanently? It was so open-ended, and unpredictable, that I couldn't bank on this just being a temporary hiatus to my senior year of college. This was full on, dropping out, and joining a band.

Rachel handed me a glass of Cabernet, but I held up my hand, and glanced at my phone for the time. It was nearing two in the morning.

I stood up, heading for the balcony. I needed fresh air, but the hot dry night offered no sense of refreshment. "Maybe you need to sleep on it." Rachel suggested when I turned back toward the room.

The thought crossed my mind momentarily, but I was realistic enough to know that even if I could shut my mind off long enough to fall asleep, I knew I'd be plagued with nightmares anyway, and that would ultimately cause more stress than I needed right now. The best course, I decided, was to continue to sort out my head until I'd reached a solid decision.

And as I sat here now in the late morning hour, deliberating over a bagel, I still had yet to come up with anything substantial. What I did know for sure was that I had obligation to at least one more show with Lull, and while that was several hours away, my head had yet to hit a pillow.

"You should sleep." Ray-Ray's voice came from behind me as he scooted into the empty seat beside me. His hair was disheveled and he'd yet to shave this morning, which made me want to run my hand over the course of his cheek. He was wearing a newer style orange and white Coma t-shirt that he'd talked Lucas into giving him the night before.

I watched as he took a sip of my tea, which had long since gotten cold. "I should," I admitted, "But I don't think I'll be able to."

We sat in silence for a while, and with each passing second, it grew harder and harder for me to focus on anything other than him. Had I known when we'd left Pennsylvania only a week ago that I'd be feeling this way about him, I might have held my heart a little stronger.

"Look," he began, "I can see it in your eyes how badly you want this. And it's a great opportunity for you, not only musically, but to be with your family again. It's what you want, Natalie, and this decision shouldn't be this hard."

It shouldn't be, I told myself, *but it is*. And it was because of him. I wasn't ready to let go of what we'd started. Even if I came back, who was to say that it would be what it is now? Who was to say that it would even be what it was before we ever made this trip? There was no way I'd ever be able to see him with another woman and be happy for him, not now, not knowing what exactly what being in love with him was like. Watching some other woman having all the best of him, while I was on the other side, just looking in, would tear at my heart in ways that I wasn't willing to admit to.

"We could try the long-distance thing, Ray-Ray. We could Skype and text until I come home."

"Are you?"

My eyes turned up and met his. "Of course. This is just for a few shows until they can find someone to replace St. Vincent." As I said it, I let myself believe it too.

Ray-Ray's eyes lowered as he nodded. Something bit

at me, deep inside, when he pulled away from me.

I offered him half a laugh. "I'll be back Ray-Ray. It's not like I'm putting my whole life into a rock and roll band. After all, I've got a promising career in Accounting."

He left the joke sit. And right there I knew. He didn't believe me.

"I'd like to tell you that I'm a hopeless romantic, Nat, and that I'd wait forever for you. But really I'm just a guy who's in love with a girl that he hasn't stopped thinking about for the last seven years."

TWENTY-FIVE
Natalie

As the plane taxied on the runway, my first thought was that I
was home. It was a strange feeling, actually. Home, in reality,
was the States. But that warm, content feeling of belonging
that I was lucky enough to experience rarely enough in my life
that it was as precious to me as gold, was here in England.
Cold, damp and dreary as it was, it was the first thing that
popped into my mind when someone said, "home".

The air was different, the smells were different, the
general feel of the country was different to me. The States
were comfortable, England was home. It was where I should
have belonged, had I grown up the way I had been intended
to. If it hadn't been for interference from my uncle, my life
would have been completely different...

I shook off the thoughts about what might have been.
There was no use dwelling in those ideas, and rightfully so,
had it not been for my uncle, I also wouldn't have met Rachel
and Ray-Ray, or my other friends, who had carried me great
distances throughout my life.

The flight had been long, and I hadn't slept as much as I had thought I would in my first class seat. It was rare that I flew first class, refusing to succumb to the luxuries that were not mine to claim. But my brothers only flew first class, and having the entire section to ourselves had a relaxed appeal. I had the entire row of cushion seats to myself, and with my iPod to keep me company throughout the nine-hour red-eye flight, I thought for sure that I would get some rest. But thoughts of Ray-Ray crept though my mind, and my heart ached to take back the last twenty-four hours that we had spent together.

As much as it hurt, the decision felt right. My destiny, my legacy, was to be on stage, one way or another, and I longed for the feeling of a guitar in my hand, a microphone inches from my mouth, and countless fans in front of me. And this flight had taken me there. I enjoyed my first class ticket a little more because of it.

Across the aisle on the plane, I watched as JT lay stretched out in his fully reclined high back Lazy Boy-on- a-plane, his head back, eyes closed, and snoring. He was meant to be here, in this crazy life of stardom and luxury. He always was, and he always would be. He never really thought about it, he didn't analyze it, he just did it. He sang, he played, he recorded, and he traveled.

On the other side of the aisle was Rylan. He slept practically sitting up in the seat by the aisle, his head resting on his hand, propped up by his elbow on the armrest. A laptop rested on the tray table in front of him, wide open with the screen saver drawing colorful arcs while he slept. There was no question that he was where he was meant to be in his life also. He had worked everyday of his life to get to where he was today. Every moment of it was a completely planned, thought-out event. None of it had happened by accident. And he protected it with everything that he had.

I found myself sleepily wondering about which one of them was most like my father. While the brief time in

England before the tour would be filled mostly with practice and preparation for our tour, I knew that if I had any hope of finding my father, this would be the best opportunity I'd had in years. I couldn't deny that it was what had kept me up throughout at least a part of the flight back home. I'd thought of hiring a private detective, someone who was an expert in finding the lost, someone who could help locate any information that might lead me to my father, so that I could finally meet him face-to-face.

As we exited the plane, I was watching the back of Rylan's shoes, and not much more, and as I walked past the airport personnel I glanced up only to give them a half-smile, since I knew they weren't so much as looking at me anyway. One thing that we didn't have to worry about was baggage claim, and at this hour in the morning, I was more than grateful for that. It wasn't like there were swarms of people flooding the inside of the airport, but even as I saw the limo parked out front, the second that leather seat crossed my mind, there were flashes from photographers lenses, and dozens of fans who flooded toward at the double glass doors at the entrance of the airport. It never ceased to amaze me how they knew where the band was at all times.

Instinctively, Rylan put his hand on the back of my head and shoved me into the limo as a large group of fans rushed the vehicle. Home sweet home, I thought, as I dived into the black leather seats and rested my head on the armrest. They could have gone a bit more low-key, I thought, but one the other hand, was more than grateful for the comfortable ride.

JT immediately began pouring the champagne the second the doors locked shut. I shook my head as he offered me a glass, then extended one to Rylan, Candace and even the driver as well. He shrugged good-naturedly and drank his entire glass without so much as a breath for air.

I wanted to sleep, I really did. It was a good hour and twenty-minute ride from the airport – a ride I knew well. Sleep continued to elude me however, and I lie wide-awake on the long end of the limo as my brothers and Candace chatted tiredly about their plans when they arrived at home.

The plans were to take a few days off before collaborating on some new music that was in the works for the next album. That didn't surprise me much. While the rest of the band was resting, my brothers were writing. It was what they did – what they lived for. They never seemed to rest. Even when they were on a break, they were working.

"It'll be nice to spend a few quiet days with JT." Candace was saying.

I could just about feel Rylan's eyes rolling in his head. "Quiet days" to him involved being locked in a room with his guitar, not spending quality time with family and friends.

I knew JT thought I was asleep when he asked Rylan, "You gonna take our girl to see Mum? She hasn't been doing too well, Kate says."

Rylan didn't hesitate. "Kate doesn't know her ass from a hole in the ground."

I heard a sigh from JT. "She's not takin' the piss, Ry. Mum's just not right anymore. We should go an' see 'er."

There was a long period of silence before I heard Rylan take in a deep breath and reposition himself on the leather seats. He might have even helped himself to some of the champagne. Somebody had, as I heard a glass clink and the sound of bubbling liquid hitting the bottom of a flute. Rylan hated champagne as much as I did, but if it was all the limo had in its reserve, he might have dove into the stock as a last resort.

"A'ight then." I heard him agree, "I'll see if Natalie is up fer it tomorrow an' we'll be over."

"Kate's sayin' she'd be better off in a community home. She thinks that it'd do her some good to be around other people with her..."

"Fuckin' rubbish."   Rylan dismissed him pretty quickly. "Kate just doesn't want the responsibility of takin' care of 'er anymore."

It got quiet again. We went over several bumps, the limo turned a bit, and I had to reposition myself as my arm was falling asleep. I was wishing that I was. The last thing I wanted to think about was the fact that my mother was losing her mind.   It had been painful enough to hear the scattered reports via email or text message from my brothers throughout the past few years, but even more disturbing was that I now had to face the reality of it. It wasn't that it was easier in another country to deal with it, but it wasn't something that I never had a say in. I was, after all, the baby of the family. I didn't get much of a say in things anyway, so I let my older siblings call the shots when it came to our mother's well-being.

When the limo pulled through the gate at Rylan's house, I forced myself to sit up. The only thought that was going through my mind was crawling into bed. I had been up for over thirty hours straight, and I felt that unless I slept for another thirty, I just wasn't going to feel normal ever again.

My room at Rylan's place wasn't just huge, it was simply palatial, and it was where I spent my summers when the band wasn't touring. Each time that I came home, Rylan gave me the option of decorating it any way I wanted. Three years ago, when I'd been here last, I had the walls painted brown, with silhouettes of guitars in a slightly paler shade, painted sporadically throughout the room. They were only outdone by the actual guitars that occupied their stands or hung on stylish brackets on the walls. Unlike my room in the States, there wasn't a single guitar hiding in the closet.

The room had a plush tan carpet, the kind that practically ate your feet when you walked across it. My bed was king-sized, decorated with high-end cotton sheets and a down comforter that matched the walls. It was adorned with gigantic fluffy brown pillows. It was girly without being too girly, and it had been a nice break from the cream-colored walls and bland dorm decor that I had to put up with back at school.

I sank down face first into the designer comforter and was in a deep sleep without a further thought.

I was pretty sure that I had slept away an entire week by the time my eyes opened slowly. My curtains were intentionally heavy, so that even during the rare bright mornings in London, the sun wouldn't so much as glimmer through. I realized that I was still laying sideways on the bed, thus the kink in my neck, and propped myself up on my elbows to squint at the alarm clock on my nightstand. It was seven in the evening.

I slid down onto the floor, laying my head back against the bed, and ran my fingers through the carpet. It felt like cotton balls. Millions of cream-colored cotton balls made up the carpet in my room. I wonder how many people would say that their carpet was their favorite part of their bedroom? About five feet from where I sat was one of my sneakers that I had still been wearing when I had fallen asleep. The location of the other one was apparently a mystery, since it wasn't in my direct viewing area.

My hands sunk further into the cotton ball carpet as I pushed myself up and made my way to the shower. My bathroom spared no luxury, featuring a twenty-two-jet spa tub, a separate steam shower, double bowl sinks and marble flooring. It was also slightly larger than my entire bedroom back in the States.

After a quick shower, I threw on a pair of jeans and a light sweater from my suitcase. I tossed my hair into a wispy ponytail and headed out into the hallway, where I stumbled upon my other sneaker. Tossing it back into my bedroom, I kept on my course through the hallway toward the stairs.

This was one of my favorite parts of Rylan's house. From the upstairs hallway, you could see the entire great room and the kitchen. There were massive windows that stretched the full three stories of the house. In the corner of the great room was a colossal stone corner fireplace, one of three in the house. There was another in the smaller living room located underneath my bedroom, and the third was in Rylan's bedroom, at the other end of the hallway from mine. If my bedroom was described as huge, his was simply palatial, taking up more than two-thirds of the second floor of the house. The third floor housed the studio, where the band would often come to practice and where Rylan's guitar collection, among other instruments, was housed.

My hand slid down the round wooden banister as I glided down the marble staircase toward the great room. Rylan was lying on the couch, his hands tucked behind his head, eyes closed, earphones in place. I wasn't sure if he was awake or asleep, so I kicked his foot. Unshaken, he simply opened one eye and pulled off an earphone.

"Let's go out to eat. I'm starving."

He blinked at me a few times, then nodded behind him. "The kitchen's that way. Why don't you go make us something?"

He started to reposition his earphone, but I wasn't giving in up without a fight. "Can we go to Waterside? Wait, no! Let's go to Albannach."

"Natalie, I'm not getting up off of this couch until I feel like going to bed. Why don't you call for delivery? Pizza, lobster, I don't give a fuck. Order anything you want."

"C'mon Ry," I pleaded, smiling at him sweetly, "We'll call it my birthday dinner."

He glared at me, and I could tell that he was having a hard time countering that argument. He sat up and stretched, then pulled his cell phone out of his pocket and tossed a resigned scowl in my direction while he made a reservation for two at Albannach.

An hour later, we were being seated on the mezzanine

at one of my favorite restaurants in London. Known for its sleek style and amazing British cuisine, Albannach had captured my interest six years ago when we rented out their private dining area to celebrate Lucas' engagement to Layna. And the last time I was in London, we celebrated JT's birthday by whisky tasting in the secluded vaults of Albannach's A-Lounge.

It didn't take long before those around us realized they were in the same room as Rylan Porter, and it was a common occurrence wherever we went to endure numerous interruptions with requests for autographs, photos, or for fans just to want to say hello. Rylan took it in stride, signing a few autographs, then turned his attention back to the waitress, who was smiling as she waited patiently to take our drink order. He asked me if I liked Bordeaux before he ordered a bottle of St-Julesn Chateau Les Ormes, which was brought out almost immediately.

Once the waitress left with our dinner order, I sat back in my chair, taking in the atmosphere of the restaurant. I wouldn't mind coming back at another time with some of my friends to enjoy the bar and the club downstairs. Now that they knew who I was, I thought with a smile.

I was casually sipping my wine, about to ask Rylan about him and Sammi and the wedding plans, when one of the restaurant waitresses came up to our table. She looked to be about forty-ish, but was just as star-struck as all of the others who had asked for autographs just a few minutes before. "I'm sorry to interrupt," she began, "But I was wondering if I could bother you for a photo?" She already had her cell phone in hand, just in case.

Rylan looked clearly agitated, but obliged anyway, as the waitress practically crawled into his lap for the picture.

He'd have been just as happy if she had just turned and went back to her tables, but she stuck around to explain. "I'm a huge fan of your dad's, and I actually saw him only two weeks ago over in Cambridge..."

"A'ight then, well if you don't mind, we'd like to get on with..."

"Right, sorry." She quickly excused herself and hurried off back to her work.

I didn't wait for the dust to settle. "What was he doing in Cambridge, do you think?"

Rylan gave me a hard stare as he finished his wine in three long sips. "Nothing we need to be bothered with."

A heavy breath escaped through my clenched teeth. This would be a tough mountain to climb. He refused to acknowledge that he had a father, and I had a thirst for knowledge when it came to the man that I never even once met. According to both of my brothers, I was better off never having known him, but it just wasn't enough for me to hear the stories. I needed to see it for myself. I needed for him to look me in the eye and tell me that he didn't care enough about me to acknowledge me.

A few years back, I had written several letters to him. I told him that I was his daughter, that my mother had given birth to me months after he left, and that I knew that he probably didn't even know I had been born. I told him that I wanted more than anything to meet him, and to maybe get to know who he was so that I could learn more about where I came from.

The response I initially received was from his agent, who wrote back on very formal letterhead that if I had issues of paternity with Mr. Porter, I should have my attorney contact his. He followed with my father's attorney's contact information, along with a brief statement that I should not continue to contact my father directly regarding this matter.

I had rationalized it with the thought that most likely, as an actor, he probably received letters like this all the time. He had people who weeded through the hundreds of letters that he received, and those of any importance were brought to the attention of his agent. In my mind, he probably never even saw the letter himself. I was sure that to this day, he had no idea that I even existed.

But when I had shared this information with my brothers, Rylan hit the roof, going into a rant of epic proportions, comparable only to those I'd seen him reserve for when JT pissed him off. And it was the last we'd spoken about it since.

"Ry," I pushed on, "Don't you think he'd want to meet me? Even just once?"

He was replenishing his glass of wine and looked up at me without saying anything, just chewing on his tongue, as though he wasn't sure whether to go into the endless diatribe that'd I'd heard over the years or just finally grace me with an answer. And while at least this time he was thinking before he was speaking, I was sure he was really just trying to prevent another three year silence between us.

I wasn't quite sure how to read the look on his face, but it appeared to be almost identical to the one he gave me after I had convinced him to come out to dinner tonight. It was the look of perfect reluctance. Maybe deep down, he knew I had every right to find our father, and to come face to face with the man who created me. But he still thought he made the rules, and it was going to be a battle of wits to get him to see otherwise.

"He's made it quite clear that he wants nothing to do with his family, Natalie. So no, I don't think he'd want to meet you, or see me or JT or even Kate again. It is what it is, and let's leave that alone."

"I can't." I pushed my napkin onto the table, leaning back in my chair, arms crossed over my chest. "It isn't fair, Rylan. It's not fair that you've all at least met him, and have gotten at least the chance to form your own opinions about him and I can't! I mean, don't you think I've the right to have a father?"

His face was reddening, I was sure his blood was boiling beneath his skin as he sat there, frozen, not even breathing for several moments as the waitress came back to deliver our plates. "Nothing about life is fair. That's something you'd be better off to learn young."

My eyes rolled before I had the chance to control myself and I spit out, "Like you have any experience in life being unfair."

He turned his attention to his plate, and though his face was turned downward, his movements were stiff and mechanic. "Natalie," he was talking through clenched teeth, "I've always found it best that if you don't know something to be fact, not to make comment at all."

Of all the nights that the dreams shook me awake, they were always worse when I was here. Here, so much triggered the memories that I longed to forget. The smell of the air, the sound of the British dialect all around me, the absence of the security of my friends, it all brought me back to when I was nine years old, and living in Hannah and Leo's house.

The exterior walls of that house encased the damp, heavy air that reeked of sweat, breath and whiskey. Hannah's green canvas couches were about the only item in the entire house that wasn't brown, beige or yellow. Not much of the décor from the house had ever exited the sixties, including the wallpaper that drenched almost every inch of the place, holding for eternity the stale second hand smoke that often hung in the air when either of them were home. The carpets, a faded shade of light brown, had a worn walking path between the small, dimly lit rooms.

It was on these floors that I'd often hear the shuffle of Hannah's feet. She never lifted them, just pushed them across the carpet as though she wore heavy skates on her feet. Leo made a whole different noise when he walked, that of which I learned to recognize early on in my stay. His feet would hit the floor with a thunderous conviction, as with each step he slumped his short and stocky stature into the ground, making his mark wherever he went.

I remember once lying in bed, hearing the slumping of Leo's feet in the creaky hallway that lead to my room. They stopped outside of my bedroom door, and I swore I'd hear his hand on the knob, his breath heavily hitting the wooden door. Sometimes, I'd hear the door squeak open, usually slowly, and if I dared to peek open my eye, I'd see the light from the lamp post outside my window illuminate the creases on his face as he looked back at me in my bed. He'd grunt happily before he pulled the door closed behind him and slump back down the hallway, and I'd be left with the ghost of his gaze hovering over me, and the smell of his excitement still lingering in the bedroom.

I remember the first time that I'd had to fight him off. Usually, he'd just come in and stare, and then leave. But he'd had a row with Hannah, drank too much of his whiskey, and ventured further past the doorway than he normally did. My body froze, as I clenched the stale-scented sheets up against my cheeks. His hand slid heavily over the cotton blankets that were the only barrier between my seven-year-old body and the thick frame of Leo. I stiffened under his fingertips, erupting a coarse chuckle from his throat as he grasped at the blanket. He stripped it away, and hurled it to the floor with an abrupt eagerness that instantly squared my shoulders back against the mattress. I brought my knees to my chest and kicked at him with enough force that it sent him staggering backward. And as if reality had suddenly hit him, he shuffled back out the door as quickly as easily as if nothing had just happened.

Every night thereafter, I slept lightly, with a desk chair propped up against the doorknob, and if I fell into a deep enough sleep, I would at least be awoken by the sound of his struggles to enter. I wasn't foolish enough to think that I could have fought off a full-blown, sober attack, but I knew that he and I were now on a certain understanding. He wasn't going to get to me without a fight.

TWENTY-SIX
Natalie

Rylan was gone by the time I made my way downstairs for breakfast. He had left me a quick note on the kitchen counter, which I found as I ran my hand along the marble counter tops, on my way to the fridge. I'd wanted to apologize to him for my comment last night. I shouldn't have let my frustration turn to anger, and I hadn't meant what I'd said.

There was a general feeling of emptiness in the house, which was okay, but I much preferred the coziness of my Pennsylvania brick townhouse. At least if I was alone in the house I shared with Rachel, the place didn't feel quite so empty.

Perhaps it was the remnants of last night's dream, but here in the empty house, I felt as if the world were watching me. I started humming the first tune that came to mind, which made me feel a little better. And before I was finished cooking my breakfast, an onion and cheese omelet, I was all-out singing the words to *Curb*, an unreleased song that JT had written years ago.

I pulled up a bar stool and sat in the breakfast nook, enjoying the view of the back garden through the seven-foot high windows. It was actually sunny this morning, and the gardens were inviting. Rylan no doubt had a team of gardeners, though I never saw any of them, but the shrubs and lawns were kept impeccable every time I came.

Most mornings that I spent in England were rainy and dreary. It was a relief to have just one that was sunshiny and bright. Even if the rest of the days I spent on this trip sucked, at least I had one that was beautiful.

I took full advantage of it, taking my plate of eggs out onto the stone patio through the French doors, and walked through the ivy-covered trellis. Rylan was very much into stonework, and most of the back garden was designed with various types of stone, from the Japanese rock garden, to the rock wall, to the antique style garden furniture. Bamboo lined the outskirts of the patio, and just beyond that ran a handcrafted babbling brook over a bed of weathered stone.

A cool breeze nibbled at my bare arms, tossing my hair over my shoulders and sending wisps of brown locks softly into my face. The air smelled of damp green grass and crisping mature foliage. If the weather held up, it was going to amount to a beautiful day.

I was finishing up my plate of eggs when the bell from the front gate rang out, loud and echoing through the house and the garden. It made me jump at the sound of it, and I hurried over to the telecom in the kitchen. You never knew who'd be on the other end. Many times, it'd be a group of fans looking for autographs. Sometimes it'd be reporters, often claiming to be a delivery person, or some other scheme that they'd cooked up.

"Package for Rylan Porter," came the proclamation through the speaker.

"Thanks," I responded, "You can leave it at the gate."

"It requires signature, Miss."

I rolled my eyes. Oldest trick in the book. "I'm sorry,

but Mr. Porter isn't available. You'll have to send it through his management company, please."

"I only need adult signature, Miss. It doesn't have to be Mr. Porter's. The law office just needs proof that the package was delivered, that's all."

Law office? I hoped it wasn't some sort of a court summons. It happened more often than the media caught hold of, artists being sued for various things. Paternity suits, destruction of property, or their music too closely resembling another artist's. The last of which had been one that brought Rylan's attorneys to court on multiple occasions.

The difference, Rylan would explain, is that his music was brilliant, and he'd made millions off of it, while the other artists that he'd allegedly "stolen" from, were hurting for money, and thereby needed to sue him to recover any legacy from their work. It was all rubbish, he'd contend, all of his music was original. With so many songs and artists out there, it was impossible to know if work he'd created resembled some unknown's music or lyrics.

I briefly wondered if I should try to phone Rylan, as I made my way down the paved brick drive, lined with flowering bushes that were changed out every season to maintain a constant rotation of fresh foliage. A large messenger truck sat just on the other side of the heavy iron gate, and outside of it stood the delivery man with a medium-sized box at his feet. He extended a clipboard and pen through the gate as I approached. "Sorry to bother you Miss. I'm just not allowed to leave estate belongings at doorsteps." His eyes focused on the large house behind me, "Or gates, for that matter."

I smiled as I signed my name on delivery receipt and handed it back to him. "Estate belongings?"

He glanced down at the delivery receipt. "Estate of Hannah Kaplan."

Goose bumps iced my skin as my eyes shot over to the box that he was picking up to hand to me. I could barely feel my own arm as it reached to the button to open the gate so he could hand me the box.

My eyes were still wide when I set the box down on the coffee table, wondering what the hell we were doing with Hannah's estate belongings. *We weren't even related by blood.* Surely she had family who would hold claim to her personal affects. Why the hell would they be sent to Rylan?

I started to dial his number, my eyes still on the box. It rang four times then went straight to voicemail. I ended the call without leaving him a message. My hands were shaking, and I tried walking away, into the kitchen. What could be in that box? I thought about calling JT, but I knew it was way too early for him. There was no chance I'd catch him awake on his day off any time before noon.

I went back to the living room to look at the box again. It was standard cardboard, held together by packing tape. It would be incredibly easy to pull the tape off and reseal it without anyone knowing any better of it. The edges of the tape were already starting to peel...

I nearly leapt out of my skin when I saw Sammi come out through the French doors in the kitchen. "There you are." Her short red hair was wispy this morning, a product-held bed-head ensemble, held back by her sunglasses.

Her presence was welcome, and I sighed in relief of no longer being alone with that box. It was like have a ghost sitting there, beckoning to me. I immediately shifted my attention to Sammi, trying my best to focus again on the living instead of the dead.

She wore a simple, curve-hugging floral print sundress that flared out at the bottom just above her knees. It was so un-Samantha Brockhaven that I found myself staring for a moment to take it all in.

Outside of work, Sammi's usual attire consisted of high end, cutting edge fashion trends. She tended to wear what the models wore, hot off the runway. And she wasn't afraid to make a bold statement. But I did happen to notice, without

saying, her curves were a bit... curvier than I'd seen them in
them in the past. I tried not to pay attention to such shallow
things, but Sammi had always been petite. And not that she
wasn't still – maybe it was the print or the cut of the dress –
but something about her seemed different.

"I'm trying something new." She said, taking a seat at
the table across from me.

I held up my hand, dismissing her explanation. She
glanced over at the box inquisitively. "I just passed the
delivery truck. Your friends sent you some stuff from home
then?"

My eyes flew back over to the box. "Yes." I picked it
up before she could see any of the handwritten description on
the top, and turned toward the stairs. "I'll be right back."

In the back of my closet, I slid the box on the floor, then
set some suitcases on top of it, hoping it wouldn't draw any
attention from the cleaning lady. With any luck, I'd have time
to take a quick peek before Rylan asked about it. If he was
even expecting it at all.

I flew back down the stairs and found Sammi in the
kitchen. She sat with her elbows on the table, chin resting on
her hands. "I thought you might want to go shopping."

I eyed her suspiciously for a moment, forcing the box
and Hannah Kaplan out of my mind. Shopping with Sammi
was like walking through a minefield. You just never knew
what you were going to get. I tossed the idea around in my
mind a bit before answering. "I guess I do need some things
to hold me over for the next few weeks."

Soon after, I found myself sitting in the passenger side
of her car, taking in the sights of my long beloved city of
London. I missed it, I had to admit. To grow up here would
have been appealing in so many ways, but I'd have grown up
jaded. Here, my face was known. While the people here
knew I was related to 7 Year Coma in some form, that
relationship was long debated by the paparazzi and fans alike.
There was much speculation, mostly due to the silence of the

band and their management, as to my true identity. Most assumed that I was Rylan's illegitimate daughter, or JT's even. Some thought I belonged to Sammi, as I spent quite a bit of public time as a child latched to her arm.

Rylan was a master at talking the press into circles, but JT's response when cornered was to come out swinging. Both methods were equally effective. And on the few occasions where interviewers got their microphones close enough to me, I had a rehearsed response for any number of the typical questions, and a sweet smile that I flashed followed by a "no comment" for those few reporters who were quick-witted enough to throw one at me that I hadn't prepared for.

The city flew by the windows of the car like scenes in a movie and I wished that we were walking instead of driving. It felt like the perfect day to take our time. But Sammi lived by a schedule, and time was a precious commodity, even on her days off. We skidded to a halt, three-wheeling it into a parking space, and Sammi's hand was on the door before she even switched the ignition off. She took her shopping seriously.

I was on her heels as we stepped into London's trendiest shopping district. Sammi's hand gripped my wrist as she pulled me into one of the stores. The moment I walked in, I instantly wanted to walk back out. Everything in the store sported a designer tag, and a price tag to match. I only had to glance around the place once to see that there wasn't anything in here that I would walk out in public in. "Sammi, are we here for you or for me?"

She was busy fondling a papaya-colored jacket with flowing kimono sleeves. "Your stage presence could use a little help." She quickly snatched a tight green halter top off the rack. "And help has arrived..." She held the hanger up against my shoulders, then nodded approvingly.

"Says the woman in the floral print sun dress." I took the top from her and added just for fun, "I don't even think my mom would be caught out in that."

I saw her smirk as she continued to flip through stage-appropriate attire. "Are you going to go see your mom?" She meant to be casual by this, but she knew the history.

I shrugged, running my finger along a black lace skirt that cost a little more than my monthly car payment. It only took Sammi a quick glance in my direction for her to pull it off the rack and hand it to me, before she continued her search. "I will, I guess. This seems to be a topic of debate between my brothers at the moment. I figured I'd let them get it sorted out between the two of them first."

"I have to agree with JT on this one though." Sammi moved on to the next round rack of clothing underneath a manikin wearing a white leather dress that looked painted on. The thing creeped me out, so I stayed put and sorted through all of the clothes that Sammi had rejected.

I tried not to let it get under my skin that she seemed to know more about my mother than I did. "I guess I'll have to see for myself. I'm not big on community homes, but if she's as bad off as Kate says she is, then maybe it's for the best. I'm not normally one to side with Kate on matters of any importance though. She's got about as much reason in her as a snail."

Sammi suppressed a laugh, handed me an armful of hangered clothing and led me over toward the dressing room. "That's exactly what Rylan said. Snail and all."

We laughed as the dressing room door clicked shut behind me. Sammi waited as I modeled each outfit, letting her give me a nod or a headshake on each piece. She was not afraid to be critical, in fact, her job depended on her good judgment, and I knew that everything that she was handpicking for me was nothing less than stage perfect and audience loving.

We visited no less than seven stores in total, and Sammi had to lean on her trunk with both elbows to get it to close. As soon as were on the road, I couldn't hold back a question that was burning in my mind since my dinner with Rylan. I was hoping that she had the answers that my brothers weren't willing to share. "Sammi, have you heard that my father was in the area recently?"

Another one of her job requirements was to keep cool under extreme pressure. The woman orchestrated concerts in front of millions yearly for one of the world's most successful bands. Calm was second nature to her. Yet I noticed as soon as the words had come out of my mouth that her shoulders instantly squared, and she gripped the steering wheel a little tighter. She quickly bit her lower lip and glanced over at me briefly, but then returned her gaze back to the road. London's streets were no place to lose your concentration. "I heard that rumor."

"So," I pressed on, "Any idea where he is now?"

Sammi was a master liar. It was in her job description since her PR days. She spun stories for the press to cover up all kinds of scandals on behalf of the band. And she was a master at it. She was one of the best in the business. But it rarely carried over into her personal life. If you asked her, "Does this make me look fat?" she'd find the most diplomatic way possible to tell you yes.

She thought a while before she replied. "I do know where he is, Natalie. I'm just not sure that I should be the one to tell you."

TWENTY-SEVEN

Rylan

"What do I think? I think its shit, mate. From the beginning, then." The temperature inside the sound booth felt ten degrees higher than normal. *Can't be good for the equipment*, I thought, glancing around me at the sea of knobs, buttons and lights. *Fuck it, I'll call the maintenance team myself if these idiots here couldn't figure out how to lift a phone.*

And the tracks they were recording weren't much better. How these sound "engineers" were still employed was beyond me. Lee Mason's vocals were sounding more like a phlegm-ridden feedback issue than a cutting-edge rocker, and it was grinding on my last nerve. I had enough to deal with in my world, yet my "hobby" was now starting to add to the stress in my life. I was bank-rolling an atrocity.

"Less bass." I told them, trying to control the low growl in my voice as I headed out for some cooler air. If Lull was going to make it to their next record, they had a long way to go. These studio sessions were a rarity, but I wanted them to get them in before we hit the road again.

Steve Cronin and Jasper McGurty were standing in the hallway, slugging down soda and chips while Lee was in the studio. The scene reminded me briefly of JT and myself, in our early days. JT being the slugger in the hallway, and myself being the one busting my ass in the studio. But I knew that these kids both had musical ability and I'd seen them work hard on many a day, so I let it slide that at the moment they were both seeping under my skin.

"It's a shame Nat's not here. We could really use her." Jasp had worded his statement wisely.

"She's only signed on for the tour, not as a member of the band." I reminded him, not holding back any impatience from my voice.

"She should be." He looked to Cronin for support, "Our permanent guitarist."

Cronin was quick to jump in, "She's exactly what Lull needs."

At least there'd be no need to convince them, I thought, and tossed around the idea of pushing Natalie a bit more to commit to the band. I'd let it rest, perhaps more than I'd intended to, during the past few days, but it might not be a bad idea to bring it up to her before the tour to get her thinking about it now.

The pair of them mistook my silence as refusal, and were quick to defend their case. "Look, Lee won't tell you this himself, but he's on board with it. He knows we need her."

My eyebrows raised, providing them only with a somewhat bored glance as I tried not to chew my tongue. "Perhaps if you spent a bit more time in the studio, and not as much out in the hallway, you wouldn't need her so much."

I had to admit, I enjoyed watching them walk away, back into the studio, thinking all the while that I was a proper dick. But I also knew they were right. I'd been tossing it around in my head a lot more than I'd wanted to lately.

There was a lot to consider having her sign on with a

band. Her life would be under a microscope. Things would be dug up. Things that had been buried deep. The paparazzi had their ways of finding those things, sniffing them out like hunting dogs, and splashing them all over the media for the public's enjoyment.   It was the last thing I'd wanted. Knowing the truth would shatter her, and I couldn't take watching that happen.

We'd done enough over the years to protect her from all the insanity that this life brought. Sending her to another country and changing her name were extreme, I knew, but it had worked better than I could have hoped.   Sure, the photographers had snapped a few pictures over the years, and the journalists had their share of questions, but in the end, our silence - and Sammi's magic - had managed to keep her identity hidden. No one knew who she was.

And when she returned to the States as she did at the end of each summer, it kept the press from following her across the ocean and hounding her at her front doorstep. That alone was worth all the painstaking efforts we'd made.

But her identity was buried under a mound of lies, and it would take little more than a few digs with the right shovel for the truth to come crawling back out. With all that had happened to her in her life, it was the last thing that I wanted to happen. She'd been through more than enough already, and I hated the thought of the past coming back to haunt her now. Not when her life and career where just beginning.

TWENTY-EIGHT
Natalie

JT wanted to go see my mother, which came with strings attached. My sister, reportedly, was now staying with my mother, claiming that she and her husband were on the verge of separation. This only added to the fire between her and Rylan, since he ascertained that this was just a ploy on her part to get claim to our mother's house. Kate was devious, nobody could argue that, but I didn't see how faking a split between her and her husband would've been the best way to go about getting our mother's house. Regardless, she was living there. Rylan had changed his mind about coming with us the moment he heard Kate was there.

When we pulled up in front of the house, it was just as I had remembered it. A small, two-story house sandwiched in between two other houses of the same size. It was wrapped in white siding, and surrounded by a beautiful landscape that had been impeccably maintained for my mother by some of the many caretakers that Rylan had hired years ago. Among them was also a cleaning service, in-home caretakers for her health and visiting nurses, and a not-so-subtle round the clock security guard stationed outside of the home, which I was sure pleased the neighbors. It was a cruel necessity, we had found out soon after my brothers became famous, as fans stalked the place at all hours, hoping for a glimpse of the rock icons.

Kate's light brown hair was beginning to show slight signs of gray, but that was just about the only tell-tale sign that she had celebrated her fortieth birthday earlier in the year. There was barely a wrinkle on her face, and other than looking ever so slightly older, she appeared exactly the same as when I had seen her three years prior. She had shallow brown eyes that tended to stare off into the distance when you were talking to her. Her makeup was flawless as ever, and her nails were freshly manicured.

She greeted us with an enthusiastic smile that revealed a perfect set of white teeth. "Natalie girl! Look at you! You're gorgeous and so grown up!" She wrapped both arms around me and hugged me gingerly. She smelled of high-end perfume, something flowery, which made me want to gag. I wanted to tell her that she should have saved her money and just rolled about in a meadow somewhere, but I was trying to be on my best behavior.

JT gave Kate a quick hug, telling her that she too looked stunning as ever. JT knew where and when to lay on the charm. Sometimes I wondered if deep down, he didn't see right through her way that Rylan and I did. It was hard to read JT.

"Where's Mum?" He asked, scanning the living room first, then peeking around the corner into the kitchen.

Kate motioned to the back. "In the garden. She's been spending a lot of time out there lately since the weather's been nice."

I followed JT out back, where we found our mother seated on a garden mat, pruning some flowering plants. Her eyes lit up when she saw JT. "John Thomas Porter, I can't believe you didn't tell me you were coming to visit me!" He helped her to her feet and embraced her frail body.

Unlike my sister, my mother had aged exponentially since I had last seen her. Her short blonde hair was now completely white, and she had lost close to twenty pounds, leaving her already slender figure now fragile.

JT shot me a quick warning glance, as he made sure that she was steady on her feet before he let go of her. He had told me before we had even decided to come visit that she was slipping fast. She had been diagnosed with Alzheimer's a few years back, but the doctors said that her mind was rapidly deteriorating. "I called you this morning, Mum."

Her face twisted in a thoughtful frown. "No, I don't recall. But no matter, you're here now." She turned to me. "Is this your wife? She's absolutely beautiful! And so young..."

I felt my heart sink with such force that I wasn't sure if the pain was from it being ripped from my chest or from hitting the floor. I was pretty sure that I had opened my mouth to speak, but I wasn't sure what to say. What kind of a world was it when your own mother didn't recognize you?

I felt JT's hand on my back. "Mum, this is Natalie."

I could tell that the wheels were turning in her head, but she continued to return a blank stare. For a second, it appeared as though the light went on. "Oh! Rylan's girl?"

I felt JT freeze for a second before he countered, "No, Mum. Natalie. *Our* Natalie."

She merely shook her head, a blank stare falling upon my face. And politely she said to me, "I'm sorry. How are you Natalie?"

She extended her hand to me, which I ignored and pulled her into a hug anyway. "Hi Mum."

I tried to tell myself that it was the disease that had her mind in shambles, and that it wasn't anything personal, but it killed me that she remembered JT and not me. And when we got back into the house, it was clear that she still knew Kate as well. I tried, for the time being, to not let it bother me and to just enjoy the time that I was getting to spend with her. But there was an aching in my heart that not only did I not have a father, but now my mother was somehow lost as well.

For the most part, my mother was quiet as Kate did all of the talking anyway. She told us all about her girls, her job as a financial advisor, and her many friends. I couldn't help but feel as though she was trying to show us up, and every time I glanced over at JT, he seemed to be equally as bored. Every once in a while, when he was sure Kate wasn't looking, he'd nod at me to get my attention, then roll his eyes dramatically and pretend he was snoring or try to make me laugh with some other crazy face.

Kate invited me at one point to tell her about myself, and as soon as I got a few words about school out of my mouth, she cut in with how she had finally been afforded the opportunity to go back to college just a few years back. Now that she had her degree in Accounting, her husband was jealous and wanted to leave her, so she told us. I made a mental note to change my major if I ever did go back to school. There was no part of me that wanted to be in anyway like Kate.

Once my mother went off to bed, Kate offered us drinks, attempting to entice us to stay. I heard JT let out a low sigh as his eyes met mine. Without saying a word to each other, I knew that we were both agreeing to only one drink, to appease our sister, and then we would get out of there.

When she handed us our glasses, I could smell the alcohol without even having to bring the glass up to my face. "It's a Vodka Tonic." She told me, as though she were serving me my first alcoholic drink.

All I knew as I took the first sip of the nearly full glass was that whatever it was, it sure as hell wasn't a Vodka Tonic. It had vodka, but I think that was all it had in it. JT laughed when he took a sip of his, and I knew that he had realized the same thing that I had. "Katie girl, there's no doubt ya got Irish in ya." He held up his glass and toasted the air in front of him before taking a much longer sip.

She laughed, and followed suit. Then she revealed casually, "So I heard from Dad."

JT nearly spat out his vodka. Choking back whatever managed to get down his throat, he set his drink down on the coffee table next to him, and sat up straight in the armchair. "You did?"

Kate nodded. "I did, straight away. He phoned me and wanted to get together. But I told him to fuck off. He didn't even ask how Mum was doing."

JT settled back down and gave her an approving smile. "Nice one. Good for you, Katie girl."

For the second time in one night, my heart sank. "Wait, do you know where he was calling from? Did he say?"

Kate and JT both looked over at me, as Kate told me, "Nah, Love. It's best to leave that one alone. He's just a bloody bastard, and no more a father than a sperm donor really. And what you want with him anyway?" And as quickly as she brought on the conversation, in true Kate form, she changed it. "I made biscuits earlier. D'ya want any?"

So he was reaching out to Kate. There was hope in that. Maybe he wanted some sort of family ties. Maybe he missed us. Well, missed them, I had to remind myself. You can't miss someone if you don't know they exist. But the fact that he wanted to get together with Kate meant that he was close enough for a visit.

When we said our goodbyes to Kate, she made me promise to call her in the upcoming days to get together. She wanted to go shopping, have lunch, or engage in any kind of sisterly act that she could possibly come up with on a whim. I bit the bullet and told her yes, more out of politeness than anything, and found it hard to say no when she asked for my cell phone number. Besides, I reminded myself, maybe I could get some more information about our father out of her. In the car on the way back home, I grilled JT. "Do you think he knows anything about me, JT? It seems strange that he doesn't even know he's got another daughter."

He kept his eyes on the road, flipping through the endless stations on his satellite stereo. He'd settled on some Zepplin before casually responding, "Dunno, Love. It's hard to say if he and Mum talked much back in those days. Everything was kind of sketchy between the two of them."

I turned the volume down before his hand was barely off the button. "But aren't you curious about him? Don't you want to know what he's been doing? Or what he looks like now?"

"Nah." JT was clamming up, which wasn't unusual when he was fighting off strong emotions. I had heard him say many times that if he ever saw our father just by chance in public somewhere, he'd need a team of people to stop him from beating him to a bloody pulp. That was typical JT talk though. Who knew what would really happen if the time ever came when he found himself face to face with the man.

But as we pulled up to Rylan's dark house, JT found an easy subject change as he nodded toward the house. "Where's he at tonight?"

"Recording studio. He wanted to make sure the crew had everything set up right for tomorrow." I glanced at the clock on the dash. It was almost ten. "Rylan Porter in a room full of musical instruments and recording devices means that he'll be there until someone drags his ass out."

"You can stay at my place then."

He turned the wheel and was about to step on the gas when I put my hand on his. "JT, I'm fine, really. I'm twenty-one, not ten."

He eyed me skeptically for a moment or two. "You still get those nightmares?"

"They're not so bad…"

He knew I was lying. And I knew that he knew. "Candace would love if you came by."

I thought about it for a moment or two. It would be nice to spend some time with JT and get to know Candace a bit better. But I was tired. I wanted to call Ray-Ray and go to bed.

"Another time," I promised, giving him a quick kiss on his stubbled cheek, "Tell her I said hi, and I'll see *you* tomorrow."

He gave me an uncertain look as I closed the car door and peeked back through the open car window with a smile. "I'm here if you want to call," he reminded me as I turned toward the house.

I was on the phone with Ray-Ray the second JT's car pulled out of the empty drive. The house was even lonelier when it was empty at night than it was during the daylight, and it made me miss my friends all the more. I was never lonely in Pennsylvania, as someone was always close by if I needed them.

"Good God, girl. I don't think I can take one more day without you," was how Ray-Ray picked up the phone. It instantly made me smile, and had me wishing that my back was nuzzled up against his chest, my head leaning back on his shoulder, and his arms wrapped around me strong enough to hold me safe against him, but placed strategically just under my breasts enough that he "accidentally" would brush up against them. God, only Ray-Ray could make me feel that way from across the ocean.

I slipped off my shoes and my jeans and traded them in for a pair of soft cotton white shorts. I was half-way through sliding on a skin-hugging peach-colored tank top when I responded, "Me too." I slipped on top of my comforter, not sure if I was ready for bed or a snack. If he were here, the decision would have been much easier. I'd simply lock my door and curl up next to his naked body just after an intense round of wild animal sex on my bed. Good God, I told myself, I needed to find a better way to occupy my mind. The impromptu sexual urges might just be the death of me.

"Ray-Ray, why don't you just come visit? Our tour is

coming up quick, and I really want to see you before we leave."

"Love, if I were to come there to visit, we'd never leave your bedroom." Ray-Ray joked. There was an air of seriousness in his voice that I hung onto, if only for a moment.

"I can have a ticket ready for you tomorrow."

There was a long pause on his end, and I knew what was coming next long before the words crossed the line. "You know I can't. School is starting in a few days." It didn't make me feel any better, knowing the reality of it. Ray-Ray spent the majority of his life breaking the rules to get what he wanted. If he really wanted to be with me now, he'd have made up the time he missed when he got back. Surely there was a way, if he was willing.

"A long weekend then. You could do a Friday through Monday trip." Hell, he could bring his schoolwork with him and we could do it together. Right now, I'd have given my left arm to be able to reconcile a balance sheet for him.

I could practically hear him smile through the phone. Or at least I thought I could.

"Send me a ticket, Love."

I went to bed that night wishing he were already here, filling the emptiness of the bed next to me. If I tried hard enough, I could smell his cologne, and feel his arm slung over me as I nestled in under my sheets. And if I really let my mind wander, I could feel the heat from his body wrapped up in the sheets against mine. I stopped there. The last thing I needed were any sexual urges creeping up when there was nothing that I could do about them.

Missing him was about the worst feeling that I could have imagined. For so long, when we had been just friends, I was content with seeing him whenever we caught up again. Sure, that was pretty frequently, but I had never had that longing before, that longing that dug deep within me and grabbed my heart with an iron fist that just wouldn't let go. No matter what, it was always there. He was always on my mind and in my heart, no matter how far away. Still thinking about him, I pulled my guitar into my lap and began strumming a tune. It was one I'd been working on for some time, on and off, and as I played tonight, I slowed the tempo a bit, enjoying the sound of the song in a whole new way.

I hadn't realized that I'd drifted off to sleep, guitar in my lap.

The hallway was dark, which I knew was wrong right away. I'd had conscious enough memories where the hallway had been well-lit. Lit enough that I could see the blood stains and his face. His face had always been very clear in both my waking memories and in those that came back through my dreams. But in this dream in particular, it was dark, which made me question how much of it was a reflection of what really happened, and how much of it was my subconscious telling me that I didn't want to see this clearly yet. I wasn't ready. Not even now, twelve years later. A part of me wanted to wake up. A part of me wanted to confront him. None of me wanted to stay in this dark hallway, not when I knew what was about to happen.

He held his arm against my neck, choking me. I froze, both in fear and in pain. But my legs wanted to kick out against him, my knuckles wanted to connect with his chest and his face, pushing him back away, into the dark hallway. Yet I stood still as his breath hung in the air in front of me, tainted with grain alcohol and tobacco and unbrushed teeth. And the stench grew stronger as he spat accusations at me. "It's your fault, you little bastard child... She and I would still be together if we didn't have you here, sucking us dry at every turn. And if your father were half the man that Hannah thinks he is, he'd be taking you on himself, not leaving you here to rot while he's out making his millions..."

Even in my dream, I knew this wasn't right. In his prime, my father was a b-rate movie actor, at best. "Millions" hardly covered his pay salary accurately. He'd have a better shot at kissing

up to my family and inheriting the windfall that my brothers were
on their way of making before he'd get a break big enough in a film to
be deemed a millionaire. Regardless, my uncle seemed to think that
his wife wanted my father - that she had some great misperceptions
of who he really was. I found it all very strange, as neither my aunt
Hannah nor my uncle Leo had ever mentioned anyone in my family.
Not even in the nights that I cried, homesick as hell, wanting to go
back to them.

   The dream faded, lingering only in bits and pieces as I
lay amongst my scattered bed sheets, hugging tightly to one of
my pillows. I wished to God that I'd listened to JT and gone
to his house. At least then if I'd gotten up and gone to the
kitchen for some tea, I'd known for sure that I wasn't alone in
the big empty house.

TWENTY-NINE
Natalie

The coffee shop near the band's recording studio was a corner coffee shop, heavily visited and prone to frequent star sightings. It wasn't unusual to run into celebrities in this area, but you just couldn't deny a busy star their expensively fancy coffee. It was lifeblood on which they existed.

I was still waiting in line when I spotted Dax, having just slipped a few pounds on the counter in exchange for his extra-large cup of cappuccino to go. He was midway through licking the foam off of his upper lip as he was about to walk past me.

He tilted his sunglasses down just a bit to peer at me over the top of them. "If I knew you were back here, I'd have bought you a coffee."

I shrugged. "It's all good." I was suddenly acutely aware of my American accent, and hoped that it didn't attract us any more attention than we were already getting. I had always tried not to let the whispers and commotion bother me, and most of the time I was successful.

"Nah, I'd never forgive myself for passing up an opportunity to buy Natalie McKinney an overpriced coffee." Dax slipped under the rope and pole barrier and stood next to me in line.

Dax towered over me at six foot two. Back in the band's early years, he was lanky, partially from the work and lack of good food, and partially from the drug use. Most of the latter had leveled off now, or at least slowed to a dull minimum. In the more recent years, Dax had invested in a personal trainer. 7 Year Coma wasn't the type to rip off their shirts in concert, but if Dax ever did, his rippling abs might cause a feeding frenzy among the women in the audience.

"I heard you're slotted to be the next takeover guitarist for Lull?" It came out of his mouth like honey, but stung like the bee that made it.

I sighed heavily and made a mental note to bitch out Rylan later, and remind him that I had not accepted any such position with his trial band. Lull was a fitting name for Lull. "That rumor is untrue, my friend. I'm just the tour-temp until they find a permanent replacement. I'm obligated to nothing more than this tour."

Dax's eyebrows raised, but he shrugged good-naturedly, "That's a shame. I thought you were a perfect fit for the role. That band just needs a guitarist with talent like yours to complete the package, and there'd be no stopping them."

My eyes narrowed, and I was sure that Rylan had put him up to this, but one look in his eyes told me that he was being genuine. He leaned in close and in a low voice told me, "Ry'll tell you that it was his idea, but don't believe it. It was all my suggestion."

I couldn't help but smile at the thought of Dax giving Rylan advice on how to manage a band. Not that he wasn't capable, it was more the thought of Rylan actually taking anyone's advice.

When it was my turn to order, Dax quickly slid money

down onto the counter, slipped his arm around my waist, and then steered me toward the door before I could object. The second we were out in the sunlight, I thought he was going to let me go, but he kept a tight grip on me as we turned in the direction of the recording studio. I was laughing at the way he whirled me around the corner, the coffee splashing in our cups, and I was still laughing when the glittery flashes from the cameras snapped our picture only a few feet from the studio entrance.

I stopped dead in my tracks, my smile instantly gone, with an astonished blank stare taking its place.

Dax urged me to move, giving my wrist a gentle tug, but my feet were frozen, allowing them to continue to take their photographs. They were shouting out their questions, which was a dead giveaway as to how their story would be twisted and manipulated to sell their lies. And I knew better.

It wasn't until JT happened to poke his head out the door and realized what was going on that I snapped out of it enough to get inside. But not before I caught out of the corner of my eye JT sucker punching a photographer, sending the camera flying out of his hands and crashing to the street. He was going for another one when Dax caught his arm and dragged him toward the studio. JT went, but shouted curses at them with every aggravated step.

Once the doors closed behind us, JT turned to us. "Let's see if *that* makes top story then." Without a second thought, he sauntered up the stairs to the studio, where the rest of the band was warming up.

I slumped down onto a stool, trying to get my blood to stop pumping furiously through my head. I had long grown accustomed to a life with cameras around. But I never cared before who was watching. It never mattered who was glancing over in the line at the grocery stores, reading the lies created about our lives, for their own entertainment. And yet today, it seemed to get under my skin. Their voices, their innuendos, their invasion of my privacy, all seemed to sting just a little more today than it ever had before. *You're just not used to it,* I tried to convince myself, *it's been so long since you've been back home, that you've forgotten how it feels.*

And by the time the band was picking up their instruments, the shakiness was dissipating, and I found myself lost in the magic of new music.

The recording studio was always one of my favorite places to be as a kid. Once in a while, during their breaks, Rylan would hand me one of his guitars, pull up a stool next to me, and he'd teach me their new songs, or a song that he was toying with on the side. He had a few dozen written that weren't quite 7 Year Coma, but were high quality songs nonetheless. I was hoping today that he might do the same, since I was loving their newest work.

But at the break, Rylan slipped off to talk to the group of recording techs in the booth. JT and Eli went out for a smoke, and I overheard Dax remind JT to behave himself. I wouldn't have been surprised if JT returned with a black eye himself. There was no doubt that the media was still buzzing around at the door.

"He's a glutton for punishment." Lucas mumbled as he headed off toward the kitchen area. "Anyone for a refreshment?"

I shook my head. I was eyeing up the Epson. There was a melody dancing through my head and chords that were itching my fingertips. I slid onto the stool, looking around to be sure that I was alone before I let the pick hit the strings. Before long, I was humming the words softly to myself, lost in what I considered to be a beautiful song, American or otherwise, I simply enjoyed my work. Just as I was about to set the guitar down, I caught Dax heading my way. He glided smoothly over to the guitars, chose his favorite Gibson acoustic, and handed it to me.

I eyed him suspiciously. "What're you doing?" There was an embarrassed laugh in my voice, and I felt awkwardly aware of my youth at that moment.

"Just take it." He told me, then turned and lifted his Epic acoustic when I finally replaced the Epson and set his Gibson on my lap. He slid a stool up next to me, and strummed a few chords of my song. He replayed the chords over again, and nodded for me to jump in.

He smiled, giving a quick nod of approval as he kept on strumming. The song had a different twist on the Gibson, and I noticed that he had slowed the rhythm down just a bit, but it was working, as the two of us played together.

"Do we have words yet?" He asked me, putting a little more force into the chords, trying it out. "Let's hear 'em then," he ordered, adding a few notes of his own for effect.

I waited until he brought the song back to its chorus, and started there, singing quietly enough that I hoped only the two of us could hear. After the first few lines were out, I found myself looking up at him. I wanted to stop there, get his thoughts.

Instead, he answered by returning to the beginning of the chorus and singing with me this time. At the end of the chorus, he strummed heavier and harder, added a faux ending to the "song" as he knew it.

"Damn girl," he said, wiping his brow and setting his guitar back on the rack, "What have you been hiding all these years?"

I was about to answer when Lucas and Eli came back in the room, smelling of cigarette smoke and carrying on past what our voices could carry a conversation over.

"Are we going to do this or what?" Rylan burst in the room like he'd been inconvenienced by the break. "Where the fuck is JT?"

Dax shot me a wink before grabbing his Epson back off the rack and returning to his post.

THIRTY
Natalie

London's airport was absolutely packed with people. I felt as though I couldn't take two steps without being run over by a suitcase-wielding maniac. I found myself an empty spot on a hard plastic bench by the baggage claim. Back in the day, Rylan or JT would meet me here when I returned home from the States to start my summer. I'd round the corner and the moment I'd see whichever was designated to meet me, I'd run full speed at them, forcing them to either catch me or be tackled. It was a tradition I'd kept up even after I was big enough to actually knock one of them to the ground if they weren't careful.

I smiled at the memory, and watched as various others greeted their loved ones at the baggage claim. Glancing at the clock on my cell phone, it was only ten minutes before Ray-Ray's flight was due to land. The flight boards predicted an on time landing, for which I was every bit grateful. I wasn't sure how much longer I could last watching other long lost lovers reunite. I tried to imagine what it would be like when he rounded that corner. I was going to cut through that crowd like a racecar driver toward their checkered flag. He wasn't going to know what had hit him.

I was a little taken back by how fast my heart was beating. Was I nervous? Anxious? I had no reason to be, I reminded myself. This was Ray-Ray. My friend. My... boyfriend. It was the last part that did it, I imagine. That last part that made my skin glisten with subtle droplets of sweat, made my eyes tear at the corners, and made my stomach flutter with a hopeless bound of excitement that could only be described as love from the distance.

The flight had landed, according to the board. The foot traffic was heavy, and the baggage claim that belonged to his flight was beginning to turn and spit out the first few suitcases. Tired travelers, the only kind to have just come off of a seven hour flight from Philadelphia, grabbed at luggage as it made its way around and around on the belt. More and more passengers pooled around the claim, watching as the bags rolled down the ramp.

My eyes fixed on the corner of the hallway. I'd see him the second that he stepped out from behind the crowd. To pass the time, I tried to imagine what he'd be wearing. Hopefully not the lime green shirt, I thought with an audible giggle. It didn't matter, I didn't plan that it'd be on him long anyhow. I had wanted to take him out to dinner, if he was up for it, but then changed my mind and decided that maybe it was best to just bring him straight home and up to my bedroom. We had some catching up to do.

About half of the luggage had been removed, and the hallway traffic was beginning to thin out a just a bit from the off boarding rush that had just ensued. Ray-Ray's first class ticket should have let him off the plane first. I looked down at my cell phone, but there was no indication of a message. Maybe he just stopped at one of the shops, or perhaps for a drink or a bite to eat. It seemed strange that he hadn't rung to let me know, but I leaned forward a bit in my seat, sure he was only a few steps from rounding that corner.

And as the last of the bags were claimed, and the belt ran around its course empty for several minutes, it began to occur to me that the happy meeting that I had imagined wasn't going to happen as I had planned. I took a deep breath and allowed myself to stand up.

My thighs ached from sitting sedentary for so long. Slowly, I walked toward the corner, and stepped into the adjoining hallway. Sunlight poured through the windows that stretched from floor to ceiling. The people mover hummed, carrying only a passenger or two. The hallway trickled with a few people, none of who I recognized.

I tried Ray-Ray's cell, but it went straight to voicemail. I started to wonder if he had gotten lost, or missed his flight. I had no waiting voicemails on my phone. No text messages. I shoved the phone back in my purse and continued walking down the hallway until I reached the line for security check. Peering past the gates, I scanned the hallway beyond, but there was no sign of Ray-Ray.

I waited a full two hours after the plane landed before I headed for the limo that I had reserved for Ray-Ray's first trip to London. I tipped the driver and sent him on his way, then headed for the bus terminal.

THIRTY-ONE
Natalie

The neck of the guitar was resting solidly on my forehead, and I strummed sideways, mindlessly. My legs loosely circled the bottom of the guitar, and found that it was actually comfortable sitting that way on the plush living room carpet in Rylan's living room. If it weren't for the fact that my left thumb kept hitting my eyebrow as my hand slid up the fret board, the tune might have actually amounted to something. If I could have figured out how to light the fireplace without burning down the house, I might have enjoyed that as well. In fact, it might have given me an outlet to burn away any memories that I had made with Ray-Ray over the past few weeks.

I strummed even harder at the mere thought of his name. Each chord was pushed not with my hands and arms, but with my entire body, as my fingers channeled what bled out of my soul. Instinctively, my guitar turned in my arms until it cradled comfortably in my lap, and without conscious thought, the music took over with a rhythm that I had only heard before in my head. It was pouring out through my heart, through my fingers and back into my head like a cruel, vicious circle.

I never even heard Rylan enter the room. I wasn't sure how long he had been there, and I didn't care. I had seen him play his heart out on stage so many times, it didn't matter to me that just this once, he had seen me bare my soul in a musical mess. As my tears dropped over the hollow wood, I finished the song. Then, with a quick sniff, I ran the back of my wrist against my damp face, hoping to sop of some of the emotion that I had allowed to spill out. But once you pull the dam, it's that much harder to hold back the rest of the river.

"Hearts were meant to be broken, Natalie. It's how we know we're alive." My eyes met his for only a moment, and in that moment, I knew that he was no stranger to what I was feeling.

That simple statement came as a surprise to me, maybe more so than any of his lyrics I'd ever heard. My oldest brother, devoid of any emotion unless it involved a guitar or vocal ensemble, was not immune to the raw emotion of a love gone awry. I knew, for the first time, that the fuel for the fire behind his voice and his talent, came from some place real. He too had experienced gut-wrenching pain. He too had experienced grief, a loss so profound that it buckled one's knees, and he turned it into music that millions could feel, every time he walked on that stage.

I left my own misery for a moment to ponder what kind of loss could possibly result in the raw emotion that sold millions of records over the past decade and a half. It was more than simply losing a father, I knew that much. There was so much more behind his performance that was not only a mystery to his fans all across the world, it was lost upon even his own sister.

And suddenly, an unexpected guilt crept in. I felt as though I were being selfish for mourning the loss of a love that I barely had but for a brief moment in time. I would heal,

I was sure, and forget in time that Ray-Ray and I had ever had a short-lived love affair. I'd get over it and would move on, I was certain of that fact. But had Rylan? I wasn't so sure, by the way he sympathized for his little sister's failed relationship.

Rylan lit up a joint, took a quick inhale and passed it to me. "Fuck love anyway, Natalie. You're too young and have too much talent to be tied down at this stage of yer life. You get out there on tour with us, and you'll be too damn wrapped up in the life we live to be thinking about love." He leaned his head back on the seat of the couch, letting the high settle in. "Don't waste another tear on him. Save 'em for someone who wouldn't leave you sitting alone in an airport."

The sweet smell of the drug hung in the air around us. I missed these moments with Rylan where we could smoke and talk and play guitar, as we'd had so many nights when I was still in high school. And under the circumstances, I found it to be a comforting distraction. "Were you ever in love before Sammi?"

His mouth fell open before he could hide his surprise at the question. In my twenty-one years, in all of the conversations we'd ever had, we had never broached the topic of his love life.

It was a long time before he answered, and he did it after a heavy exhale of smoke. "Once. But it was a very long time ago. I was too young to know how to love the way it's meant to be done. It's a game that's meant for later in life, not when you're just barely out of your teenage years. Those years are best spent on discovering yourself, not divulging your heart into someone else's."

I looked at him inquisitively, questioning not what he said, but the integrity behind his words. His voice may have been convincing, that air of confidence that the public often mistook for arrogance, had saturated his breath. Yet the way his eyes blinked rapid fire as he spoke told a different story altogether. I had seen him mislead the media enough to know what his tell was.

And it was that very moment that I realized that if I were truly just like him, I was headed for the same fate. One day I would wake up and believe that music was all I would ever have time for. I would never love anything more. I would never feel anything more intense with any other human being than what I felt when I played my guitar or projected my voice into a microphone. Nothing could compare. It was both a gift and a curse.

With a heavy heart and a tired mind, I nodded in acceptance; not just at the idea that love - for him - was a thing of convenience, but that for me, it was just best that I stay out of it altogether. I didn't need the distraction of the raw emotions and heartache that love brought along with it. I had a career to focus on. A career that wouldn't leave me standing alone in an airport, my emotions raw, wondering if I'd ever put the pieces of my heart back together. Love could come later. Or not at all. It didn't matter to me anymore.

"Hey Ry," I told him, "I'm in. I'll sign on with Lull."

THIRTY-TWO
Rylan

You never knew what you were going to walk into when you opened the door to JT's place. By mid-morning you could find a party in full swing or leftover stragglers from the night before. Once I found the place completely devoid of life save for a bulldog - which didn't belong to JT - a kayak, and about half a dozen articles of clothing strewn all around the room.

I prepared myself for the unexpected as I stepped out of my car in his large circular drive and walked toward the front door. JT had spared no expense when he built this house. An aerial view would reveal the home's crescent shape, though from inside you could never tell. It was set off the road about a half-mile in a neighborhood that was shared by equally eclectic celebrities.

The solid mahogany door swung shut behind me, and I was greeted by the smell of wood smoke and cleaning product. I could never remember the name of the plump Russian woman who cleaned his house, though he'd brought her with him when he moved from the city a few years back.

But the old woman greeted me with a smile and I humored her by returning the hug she bestowed upon me before she shooed me off toward the living room where she said I'd find JT. "He's not doing too well, you know," she called over her shoulder. "I think he started up with the Charlie again."

I'd have thought her to be a meddling old woman except for the fact that I knew she was right. But JT was a big boy, and could hold his own. We'd all dabbled, it was no secret, but JT's emotional condition didn't always agree with the various drugs that were out there, and while I'd be the first to admit that it usually made him more tolerable to deal with, the crashes were that much worse for him.

JT was at his piano, a gorgeous baby grand that would have to be air lifted if it would ever have to leave the house. Several notebooks stood in a stack on the bench next to him, with one cocked open before him, resting on the piano and laden with scrawl. I hadn't heard a single note played since I had walked in the door, and with this piano, I'd have heard it coming up the drive.

I could tell he had something in the works though, a melody in his mind that he was carefully plotting out. He had that far off look in his eye, like he was in a place other than here, where music and words were heard not with the ears but with the soul. This was the birth of about fifty-percent of Coma's songs.

"Grab a guitar." He told me, and though he was looking at me, I wasn't quite sure he was even seeing me. His pen scratched along the paper, then he tapped the top of it rhythmically, stopped, chewed on the top, and tapped a bit more before writing everything down again.

I swung a chair around to face the piano, sinking in comfortably. There wasn't anything in JT's entire home that didn't have a soft surface. "I didn't come here to write."

"Quick." His voice held a certain impatience, and it got

the better of me. Who was I to mess with something that could possibly bring us our next big paycheck?

He began channeling the notes from his head to the keys, repeating the first few until I had a guitar on my lap and could follow along. It sounded almost like a slower version of *Strawberry Fields*, until he added a few lyrics.

Another day, another night
Gone without a second thought
Until broken shadows crossed your eyes
And night eased the pain she brought
She stood in silence behind your screams
You stood and watched her shatter dreams
All in a memory
All in a memory
She's a broken memory

It took a little more than three hours, and a complete rewrite of his lyrics, but we had a solid tune by the time he put his pen down and I set the guitar back in its stand. It would go on our next album, the second that would come out under my new record label from Coma. After that, it looked like we might take a year off from touring and recording.

I had about half a dozen other bands that were signed under my label, some of which were producing mega songs. I figured even if two or three made it big, it was a solid venture.

JT and Dax had each announced in the past six months that they wanted to produce solo albums in the coming year, while Lucas and Eli were planning families. And I couldn't escape the hints that Sammi was subtly laying track that she was ready for a break as well. I looked forward to spending some time off with her, and play "normal" as much as we could. We had a wedding to plan, after all, and I wanted her to be able to devote some time to that. And me, I'd indulge in it with her.

It had been too many years since I had been in love

with anything other than music, and music took away from the need for companionship. I dove, headfirst, into writing a song and it consumed me. At that moment heaven, if there was such a thing, collided with earth, to form the perfect consummation of sound that would echo through my ears and course through my veins to grasp a hold of my heart in a way that no woman could ever touch.

Until Sammi, love was a disaster that I hadn't been looking to repeat.

It had begun over twenty years ago, but it haunted me every day. I had met the woman fast, fell in love even faster, and nine months later learned why they made birth control so readily accessible. At least with Sammi, she was clear that she didn't want kids, so I didn't have to worry that it wasn't my intention to go down that road again. Not that it didn't work out alright in the end, but I wasn't interested in surrendering my life to nappies, and the only bottles I wanted in my future were those filled with alcohol. My career didn't allow for child-raising. Not the way that it should be done.

JT scraped a credit card against a sheet of glass on the piano bench that he was now straddling. "Celebration," he told me, as he handed me a rolled up paper bill, "for another successful million." It would most likely take two to three years before we saw that million from our song, but it would be a million nonetheless.

"Your housekeeper's got her eye on you." I told him, leaning back and letting slow burn in my sinus cavity creep into my brain as he lit up a joint, "Wouldn't be surprised if she hasn't got the press on her speed dial."

"Essi?" JT blew out a stream of smoke, "She's got some bug up her crawl. Pay no mind." For the first time since I'd arrived, the creases in his forehead released as the drugs filtered through his system.

I raised my eyebrows when I noticed he caught me staring at him. "What's up with you?"

He blinked several times, as if to clear his mind more so

than his vision. I tried to ignore the fact that he was tapping his foot less than rhythmically on the carpet, and tried even harder not to let it drive me to a slow insanity.

"My missus is gone. Won't be around anymore."

He said it with a sullen casualty that I would have thought this had happened months ago had I not seen her only last week hanging all over him. I thought maybe he was just taking the piss, so I shrugged it off as a joke. "Ran off with a roadie, did she?"

The hard glare he gave me told me that I had hit the nail on the head, and I felt a bit guilty as I realized the impact of this on him. "Two nights ago," was the only explanation that he offered. His foot stopped tapping and he switched to chewing on a fingernail, a rare habit that he reserved only for the presence of those of us who knew him best. JT was nothing if not particular about how people saw him. I was sure it took a great deal of energy out of him, which he had to spare, to keep track of his public self versus his actual persona.

I mumbled a quick apology at him, then asked, "Did you get an explanation?"

"Didn't need one. Stepped on the bus and found 'em goin' at it on couch."

I raised my eyebrows. "Didn't see that one coming."

He looked away, and resigned from any kind of neurotic body movements. Perhaps I should have been the one to give him advice, being as I was the older brother, but I didn't feel qualified for the role given my own history. The two of us were on our own when it came to figuring these things out.

But I wasn't immune to his pain, or how it felt when your heart hit the ground after a fall from a thirty-story building. I felt for him, knowing that he thought he really loved this woman.

Over the course of the past fifteen years that we had been touring, JT had hundreds of women. He'd had a few girlfriends as well, none lasting longer than a year, and none serious enough to move in with. I always assumed it had more to do with our lifestyle than anything else, and we never talked about it. Our band mates up and got married and maintained their relationships both on and off the road, but until Sammi, it wasn't the life I wanted to live, and I've always assumed that it wasn't for JT either.

I looked up at JT. "It's nothing you need to worry about now. We'll focus on the rest of the tour and the next album..."

He cut me off abruptly. "Fuck her." He pulled a pack of cigarettes from his jacket pocket and offered me one, which I took. He lit up right there in the house, took a sharp drag, and let the smoke flow easily through his lips.

He had already moved on.

THIRTY-THREE
Natalie

We had practiced for hours, every single day for an entire
month. But truth be told, we could have used the practice
even in the time that we had taken off, which seemed to be
only to sleep and eat and occasionally swing by a bar or club.
It wasn't even the music that we had to get right. The songs,
they were easy enough, which pissed me off considerably
since we were opening for one of Britain's top bands. We
lacked the chemistry that made a band great. Lee and I fought
like an old married couple, which was ironic because the rest
of the band revealed to me one night over drinks that Lee was
gay.

The whole idea of Lee's sexuality didn't surprise me,
but it did piss me off that he didn't feel forthcoming enough to
tell me himself. Was it supposed to be a big secret? I had
heard that sometimes band's managers forced band members
to hide their sexuality so that they could market themselves to
the female audience, but with Lee, it seemed to all be self-
induced just to produce the drama that he loved to envelope

himself in.

"Maybe you could change his mind, Natalie." Jasp suggested. He wasn't looking at me when he said this, he was looking to my right, and when I glanced over my shoulder, there was a blonde in a mini bending over the pool table so far that her thong rode up to her damn chin.

I snapped my fingers at him, drawing his attention back to my eyes. "Let me say this only once. If you ever suggest such a preposterous notion again, you'll be playing bass with the strings tied around your bollocks."

I firmly believed that sexuality was not chosen by you but chosen for you, long before you were birthed into this crazy world in which we lived. It was no more a choice than the color of one's eyes. My issue with Lee was deeper than sex. It was his attitude; his core being as a person. I distained those who treated others with malice, especially when one of those people was me.

Jasp only rolled his eyes at the empty threat and finished off his beer. I had to smile, thinking for a moment that he reminded me of Ray-Ray in a strange way. Not the most recent version of Ray-Ray that I said goodbye to back in the States, or the new version of Ray-Ray that in my mind I both loathed and missed dreadfully. It was the best friend version of Ray-Ray that I found myself missing even more than the romantic Ray-Ray. And it was this version of Ray-Ray that I found similarities of in Jasp. I groaned at the thought of any version Ray-Ray. The pain was still there, even though months had gone by. It wasn't any easier to think of Ray-Ray now than it was the night that I came home from the airport.

I quickly forced myself to conjure up thoughts about our tour, which started in the morning, in a last-ditch effort to keep my mind from sinking into depths of depression and gloom. We'd be flying out of London for Amsterdam, and from Amsterdam to Germany. From there, it'd be seven weeks on the road, followed by three weeks at home, and another seven weeks on the road before the tour ended in Japan. I was excited about being on the road again, though this time, I'd have my own band to be touring with, and it would be work, not fun, like back in the days when I rode along with my brothers' band. At least I got along okay with these two, I decided.

I looked over at Steve, who was eyeing up the bartender, a cute brunette with cleavage that could swallow a man whole. "Just go talk to her." I reached into my back pocket and threw a few crumbled up paper bills at him. "Here, go order me a drink."

His gaze fell back to me for only a moment, testing to see if I was serious, then he took my money and stood up. As he left, Lee came sauntering in and took his drummer's seat. He wore an arrogant smile, and his skin glistened with a coating of sweat. He eyed me up and down, then turned to Jasp without so much as a further acknowledgment in my direction. "So Jazzy, did you score anything good to take on our road trip?"

I had too much of JT's pride not to let someone blatantly push my buttons. "Yeah, Jazzy. If we're gonna play with the big boys, we better be able to score some good shit."

Jasp bit back a laugh, and flashed me a warning look while Lee was busy glaring me under the table.

"Don't be such a bitch." Lee hissed, to which I responded only by rolling my eyes, a reaction that I wasn't even aware of until he started to flip out. "You know, there's something to be said about nepotism. Maybe you should just take your Martin guitar and go home to the States, you wanna-be Yankee bitch."

Jasp wanted to interject, and put his hand in front of Lee, who was now standing up and acting like he was going to come at me. If I had no self-control, I'd have been laughing. Lee was about as scary to me as one of those ankle dogs that barked a lot, but you could step on like a bug if you really wanted to.

"My Martin is back in the States where it's safe, so don't worry." I wasn't sure if he was trying to insult the fact that I had resided in the States for most of my life, or the fact that I had money. Either way, I wasn't letting him get one insult in unanswered. "Although I could always borrow your brother's, since that's what he plays on stage." I slid to the end of the booth and started toward the bar to get another drink, since Steve had apparently forgotten why I sent him up there in the first place. I couldn't help but add, "Quality guitar though. You should try it sometime."

From behind me, I heard Lee shouting, "Leave my brother out of this! You don't know *shit* about my brother!"

I took a seat at the bar, thinking that was rather funny since I probably knew Lucas better than he did. *This was going to be an interesting tour.* As I was glancing down the bar for a bartender that wasn't wrapped up in getting my band mate's phone number, I happened to spot Dax sitting on a bar stool about seven over from me. My eyes scanned the rest of the bar, but I saw no sign of my brothers or the rest of their band.

Since I wasn't being waited on yet anyway, I slipped myself in between Dax and the person at the bar stool immediately next to him. "The last guy I asked to buy me a drink got the bartender's phone number instead."

A smile quickly crossed his face and he wrapped an arm around my waist, pulling me close to him. I was enveloped in the immediate sudden warmth that was radiating off of him, and the not too subtle scent of his expensive cologne. It was a new cologne, I noticed, and it worked for him. "Doll, I'd never do that to ya." He held out a crisp bill toward one of the bartenders. "Make it a double, Kelly."

My eyebrows raised with mock impression. "First name basis already? The relationship's only what, a half hour old?"

"Twenty minutes," Dax said, matter-of-factly, his accent strong, "And its already going better than my marriage."

Wincing a bit, I took the bar stool that opened up on the other side of him. "Sorry to hear about you and Jules. I mean that Dax." The news that the two had separated came just a few days prior. It had been long rumored that Dax wanted to see other women, but that had been a complete fabrication by the media, founded on more than the stories they wanted to sell and the stories the public wanted to read. The two had tried very hard to make the news of their separation a private affair, but as many things with the band go, everything was subject to public scrutiny or approval. And with that came the media and their lies. The truth was, as Dax had relayed it to us at Rylan's place the night after they made the mutual decision to split, was that Jules was tired of touring, and wanted to settle down and start a family. Dax didn't want to give up touring, and certainly did not want to raise children on the road. It had been an ongoing battle for years now, he confessed, over an open bottle of Glenfiddich.

Rylan was somewhat less than supportive, and did a fine job in convincing his friend that the split was for the better. By the time Dax left Rylan's place in the early morning hours the night it had happened, he was sold on the fact that marriage was an institution that was not only completely unnecessary, but confining to the creative spirit and constricting of the musical soul. The experience of love and loss would bring him back closer to who he truly was inside, and he should thank the heavens that he wasn't longer vested in the relationship, lest he be forced to dig himself out of a deeper spiritual deficit. The second Dax left, Rylan and I had gotten into it pretty heavily.

"Are you fucking mental?" I'd shouted, shoving him a bit harder than I'd originally intended. "You're engaged, last I'd heard..."

His eyes had widened and he had put up his hand to block any further attacks. "And I still am, a'ight? It was simply said to help him get past these next few months. Nothing more..."

"'Love will suck the life out of you and leave you bleeding on the street?' Those were your exact words, Rylan Caleb Porter. I hope to God that you're not writing your own marriage vows."

"It's all relative, Love. You'll find this as you go on in life. There'll be times when your heart's been beaten down and trampled upon by someone that you loved and trusted, and you'll wonder why you'd ever bothered with it to begin with. It takes a lot out of you – heartbreak. It's a right bitch." He finished off his glass and set it on the marble top counter. The morning sun was peeking through the blinds all along the side of the house, and even through his tired eyes, I could see that he was more serious than he'd been all night. "But when it's right, it's the most amazing thing you'll ever experience. When you can put your trust in someone entirely, and they in you, well then, that's a thing of beauty right there, innit?"

Dax took a long, slow sip of his liquor. "This life just ain't for everyone, ya know?"

I gave him a half smile, wanting to tell him that I didn't necessarily agree with what Rylan had told him the other night. I wanted to assure him that if he truly tried hard enough, he and Jules would be able to make it work. But I was pretty sure that Dax only saw me as his best friend's kid sister, not someone who could offer any kind of substantial advice or guidance, just inexperienced opinions based on nothing more than girlish fantasies about how I surmised love to be. After all, Dax had lived those dreams. He had been married, had been in love, and by all accounts, probably still was.

And suddenly, I wanted to change the subject. The thought of being caught in a conversation about love with Dax made me shift uneasily. Even the prospect of offering that he'd find new love, if not in Kelly the bartender, but from some other viable source, seemed disconcerting at the moment.

Dax's eyes looked tired, but still bright. As a kid, I always thought that Dax had happy eyes. When he smiled, they lit up the room. It was hard to find the guy in a bad mood, which was substantial considering my brothers were his best friends. Those two alone when they got to quarreling over something were enough to drive anyone mad. But Dax held up better than the others with them on tour, maintaining his constant good spirit.

"What time does our flight take off tomorrow?" I tried to gracefully hide the fact that whatever drink Dax had ordered me burned my tongue and my throat, and was now causing an inferno in my stomach. I glanced quickly at him to see if he noticed, but he didn't seem to be paying attention. Maybe Kelly was distracting him slightly, as she was bending over to reach a bottle on the bottom shelf.

He answered me without missing the show. "Eight a.m. Which makes sleep tonight pointless if we have to be at the airport at six." After a quick glance at his watch, he followed, "Five more hours of fun. Then we're back on the clock."

I couldn't help but smile. "So are you hanging out in the pub until then or are you going back home?"

Dax shrugged. "Ry's place is closer to the airport than mine, so I'll probably just follow your lead, Love." As he said this, I was subtly aware that his smile was sweet and soft all at the same time. I wasn't sure what it was about him that just sucked me in every time, but whatever it was held me to him. Maybe it was that girlhood crush that I had retained, pining after a rock star that I had no chance in hell with, but secretly imagined that those eyes sought out only mine in the audience of thousands.

By the time I got around to saying goodbye, Jasp and Steve had invited themselves to come back to Rylan's place with us. We settled into the living room, experimented with breaking decibel records on Rylan's top of the line stereo system, and cracked open the liquor cabinet to finish off the night. Steve and Jasp were utterly impressed by Rylan's place. But the novelty wore off quickly, and soon we were divulged in corrupt conversation and frequent bouts of marijuana-inspired laughter.

Sitting next to Dax on the couch, I was ignoring the fact that every time I laughed, I moved just a little closer to him, until eventually I felt his outstretched arm encircle me and pull me in against him. Either Jasp and Steve weren't in any mental condition to notice, or it just didn't faze them, but inside I was silently freaking out. On one level, this could be no more than a friendly embrace, but everything inside of me was telling me otherwise.

I tried to ignore the fact that the warmth of his body and the smell of his aftershave were inviting me closer. I needed to not delve into the thoughts that guitar players had strong hands and eager fingers. And the feeling of his digging into my shoulder muscles in a seductive massage that I swore bore a rhythm to that song we had spontaneously created back at the recording studio not so long ago wasn't helping either.

I needed to move. I needed to find a way out of this, and quick. The last thing I needed was to get involved with Dax. It would only complicate the tour, not to mention his situation with Jules.

"I'm going to bed." The announcement forced itself from my lips before I could compose a more plausible exit. It wasn't graceful, but it had worked.

Dax wished me good night with a wink. I sent back a quick wave and fled up the stairs, cursing myself the entire way for acting like a teenager on her first date. *Lame*, I convinced myself, *I was acting like a damn child...*

It was the first time in months that I had thought of a guy in any sense other than strictly platonic. And even then, I felt as though I were cheating on Ray-Ray in some distorted sense. How he even had any business lingering in my heart was beyond me. He should've been properly exorcised the moment that the plane that he failed to board took off out of London airport. Yet in the decade that I had known him, the fact that I had grown to love him on so many levels was not as easily erased as I'd have wished it to be.

My door clicked shut behind me, and I looked around my empty room, relieved to be alone. On tour, there'd be precious few moments of alone time. Scanning my room briefly for anything I may have forgotten to pack, my eyes fell to the back of the open closet, and set upon the box that now sat there uncovered. The box that belonged to Hannah Kaplan.

I shouldn't, I told myself. I should slip the box in Rylan's office downstairs before we leave. It wasn't my business. But so many years of having lived in the hell that was Hannah and Leo's made it my business.

I pulled slowly at the tape. The flaps of the box fell open, revealing neatly packed contents. A music box, one that I remembered used to sit on Hannah's dresser, was placed sideways near the top. Some figurines, carved from wood and shaped like whales, had been wrapped carefully in tissue paper and bubble wrap. There was a photo album, one that I remembered used to sit high on a shelf in the living room. I remembered Hannah showing it to me once. It had old pictures, edges frayed and color faded, of Hannah when she was a young girl, of her parents and grandparents, all who had already passed before her. And wrapped in more tissue were some framed pictures. These I'd never seen before. The one on top caught my eye instantly.

It was a woman in the hospital, looking exhausted and haggard just after childbirth, holding a newborn baby who was peacefully sleeping on her chest. The woman resembled Hannah so much so that I had to blink several times to clear my eyes. Hannah's mother? The picture seemed so much more recent and brighter than the pictures in the album. *It couldn't be*, I rationalized. And Hannah didn't have any sisters, she was an only child. But the face was unmistakably Hannah's face. Just as I remembered her, perhaps a bit younger.

Hannah had a child? Perhaps something had happened to the baby? Had she given the child up for adoption?

Remembering the years I'd spent with Hannah and Leo, that baby was far better off, no matter what the outcome. Surely Leo wouldn't have bestowed upon his own child what he'd done to me. But I wouldn't have put it past him either. And Hannah had known what he'd been doing all those years. She'd seen my tears, the bruises, heard my muffled screams in the middle of those nights. And yet she'd done nothing to protect me. Nothing to stop him.

I ran my fingers over the glass covering the baby's face. Yes, that baby was far better off without her.

THIRTY-FOUR

Rylan

It wasn't my first time playing in Amsterdam, though I had to admit, I couldn't remember any of the last three times we'd played here. The most recent was at least five years ago, perhaps more, and fuck it if I hadn't spent the better part of those years in a haze. I'd either have been hung over or buzzing off of whatever powder had found its way into our dressing room before the show. So Amsterdam was like a whole new country to me.

Sammi mentioned something about tulips, and I tried to counter offer with canal boats. They weren't really quite my thing either, but it sounded a little more exciting than looking at flowers.

"No boats." Sammi was lying in my bed, her head propped up on pillows and nursing a bottle of water. In all the years I'd known her, I hadn't seen her sick once, but she'd been looking quite pale since the moment she stepped into my hotel room.

I held my gaze on her a moment longer, deciding she looked a bit too ill to argue with, then turned to the closet. As I pulled my jeans on, I turned back to Sammi. "We can go see the lilies if you want to." I crawled into the bed next to her, and she rolled onto her side, sliding her porcelain fingers along my bare chest.

"Tulips," she corrected, her voice murmuring as she buried her face into my shoulder and curled up against me, "Amsterdam has a lovely Tulip Museum."

My hand slid into the small of her back, holding her against me. There was nothing more peaceful to me than holding her in my arms, such a calm serenity that baked warmth over the two of us as we lay on top of the cushioned satin-lined hotel comforter. I would lay here all day with her if she'd let me.

I brushed my cheek over hers, enjoying the soft of her skin against mine. But the enjoyment was short-lived, and she sat abruptly, running her hands through her hair. She looked like she was about to get sick. I sat up quickly, just in case.

But she regained her composure, drawing in a deep breath. Her green eyes turned up to meet mine, and I knew right then and there. Before she ever even said the words. All of it slammed together in my mind faster than I could comprehend the meaning of the words.

"I'm pregnant."

THIRTY-FIVE
Natalie

Our tour started off with a bang. Literally. The stagehand who was assigned to my guitars dropped my new Epic right out of the case. If he had muttered even one apology, I wouldn't have minded so much, but every time thereafter that I saw the bruise just below the body, it brought me back to that day.

We were playing at Heineken Music Hall, the first of two sold out concerts in Amsterdam to lead off the tour. Arriving at the stadium in early afternoon for sound check, we had ample opportunity to check the place out while it was empty.

Our band's name was printed in bold typeset on a white sheet of paper and taped to our dressing room door. Steve snapped a few pictures of the thing, then made us all pose next to it before we went in.

Lee had burst through the door like he was on fire, jumped up and ran across the sofa, crashing into the cement wall on the other side. Jasp followed in similar fashion, letting out an excited shout as he did. I smiled at the two of them, shaking my head as Steve came up behind me and grabbed me around the waist, swinging me in the direction of the back room. "If you need us," he told the other two, "don't bother. We'll be busy."

"Benefits of having a chick in the band..." Jasp called back to him.

I wriggled my way free. "We're on tour for one day and you're already throwing Megan out the window?" Hell, I thought sadly, it was probably for the better if he had. Love didn't seem to be a concept our lot could maintain on the road.

He gave me a gentle push back in the direction of the sofa. "Nah, I'll wait until next week maybe."

While the guys dove in to the stocked mini-refrigerator, I stole away to go check out the stage. From here, the arena looked larger than it did from the audience. I had seen Coma play here several times before, and it never ceased to amaze me how many people you could pack onto a football field.

Our instruments were already set up, awaiting our upcoming sound check. I ran my hand along my Les Paul, one of the two guitars I had sitting on stands over on the left side of the stage.

"There's something to be said for instrument selection." I heard Dax's voice come from behind me. "It says a lot about a woman."

"Or a guy." I nodded toward the Gibson he had hanging from the strap around his neck. Glancing down, he returned a laugh, pulling up a stool.

The first few chords that came through the speakers struck me as oddly familiar, and it wasn't until he repeated them that I was able to recognize them as my song. My song, the one that I had played for him at the recording studio a few weeks prior, transformed slightly into a slower version of its previous self, but my song none the less.

"What is this?" I laughed, as he played along.

He looked up and smiled, finishing a few more notes before responding, "Every time I see you, this tune pops into my head."

I strummed along with him, getting lost in the familiar melody that we began to create. Dax nodded in my direction. "That's good, let's slow down the pace a little. Just like that."

Getting into it, I started to hum along, throwing in some of the lyrics that I had held back the last time we played. Dax picked up quickly on the backup while I sang, and jumped in to take the lead vocals on the chorus. Then he stopped suddenly. "We should be writing this down."

"It's pretty good."

"I don't have a pen or paper."

A smile formed on my lips. "We'll just have to remember it then. It's bound to be a hit."

"You'll be famous, Love."

"*We'll* be famous." I corrected him.

I laughed, whole-heartedly, and enjoyed the feeling of the crisp air flowing in and out of my lungs freely. Dax had that effect on me, making me feel like nothing else in the world really mattered other than the here and now. It was a place that I wished I could always be in my life. Here and now. After all, wasn't that what it was all about? Why worry about the future when we weren't there yet? I didn't need to constantly plan out every little detail of my life, sometimes, I just needed to live in the moment and enjoy it for what it was worth.

"Come on." He reached out his hand for mine.

Inquisitively, I stared back, but only for a moment, before my fingers interlaced with his.

"Take that look off your face," he told me, "we're getting some coffee and writing this down before it slips our minds."

I laughed again, pulling my hand back. "I've got sound check in a half hour."

"I'll have ya back in plenty of time, Love. We're just

going across the street."

'Across the street' led into down the block, on the train and into a small pub crafted in heavy stone, the kind that protected you from a hard, cold winter. A woman in a beret, leaning heavily on a thick bearded man in an overcoat, laughed heartily as her eyes adjusted to the sun when the pair of them stepped onto the cobblestone outside the pub.

Dax caught the heavy wooden door in his free hand, and led me into the dim light with the other.

THIRTY-SIX
Rylan

There weren't enough pain-killers in the world to squelch the ache that resounded behind my eyes and shot down the back of my neck. It was stress-induced, nothing more. I hadn't touched any alcohol in twenty-four hours, for fear that it would cloud my judgment.

Sammi's revelation had me spinning. I couldn't deny it. I couldn't accept it. I was caught in a world spinning out of control beneath me, and I wanted to take the next exit off. I found myself at every quiet moment losing my breath, my chest caving heavily at the thought of how my life and career were very quickly going down the toilet. Everything that I'd worked over the past two decades was about to end. Everything I'd given up along the way was for nothing.

How could I have let this happen? I had spent my entire adulthood being beyond careful. One slip up, *one*, and this is my punishment?

How the hell were we going to raise a baby with this

kind of a lifestyle? It wasn't possible. Babies didn't belong on tour busses, or growing up in hotels. And the media would be all over it the second this slipped out. There was no way Sammi, for as good as she was at public relations, could cover this. And her career was officially over. I couldn't have her doing all of what she did for us while carrying a child. *My child.* I didn't think I could ever get used to thinking that way.

Hell, last time I hadn't the privilege of the nine months prior to prepare for a baby.

I shut out those thoughts as quickly as they entered my mind. I couldn't let what happened decades ago cloud my decisions today. That was a lifetime ago. Things were different now. I was older. My career was stable. I had no excuses this time around.

I pressed my palms against my temples, wishing I could crush the pain away. I couldn't think any longer about it. It was beginning to make more than just my head hurt. My entire body was aching with tensed muscles. I needed to focus on what I could control. Hard as that may be.

I was on the brink of firing Lull full stop at any given moment. They were a detriment to my good name, and even as the reviews were pouring in on Coma - and for Christ's sake, even Lull's opener – Lull was still tanking out at every show.

Not to mention that the little rat of a lead singer had been caught red-handed making out at an after-party with a stagehand on the first night we played in Italy. "Just come out with it." I told him when I had caught him without his band mates. I had enough secrets in my own personal life, I didn't need someone else's skeletons clouding my profession. "I don't have the patience or the resources to cover for you at every turn."

He promptly cursed me out before storming back to his hotel room, a sullen tail between his legs. He'd get over it. Or he wouldn't. It mattered none to me. My concern was simply for the success of his band, and the return of investment that I should be seeing back in my bank account.

But for what it was worth, I knew that I was partially to blame for the band's lack of success. I had thrown Natalie in, completely unprepared, hoping she'd hold her head above water, but having the distinct displeasure in watching her sink miserably, musically speaking. She'd needed a few months more practice before she was tour ready, but we didn't have the luxury of those precious weeks. As a result, I'd set her up for failure.

It was no wonder that she was missing, or late, for sound checks. She'd slipped into the last one fifteen minutes before the band was wrapping up, claiming that she had lost track of time. I had been sitting in the back of the arena, trying to gauge what it was about this band that had me continuing to fund them, almost entirely, and open for my band when they weren't fit to be an opener's opener. But the answer was summed up in one word: Natalie.

I had always tried to protect her, whenever I could, from the emotional roller coaster that her life could easily become. Not one for being outwardly emotional myself, I tried to instill a sense of rationale within her, and had always tried my best to model self-control when it came to matters of the heart. Hers could be easily shattered - like glass on a train station floor - and if it sucked the very life out of me, I was going to keep her from having to experience that pain ever again. I had let her down once, I'd be damned if I was going to do it again.

So maybe there were secrets. So what? Didn't she deserve a sense of peace in her life now? The truth would only tear her apart, possibly far beyond what I had seen lying on the floor at Waterloo so many years ago.

It was a delicate balance.

The moment the headache subsided enough that I could focus my vision without the overwhelming nausea, I stepped out of my hotel room and headed toward hers.

If I worked with her at every breaking moment, she just

might come around enough that she could pull this band up to where they needed to be. I just needed to get her to see that all she needed was some concentration and some inspiration, and she'd be there.

As my knuckles tapped her door, I considered for a moment that perhaps I should have called her first. She might have been out, shopping or doing whatever it was that kept women busy when they weren't busy. But the rustling and hushed voices on the other side of the door told me otherwise. I waited for another brief moment before knocking quite a bit louder. Common sense should've kicked in to tell me to head back to my room, and in retrospect, that would have been my best option.

"Natalie." It came out a bit more forward than I would have liked.

I found her sing-song response of "Just a sec…" somewhat like the effect of an out-of-tune guitar, and it made my skin crawl with icy bumps. The fact that it was taking a lot more rustling, a few more whispers, and another thirty-seconds to open the door had me really going - so much so that by the time she pulled the door open, I was practically walking through it anyhow.

"What's going on here?" I immediately started walking through her suite like I had all of the time in the world.

The room was practically pitch black with the heavy shades pulled shut, the bed sheets and comforter were falling to the floor, and an Epson Acoustic was propped up on the armchair.

Other than that, the place was completely in order, which was what I'd expected from her. We'd shared the family gene of OCD, if there was such a gene – fuck if I knew – but we both had it enough that nothing in our lives could be out of order. Beds were made shortly after exiting them, pillows aligned systematically and sheets tucked with hospital-bed precision. It was a horrendous way to live, particularly for a rock star, but I'd learned to adapt enough to let the hotel staff tend to the empty bottles, cigarette butts and the rest the day after a show.

Natalie didn't try to hide the appalled tone in her voice. "I'm composing," she snapped, and her eyes followed me as I poked my head into the kitchenette. "Can I help you find something?"

Turning to face her, I said, "Who else is in here with you?"

She didn't answer. She stood there, her hair still tossed from sleep, in a tank top, pajama shorts and bare feet. I wasn't buying the 'composing' bit for a second, even though I'd known for years that both she and I did our best composing both upon waking and just before bed. That too was apparently genetic.

"I heard voices. You're not alone. Who else is here?"

She didn't need to respond, as my eye caught the neck of a second guitar propped up behind the armchair. A Les Paul Semi-Acoustic, in cherry wood. I knew that guitar very well. I had given it to Dax two years prior, during our 'Wrecked and Bothered' tour.

My eyes went from the guitar back to hers, only for a moment. I expected a rash of excuses, perhaps some pleading, none of which I got. I couldn't pinpoint if that fueled my anger, or if it kept me from exploding into the bathroom, the only other place that he could be hiding out of sight.

"We're working on a *song*, Rylan. We're not sleeping together."

The mere sound of those words in the air were enough to make my fists clench and my face burn. *"You're a child,"* I wanted to say to her, *"And he's my age. Of course you're not..."* But the realization came crashing into my head quicker than I would have liked. She was twenty-one years old. *By the time I was twenty-one I'd already had a four-year-old child.* I quickly dashed the thought from my mind. It wasn't something I wanted to dwell on right now, not when my best friend's guitar was sitting in Natalie's suite.

I turned without a word and flung the door shut behind me with such force that the hallway shook, and adjoining doors rattled. It was the first time in my life I believed a spin from a tabloid.

THIRTY-SEVEN
Natalie

Once again, I found myself pouring my heart out before our sound check ever started. Playing with my own band, there was a reserve that I found to be holding me back slightly more than during any of the times I'd played with Coma. But I found the time before the sound check to be relaxing and freeing, enough to give me the outlet that I so desperately sought these days. I was lost somewhere in between chords or my own voice as I stood in Lee's position at the front of the stage. It was most familiar to me, being in the front. It was here that I could confess my innermost emotions to my empty audience, purging my inhibitions before actually appearing onstage in front of the thousands who would show up early for the real deal. Our band was just background noise for those who wanted to get a good buzz in when 7 Year Coma hit the stage.

I wasn't aware as my hand moved across the fret board, the vibrations from the strings pressing into the first few layers of skin, and my vocal chords stretching to reach notes

that I hadn't thought I could reach before, that my audience
had grown by one. In my head, I was hearing my drums
behind me, my bass player to my right, and my lead guitarist
off to my left.

The music was mine, and mine alone. Every note
belonged to me. And I found myself confessing, as my voice
projected through the empty arena, and my guitar strings
played into the abyss. My soul emptied into the vacant seats,
letting go of my longing for Ray-Ray. I was content - for that
moment - in that it had ended. I didn't have answers; I didn't
have truth. But I had that moment. I had love, and I held it
once, before it was gone. And I let it go. Out through the
music. The melody carried that pain across the open air and
let it fall out into the empty crowd before me.

It was just me, alone, with my music and my soul.

But as my song came to an end, and I reached for my
now warming bottle of water next to my amp, my eye caught
a glimpse of Lee walking toward the stage from behind the pit
seats, far off to my left. He lifted himself onstage, and with a
cocky swagger, sauntered across the wooden stage planks
toward me. I braced for a snide comment that never came.

Instead, he stood about five feet from me, his head
slightly cocked to one side, almost as though he were seeing
me for the first time ever. With my guitar still hanging from
its strap around my neck, I dabbed the sweat from my face.

Lee stretched out his hand to me. "Lee Mason. Want
to play in my band?"

He had forgone the eyeliner that would no doubt be
adorning his eyes later that evening. He still had a fair
amount of metal pierced into various places on his head, but
only wore a simple white t-shirt with a plain black logo on it,
and un-ripped jeans that were covering his black metal toe
boots. His hair was wet, as though he had just emerged from
the shower, and not like usual, when it was coated it mouse
and gel, enough to stand it up into the spiky mess that was his
social presence. Instead, it was simply hanging on his

forehead and ears, curling just a bit at the ends. With the scowl missing from his face, I actually found myself thinking that he wasn't all that bad looking.

I wondered what had brought him out of his hotel room in such loose form, but didn't ask. Instead, I removed my guitar strap and placed the instrument gently down on the stage as I began flipping switches on the amplifier.

Lee readjusted his microphone as I took another long drink of my water. It was going to be a hot night, judging by amount of sweat I had already lost. I desperately needed a shower even before our sound check, and was about to head in that direction when Lee wondered aloud, "Where's that girl when we're playing on stage?"

I shot a quick glance in his direction. "I play the same no matter where I am." There was an air of indignation, perhaps stubbornness to my voice, that I wasn't able to hold back before it came out that way.

Before I turned my attention back to my own equipment, I saw him shake his head. "Not from what I just saw a few minutes ago, you don't. There's a bit missing when you're up on stage with my band."

As much as he probably hadn't meant to, there was a slight emphasis on the last two words. Therein lied the animosity between us, I realized. It would always be Lull, and maybe that was the crux of our problem. In essence, I wanted my own band. He had what I had wanted all along. No, I corrected myself. I wanted what Rylan had. But at least Lee was well on his way. I was only his backup, and as long as I was in his band, that's all I would ever be. But if Lee could see a difference, then so could everyone else. And that included Rylan, the one person that I wanted to believe in me the most. Though it seemed now as though our relationship was straining more and more with each passing day.

The show that night proved to be just as lack-luster as

the others to date. We seemed to fall flat at every turn, our timing was still amazingly off, and though we received cheers from our audience, I wasn't so convinced that they weren't just patronizing us.

The rest of my band headed back to our dressing room, and I swung by Coma's, as they waited for the stage crew to finish the set change. The air backstage prior to a show was intense. On the other side of the closed door to their room, crew was running around chaotically, trying to ensure that every little detail was tended to. The door to the band's room was constantly swinging on its hinges. Still, the guys lounged about, smoking, drinking, laughing, and gearing up for the show.

While I sat on the overstuffed couches with the rest of the band, JT buzzed about the room, air drumming on Eli's head, tipping over a folding chair, smoking a cigarette, or singing in his best imitation of a Spanish symphony that he could muster. Rylan was doing his best to ignore him, and nodded over in my direction. "Rough night again?" He didn't need to tell me that he had been watching. I had seen him stage side, just out of sight of the audience.

I raised my eyebrows and exhaled a long stream of smoke, but didn't answer him. Instead, I turned my attention back to JT, who was shadow boxing a little too close to the door, and had just about clocked Sammi as she came in to report that there were three minutes left before they were due onstage.

"I'll work with you on Wednesday," Rylan informed me dryly, as he stood to stretch and get ready to go on stage himself. "Get you to where you need to be."

I nearly choked on my cigarette. "I'm sorry?" I was hoping I hadn't heard him right. I sat there, too shocked to move, watching him swing his arms back and forth as he walked around the makeshift coffee table in front of the couch.

"It's alright Natalie, sometimes we all get in a slump.

We just practice a little harder and work our way out of it."
He gave me a quick wink before disappearing out into the
hallway.

A fire was burning in my chest, one that I couldn't calm
with the melted ice-water-and-lemon that I had been sipping
for the past fifteen minutes that I had been off stage. A rare
lump was forming in the back of my throat, followed by an
undeniable pressure behind my eyes, and I squeezed my eyes
shut hard to fight back the tears.

It didn't matter to me that the entire audience wasn't all
that engaged. That could be easily tossed off on Lee's over
stimulation, or Jasp's tendency to be slightly off count with
Steve's superfluously loud hammering of innocent drum
skins. But the fact that Rylan was calling me out cut me to the
core. And I was sure it had everything to do with him finding
Dax in my room. He was simply misdirecting it at my music.

After all, hadn't he taught me everything I knew? At
five years old, I was playing chords that rivaled most of what
even the best bands today could produce. Whether it was
genetics or coaching left open-ended questions, but there had
never been any doubt that I had an undeniable talent that
most could only dream of. And Rylan had molded that talent
into something spectacular, from an early age. Years later,
when I was in the States, he still served as my role model,
providing me a level of talent that I would strive for.

It was killing me to think that he saw less than himself
in my performance. And while a part of me wanted to stick
around to confront him about it after the show, the rest of me
knew that this was his show tonight, not mine, and as both an
artist and his sister, I knew better than to squelch his post-
show high with melodramatics. These things could be settled
Wednesday, in a neutral forum.

Dax was the last one out. "Ignore him, Nat. He's twice
as hard as that on himself. It's just the way he's wired." He
was leaning over the back of the couch, his face only inches
from mine, smelling like proper sex, drugs and rock and roll.

He almost made me want to go out there and watch him play tonight. But when he leaned in and brushed his lips against mine, every decent thought I had rushed out of my head.

Sure, it wasn't anything that he hadn't done before. Theoretically, I had kissed all of the guys in the band. They were my family. But there was something about the way his mouth lingered just a bit longer than it ever had when I was growing up. There was something more to that particular kiss that made me realize all too much that I wasn't twelve years old anymore.

Before he slipped through the door, he gave me a quick wink and told me, "See you after the show."

THIRTY-EIGHT
Rylan

Sammi's hands had barely touched me all night, yet I was finding myself seconds away from slipping away from the party and into my bedroom with her at the slightest of glances. She was buzzing about, as though she were hosting the party herself. Occasionally she'd have difficulty punching out of the proverbial time clock, which seemed to be the case tonight.

She hadn't yet begun to show, and was still able to pull off the figure-hugging short dresses that I loved so much. Tonight it was one that dipped deep into her cleavage and hung loosely just above her mid-thigh that when she walked I could imagine the material giving way with each step to reveal what I knew was a perfectly tight ass.

I finally caught her around the waist, when she stepped close enough, swinging her around so that her face settled in only inches from mine, and despite her disproving stare, slipped a quick kiss on her cherry flavored lips. The kitchen was empty at the moment, but she shifted uncomfortably. "Ry..."

I had a hard time letting her go, but she had a convincing tone to her voice. It was important to her reputation that our personal life and business didn't mix. And though this was only a private party, there were enough people outside of our immediate circle crammed into my hotel room tonight to make this "business" for her. And considering myself a professional as well, I respected her wishes. As hard as it was sometimes.

A low growl escaped my lips, and she responded with a quick wink and a less than subtle swing of her hips as she carried two full glasses with her back into the general area of my hotel suite. I settled on a sip of Siglo de Oro and let it warm my tongue before swallowing. A cold shower might have been preferable at the moment, but the liquor did the trick.

Stepping back into the main room, I was beginning to wish that we would have parties in someone else's suite. It would take all night to clear everyone out of here, and I didn't know the half of them. Most of them belonged to my openers, and I had my doubts that even they knew most of these people.

Lee and Jasp were arguing in the far corner, hopefully over Lee's stage appearance, though I knew that was a long shot. The fucker had the nerve to present himself before my audience with purple lipstick on. It was hard for me to follow the dramatics that that kid carried with him everywhere he went. He was the gay version of JT, minus the talent.

Eli, Dax and Lucas were drinking heavily over by the sound system, with Natalie and Steven Cronin, the drummer from Lull. She was standing in between Steve and Dax, and from my angle, it looked as though Dax's hand was on her lower back. She stood eerily closer to him than she did to Steve, her own band mate. This wasn't, of course, entirely suspicious since she had grown up with Dax and the rest of

Coma, but she had been spending an unordinary amount of time with Dax over all of us. Even when I had invited her out for dinner at a well-renowned restaurant the other night with me and Sammi, she turned me down. Later, I found that she had been down the road a bit at a seafood place with Dax and Lucas.

Sammi had tried to convince me that it was all very innocent, mentioning that Natalie had told her that she and Dax were working on a song. *A song...*

Really, the two of them, composing. Now that was one for the record books. But Sammi thought that their song had promise, and yes, she'd had a listen, at least Natalie's part, and thought that it was rather good. She'd even suggested that I ask Natalie about it at some point. Maybe my showing interest in it might help to get some insight on her musical direction. What musical direction? Hadn't I bred that musical direction in her already? She was clearly Coma-inspired. I'd heard her work over the years, I knew what she drew from. I couldn't imagine that anything her and Dax were coming up with would be far off from my standards.

And why wouldn't Natalie have come to me if she'd wanted me to hear their song? Why would it be up to me to approach her about it when she had never mentioned it once to me?

Another sip of my drink had me shifting back over to Sammi. She stood, thin yet comprise, commanding and elegant all at once. She was center of attention, even with our lot in her presence.

At one point, she caught me staring from where I was leaning in the doorway, and her eyes held mine for just a moment before they turned back toward some of the wives that she was speaking with. A smile, a nod, and a quick laugh later, she placed her hand on one of their arms, excusing herself politely, then swept across the room back over to me. She leaned in, placed a determined, yet sensual kiss on my cheek, whispering, "I *cannot* wait to get you alone."

I shook my head ever so slightly. "If you only knew..."

I wanted to ravage the woman right there on the living room floor, regardless of the company, but the majority of those outside our band had absolutely no idea that there was anything at all between the lead guitarist and his manager. Let alone a baby...

But I was quickly distracted by JT's grand entrance. He flung through the door, sauntered across the room and straight out to the balcony, threw up over the edge, then swaggered back in the room as casually as someone who'd been there all night. He grabbed the bottle right out of Eli's hand, guzzled it down in a long swig, and handed it back to him, wiping his mouth on his sleeve.

I knew this side of JT and despised it. Long after we were kids, I was still his keeper. It was the side that the rest of the world read about on the front pages of the tabloids for weeks on end. It was the side of him that couldn't be reined in, no matter how hard any of us tried. Once the beast was off its leash, anything could happen. And it often did.

I kept a close ear on him the second that I caught Natalie pulling him by the elbow over toward the corner of the room. Trying not to let on that I was listening full on to their conversation, I kept just out of sight, with my back against the door frame to the kitchen, sipping my drink and kept my eyes focused enough out of their direction that they were only in my peripheral view.

"She's not worth it JT, alright? You have nothing to prove to..."

He cut her off quickly. "I'm over it, Love."

I caught myself cringing, and had to turn the corner in case I needed to run interference. She hated being lied to, but her voice was soft when she said, "Don't let her get the best of you." She squeezed his arm, "I mean it."

He laughed and pulled her into an affectionate headlock. "Ah, Natalie girl, the press'll say wha'ever they want anyway. Why not give 'em something to write about?"

Wriggling free, she pleaded with him. "Please JT? Just listen, if you don't give her anything to go off of, it hits her harder than if she gets to read about you in the morning news."

He seemed to consider this for a minute, then brushed his lips against her forehead and promised that he'd behave himself. And much to my surprise, I actually saw him later pouring himself a tonic water with a lime. What power she had over him was unbeknownst to me, but I was reluctantly grateful for it.

Reining JT in was a responsibility that I had long shared with no one. As much as I hated any of the accountability for his actions being on her, I also knew that she had a way of working him that I didn't, and right or wrong, it got results. And these days, I needed all the help I could get with him. But to be honest, I'd rather her only responsibility be her band, and nothing more.

THIRTY-NINE
Natalie

"Sing your part on *Slipped Up Again*." Rylan instructed. He was sitting on the stage, his arm draped casually over one knee, while his other leg stretched out comfortably in front of him. This was how he did his best work with bands, he told me once, listening to the music raw and unplugged, feeling the melody course through his body via the vibrations in the stage. A clipboard and a pen off to his side, he occasionally leaned over to take random notes, and from time to time, I'd see him either nod or shake his head, as though he thought I couldn't see him.

I played the rhythm of the song on my guitar, singing backup without the benefit of Lee's lead vocals. Rylan stopped me about half way through by holding his hand up. "Let's hear your lead on that one." I narrowed my eyes at him, but when I got no reaction, I placed my left hand fingers on the fret board and began with the opening G chord. I didn't have quite an entire verse out before he was stopping me again. "How about one of my tunes? Lead on *Drought*, voice only, no guitar." I took a moment to get the tune in my head. It was a rare B-side that they never played live, but was one of my favorites. I found myself struggling a bit to get the pitch right, but as soon as I did, I took off with it. I enjoyed hearing the sound of my voice alone project through the microphone and come back through the speakers. I was about to hit the chorus when Rylan bolted to his feet.

"No, no, no, no, *no*..." He knocked the microphone stand clear to the ground, and continued walking, right past me, then swung back around again, dragging his hand through his hair. The creases around his eyes deepened, which happened nowadays when he was agitated. Part of it, he told me when I had pointed it out a few years back, was the constant stress and long hours of his job, and the other was attributed solely to me.

There was no doubt that he had played the role of a father figure in my life. It was always Rylan who made the arrangements for me to travel back and forth, had enrolled me in school, and had been the one that the dean had called the few occasions that I had gotten in enough trouble to call my parents. But that was his own doing. I had never asked him to assume that duty. I'm sure a lot of it also had to do with JT's lack of maturity and Kate's refusal to play any part in my upbringing, but I was sure a lot of it was Rylan's inability to let anyone else to make decisions. So he had no one to blame but himself if he didn't have the dashing good looks that he had a decade ago.

"It sounded good to me." I knew as soon as the words fell out of my mouth that he was going to trample all over them. He didn't take excuses from his band, and I knew better to have thought that he'd handle it any different from me.

But something softened a bit in his voice when he said, "Natalie, you're a damn good singer. You have been since you were a kid. But you just don't have that raw passion in your voice anymore. Or your guitar, for that matter." He replaced the microphone stand and readjusted it to his own height before he went on. "You need to dig deeper into your soul and just pour it out there all over the stage for your audience. They want to feel your pain, they want to feel your elation every time your voice hits that microphone or your pick touches the guitar string. They paid good money for that feeling, and you owe it to them."

Irritated, he held out his hand for my guitar, which I handed over to him without losing eye contact. The first few chords to *Drought* echoed through my chest. I could feel the strings on the tips of my own fingers as I stood watching him play. And as he sang the first few verses, I immediately heard the difference. His voice started out as velvet, strong and smooth, then as he neared the chorus he simply let go, strumming the guitar like he was about to saw it in half, and stretching his vocal chords into notes that cut deep into my soul. While he sang, his eyes were open, occasionally blinking swiftly, but I could tell that his focus wasn't on anything visual. He was drawing from something that was somewhere behind his eyes. I doubt he even saw me. And occasionally he'd close his eyes hard, shutting the audience out for a brief moment, as if to further project that passion from within him. But he always returned to viewing the audience, reading them as much as he was reading himself. Even tonight, when he had only an audience of one, he was reading me.

He stopped just short of the chorus, in the exact spot where he had interrupted me. Yet this time, chills had crept over my skin and my pulse was racing. I felt instantly transformed into the likeness of a fan in the crowd. There could have easily been a crowd of several thousand around me, I felt just as much energy standing there alone.

I found it hard to speak the moment that he handed me back my guitar and walked over to the edge of the stage to take a sip from his bottled water. But I had to know. "How do you do it, Ry?" The guitar strings still seemed to be vibrating, or maybe it was my hands shaking. "Where do you get it from?"

He went back to his spot sitting on the stage, and motioned for me to join him. "I've got a lot buried that I draw from." He finished his water and chucked the bottle into the stands. I resisted the urge to leave and go pick it up.

"Like what?"

He gave me a half smile and shook his head. "It's all in the music, Natalie girl."

I should have known he was going to give me a cryptic answer. I felt like there was a lot more that he should have been saying just then, but was choosing not to. Frustrated, I turned away, stretching my legs out in front of me on the stage. I ignored the fact that my new jeans, the ones that made my butt look cute, were touching the same wooden planks where people walked. I doubly ignored the fact that my palms were pressed into the same wooden planks, and were now sticky to the touch. "Right, it's always about the music, innit?" I replied, surprised to hear my British accent seeping through stronger than it'd been in a long time. "Nothing else matters to you, does it?"

He looked taken back. Perhaps a little too much, and instantly I felt the sting of remorse. Maybe there were things I didn't know about, I was sure there were, but maybe there were things I didn't want to know. A lot had happened before I was born, and a lot happened while I was in school and he was on the road. It was entirely plausible that he had been in and out of love and just never mentioned it. Then again, it was also likely that whatever emotional bank he was drawing from had nothing to do with love at all. I was beginning to hate the fact that he couldn't just open up and share like a real human being, and that I was left to decipher, much like the rest of his fans. How was I to learn that way?

FORTY
Natalie

I was craving a Yuengling Lager like there was no tomorrow. Europe had some of the best mixed drinks I've ever had, but I missed the local beer back in the States. Standing here by the closed hotel pool, sipping a Stella, I realized how much I cherished my alone time.

While the rest of the band was enjoying yet another post gig party, I had escaped to the serene calm and chlorine saturated oasis that surrounded me now. The air hung heavy and wet, clinging to my hair and skin. I didn't mind. I was at peace. The water danced at the surface from the jets at the far end of the pool, and glints of the neon white lights reflected off of the tiny waves that crashed against the blue tiled sides.

Serenity.

And just as I was about to consider myself lucky for the entire five minutes that I had been here, the creek of the swinging door behind me etched through my privacy like nails on a chalkboard.

Lee stood less than an arm's length in front of me,

closer than I liked him to be. He smelled lightly of Dom Perrier, probably left over from the night before. I imagined him, pinky up, sipping from a delicate long stem champagne glass with whoever he had picked up after the show. He played his cover well, entertaining women under the watchful eye of the camera, and behind closed doors leading his secret life.

I let out an impatient sigh, then emptied my bottle in one last bitter swig before giving it a careless toss in the trashcan.

"I'm surprised you're not practicing." He told me. "After the atrocity that we saw on stage tonight, I'd have expected you to be doing everything you can not to let it happen again."

My eyebrows raised, but I said nothing. My fists clenched instinctively, and I shoved them in my back pockets before they could react without my mind telling them otherwise. Instead, I found it more amusing to look him in the eyes, which was making him shift somewhat uncomfortably in his designer shoes. It was a damn shame that no one had been using the pool recently. I was hoping that he'd slip on a stray puddle and land on his overdone face.

Something about his eyes struck me tonight in a way that I hadn't noticed before, not even that night that we had shared a microphone. Behind the eyeliner, I saw a striking resemblance to Lucas. It was the first I had really ever noticed it, but he did share the same salient green eyes that his brother had. Even more surprising was the way I found myself studying the rest of his face as though it were the first time I had ever seen him.

Then I caught him doing the same, his eyes glazing over my face, as though he were focusing on every detail, until our eyes finally locked. Instinctively, a fury bubbled up within me, wanting to shout back at him, defend myself against his attacks. He wasn't being fair. Our entire band sucked, it wasn't just me. We had no symmetry, no chemistry

as a band. And the worst of it came from Lee and myself. We
repelled each other.

But just as I was about to open my mouth, Lee closed
the gap between us and pressed his lips against mine. It was a
hard, angry kiss, his hands grasping my upper arms to hold
me from falling backward as he leaned in and attacked my
lips with his. And as much as I wanted to push him back,
scream at him for being a jackass, I found myself pushing
closer to him, kissing him back, with just as much fury.

And soon he had pinned me up against the wall of the
poolroom, the thick air moistening our skin. He tore at my
shirt, and I at his until we were ripping and shredding our
clothes off of each other. A million things could have run
through my mind at that moment, but all of it went to the
wayside as the two of us fulfilled a need that I hadn't felt in
far too long.

It was anything but gentle, as his painted black
fingernails left painfully pleasurable trails on my skin, and I
bit into his neck and shoulders with deep purple kisses. By
the time we picked ourselves back up off of the tiled floor, we
were both bruised and breathless.

Lee buttoned his jeans, but his t-shirt, which was now
in shreds, went sailing into a nearby trashcan. My bra was a
lost cause without its clasps, and followed the fate of his shirt.
He sucked at the drops of blood on the back of his hand where
I may have bit a little too hard.

"What the hell was that Lee?" I ran my hands through
my hair, most of which was now wisping out in all directions.
I was finding it hard to catch my breath.

He shook his head. "Just sex. That's all."

My eyes narrowed, and the blood that was pumping
through my heart at an accelerated rate began to run hot.
"Don't give me that bullshit. You know what I mean."

He drew in a deep breath, letting it out hard. "I'm still
gay, if that's what you're asking."

"Well I'm not one of your cover girls, and there aren't

any cameras in here, so again, what the hell was that all about?" I was feeling as though my femininity were being insulted.

"Why don't you tell me? You were an active participant in the whole thing."

I bit my lip and fired back. "The difference, you asshole, is that I'm straight and you're a guy."

He squatted down to tie his shoes, looking up at me as he did so. I could see it on his face, hear it in the pitch of his voice. "I don't know, Natalie. It's not even like I'm bi. It just happened. I can't explain it any more than you can."

I couldn't help but feel like he was just as lost as I was. Maybe it was the secret life style that he had forced himself to lead, or the loneliness of being on the road and missing someone at home, but he had that same emptiness in his soul that I felt every time my thoughts drifted back to Ray-Ray. The ache in my heart couldn't be eased by a one-night stand, but it did help to satisfy the physical urges.

I watched Lee walk out into the hotel hallway. His green eyes had iced back over, and I could feel mine shut him back out just as quickly. Whatever it was that had just happened between us was a fluke. It was a mistake. A one time, completely undeniable error in judgment.

FORTY-ONE
Rylan

When Sammi slapped the pages of the newsstand tabloid down on the table, it didn't take but a second for me to realize where she was about to go with it. "Are you going to talk to her?"

"Her? What about *him*?"

A picture of Dax and Natalie sitting too close for my liking in a booth at the Ha'Penny Bridge Inn in Dublin, from two nights prior, was taking up the entire cover. *Damn it*, I knew I should have gone to that club. Instead, Sammi and I had retreated off to my hotel suite early.

"I'll handle him. You handle her."

I squinted a bit at the smaller pictures on the side of the cover, then grabbed the thing off the table for a closer look.

Sure enough, there were more pictures of Natalie, with Dax leading her by the hand into a doorway that I couldn't make heads of tails of what building it was attached to, but it could have very possibly been a hotel. Above it were a series of pictures, obviously shot in continuum, of the two of them laughing, with him holding her close. Regardless of the reality, I didn't like the implications, and the longer I stared at the photos, the easier it was to believe them over what she had insisted in all of our previous conversations.

A long stream of curses flew past my lips before I could gather my sense. *What the hell was she thinking?* She knew better. My hand swung around and knocked over the small table lamp before I could control it.

"She's young Ry, and naïve. This is all new for her..."

"Uh uh," I cut her off, "She's been on tour with us for too many years to know that there are certain things you do in public and there are certain things you don't. There are certain relationships that are kept private."

"Like ours."

"Exactly." It had slipped off my tongue quicker than I could retract it. *Damn it.* Usually my head was quicker than my mouth. Her lips tightened and I knew she was seconds from laying it out for me. We both knew this business well. There was no privacy. No matter how hard you tried, they saw everything, and they knew everything. It was only just a matter of time.

I reached my hand out to her, instantly loving the way the soft skin of her slender fingers fit perfectly in mine. The woman was nothing if not the epitome of class. I pulled her into my lap, lowering my head to her ear. "You know I didn't mean what I just said." I nuzzled her neck, enthralled with the way her breath caught in her throat and her head titled back ever so slightly.

She leaned into my kisses, arching her back, running her hands through the back of my hair, rubbing her thigh against me as I hardened instantly for her. There wasn't an inch of me that didn't want to be up against every inch of her, and again I lost control of myself as my hands slid up under her blouse, grabbing at her breasts hungrily. She was the only person I ever truly needed in this world. And I needed her in every way imaginable. I needed her in ways that no man wanted to freely admit to, and I'd do anything to keep her happy, even if it meant jeopardizing the most precious thing in our relationship - our privacy.

I'd long believed that marriage was an institution in which I never belonged. My career choice didn't support a true commitment to anything other than the music. And if I couldn't commit one-hundred percent to something, there was just no use in going through with it.

Not that there were other women that I'd have wanted a relationship with. Not in years of late, at least. Early on, sure there'd been plenty. Too many. And that's how mistakes happen. You learn all too quickly that being careless is a lifelong obligation, and not just a financial one. There are those calls that come through that management is able to quickly squelch, but not before the tabloids and the press are all over it with their speculations.

And then there are those that simply can't be denied. When you look into those eyes that mirror your own, there's precious little that can be done at that point.

It lay underneath the surface of everything I did. It was always there, haunting me in ways that no one would ever know. Not the fans, not the rest of the band, hell, not even JT or Sammi, who both knew more than anyone else, knew the whole story and how much it really affected me and everything that I did. I'd spent so long covering it up, that I eventually began to believe my own lie. But it ate at me every day. And bled into everything that I did, every relationship that I had.

FORTY-TWO
Natalie

I wasn't feeling myself when I followed Jasp and Steve on stage the night we arrived in Madrid, but they were doing their best to snap me out of it. As our feet hit the stage and our crowd cheered, Jasp swung his arm across my shoulders and pulled me past my microphone, over to Lee's in the center of the stage. With me practically in a headlock, he addressed the audience.

"Doesn't she look lovely tonight?" Cheers and whistles resonated from the crowd, half of which were still filtering into the stadium. I wasn't particularly dressed up, wearing a pair of skinny jeans, boots and an incredibly low cut, breast-hugging white top. My makeup artist had done wonders to erase the lack of sleep from my eyes with some color, and my hairstylist had let me go on with a fresh just-out-of-bed look. "Wait'll ya hear her. She's just as talented as she is prett'y." He then gave me a less than gentle shove back toward my post, and headed off across the stage to his, just as Lee made his way out and the crowd burst into a roar.

Our performance tonight was our best yet. Lee and Jasp blew the audience away with their chemistry, and Steve kept a hard steady beat on the drums. And I lent a light melody and heavy soul that I didn't know that I had.

Maybe it was the fact that the whole time we were on stage, my mind was drifting to a million other places. My mother's mental condition was deteriorating each day it seemed. JT and Rylan were constantly arguing with Kate over what should be done. Kate felt a group home was best, but my brothers didn't seem to agree. At least not until Kate found that my mother had wandered off. It had taken us almost half a day to find her, and when we did, she was moments from stepping onto a bus.

As much as I hated the idea of my mother in a group home, Kate insisted that her doctors felt it was best for her. Rylan still didn't seem sold on the idea, but JT was now siding with Kate, which wound up Rylan even more. And every time I opened my mouth, it seemed a lost cause. So I kept my opinions to myself and let them handle it.

I talked to Rachel about it the night before, and she thought I should just let it be. If I didn't have a strong enough opinion to fight about it, then why even worry about it? In the end, it was going to be Rylan's money that made the decision, so it didn't seem like any of us really had a say in the matter.

I tried to focus on the music, on the crowd, on anything that would keep my mind on my job. But I noticed that the more distracted I was, the better I was playing. Maybe Rylan had a point, digging deep was benefiting my performance. My eyes strayed over to Jasp, who was lost in the moment with his guitar. He entered another world when he stepped on stage. And his performance never faltered. Steve was looking like he was having the time of his life, sweating profusely under the hot lights, and pounding away on his drum skins. Lee even looked like he was feeling the crowd in a whole new way tonight. They certainly loved him, and surprisingly, were actually singing along with his lyrics.

Still, even when we left the crowd cheering for more as we exited the stage, Lee couldn't help but take digs where he could. We were making our way back through the hallway toward our dressing room, with Lee leading the way, walking backward.

"Can't you count?" He wasn't masking anything in his voice as he practically growled the words at me. "'Cause there were at least two songs that you completely missed your timing on the intro."

"Lay off, Lee. She was amazing." Steve was quick to jump in, and Jasp to follow.

"*Fucking* amazing. We all were. We rocked the house tonight!"

Lee wasn't satisfied quite yet though. "We've got a long way to go."

I brushed past him and stopped short at Coma's closed door, knocking loud and quick before peeking my head in. Before I stepped in, I nodded back in Lee's direction. "Talk to me when you're not coming in a half-beat too early." I ducked into Coma's dressing room before he could respond.

Eli, Dax and Lucas were playing cards, half-heartedly, with some of the road crew, around a small coffee table in the center of the room. I whisked a cold beer out of the fridge and twisted the top off with my shirt before taking a seat between Dax and Lucas. Perhaps I was sitting a little closer to Dax than Lucas, but wasn't fully aware until Dax's arm slid around my waist and pulled me even closer. He tipped his hand in my direction. "Any advice for a dying man, Love?"

Not even sure what game they were playing, I saw that all his cards were below a seven and advised, "Drop the queen on your next turn and keep the pair of tens."

Four of them threw down their hands, with Lucas rolling his eyes. "This is what you get for letting a girl in the room before the show. Coma's dressing room is no place for a woman..."

I blew him a kiss. "You sound like your brother." I

laughed as he flipped me off and stood up, guzzling what was left in his bottle.

Eli was the only one left still holding his cards. "I had three tens, you cunts."

Dax held a firm grip around my waist. "I monkeyed around with some of our lyrics last night. Care to hear 'em after the show then?"

A deep breath filled my lungs before I could gather my thoughts enough to respond. Something about the way he held onto me, the way that his breath shared the same air as mine, the way that it was so wrong for the two of us to be sitting in such close proximity, I tried not to let it turn me on as much as it was as that very moment. The warmth of his embrace was not quite as safe as when Ray-Ray had held me, but more so protective with Dax.

I reminded myself that while I couldn't help the feelings that were coursing through my blood at that very moment, or control my heart from skipping beats, I could control the fantasies that were about to take over my mind. I needn't go there, to a place where there would be no return, to a decision made in a split second that I'd regret for the rest of my life. Dax was a married man, separation or not, and my brother's best friend. Those were two relationships that I refused to betray. Jules deserved the respect of a clean divorce, and Rylan, he deserved the respect of his sister not crossing the lines that divided friends.

There was a trust between Rylan and me that would never be shattered. He had taken me in, and acted as a father to me when my own father wouldn't. Over the years he had provided me with the home that I called my own, a bedroom where I learned to compose my own music, and the only familial stability that I'd ever known. He'd taken care of my schooling, my finances, and my every need since I was nine. He'd guided me through life, offering the best advice that he could, and all without anyone asking him to.

Perhaps that was the reason why he resented the fact

that I'd searched for our father all these years. I wondered, as I pulled away from Dax and crossed the room toward the minibar, if somewhere deep within him, Rylan wasn't upset at the fact that I didn't appreciate all he'd done for me over the years.

"Can't Dax, sorry. Another time maybe."

I wished them all a good show and headed back to my hotel room. I was just stepping out of the shower when the knock came at my door. Still in my bath towel, I cracked the door open just enough to peek through it.

"Busy?" Lee stood in the hallway, his hair still wet from just coming out of the shower himself, dressed in a black and white horizontally striped long sleeved t-shirt, black gloves with the fingers cut out, tight dark colored jeans, and leather boots with metal spikes running up the sides. If I didn't know him, I might have thought he was here to steal my purse or jewelry.

I slid the door open with my bare foot and as soon as he stepped into my room, I used the same foot to kick it shut again.

"I didn't mean to catch you indisposed." He said, noticeably eyeing me up and down before helping himself to a seat on my bed.

"I didn't think I had much to worry about. It's not like you're here to molest me or anything."

He raised his eyebrows and cocked his head slightly to the side. "You sure about that Sweetheart?"

I gave a quick laugh, more annoyed than amused, and dropped my towel. "You're still gay, remember?" It was something he had reminded me of after almost every encounter that we'd had since that night in the poolroom.

"And you're not my cover girl." He watched as I pulled a red G-string out of my suitcase and slid it on.

I stood in front of him, my bare breasts parallel to his eyes, and let him run his hands on them as he stood up in front of me. "Still think I'm half a beat behind?"

His arms wrapped around me, and he bit his lip seductively. The lip ring turned me on. "Come on, Baby Blue," he moaned in my ear, "let's not mix work with pleasure."

I pushed him down on the bed, and then crawled on top of him. "Because God knows there's no fun in our line of work."

He stopped talking, and I covered my mouth with his, sliding my legs up on either side of his chest, and pulled my fingernails up under his shirt, leaving a trail of scratches. Lee Mason was the type of guy you look at, with his piercings and leather, and you expect that he would like his sex brutal, just as it had been between us in the many times we'd been together since that night in the poolroom. But he took me by surprise when he grabbed both of my wrists, pulled them to his mouth, and placed gentle kisses on each one. He followed with a trail of kisses up my left arm, slow and soft, until he reached my neck. Just when I thought that we were going to slip into a slow, soft, effortless round, he again shifted to deep hard bites and clawing. He had my mind spinning and my body aching but screaming for more.

The entire time, he interrupted the sparing match that we had become accustomed to with brief intervals of soft, tender moments. It was both intriguing and frightening to me that he had shown anything other than just a sexual desire.

And suddenly, without warning, he'd returned to his rough, aggressive tendencies that had dominated our encounters. And when he did, he brought it on full-stop, no holds barred, wrapping both hands strongly around my wrists, slamming them back against the wall, his knee pressing into my hip until I was flat against the wall. His teeth bit at my lips, a hungry growl spitting through them as he forced himself against me.

In the cusp of his grasp, my vision started to blur, just ever so slightly, and no amount of blinking was bringing focus to what was unfolding before my eyes. I shifted, becoming uncomfortably aware that I was slipping out of reality. A hot sweat dripped from my forehead, and I felt my pulse rise.

Replacing Lee's small stature suddenly stood my uncle Leo. Heavy hands where holding me against the wall, not in my own hotel room, but in Leo's hallway, just outside his bedroom. My blood turned icy in a matter of seconds and pure instinct took over as my knee came up swiftly into his crotch, and the second he doubled over, my knuckles drove into his cheekbone. I went to push him back, run out the door, as I had done many years ago, but he caught me around the waist, and I hit the floor hard.

"Natalie, what the *fuck*?"

I was staring up at Leo, but hearing Lee's breathless voice. My head was aching fiercely, and I was having trouble catching my own breath. It had never been that vivid before. The memories, in my dreams, the images had never come to me like that before. I blinked several times, trying to clear the ghostly image from my vision.

I took a deep breath and pulled myself up from the floor, then went to the mirror to inspect the damages. I already looked like I had been in a fight. And in some regards, I felt like I had been as well. But as I looked into that mirror, what was staring back at me was a face I had seen before. Not as a twenty-one year old woman, but as a nine-year old girl. It was an image that wasn't fading, no matter how many times I blinked.

Feeling the emotion bubbling to the surface and drowning my eyes without warning, I sniffed quickly. "Get out Lee."

He wanted to hold back the look of bewilderment on his face, I could tell. His mouth hung open as though he were about to say something to me but thought better of it at the last second. Instead, he slipped to his feet with a grace that only Lee Mason could possess – catlike and gruff, all at the same time. His eyes were locked on me as he crossed the room, still in silent awe, as though this were the first time he'd ever been kicked out of a hotel room. Hell, maybe it was, but that wasn't my problem.

The second the door slammed shut behind him, I raced to lock it, then let my back slide down the wall, until I was hugging my knees. My body was shaking, repulsed by the taste of my own blood on my tongue and the throbbing of my skin swelling where we'd gotten too rough.

I'd felt this way before. Outside of the nightmares.

It came back like a flood, that I wasn't able to stop. They were memories, not dreams. And they were all too clear this time.

I had come home late from a friend's house, and ran through the rain of a storm just starting to brew in the night air. I knew I was past curfew, and if Hannah and Leo were up, I knew was going to be in trouble. But I'd lost track of time, and knew that not coming home at all would leave me in a worse predicament. He'd know. He'd find my bed empty when he slipped through the door in the midnight hours.

I had tip-toed through the kitchen, and down into the hallway where the bedrooms were. I thought I would just slip into my room, and pretend like I'd been there all along. But my bedroom door was closed, light spilling out onto the floor of the hallway in front of my feet, and I felt like I should just turn and run.

But something pulled at me. It was all so terribly out of place. I had to open that door. I felt like I had to know.

Hannah was sitting on the edge of my bed, two suitcases at the foot, and Leo was holding a kitchen knife just inches from her face. Neither of them saw me, and I stepped back, trying to see yet also remain out of sight. Hannah was crying, begging him not to do this. He told her that this was the only way to keep her from leaving, that he couldn't trust her anymore.

He pushed her down on the bed, told her to get undressed. She started screaming my name, begging me to help her. He told her she was going to die, that he'd slit her throat if she didn't listen to him, and she'd bleed to death all over the new sheets they'd just bought.

But she kept screaming for me to help her, as if she knew I was there.

And I knew at that moment what she knew. I was her only hope.

She started to take her clothes off, and he kept screaming at her to go faster. That he wanted to have her one last time before she died. She screamed for me again, and I just couldn't take it anymore.

A small cry escaped my throat. And it was enough to make him jump up and turn.

Hannah grabbed him from behind, but he turned quickly, plunging the knife into her chest. I knew she was trying to scream, but the only sound that came out was a muffled, gurgled gasp, barely vocal. It was the most painful sound I'd ever heard. Until I heard him pull the knife from her, and stab it into her three more times, rapidly, angrily.

Had I thought to run, I would have. But I stood there frozen, unable to move my feet.

It wasn't until he turned to face me, his face and hands and clothes stained with her blood, that my feet allowed me any movement. And it was a clumsy sort of turn and run that allowed him to catch me so quickly.

He had me up against the wall in the hallway before I could regain my balance. My head ached from being slammed so hard against the plaster, and I can remember tasting the blood in my mouth when I bit down on my tongue. I could barely make out what he was saying.

"You think you two can run off and have a better life without me?" His speech was slurred and his breath reeked of stale bourbon. "You bloody little bastard child... She wants to leave me for your father? Let's see her get his money now... Fucking wants to be a millionaire, does he? This'll bring him fame a lot faster..."

He kicked his knee into my stomach, and I remember gagging. Hannah was dying, and all I could think about was trying to get away from Leo so that I could do something to save her. But he continued to kick at me. I tried to fight back. I punched him once, kicked out at him a few times. He took a step back, and I thought that he was going to walk away, maybe go back after Hannah. It all happened so quick. But instead, he took his knife, and swung it at me. I had tried to move, but he caught me in the side with the blade. The force of his thrust knocked him off balance, and as he fell over slightly, I kicked him as hard as I could. He hit the ground, cursing me, and before he could stand, I kicked him again, in the face. I kicked him as many times as I could before I realized I needed to run. There was nothing more I could do for Hannah. I had to save myself.

I wasn't aware of the blood I was losing, or the pain that was anguishing my body as I ran through the stormy night. I cut through the park, and made it as far as Waterloo Station, where I'd slipped inside and called JT from the row of payphones. As I waited by the glass wall, watching the rain come to a slow trickle, the thunder and lightning dissipated, I began to become weary. I knelt down on the row of chairs against the window, backwards, so I could watch for JT's car.

And a slow realization hit me, as the picture became more and more clear. It wasn't a lightning bolt that hit the window. It was a bullet. For the first time, I could see clearly Hannah's car, sliding sideways around the corner. I stood, at first thinking that it was Hannah, that she'd somehow survived the wounds, and had been following me. But then I saw the gun pointed through the open window, and Leo's face glaring back at me. It was only a split second before the white flash, and the windows at Waterloo were shattered, the impact sending me flying back against the tile floor.

Sitting on the floor of the hotel room, I wished I had been dreaming. I wished that I could open my eyes, and toss it away as another nightmare that meant nothing. But it was all too real.

FORTY-THREE

Rylan

The morning paper that was slid under my hotel door was my only reminder some mornings of what country we were in. Madrid. It had to be. The damn thing was in Spanish. I tossed it aside and pulled open the curtains to inspect the view. Below stood a majestic fountain, surrounded by architecturally prominent buildings, all of which I'd never get to see beyond the view from my window.

Rarely did I get enough time in the cities that we visited. In the early days, before press conferences and interviews and radio contests, we'd go shopping or drinking, and mull about the streets, seeing sights that the average person would only catch a glimpse of in pictures on the internet or in a travel book. I'd seen it all; The Eiffel Tower, Grand Canyon, Mount Olympus, shit that never really mattered to me at the time. Nowadays, I'd give anything some days just to go to the corner shop and grab a tea to go.

Our Girl would delight over the pictures I'd send her.

So much so, that when we brought her on tour with us, I'd make sure we'd go see some of the places she'd requested. But she was never so happy as when she was old enough that I let her come to shows. She marveled at being in the crowd, watching the other fans, getting caught up in the energy and the music.

She'd want to know what it was like being on stage. Not in general, but that night. What was it like *that* night, playing for *those* fans? Was it a good crowd or were they rather flat? Did I notice that everyone started cheering during the guitar solo for 'Runaway Life'?

They were all questions that I had wondered myself as an inspiring artist. They were the type of questions buzzing around my head, twenty-four-seven, making it impossible not to pursue the dream that was now my reality. It was far beyond a hunger, stronger than any need to achieve; it was a necessity, equivalent to breathing. I wouldn't have been able to do anything else with my life if it didn't involve holding a guitar in my hand.

She was just like me, and whether that was inherent or intrinsic, I'll never know. What was becoming painfully apparent though, was that I wasn't able to hide the truth from her any longer. That same drive that we shared for music, she applied to everything that she pursued. There wasn't much that I could do anymore to keep the truth hidden. And it was better it came from me than she find out on her own.

I had Sammi arrange for our next break to take us back home to London. With my mother's mental state deteriorating rapidly, it was best that we take a few days anyhow to take care of business with her.

I flipped through a few of the pages of the paper, about to set it down when a photograph, no larger than a playing card, caught my eye. The only words that were in English were the name of my band and our guitarist, but the picture needed no explanation to me. Dax's arm was wrapped around Natalie's shoulders, and his lips were pressed against her cheek, dangerously close to her mouth. There was a crooked smile resting on her face, and her eyes were half-closed, as she seemed to be pulling away from him just as the camera had appeared.

Without the benefit of Sammi being able to slow me down, I flew full steam down the hallway and pounded my fist against Dax's door. I caught the attention of security, but only enough to make him look up, notice who was the cause of the raucous, and look back down at his own morning paper. This was one of the benefits of being who I was. I got away with things that others didn't. It was a damn good thing for Dax that I wasn't capable of murder, but he was about to find out that I could come close.

The door flew open, and a half-awake and barely lucid Dax appeared with a dark room behind him. "What the hell's going on? Everything alright?"

"Is everything alright?" I repeated, shoving the paper into his chest and pushing him back into his room. I flipped the light on. "You fucking tell me."

He rubbed his eye with one hand, and glanced down at the paper that was in his other. Immediately, he rolled his eyes. "It's not what it looks like, Ry. C'mon, you know that."

"Do I? 'Cause everything I'm seeing is telling me otherwise."

"We're writing a song, that's all there is to it. I'm helping her out."

"Yeah? Well she doesn't need your help. Not when it's like that."

"Like what?"

"You fucking well know what I mean 'like what'. Are you fucking sleeping with her?"

He took too long to answer, and I started toward him. He took a few steps back and defensively, "*No!* No, I'm not sleeping with her."

I chewed on my tongue a moment, trying to talk myself into turning and walking away. The alternative was to slam him through the wall. It might not solve my problems, but it sure as hell would make me feel better at the moment.

"And even if I was, she's a grown-woman, Rylan. Like it or not, if I wanted to have sex with your sister..."

My hands exploded onto his chest, and his shirt crumpled into my fists as I threw him against the wall. My head was not connecting with anything else in me at the time, and anger was taking complete control over everything, including my mouth. "She's not my sister, you fucking cunt!"

Shocked at the words that had just exploded off my tongue, I let go of him, and took a step back. *Fuck*, I thought, *what had I just done?*

Dax didn't move, and I myself stood frozen. I couldn't take it back. I couldn't move forward. I was literally frozen.

"What the hell are you talking about Ry?"

I looked up at him, directly into his eyes. A part of me was sure that he had to have known all along, or at least suspected, but the other half of me knew that it had all been so carefully hidden that there was really no way he, or anyone else, would ever have had a clue.

And as the realization came over his face, I knew it was the latter.

Slowly, he asked me, "She knows this too?" And when I didn't answer him, when I couldn't answer him, he stepped back toward me. "Rylan, you need to tell her."

I set my hand on my forehead, shading my eyes from the now-glaring morning sunlight that was piercing through a sudden headache. A deep breath later I resolved, knowing full well he was right.

"I will."

My hotel suite wasn't large enough for the amount of ground that I needed to cover, but it would have to do. I couldn't be around anyone right now. I needed the time alone to think, to get everything sorted.

Dax wouldn't say anything to anyone, I was sure of

that, particularly not Natalie. I didn't have to worry there. What did concern me was that Natalie needed to know – that was clearer than ever now. I couldn't live with the fact that people outside of our family knew and she was still in the dark.

But could she deal with the truth? *Would she even believe it?* Her mind was so damaged from all of the trauma – and she was still sorting through all of that herself. I knew about the nightmares, knew that they still haunted her. And why wouldn't they? What I'd heard from the court hearings that I'd attended on her behalf - what they were able to piece together from the evidence that they had - was horrifying. I'm not sure a full-grown adult could process what had happened in that house, let alone a nine-year-old child.

It all seemed so far-fetched now, so distant from when the lies were created in the first place. The lies were necessary, to protect her, and to give her the life that she could never have if she had remained Natalie Porter. She'd have always in the spotlight, always having to face the media, answering questions about what had happened to her as a child, what he'd done to her. But she might not see it that way, not see it as a necessary step to protect her.

I was torn.

Even when the frantic knock came at more door, and I saw her standing there, tears soaking her flushed face.

God, she knew, I thought, *that bastard told her.*

I pulled her inside the room, closing the door behind us. I wanted to speak, but the words wouldn't form on my lips. I wanted to apologize. I wanted to beg her forgiveness. I wanted to tell her so much so quickly that the words just froze somewhere deep in my chest. The sight of her, so exasperated and tormented by her own emotions, brought me back to a place I hadn't been in twelve years.

"Ry, I remember." And the eyes that were staring up at me were those of a nine-year old child's, not a twenty-one-year old woman's. "That night. I remember what happened."

We sat, at the same time, across from each other. She sat in as near a fetal position as she could on a couch. Her bare feet rested on glass top round table that sat between us, her elbows on her knees, and her palms pressed tightly against her forehead. Her dark brown hair spilled over her face and her hands, and though I couldn't make out her face in the whole mess, her labored breathing told me she'd surpassed tears some time back.

I thought about reaching across to her. Offering her comfort, taking her in my arms and holding her until she believed the pain would subside. But instead I sat. Waiting, however much it killed me, for her to pull together the courage to tell me what she'd been hiding inside for twelve years.

"I know why he wanted to kill me and Hannah, Ry." Her voice was steady as she raised her head, her eyes locking with mine. "She was having an affair."

My heart shattered into a thousand pieces at that very moment. I couldn't bear to hold eye contact with her anymore as my gaze shifted to the floor. The words were more than I could handle. I simply nodded.

And it didn't go unnoticed. "So you knew about her and Dad?"

My head shot up. "Dad?"

She was quiet for a moment, as she tried to read my face. Then she began her story, recounting in horrific detail the events that had played out that night. The investigators had been surprisingly accurate about most of what she confirmed for me there in that hotel room. Though the pieces that they couldn't know were what he'd said to her. What'd he'd said to Hannah. The pieces that I'd paid a heavy price to conceal. Motive.

"Hannah was sleeping with Dad," she finished, "and Leo just went crazy."

We sat there in silence. For the longest while we sat there absorbing each other's information. She'd even offered an apology to me, at one point, thinking that I'd been unaware of the affair.

I held my hand up to her, still unable to speak, as my cell buzzed off the end table beside me. Moments later, the hotel phone was ringing. It wasn't until Natalie's phone buzzed that I actually shifted my attention from our conversation.

She held up the text message. "It's JT. 911."

FORTY-FOUR
Natalie

The decision had been made. My mother was moved into Granby Mede's group home for Alzheimer sufferers.

Kate had called JT in a panic, telling him that our mother had wandered out of house and was nowhere to be found. We rushed home from our final show in Italy to find that she'd been turned in at the local hospital. An younger couple had found her wandering about the bus station, asking to buy a ticket to the States. The hospital had been unable to determine her identity when she couldn't even recall her own name.

But at Granby Mede, she now had caretakers in a less-than-hospital-like setting, tending to her every need. Rylan had insisted that he would choose the facility, and Kate agreed, though I was sure that since it was Rylan's money that would be paying the bill every month, and Kate didn't have a leg to stand on if she disagreed anyhow. JT as always, remained impartial, and of course I wasn't even asked my opinion, so I kept it to myself.

The matter of going through the house to prepare it for sale was to be a family ordeal, however. Rylan didn't trust Kate to do it alone, and Kate, in turn, didn't trust Rylan. So it was agreed between the two of them that the four of us would do it together. It would be the first time in almost a decade that Rylan and Kate would be under the same roof.

JT swore he was going for the sole purpose of the entertainment factor, and offered that I should surrender myself to the same expectations. Anything more, he warned, would be setting myself up for disappointment.

And for me, it was enough to keep my mind off of rush of memories from the other night in the hotel room. I felt bad about Lee, in a strange sort of way. There were rumors flying around in our group that we'd gotten into a fight, and neither Lee nor I addressed any of it. We hadn't spoken since our last encounter, but I highly doubted he'd be stopping by my room again when we resumed the tour.

When we pulled up to the house, Rylan swore under his breath as he slammed the car in park. Kate's car was already in the drive, despite Rylan's insistence that we were all to arrive at the same time. There was no sign of JT, who had sworn that he'd be there at least five of ten.

The sun was hanging high in the morning sky, casting a warm glaze on my face as I got out of the car and stepped onto the walkway. The realtor had already been by and a neatly placed sign stood fresh in the front yard. I tried to picture someone else living in the house where my brothers and sister grew up, but I just couldn't bring myself to fully visualize another family settling in here. Strange as it was, it was home to my earliest memories, and I just didn't know if I could let that go so easily. I wondered if my siblings felt the same.

I followed Rylan up the drive, and was on his heels as he pulled the front screen door nearly off its hinges then burst through the thick mahogany door with the quaint window cutouts at the top. I imagined that as a child, he'd often do the same in reverse, running out to the yard to find his friends.

Kate was sitting in the living room on our mother's favorite rocking chair, sipping from a steaming mug. She seemed unaffected by Rylan's grand entrance. "Good to see you, Rylan. How've you been?"

Rylan didn't hold back. "We agreed on ten, Kate. Ten a.m., outside in the drive."

Kate sipped again, then gave him an inquisitive look. "Did we? I thought we said nine-thirty. Well, no matt'er, is it?" She set her mug down. "Did ya have breakfast yet, Natalie? There's some muffins in the kitchen..."

Rylan walked into the dining room to peer out through the front curtains as JT's tires screeched out front. "We ate already," he called back to us. Kate shrugged, and I suppressed a laugh.

JT's arrival seemed to distract Rylan enough. He was practically pulling JT toward the basement, as though he had some other agenda outside of sorting through boxes. "You two can focus on the attic." He told us, the basement door clicking shut behind them.

Kate and I looked at each other, eyebrows raised, then headed up to the attic. "I think there's even some of your childhood stuff up here, Natalie girl."

I was actually more interested in stumbling upon anything that might have to do with our father. Perhaps among the endless boxes was some meaning behind his affair with Hannah. Some clue as to what had conspired between them, hidden amongst the memories and the photos.

My mother's attic was anything but dusty and creepy. It was actually quite the opposite. She'd had it finished a few years back, painted a nice light shade of pale blue with white trim. Skylights lit the room quite well, especially in the late morning. The room itself had a slight scent of lemon, making me wonder if it had been just recently cleaned.

Whereas most attics might contain cardboard boxes full of memoirs, holiday items and seasoned clothing, my mother's contained blue plastic tubs, snapped shut with a matching blue lid. There was a label on every container with a name, a brief description of what was inside, and a date that it was placed into the attic. In her better years, my mother had been quite the neurotic organizer.

Kate motioned for me to follow her to the far end of the room, where the oldest of the tubs were located. These tubs were gray with gray lids, which were the only kind that they sold at the local hardware store back when she first moved into the home, many years before I was born.

Soon, both Kate and I were sitting cross-legged on the plush carpeted attic floor, going through each tub, and sorting the items into new tubs that we would either keep or throw away. I glanced up at her face from time to time, to see if there was even the remotest of possibilities that selling that house that she grew up in was striking a sentimental note in her. But she wore that same stoic, faraway glare in her eyes. Occasionally, I thought her face softened just a bit when she'd come upon a memento, a small token of her childhood, and every so often she'd smile and tell a quick story about whatever memory the trinket would conjure up.

She laughed when she pulled a ceramic, bowl-shaped item, out of bubble wrap. My mother had always kept everything neatly preserved. I wasn't sure what it was all being preserved for, as none of the items were ever displayed, but if they were to make it to a museum someday, they'd all go in pristine measure. This particular work of art was painted in bright purple, finished with some sort of glaze, and had Kate's initials scratched into the bottom. "It's an ashtray." She announced proudly, with a hint of sentimentality in her voice. "Back when smoking wasn't so bad for ya. I made it for Mum and Dad in my primary school art class."

I smiled back at her, slightly jealous at the mention of our father. I tried to picture the look on his face when she brought this project home and presented it to him. However since I had only seen his face in pictures and the one movie that he made it into, I didn't have much to feed my vision. I was sure he loved it though, as I was always told by my brothers that Katie was his favorite. "Smoking's bad for ya?"

She rolled her eyes and laughed. "D'ya smoke Natalie?"

"Rarely." It was half-true. "Only around JT and Rylan, really."

I heard Kate grumble just a little. "What's with Rylan anyhow? He seems more irritable than ever today."

I wasn't about to bring myself to tell her. After all, it had been Kate who'd sent me off to live with Leo and Hannah in the first place. It had been she who'd fed me to the wolf, so many years ago, when I couldn't fend for myself against Leo's attacks. I didn't blame her, not entirely, only because she hadn't known what he was capable of. But I hadn't brought myself to forgive her fully yet either.

It didn't seem to have affected Rylan much when I told him. He'd sat there listening, stone-faced as always, and offered a hug and an apology, which I told him was unnecessary on his part. What he had given me in the years that I lived with him were far more than he ever needed to, and I was grateful for that. He'd been the father to me that I never had through our own. And that meant more to me than anything.

I hadn't intended on ignoring Kate's question, but when I opened the next tub and discovered it was mine, I'd already forgotten about Rylan.

The label had read "Natalie", the date two years after I was born, and was described simply as "Memoirs", but somehow I had been too enthralled in conversation at first to notice any of those details. Yet right there at the very top of the inside of the tub was my original birth certificate.

It was actually framed, which was quite an honor, I thought, given the circumstances that my mother and father weren't living on the same continent at the time of my birth. For a single moment, I actually felt that maybe I had been a welcomed being into this world. And that maybe, if for only the time that it took to put the document into a black frame, I really was wanted into this family.

I pulled the frame from the box, and suddenly anything that Kate was mumbling about was going in one ear and out the other. I had to hold the frame sideways slightly, as the light pouring through the skylights was causing such a glare. I ran my finger over the glass covering my name. Natalie Christine Porter. And right there was the only documented proof that I had ever once been a Porter.

I was sure that the rock-like feeling in the back of my throat were tears that would have longed to escape. But years of saying goodbye to Natalie Christine Porter had given me enough decorum to hold them back in front of Kate. Sure, I might shed a stray tear or two, but it would be much later, when no one was around to witness the silent pain that still lingered occasionally for my absentee family life.

I was almost about to set the frame aside and dig through the rest of the box when something else caught my eye. Listed as my mother was the name Hannah Cole Kaplan. *Aunt Hannah.* My stomach turned violently as I gripped the frame tighter.

And then I saw what was written in the space for my father's name and my stomach turned again.

Rylan Caleb Porter.

"Kate..." I was having a hard time catching my breath. The letters behind the glass frame were swirling in front of my eyes. Kate would have an explanation, I assured myself. *Stay calm, don't panic.* There was logic involved somewhere, I was sure of it. Logic that escaped me at that very moment.

I shoved the frame at her, taking slow deep breaths, trying not to hyperventilate. I reached back, steadying myself on a stack of boxes behind me.

An inquisitive, almost annoyed look was painted on

her face until her eyes fell upon the pink watermarked document that was held within the frame. Realization seemed to hit her instantaneously as her eyes shot back up to meet mine.

The air was sweeping out of my lungs harder than I could pull a breath in. I could feel the blood pumping through my veins faster than I could control, and a heavy weight was pushing down on my chest, crushing my ability to think straight. "Why is Rylan's name on my birth certificate?"

Kate didn't say a word. Instead, a pitiful look crept across her eyes, and if I didn't know better, I would have thought that she was trying to suppress amusement. A moment went by before she asked, seriously, "You mean you don't know?"

My eyes narrowed. My blood ran hot through my veins, but a cool sweat was crawling over my skin. "What, Kate? Don't know what?"

I swore that for the life of me, she was hiding a smile behind her pursed lips. She must've realized this as well, as she immediately regained her composure. Leave it to her to be amused by my confusion. Kate loved to have the upper hand.

And like a light switch, she was immediately calm and caring, mother-like, in a way. She set the frame aside and wrapped both arms around me, sighing heavily. "I'm so sorry, I thought you knew about this years ago."

The answers weren't coming quick enough for me, and the thoughts that were going through my head were far worse than what I hoped was not the reality of the situation. I pushed her back and walked across the room, hands on my hips, then when I felt that I could no longer breathe, my fingers slid down along my thighs onto my knees, as I bent over, gasping for air. My knees felt weak, but I forced myself to keep calm. I straightened up, forced air into my lungs, and began pacing again.

I wanted to strangle the words from her throat, but

instead, snatched the frame back out of her hands to be sure I'd read it right. I slid down the wall that I had been leaning against, my chin landing on my knees, and my palms instinctively pressing against my forehead. My stomach was turning, and I was fighting the urge to throw up. Squeezing my eyes shut, I tried not to think too much as Kate began talking.

"Rylan never really had much of a sense of responsibility, let alone knowing how to raise a baby. Always like Rylan, just walking away from his problems." She looked at me for my reaction, but I had none to give. She shrugged, like it was all no big deal, and actually continued going through the box she'd been working on while she rambled. "He'd paid her to take care of it, but she wasn't having anything to do with an abortion. She took that money and ran. That's what I told Mom when she dropped you off at our doorstep. That Hannah was a greedy woman. But it wasn't right for me and Mom to raise ya when you weren't our problem to begin with. We tried for a while, but it was hard work raising someone else's kid. And Mom was losing her mind. It was a lot to deal with. That's the only reason I called Hannah to come and get you. If Rylan wasn't going to take responsibility, she had to. No one ever expected all that nonsense with Leo to happen. If it hadn't been for that, you'd still be with 'em today I'm sure."

I could no longer fight the violent turns in my stomach, I had to run down the stairs to the bathroom, still clutching the frame tightly. Lunch was suddenly no longer an issue. I rinsed my mouth and tried to drink a Dixie cup of water, hoping it would help to settle my stomach.

As I looked into the mirror, and for the first time, I saw what everyone else saw. Rylan's face. How could I not have known? Every day I looked at my reflection and saw the same thing. Everywhere around me, people who knew us commented on how much I looked just like him. Never JT. Never Kate. Always Rylan.

Tired of fighting urges, I didn't try to stop my hand as my fist hit the glass, shattering my reflection. I never felt the pain, or saw the trickles of blood that spider webbed around my knuckles. Grabbing the frame off of the vanity, I exploded through the door and down to the first floor, then circled around and stormed down the basement stairs.

"*Rylan!*"

"Natalie, what's wrong?" JT was at the bottom of the stairs when I came flying down them, and caught me by the wrist the second he saw me, blood staining his own hand as he gripped my arm. "What the hell happened to you?"

I hadn't noticed the mess of torn skin or shards of glass that were left behind on my hand. It was the last thing on my mind. I yanked my arm back and started toward the back room in the basement. "Where the hell is Rylan?"

I didn't have very far to go; he was already rushing toward us, a look of concern painted on his face. "What's the matter? Good God, you've got blood all over ya. What's happened?"

"You tell me." I said, shoving the frame at him. He glanced down at it only for a minute, and I didn't give him time to respond before I fired off at him. "Why is *your* name on *my* birth certificate, Rylan? Why don't you explain that one to me?"

His eyes seemed to search mine, looking for more than what I was giving him. Maybe he was trying to find a way out of this, but I wasn't about to give it to him. Patience wasn't a luxury I could afford at that moment.

"You know what? Never mind. You don't need to explain. Katie already did." I grabbed the frame back out of his hands and threw it on the concrete floor, smashing the glass into a thousand tiny pieces at his feet. "I just wanted to hear it from you!"

Rylan never took his eyes off of mine, though I could tell the wheels in his head were turning fast. But I wasn't the press and this wasn't an interview. I was his daughter, not some stranger with a recorder. And I deserved the truth.

"What exactly did Katie tell you?" He took a large step past me, trying to avoid stepping on the broken glass.

Each breath I drew in felt as though I was fighting against a weight on my chest, and I forced the air out of my lungs through gritted teeth. I let the words just snap off of my tongue. "Everything Rylan! Everything that you hid from me all these years. You paid Hannah to have an abortion..." It took the breath out of my lungs to say it out loud, and all that remained was a shakiness in my voice that threatened to take over the rest of my body. I was struggling to keep my knees from folding underneath me.

He closed his eyes and clenched his teeth so hard his jawline went white. I wasn't sure what I was expecting from him, what words he could possibly offer at this point to take it all back, but he and I both knew that I was going to shoot him down no matter what came out of his mouth. "It's a lot more complicated than that Natalie. I was a kid. I had no idea what to do with a baby. And I was about to go on tour..."

That was all I needed to push past him and burst right back up the stairs and out the front door. I wanted to keep running, but I wasn't sure where I'd even run to. Instead, I stood in the front yard, feeling like I should be fighting him and not the tears that were brimming around my eyelids.

From in the house, I heard JT's voice issue a quick warning back toward Rylan and Kate, "Try not to kill each other, would you..." before the front door slammed shut again. I spun around to face him, and he had his arms around me in an instant.

I should break down, I thought. I should cry. But the tears refused to spill over. I tried to talk, tried to explain what I felt inside, but there were no words that I could put on what I was feeling. JT offered no advice, didn't promise that it was going to be okay. He just held onto me tightly. I was sure he was convinced that if he didn't, I was sure to run.

When I thought that I could stand on my shaking

knees, I pulled away, and he led me to the back yard. We sat on a wooden bench swing that was seated on the stone patio just outside the back kitchen door. It was a beautiful backyard, with pristine landscaping and neatly cut grass. It was such a happy place to be, and I felt a tinge of guilt for being so miserable there. It almost made me laugh, in a sick sort of way, the vision of me sitting in this beautiful garden, looking so sad and pathetic.

I sighed and looked up at JT. "You're not even my brother, JT. You're my *uncle*. How fucked up is that?"

JT answered quickly. "You're my sister, Natalie. For twenty-one years, you've been my sister and I've been your brother. Doesn't matter that a piece of paper says otherwise." He lit a cigarette, handed it to me, and lit another for himself.

I took a hard drag on the cigarette and blew out the smoke slowly. I was hoping that it would settle the nausea, but it didn't seem to be working. I had so many questions, most of which I wasn't sure I wanted answers to. And I wasn't about to trust the answers that I would get from anyone other than JT.

"Does everyone know? I mean am I the only one who's been in the dark about this?"

JT shook his head. "The only ones who know are our family and Sammi."

New questions were sparking around my head like July Fourth Fireworks. "Hannah? Rylan and her…"

JT snuffed out his cigarette. "I think that's a conversation that you should have with Rylan, Natalie. Don't put too much faith into all Kate tells ya. She's got her own agenda, alright? Just talk to Rylan."

And my shakiness and nausea were replaced quickly with anger all over again. "I'm finished talking to Rylan."

"You should at least give him the chance to explain."

"He had twenty-one years to tell me anything that he wanted to. I think he's missed his opportunity."

"Give him the chance." JT repeated, nodding toward

FORTY-FIVE
Natalie

However it was that JT got me into the house and Kate out of it was beyond me. I found myself standing across the kitchen from Rylan, caught halfway between wanting to bolt out the back door and wanting to jump across the table to strangle him.

Rylan looked uncomfortably complacent, like he wanted to bolt himself. I knew he wanted a cigarette, the way he was grinding his teeth, and the vein on his temple was pressing out from under a stream of sweat, the way it did when he was onstage singing for any period of time. He was leaning all his weight on one shoulder against the wall, as though he alone were holding up the house.

The kitchen had always been one of my favorite rooms of the old house. The décor was timeless, an age-old country cottage look, complete with a brick fireplace that Rylan was currently standing in front of. But for as many times as I'd enjoyed the warm feel of the room, I wanted nothing more than to run as far away as I could from anything associated with him.

He shook his head ever so slightly as he took a deep breath in, glancing up at me only for a moment, then shifting his gaze back down to the wood-planked floor. "I'm sorry you found out this way, Natalie. I really am."

"Don't fucking apologize to me." The words snapped out quicker than I had anticipated, and I began to hate JT for talking me into coming back into the house.

Rylan's eyebrows raised, and he opened his mouth to fire back, but thought better of it, and quickly bit his lower lip instead.

"What you owe me is an explanation. Then you can pay for the years of therapy it's going to take to undo the damage you've done."

He nodded, and his voice was quiet when he said, "Whatever it takes, Love."

I wasn't about to filter the sarcasm, or anything else for that matter. In my mind, he deserved everything that he got from me. "Hannah? *Really*, Rylan? She was what, twice your age? And you were what, like seventeen when…"

He was quick to jump in, "I was sixteen, and yes, she was in her early thirties, I believe."

"You don't even *know* how old she was?"

"She told me she was twenty-five."

"And you believed her? Did she tell you she wasn't married either then?"

"She was separated. She left me to go back to Leo."

My stomach turned. It only ever took the mention of his name for that to happen. I had to put my hand on the table to steady myself a bit, and in the time it took me to calm to sudden wave of nausea, I realized what he had said.

"She left you? So you were *together*?" My voice was shaking now. In the precious little time I'd had so far to put things together, I had been assuming I'd been the product of a one night stand. Never would I have thought that there was more to it than that.

Rylan nodded slowly as he chewed on his tongue, a habit he had during interviews he didn't want to be at. He looked up at the ceiling for a few moments, probably debating whether he even wanted to continue the conversation.

Finally, he let out a deep breath and looked me in the eyes. "I was in love with her."

I held back. As much as I wanted to drive my fist into his face, I held back, hoping that he'd have answers to questions that I didn't even know I had. It was all still a swirl of emotion boiling up inside of me, and nothing was making sense. But one thing kept coming to the forefront of my mind. Leo's voice, as he had me pinned against the wall in the hallway. Just after he had killed Hannah. And was trying to kill me. Slowly. Painfully.

She wants to leave me for your father?

My voice, barely above a whisper and raspy from the tears that I'd been choking back, caught him off guard. "She was going back to you."

The look in his eyes told me he knew. Of course he knew.

He said nothing as I continued, realizing with every passing second more and more of what Rylan had never told me over the years. "You were the reason Leo snapped that night. He found out she was leaving him for you, and he killed her, and then tried to kill me."

He closed his eyes, nodding only slightly, and a heavy tear slipped down his cheek.

"No!" I shouted, slamming my hands into his chest, "You don't get to fucking cry. Not now. It's too fucking late for that!"

I didn't give him time to react as I lunged at him, both my hands shoving him back against the wall. I ignored the crack of his head against the brick. It was probably very similar to the sound of my own head when Leo had thrown me against the wall in the hallway back when I was nine years old. Just before he beat me until I was moments from death. It probably sounded just like that. Which made me want to lash out even more. It made me want to hurt him.

I hit him hard, connecting solidly with his jaw. I threw a second punch and was nearly inches from his eye when he shifted quickly to the side, and my already-bloody hand hit the brick wall.

I felt a pain like no other sear from my knuckles to my shoulder, across my chest and strait through my head. My knees went weak instantly, and I found myself reaching for anything I could to steady myself. My vision was blurring as I slipped to the floor, cradling my throbbing hand. Eyes closed, I was all too aware of the blood trickling through my swollen knuckles. And the only thought that crossed my mind as I doubled over in pain was that I wouldn't be playing the guitar for a very long time.

FORTY-SIX

Rylan

"Do you realize the gravity of what you've done to her?" Sammi asked, taking only a brief moment or two to let the dust settle. She checked her buzzing phone briefly, then tossed it onto an end table nearby. Running her hand through her hair and pacing a bit she asked, "Where is she now? Is she alright?"

Seeing Sammi in a near panic was something that I was not used to. And it wasn't doing anything to help calm my nerves either, so I opted for the next best thing: Scotch. I let the slow burn do the best it could on me. "She's with JT. He'll make sure she's alright."

Sammi was wearing tread in the carpet, a rarity for her. She was just beginning to show, the slightest hint of a belly pressing against her loose fitted shirt as she took each step on the plush carpet beneath her heels. I hated seeing her like this. And I realized at that moment that it wasn't just Natalie I needed to sort things out with.

Sammi had known about Natalie shortly after she came to work with us, when Natalie was about ten or so -there was simply no way I'd have been able to hide all of this from her. There had been too much involvement with the courts for Leo's trial, and endless calls from lawyers, breaks in our tours for me to be able to attend the court hearings on Natalie's behalf, and paperwork that needed to be completed to be able to fly Natalie back and forth from school in the States each year. I had intertwined Sammi in this, and never once had I told even told her the full story. Not the part that mattered at least.

I set my glass down, and turned to face her.

"I paid for Hannah to have an abortion." As I said it, I fully expected Sammi be furious. I expected her to throw something at me. To slam the door. To walk out of my life and never come back.

But instead her eyes carried up to meet mine. A brief sigh escaped my lips, and I hadn't realized until the words met the room how hard it had actually been for me to admit that simple statement.

"I didn't realize Hannah had changed her mind until she showed up at my door with a three day old baby in her arms. She told me she decided that she wanted to work it out with her husband Leo, and if he found out she'd been with someone else, he'd kill her. I was seventeen, and had absolutely no clue what to do with an infant.

"My mother thought it was best that she take care of Natalie, and we'd figure it out when the tour ended. By the time that happened, she already had it planned out that she'd raise Natalie as her own, and it just seemed like the right thing to do at the time. I was never home, and we were traveling by van back in those days, which sure as hell was no place for a baby.

"By the time our second tour had started, Natalie was four, almost five. I was in Japan, about to go onstage, when Hannah calls me to tell me that she wanted to see Natalie. I told her to fucking go to hell. She threatened to just take her, and since there had never been any custody agreement written up with the courts, there was nothing I could do. She told Leo that Natalie was her niece, so I agreed to let her take her under those conditions. It was just supposed to be temporary, but Hannah kept insisting that Natalie was happy with her and Leo."

I took a long slow sip of the whiskey, and, noticing that my hand was shaking, set the glass back down on the table. I was no stranger to the feeling, but the taste of tears in the back of my throat was one that I hadn't known for a very long time.

Sammi's face softened. "You couldn't have known that. It wasn't your fault what happened to her." Sympathy gripped her face.

"Wasn't it? Wasn't it my job to protect her? Had she been with me - where she belonged - she'd have been safe. And who the hell knows what happened in the four years before that night? God only knows what she went through..."

I bit off the sentence before I lost it. I couldn't go down that road. Not now. Not all these years later, when the thought of all that I'd learned during his trial still clenched my stomach in knots and tightened my fists into weapons that no longer could reach their target.

I drew in a deep breath and looked at Sammi. Her eyes were locked on mine, but were soft and warm and everything that I needed at that moment to fall into. My voice was shaking as I continued to tell her what I'd told no one, not even JT.

"On Natalie's eighth birthday, Hannah brought her over to my place for the weekend. She was just supposed to drop her off and leave, but Hannah ended up staying. Natalie had long gone off to bed, and Hannah and I ended up talking for hours. She'd told me that she was planning to leave Leo. For good this time. I can't say that I really believed her, not at that moment, but damn it, I was in love with her. I'd been all along. And as the weeks went on, things got more and more serious. She'd sneak out of her house and come over to mine. God Sammi, I knew at the time it was wrong..."

Anger and guilt shook my voice. I didn't need to tell Sammi what that all implied. And it went well beyond the fact that Hannah was still a married woman. While I was cheating with her mother, our daughter was left alone in the house with Leo. And the thought of that tore me up inside.

"I proposed to her without a ring. It would've been an instant give-away to Leo and to the press. I promised her that as soon as she left him, I'd buy her whatever diamond she wanted. She just needed to take that step and leave him. She'd told me how terrified she was of him, and the more we talked, the more I knew I needed to get them out of there. We'd planned on making the move the following weekend.

"When they found Hannah, she had suitcases packed for her and Natalie. She'd left me a voicemail that morning, but I hadn't gotten it until days after the fact. If I'd just checked my messages, I could've stopped all of this. I could have gotten them before he..."

Sammi's hand hit the table, probably harder than she'd realized. "You can't dwell on that Rylan, and you've got to stop blaming yourself. What's done is done. You've done the best you could to protect her, but you've got to pull your head out of your arse and realize that it's just not your job anymore. She's been asking you for the truth for years now, and you've done nothing but deny her of it."

Hearing her raise her voice at me, talk to me like I was one of the stage crew, or hell, JT even, it made me see her in a different light. For so many years this woman had stood by and kept silent, but all along had felt so passionately about my secrets that I'd been asking her to keep. Never once had I asked her how she felt about it, and she always just carried on, as though it were part of her job.

I stood and studied the mirror, and for a long time looked at the face of a man who'd created a world of lies. The rest of the world saw a legend, a songwriter, a musician.

An idol.

Yet all I saw was an empty man who looked like he'd just been in a bar fight. And nothing of what I saw resembled a father. Or even a father-to-be.

Our Girl had quite a right hook, I realized, as I inspected the purple bruise forming below my lip. She may have been my daughter, but she had JT's DNA when it came to anger management. There simply was none.

As I stood, I became increasingly aware of the fact that my back was also beginning to tighten and kink up. Most likely the result of being jacked up against a wall. *Jesus, the girl could hold her own if she ever was attacked...*

And it began to hit me. Like a slow trickle, then a wave of revelation.

She wasn't the fragile, breakable young girl I'd seen her as on the floor of the station so many years ago. Everything she'd been through with Leo, with not having a family, a mother or a true father to guide her through life, had made her into a strong, independent, self-surviving young woman.

Sammi was right; she didn't need me to protect her. I was the one she needed protecting from. The lies, the deception, it all came at her at once, and the damage I had done by holding back the truth all these years was far worse than the scars that Leo had given her.

Sammi's phone buzzed again, and this time she answered it. She listened for a few moments, then responded, "Thanks JT. I'll let him know." She slid the phone into her jacket pocket and sat down next to me. "Natalie's off the tour. She has seven stitches and a broken hand."

I shook my head. The tour didn't matter anymore.

It was only music.

FORTY-SEVEN

Rylan

A week later we were to play Philips Halle in Dusseldorf, Germany.

My hotel suite held a somber air that was akin to a wake. I'd spent the last twenty-four hours letting Sammi try to talk me out of this. And when that failed, I'd let JT take a crack at swearing, threatening and even taking a swing or two to convince me that I was crazy. But in the end, what mattered most to me was that I knew what I needed to do. It was for the best. For Natalie. For Sammi and the baby. And for me.

So while Sammi sat behind the kitchen island, sipping from a steaming mug to try to hide the fact that her eyes were smoldering from holding back tears, JT slouched in the far corner of our group, his lips tight and nostrils flared as he sniffed back his morning's fix.

The rest of them – Lucas, Dax and Eli – held their gaze on me, expecting news that I'd be taking a break, a hiatus from the band, until I could get things sorted with Natalie.

But it stemmed far beyond Natalie. I needed to get myself in order. Years of living the lies had me second-guessing every relationship I had, including Sammi. Hell, I didn't even trust myself anymore.

"There's no easy way to say this," I looked them in the eyes. It was the least I could do after twenty-two years. "I'm out. I'm done Coma."

No one spoke. Twenty-two years of music, of work, of traveling, and it ended just like that.

I expected protests. I expected arguments lined with a string of swearing.

Lucas stood up, put his hand on my shoulder, as if to say he understood. "It's been a good run Rylan."

I nodded, turning my eyes toward the other two.

"We'll be back at in again in ten years." Eli quipped, "The reunion tour'll make us millions."

Dax chimed in, "Only if we can get a break from our solo projects. Right JT?"

He didn't look up, just uttered a barely audible, "Yeah mate, whatever."

Sammi took her cue and joined the group. She had the slightest hint of a belly pressing against her designer top. She would fight the maternity wear for as long as she could, and even then, we'd have a designer plan her wardrobe to fit her ever-changing penchant for style. "Listen," she began, "there's a lot to be sorted before we make any announcements to the public. We don't want the press digging into why the band is splitting before the end of the tour, and there are going to be a lot of upset fans from the cancelled shows, so we've got to work on press release immediately."

I put my hand up stopping her. "Because I'm leaving the band, that's why. That's all the public needs to know." The last thing I wanted, or needed, was more lies to have to sift through. I was done.

"And the second that hits the media they're going to start digging on *why* you're leaving the band. People will be more than willing to offer up information when news this big hits, and everybody's going to want to tell a story."

"Let them."

"You want the press to be all over her front yard too? Her leaving Lull hasn't been in the media for more than forty-eight hours and rumours are running ramped as to why. Trust me, when the story breaks of you leaving Coma, it wouldn't take that much digging for them to find out Natalie's your daughter, and there'll be cameras in her face before you could lift the phone to warn her."

Not that she'd take my calls anyway. I closed my eyes. *Fuck.* I hadn't even been thinking about how quickly the news was going to hit. *Damn the media,* I thought, it wasn't fair that the reporters and their twisted stories could get through to her when I couldn't.

I was beginning to realize that over the past twenty-four hours I hadn't eaten one meal, and my stomach was beginning to turn in waves of nausea. We were only a few short hours away from our scheduled sound check at the venue. The longer it took us to pull the story together, the longer it would take Sammi to contact the venue and to get the press release out. The last thing I wanted was for fans to be showing up at the venue waiting for a show that wasn't going to happen.

My head was clouding over with every wasted moment, yet a reasonable solution was failing me. Fucking hell, I was beginning to sweat, and it wasn't even hot. I bit back the stream of curses that I wanted to let fly. It would do absolutely no good, and anyhow, I had no one but myself to direct them to. *I should eat something,* I thought, *settle my stomach.* But I couldn't bring myself to move.

JT stood. "We'll say it's me. We'll say I'm the one leaving the band. We'll say it's because of the breakup with my missus or the drugs, or whatever the hell you wanna say. Put it on me."

I gazed up at him. His eyes held that steadfast

reassurance that came through whenever the drugs and depression didn't have hold of him. For the first time in a long time, my brother was back.

But Sammi wouldn't have it. "The breakup with Candace was months ago. In order for you to leave the tour and the band suddenly like this, you'd have to have been committed to an institution to maintain credibility with the press or the fans. And I'm not even going to venture down the drugs path. It's too close to the truth and unless you're going to follow up this story with rehab, we're in the same predicament as with are with the breakup."

We all froze. The whole lot of us. No one had ever slapped the issues in JT's face like that before, and had the circumstances been otherwise, we might have followed it through with a full-blown intervention. But Sammi was quick to keep focus, ignoring the sullen look that fell upon JT's face. I held my eyes locked on his, even as Sammi began speaking, but he continued to stare past her as she carried on.

"The best I can come up with at the moment is an argument between the two of you. Not just an argument, but an epic blowout. We plant that this has been ongoing for quite some time, as there have been enough history of fights between the two of you, but nothing of this scale before. The two of you refuse to work together any longer, and you all go your separate ways. No one needs to know details; we can work that out later if we have to. It's enough of a distraction to keep the spotlight off of anything that relates to Natalie."

I looked at JT, who gave a slight nod. This could work. This would give the media and the fans enough to go after, and keep the spotlight off of Natalie. It was a hell of an ending for 7 Year Coma, and in some ways, maybe the perfect kind of an end for a rock and roll band.

FORTY-EIGHT
Natalie

I slipped in the back of a waiting taxi just outside of Philadelphia International. The driver looked at me through the rearview mirror, but instead of giving him a destination, I only asked, "What time does your shift end?"

His eyes raised questionably in the rearview as he answered, "I'm on until eleven."

With my good hand, I slid five one-hundred-dollar bills through the window separating the seats. "Just drive."

I leaned my head back against the seat. I'd had the last three days to come up with a plan, and this was the best that I'd come up with. I hadn't left JT's spare room for two of those days, wallowing in my own misery and whatever random concoction JT would mix up for me to try to get me through the hour. Everything felt like it had been bottled up inside of me for so long that I couldn't possibly even sit for another moment. It was barely six in the morning when I scratched out a left-handed note for JT and left it on the kitchen counter for him. I didn't tell him where I was going -

hell, at that point, I wasn't sure myself. I only told him that I'd call him when I had everything sorted.

I just wasn't sure when that would be.

Hearts were meant to be broken, Natalie. It's how we know we're alive.

Rylan's words echoed in my head, over and over. Which was why it was so easy for him all these years, to paint the lies on top of the lies, because in the end, it didn't matter if it all broke my heart. At least I was alive. It was my pain, not his, and it was mine alone to deal with. Hell, that was how I'd dealt with my pain in the past. On my own. I didn't have parents to confide in, to guide me through it. To pick me up when I fell.

I had my friends, that's what I had. The five of them had been there when I'd fallen. They'd dried my tears, laughed me through the tough times, celebrated the good times and stuck by me at every turn. It didn't matter that I was flawed, it didn't matter that I was different. It didn't matter that I had secrets. They still loved me. They still forgave me.

Your family is what you make it, JT's words that day on his bus back in Texas hit hard, even as the torrents of rain beat down against the windows of the taxi. JT was right. I'd made my own family over the years. It wasn't a 'normal' family, but it was mine.

And right now, that family was torn apart. It had been for a long time, and I was to blame for that. I'd had my own string of lies, and in my absence, that had made the gaping hole in my heart even deeper. I could only imagine what Ray-Ray had gone through all this time, putting the pieces of it all back together on his own, and coming to the conclusion that I was not who I'd pretended to be. I knew exactly how he must've felt; right here in this moment, I knew that heartache well. I had delayed setting things right for too long. I owed him an explanation. I owed him an apology. I owed him so much more.

For hours in that taxi I beat myself up, tore myself down, blamed myself for every minute of every hour that I'd kept the truth from them. And I hated myself for the fact that they'd all forgiven me so easily when I'd come clean to them, and yet I left them anyway. And for what? For music?

I was no better than Rylan. The taxi finally came to a rest in front of the townhouse. I thanked the driver and pulled my backpack over my shoulder as I ran through the pouring rain to the front door.

A chill swept across my skin when I stepped into the dark and empty house. I had hoped to find Rachel's car in the drive, and when it wasn't, I was sure that maybe she was just out for evening, but the heat was turned down far too low for just a night out.

I peeled off my wet jacket in a one-handed struggle over my cast, and shivered down the hallway to raise the thermostat. The heater kicked on in angry protest, and I relieved a little with the sound of the motor pushing hot air through the vents in the old house. If nothing else, it helped to offset the drumming rain and claps of thunder.

I sniffed hard, holding back the tears that were starting to spring to the surface, choking my breath and stinging my eyes. *Hold it together*, I told myself, climbing the stairs as yet another flash of lightening illuminated the windows peeking through the open doors as I slipped down the hallway to my bedroom. The door clicked shut behind me and I pulled the curtains closed. It was going to be a headphones kind of a night, I decided, as my hand slipped into the drawer next to my bed to find my faithful iPod waiting just where I'd left it.

As I settled back onto my bed, finally dry and attempting warmth in a pair of flannel pajamas, I slipped my bare feet under the covers and rested my head back against the wall, earphones intact and eyes closed. I let the music flow through my body, shutting out the world, my thoughts, and my life, as the bass resonated through my head. There was no better escape. Except, perhaps, making that music myself. My fingers wiggled in the cast on my right hand, longing to be holding a pick and strumming against the guitars that were still hidden in my closet.

How I missed it already.

A part of me was dead without it. And I didn't want to think about it, even as the music streamed through my ears, bled through my veins and strait into my heart. I couldn't make music for the next six weeks, when I needed it most. All in a matter of moments, I had lost my identity, my family, and my music. Maybe it was more than part of me that was dead. Maybe it was all of me. Maybe I needed to start completely over. Hell, I'd already changed my name once, what was so wrong about doing it again? I could be anyone I wanted this time around. I had the opportunity and the ability to create my own me this time.

And while I was at it, nothing was really keeping me here in Pennsylvania. I had a bank account large enough to take me anywhere in the world that I wanted to go. I could actually start over. For real this time. I didn't have to be sibling/daughter/whatever to a famous musician, or ex-girlfriend to her former best friend, or "that girl from that band that opened for Coma". I could be anyone that I wanted to be.

I could be an Accountant.

My good hand punched the bed beside me and a heavy sigh had my head falling back against the wall. I'd been down that road. I'd had that chance already. It didn't make me happy. I didn't want that life. Maybe normalcy wasn't for me. I loved being on stage. I enjoyed playing music for people. I loved watching them sing along in the crowd, hearing them cheer when I played a guitar solo. Hell, I even enjoyed singing backup for Lee Mason.

And for a while, I had loved being with my family. Whatever it was that they were to me...

My fingers slid over the volume button on the iPod, raising it above the sound of the thunder that I could feel pounding against the wall at my back. I elbowed the pillow up higher to cushion the vibrations and pulled the comforter up over my shoulders as I pressed the earphones against my head with a palm and a casted hand. I let the music take me in.

I wasn't sure how long I'd been playing the same song over and over again, but as the storm strengthened outside, a chill swept over me, as though from deep within, and my eyes popped open to see my bedroom door swing open.

I may have jumped, standing on my bed instantaneously, but I do know that my heart jumped to my throat and I threw my iPod at the intruder before my eyes had time to register who it even was.

"What the *fuck*, Natalie! What are you doing here? Jesus, you scared me half to *death!*"

Ray-Ray's eyes matched mine in horror and astonishment. He had a backpack slung across his shoulder, and his hair and crimson-colored St. Joe's University sweatshirt were soaked.

"I live here! What the fuck are you doing here?"

He bent over and picked up my iPod and tossed it onto my bed. "Rachel asked me to look after the house while she was gone."

My cheeks flushed with the sudden rush of adrenaline. Or at the sight of him after all this time, standing in my bedroom. God, how I'd missed him. His deep brown eyes, warm and round, staring into my soul like they'd done for the past eight years of my life. How I'd longed for his arms around me, holding me tight against his chest, his breath against my neck, breezing through my hair as though a day hadn't gone by and things hadn't gone all wrong between us. *And Sweet Jesus, what was I thinking?*

"Oh." It was all I could manage myself to say. It was the only word that could form on my breath without a waterfall of tears that wanted to slide away past my eyes and down my cheeks. I slid down to my knees on my bed.

He slid his backpack off his shoulder and onto the floor. "I've been staying here on weekends while she's in Boston."

"Boston?"

"With Nathan..." He shook his hair with his hands, sending a sprinkle of water drops cascading in a perimeter around him. "Oh shit," he stood suddenly and looked at me wide-eyed, "you didn't know."

I shook my head slowly.

Caught between the past and the future in one collaborative moment that seemed to freeze time around us, neither of us spoke, as we stood staring at each other. The sight of him still took my breath away, as though not a moment, let alone a year, had passed between us. Every emotion that I'd felt for him over that past year was raging through my heart in a matter of seconds, and I prayed that he couldn't hear the pounding through my chest.

He had come bursting back into my life at a time when I couldn't possibly handle any more emotional turmoil. He was the last thing I needed at that moment. *And the only thing I needed.*

His voice echoed through the shadows of memories in my head. "Breathe," he told me, with a slight laugh.

I blinked. "Huh?" It was so soft off my lips that I don't think he even heard me.

"It's just me, Natalie." A crooked smile played at his lips, but he never looked so sincere, as those dark eyes warmed me in a way that was so deep and comforting that I wanted to fall into his embrace right then and there.

I fought to keep my voice from quivering as I shook my head. "It could never be just you, Ray-Ray."

His eyes narrowed for a moment, as though he were waiting to see if I meant what I'd just said. He cocked his head to the side and gave me a wink, "Get over here...."

I slid off the bed and into his arms, letting him wrap me up tight against him. I was sure it was his heart, not mine, that I could feel against my chest, but as I buried my face against his neck and let him kiss my hair softly, I wasn't so sure there was a difference.

FORTY-NINE
Natalie

I told him my story. All of it. Even the rounds I'd had with Lee. I'd expected him to be mad, to walk out, put his hand up and tell me to stop – anything. But he sat, listening intently as I poured my heart out before him. I wasn't sure what I was expecting of him. Hell, the situation was so obscure, so profound, that I couldn't wrap my own head around it even after almost a week of absorbing the cruel details. How could I possibly expect him to have any answers?

His hand slid across my shoulders, pulling me carefully against him. His lips touched the top of my head, almost so lightly that I could barely feel the kiss through my hair, then he rested his cheek on my head, holding me a little tighter.

It felt like home, a year ago. And it made me wish that I'd never gotten on that plane in Texas.

"Hold on one second," he told me, standing up suddenly. He slipped out of the room, and I could hear his footsteps on the stairs, and moments later he returned with a bottle of wine.

\

I eyed him curiously. "No glasses?"

He pulled the cork, took a sip and passed me the bottle. "Between us? No need..."

I tossed him a quick smile, and held his glance as I took a slow sip from the dark bottle, letting the rich velvet liquid slide down the back of tongue. It had been a while since I'd drank wine, but I could tell a Cab-Merlot mix by taste alone. It loosened the strings just enough for me to let go of my emotions.

Forward was a direction that I feared intently, an unknown realm of which I dared to enter without being able to put a final resolve on my past. And my present stood but a brief blink in my own mind, a mere transition of what was and what would be, yet represented also a great divide, one never to be crossed again. That was my ideal, if I were to have it my way. I'd go onward, never looking back. Everything that had been on the other side of the ocean had passed and was to be forgotten. I had no idea what to expect of tomorrow, nor did I want to entertain it either.

Ray-Ray's voice cut through my thoughts. "I owe you an apology Nat. I should have known better than to think you and Dax were sleeping together."

I looked down at the floor for a moment. It felt like years ago from where we sat tonight. It was an entire lifetime away. "I lied to you Ray-Ray," I looked back into his eyes, "For so many years, I lied to you about who I was. You never gave me a reason not to trust you, and I still kept my life a secret. I never realized how much that would hurt you, or Rachel, or anyone else." I swallowed hard, thinking of Rylan, and feeling my stomach clench like a fist. "There aren't reasons enough for lying to your best friends, and I'm so sorry."

Ray-Ray thought for a moment, contemplating in an almost agonizing silence. He moved his head back and forth, as though silently mulling over his options, then, with eyes closed, he nodded, as though he'd come to some internal resolve. Finally, he looked at me, a wide smile on his face, and I couldn't help but laugh. "See? Right there..." He pointed a finger in my face. "There it is!"

"What?" I laughed, swiping away a runaway tear.

"You know you've forgiven someone when you can laugh with them."

I let my head fall back as I laughed. It was ludicrous. Absolutely insane. And that was Ray-Ray.

"Speaking of which..." he stood abruptly, walking over to my desk. Above it hung the prized 'Coma Trivia Challenge' trophy, the guitar pick that Ray-Ray treasured from his first 7 Year Coma concert some eight years ago. Rachel had hung it up for me. With a quick swipe, Ray-Ray yanked it from my wall, sending the hook and nail it had rested on flying across the room.

I wasn't sure if I should laugh or not. "What the hell was that for?"

He unzipped his backpack, sliding it in. "This baby is going back to its rightful owner. After a careful review of the last challenge match, it's been determined that the final question was answered correctly after all, and therefore, I still hold the reigning title of 'Coma Trivia Challenge Champion'."

I threw my pillow at him, missing him by a mile. "You're an asshole Ray-Ray..."

He laughed, grabbing the pillow and shoving me back against my bed with it. "Who doesn't know that Rylan Porter only has two siblings? What'd you say again... three? Don't you know *anything* about the band?"

I wanted to tell him it was too soon, but hell, he had me laughing at my own tragedy. That was progress in and of itself.

"It's okay," I told him, recovering my breath, "That's not Rylan's guitar pick anyway. It belonged to the opening band."

Ray-Ray bit his lip, trying not to laugh, which made me laugh instead. "See that?" He reached for the bottle of wine, took a quick swig and handed it over to me, "If you can laugh, you can forgive."

I took a long sip, letting the wine warm me inside and out.

Rylan had his reasons. I couldn't pretend to understand them fully. I couldn't say I'd accepted them. But I believed him when he told me he'd had good intentions. His heart was in the right place. I didn't doubt that. Whether or not I wanted him back in my life, it would be a long time before I could conceptualize that idea at all. But I knew that someday, if he ever came to the realization that his band wasn't everything to him, that there were more important things in life than making music, then I might find the opportunity in my heart to forgive him.

ABOUT THE AUTHOR

By day, Casey Mansfield is a wife, mother of two young children, and a Human Resources professional who specializes in Benefits, Payroll and Corporate Wellness. By night, she lives, breathes and sleeps writing. She is an avid fan of music and concerts, and has spent the last six years delving into the British rock group Oasis. Having resided in Pennsylvania the majority of her life, she now enjoys the sunny skies and warm weather of Florida.

Made in the USA
Charleston, SC
20 October 2014